HER RULING PASSIONS

The father whose sin shadowed Alycia's life . . . the husband whose ravenous ambition devoured Alycia's perfect marriage . . . the father-in-law whose shocking proposition Alycia could not turn down despite its price . . . the lover who taught Alycia the power of her beauty and the hunger of her body . . . the son whom Alycia desperately tried to keep from following in his father's footsteps . . . and the man who joined with her in a powerful and dangerous love . . .

All were part of the ultimate decision this woman of fabulous beauty and fortune must make . . . as she thought about how much she would have to give up for love . . . and then, how much she stood to lose without it. . . .

FAMILY MONEY

FAMILY MONEY

Michael French

A SIGNET BOOK
NEW AMERICAN LIBRARY
PUBLISHED BY
PENGUIN BOOKS CANADA LIMITED

For Edie and Marshall,
two special people,
with love

PUBLISHER'S NOTE

This book is a work of fiction. Names, characters, places, and incidents either are the product of the author's imagination or are used fictitiously, and any resemblance to actual persons, living or dead, events, or locales is entirely coincidental.

NAL BOOKS ARE AVAILABLE AT QUANTITY DISCOUNTS WHEN USED TO PROMOTE PRODUCTS OR SERVICES. FOR INFORMATION PLEASE WRITE TO PREMIUM MARKETING DIVISION, NEW AMERICAN LIBRARY, 1633 BROADWAY, NEW YORK, NEW YORK 10019.

Copyright © 1990 by Michael French

First Printing, March, 1990

2 3 4 5 6 7 8 9

SIGNET TRADEMARK REG. U.S. PAT. OFF. AND FOREIGN COUNTRIES
REGISTERED TRADEMARK — MARCA REGISTRADA
HECHO EN WINNIPEG, CANADA

SIGNET, SIGNET CLASSIC, MENTOR, ONYX, PLUME, MERIDIAN and NAL BOOKS are published in Canada by Penguin Books Canada Limited, 2801 John Street, Markham, Ontario, L3R 1B4
PRINTED IN CANADA
COVER PRINTED IN U.S.A.

In my father's house are many mansions; if it were not so, I would have told you. I go to prepare a place for you.
—John 14:2

Reverend Father, I promise you obedience in all good things unto death.
—Trappist vow, from *The Holy Rule of St. Benedict*

Hollywood is where not only you must succeed, your friends must fail.
—Anonymous

PROLOGUE

The three boys, skinny as toothpicks, watched with curiosity as the monk stepped from his dugout and negotiated the incline of the riverbank. He sank to his knees in the thick mud but had the strength to right himself, with dignity, and continue up the embankment. Rickety houses on stilts hovered near the bend in the Amazon, lopsided as wind-bent trees, their rafters draped with colorful wash. Behind the houses sat an unending, wavy green ribbon of jungle.

Brother Andrew spoke Portuguese to the three boys. He wiped his large hands on his coarse linen habit and gestured to show his concern. His audience smiled politely but looked uncertain.

"My good friend is missing—her name is Alycia," the monk implored again, locking gazes with the oldest boy, no more than twelve. Naked but for tattered blue shorts, his skin had the sheen of worn copper. Suddenly he beamed in recognition. "Oh, da white lady . . . nice lady . . ." He spoke in Pidgin English to please the American missionary. "Fadder, she here. Then she gone wit a man."

The monk straightened at the news. At full height Brother Andrew was imposing—tall, broad-shouldered, athletic-looking. He was fit enough to handle physical danger, and over the years, working with the poor in city slums, had saved himself and others from harm more than once. He was in his late fifties, but his angular, rugged face looked younger, and revealed an intelligence and warmth along with an unflagging energy. He walked with the purposeful bounce of someone burdened with more appointments than he could possibly keep.

"What man?" Brother Andrew inquired. "It's urgent that I find my friend. She's not well . . ."

The boy turned uneasy, not wanting to deliver bad news to someone as kind as Brother Andrew. "Gone yesterday," he said, averting his eyes. "White man took her to Rio."

9

The monk's brow folded in concern. Only three days ago he had returned from church business in Belém to discover that Alycia Poindexter had disappeared from her village. A midwife had last seen her, headstrong as ever, hitching a ride somewhere on a supply boat. Normally calm, Brother Andrew had been beside himself. He had brought with him a Swiss doctor, who, ready to treat Alycia's worsening malaria, was annoyed by her rude disappearance and had flown back to São Paulo. Alone now, the monk had been traveling by dugout over a hundred kilometers downriver, stopping at every settlement regardless of size.

"A white man?" Brother Andrew clarified. "Tall? Short? Young? Old?"

"Yes, Fadder."

"Which one?"

The boy shrugged. "Big man. Young. Not so nice." His friends giggled softly as he made a sour face.

When he could extract no more from the boys, Brother Andrew thanked them with the few cents in his pocket. Others in the village confirmed the story—a white man nobody knew had intercepted Alycia on the supply boat and taken her into an awaiting river plane. The pilot, they said, was from Rio.

Under the blinding sun the monk marched back to his leaky dugout. Somehow he would have to get to Rio, though he had no idea where to look in the sprawling city. For a long minute Brother Andrew bowed his head. He prayed that his despair and anxiety would not get the better of him. He prayed that the woman who meant more to him than anyone realized would be safe. And he prayed that the secrets they shared together would be left in the dark, untroubled corner in which they had languished for so many years. Finally he asked God to show his mercy and forgiveness.

By late evening a motorized launch had carried Brother Andrew upriver on the green, flowing waters to his village. He was exhausted but his mind refused to shut off. For almost forty years he had faithfully done the bidding of his abbot and worked among the poor. Otherwise, Trappist vows demanded a strict separation from the material world and its temptations, which required a life of prayer and meditation within the walls of Brother Andrew's New England monastery. His selfless temperament suited him well for both callings. It was some fifteen years after he had joined the Order of Cistercians of the Stricter Observance that his duties were one day altered. His abbot, Brother Manning, facing dwindling contributions from the outside world, and knowing he had a jewel in someone as bright and personable as Brother Andrew, had dispatched the monk on a highly unorthodox mission. In his simple frock, Brother Andrew was sent out to mingle with the wealthy and powerful in their sumptuous homes and at black-tie balls. He had eloquently and successfully stated the Trappists' cause. Alycia Poindexter had not been the only one to be impressed by his wit and sincerity, or to write the Trappists a substantial check, but to the monk she was the most memorable. She had been a woman of remarkable physical beauty, of course, but over the years, as their paths crossed more than once, it was her courage and perseverance that had impressed him so indelibly.

Perhaps he had been too impressed, Brother Andrew thought now. He had always pleased others by doing as he was asked, but as he dropped onto the splintered boards of the cabin deck, he felt no satisfaction, only a deep and abiding frustration.

It took another two days to reach the bustling, overcrowded port city of Rio. From atop Corcovado Mountain the massive stone statue of Christ the Redeemer induced in the monk a flicker of hope. At local churches he enlisted the aid of several priests, who promptly did whatever Brother Andrew asked. They canvassed the docks, the public squares, the cafés, the hotels. Most *cariocas* wanted to be helpful but knew nothing. At the international airport Brother Andrew inquired of the customs officer if he might examine recent exit cards for the United States. Permission was politely denied. The log of outgoing private aircraft was also unavailable to him. The monk knew the captain had been bribed, and bribed well, but had nothing himself to offer. At several hospitals and clinics he showed his one tattered photo of Alycia. No one had seen her. The entire week unfolded with the same futility. The task of locating one stranger in a city of over six million was impossible.

On the dilapidated ferry home, the monk stayed away from the cheerful crowds. He was increasingly bothered by the thought that, with Alycia unfound, his troubles might only be beginning. He did not think of himself as a man who took too many chances, but perhaps the seeds of his current problem had been planted long before he met Alycia, even before he entered the Trappist monastery on his twenty-first birthday.

He fixed on a memory of sailing his own skiff on Long Island Sound on a cloudless summer afternoon, a mere youth, rich and petulant and filled with merry contempt for the rest of the world. Two years later, not even out of college, his circumstances had changed radically, and so did the rest of his life.

For many years, living at peace with himself, the monk had been convinced he'd made the right decision in joining his order. Now, worrying about Alycia, he wasn't as sure. He wondered if trading cynicism for idealism had not been some elaborate self-deception. He considered the tyranny of ideals when they are set too high, however innocently, and his punishment—the chamber of hell to which he was in danger of descending.

The emergency-room interns were gathered around a thirteen-inch Sony, swilling coffee and groaning at they watched Boston clobber their underdog Angels in the 1986 playoffs. When the ambulance arrived, the young men and women sprang to duty around the semiconscious female. "Whatta we got here, Howard Hughes *redux*?" one quipped. The woman's face was shrunken and shriveled from the sun, her dark hair hopelessly knotted, the long fingernails chipped or broken. A pudgy-faced younger man, in dirty jeans and a ragged T-shirt, straggled in behind and gestured brusquely at the doctors as if they were so many vultures in waiting. "Don't go near her—that's my mother!" he thundered with godlike authority, intimidating the normally unintimidated. With only a whisper to someone in Admissions, the blond man had his mother wheeled straight to ICU. The interns groused about the unorthodox entry, wondering who the man was to own a platinum VIP card.

Cedars-Sinai Medical Center sat on the corner of Beverly and San Vicente, in the heart of Beverly Hills. It was a well-known haven for celebrities who swallowed too many amphetamines or took razor blades to their wrists or contacted embarrassing sexual diseases. Besides the finest medical care this side of Mass General, the hospital offered the strictest privacy for its patients. Jean Poindexter needed both. The thought of his mother possibly dying sent him into a frenzy. Just as nerve-jangling would be a glory-seeking reporter unearthing Alycia Poindexter's identity. On his private jet from Rio, Jean had radioed the hospital his approximate arrival time, demanded an ambulance be waiting, and registered his mother under a false name. He made Admissions swear that nobody but primary-care physicians and appropriate nurses would come within a country mile of her.

Through the door window in an ICU unit he watched now as the hospital's top parasitologist and pulmonary specialist went to work. Blood and sputum were quickly cultured. A nurse informed Jean of a malarial infection with persistent hepatosplenomegaly; spleen damage indicated the illness had ravaged her body for years. Her trachea and bronchi contained pockets of serosanguineous fluid and the lungs were partially collapsed. Chloroquine, quinine, sulfonamide, and pyrimethamine were hooked into her IV. For the pneumonia, a microbial therapy that included Penicillin G and tetracycline was started.

A young doctor with hooded eyes and a jaw squarer than Dick Tracy's approached Jean after a few hours. "She's a tough old girl. We'll see how she reacts."

"I'm staying in the lounge here. I'm keeping a vigil," Jean answered, to prove he was the dutiful son. "My sister, Felice, is flying in tomorrow from New Jersey. We'll pull Mother through this, with our prayers if we have to."

The doctor lowered his voice to a worried, confidential whisper. "What happened to your mother in that jungle—did she go a little crazy?"

Jean, even when scruffy and unshaven, had the soft features and good looks that caused the curious to mistake him for Tab Hunter, and when the occasion demanded it, he could be as polished as a diamond. He seized his opening. "My mother was exploited, if you want to know. She spent over ten years in a godforsaken Amazon settlement, manipulated by a self-serving monk. Mother wanted to do some good for the world, I suppose, but she ended up the monk's slave. Her health deteriorated. So did her judgment. The monk never brought her to a doctor. *I* had to go finally and save her—"

His listener drifted away, but not before his glance registered dismay, even shock. The doctor was too young to remember much if anything about Alycia Poindexter, even if he'd known her true identity. In the late fifties and early sixties her extravagant parties had headlined the Los Angeles *Times*'s society section on a predictable basis. The story of how a bourgeois girl from Paris had married correctly to become a wealthy Los Angeles socialite was well-documented. What was not as clear was why one day she'd given up everything she owned to live and work among the poor in a mosquito-infested jungle.

Only it wasn't quite that way, Jean knew as he paced the waiting room. There was one thing his mother hadn't given up.

For three days he stayed in the hospital, living on coffee and sandwiches, refusing to shower or change his clothes, not even checking with his office. His mother was moved from ICU to a private room on the top floor, with sweeping views of Los Angeles. After she was bathed and groomed by the nurses, her beauty and radiance began to return. Jean positioned himself across from her room to watch the endless stream of doctors, nurses, and orderlies parading in and out. On the third day he caught a young man with tortoiseshell glasses lingering suspiciously by a drinking fountain. Smelling reporter, Jean chased the kid away, then read the riot act to hospital security for not keeping a tighter ship.

With each day, Jean grew more anxious. His mother was now conscious and alert, but she refused to utter a word to anybody. A Harvard-trained psychologist cajoled and pleaded for her cooperation. Candy stripers brought magazines and writing paper. Felice, her favorite, flew in and spent hours with her mother, but still the room was flooded with silence. At least twice a day Jean hovered by her bedside with fresh-cut flowers.

"I love you, Mother," he would say. "You know that. Don't be angry with me for taking you out of that jungle. It was for your own good. You should thank me. You would have died there. Now, please, we have to talk . . ."

The proud, stubborn silence would not be punctured. Frustrated, Jean appeared one morning determined to make the issues clearer. "Mother," he said, his hands gripping the safety railing of her bed as his charming smile evaporated, "time is running out. You can't stay in this hospital forever. You know what this room is costing me? Over a thousand a day. ICU alone ran twenty thousand. And who knows what those gods in white smocks are going to stick me with. They say you're improving, you can leave anytime. Now, you and I have urgent business . . ."

For a moment his mother's deep blue eyes flashed defiantly. Jean leaned even closer, and his voice dropped to an insistent, angry whisper. "You think you're fooling anybody by playing possum? Maybe those doctors, but not me. I know everything now. I know all about the money. You're wondering how your little secret finally got out, aren't you? Well, I'm not going to tell you. But I know every detail, Mother. After Grandmother Harriet's funeral, I looked through her house. In a chest in the attic, under the folds of blankets and linens, there was your scrapbook. Full of clippings from the *Times*. You saved everything that involved you, even if it was negative, didn't you? All those embarrassing scandals. Then I found Dad's letter, the one you never wanted me to see . . .''

Jean watched as his mother's head stirred uncomfortably on the pillow. His smile reappeared. He was getting through.

"Why so many secrets, Mother? Why did you keep all that money that was really meant for me?'' He waited, but there was no confession, not even in her eyes. His mother had always been stubborn. "I'm taking steps to get the money back," he promised, his hands turning white on the bed rails. "I've got the Catholic Church looking into this, and I'm starting at the top, Mother. I mean *Rome.*''

Alycia Poindexter closed her eyes.

"You might think about cooperating," Jean said as he stepped back in disgust, "just this once, just to save everyone from more scandal and embarrassment. As a family we've suffered more than enough of that. You can't run away this time. And dear Brother Andrew isn't going to find you.''

Long after her son had left, Alycia Poindexter rose and maneuvered to the window that framed a view of the city. Her memories came in violent and unpredictable waves, but her thoughts about Los Angeles were the harshest of all. She despised the city. It was sprawling and dirty and incomprehensible, crowded with ambitious, pretentious people, which was why she had left in the first place. Her old friends had not understood her leaving then—nor had they particularly cared—and they would not be pleased by her return. She was totally alone here. Jean was right about that. There was nowhere to go.

For a while she paced the room, feeling her strength return. She would have to do something. Jean would be as persistent as his father to get what he wanted. Weak from malaria, Alycia had been unable to stop him from making her leave Brazil, and though she felt stronger now, she knew she was still helpless against him.

A sheet of hospital stationery was retrieved from the bedside drawer. Alycia perched on the bed and lifted a pen. No doubt Jean had alerted everyone to watch her. Somehow the letter would have to be sneaked into the mail.

"*My dearest Andrew,*" she began with a trembling hand.

Alycia made herself think clearly and carefully. There was so much to remember, of course, so many things to sort through and put in their rightful places. And so little time to do it.

BOOK ONE

BOOK ONE

On the last Friday in July 1947, the afternoon sky over Paris was a dark, rumbling canopy. Humidity had been building for days, promising rain that instead stayed locked in listless clouds. In his wrinkled khakis, a United States Army captain named Red Poindexter shuffled with several fellow officers up three flights of stairs in a gray stone building on the city's Left Bank. The Ecole des Beaux-Arts, like its Latin Quarter neighborhood of narrow, winding streets and historic buildings, had been largely undamaged by the Germans, a fact that Captain Poindexter acknowledged would save U.S. taxpayers and the Marshall Plan a tidy sum. To the captain, the war's aftermath had become an exercise in dry, inexorable number-crunching, which the bored officer had come to resent almost as much as the mandatory goodwill visits to French schools and parish churches.

Only a few years earlier, Red Poindexter had commanded one of George S. Patton's tank companies and had quickly found himself a personal favorite of "Old Blood and Guts." It was not an easy niche to fill, in light of the general's fabled temper, but the strawberry-blond officer had been blessed with boyish good looks and a brash, defiant optimism that the general had warmed to immediately. Red had led his own company from North Africa into the boot of Italy and then all the way to Berlin, helping drop the curtain on the European theater. The close-quarter fighting had earned him numerous decorations for bravery, including a Distinguished Service Cross and two Silver Stars. The respect of his enlisted cadre bordered on reverence. The more brushes with death the captain shrugged off, the more chances he was willing to take. As a child he had been pegged with the nickname "Red" for his hair and for his Christian name, Alfred, but combat had redefined it for personal valor. The thirty-year-old captain, whose blood had been spilled on four separate occa-

19

sions, was possessed of an almost childlike faith that he was not meant to die in this war because his destiny lay elsewhere.

What that destiny was, however, had never been exactly clear to Red. When the war ended, most of his friends resigned their commissions and headed stateside. There was no wife or girlfriend back in Los Angeles who beckoned, and Red had no idea what he wanted, so he remained in the service. Assigned as an aide to General George Marshall, he became a roving goodwill ambassador who constantly criss-crossed France and Belgium. The travel hardly alleviated his restlessness. Even though he looked forward to these ten days in Paris, his general routine was so inflicted with tedium that he had begun to think that only another war could save him.

At the top of the stairs Red was ushered into a college classroom, where he found several dozen undergraduates. A mixture of young men and women, they were hunched over drafting tables in typical *lycée* blue smocks, manipulating compasses and T-squares in silent concentration. The affable professor informed his American visitors that the neophyte architects were assisting in the rehabilitation of neighboring towns less fortunate than Paris. Red scarcely heard the words. His gaze fell in and out of focus. How long would this take? After a few minutes he started to the door, when his glance fell on a girl in the back row.

Perhaps she was just taller or more striking than the others, but his eyes remained fixed. Unlike her peers, the girl wore no makeup. She didn't need any, thought Red, because her complexion was flawless. Her mouth was full and sensual, and she had a high forehead and earnest steel-blue eyes. Her hair, which made Red think of autumn, was thick and full with a natural wave. The girl's face was distinctly European but somehow different, too. There was something uncommon about her, almost aristocratic, even though the Beaux-Arts was a public school. Red studied the way she worked, the precise, economic movements of her hands, and he wondered if the same efficiency spilled over to the rest of her life—whatever that was like. He considered himself a quick and accurate judge of character, but none of the speculative journeys his imagination took led him to a satisfying conclusion. Snapping from his reverie, he realized the rest of his entourage had left the classroom. Undaunted, Red moved to the girl's table.

"*J'aime votre travail,*" he said boldly, leaning over her

drawing. His French was embarrassing, but not enough to inhibit him. Nothing really stopped Red when he wanted something.

The startled girl jerked her head up. Her face flushed as she took in the American. Red realized she was older than he'd first thought. Not a girl, a young woman. Twenty-three or four, he guessed, which only deepened the mystery about her.

"I also like the architect who made the drawing," Red continued, still speaking French. "Would you accept an admirer's invitation to dinner?"

Red's smile always came easily. His confidence was unlimited. His soft, round face had clean, chiseled features and his smile alone had opened more doors and hearts for him than any flowery words. In college there had always been a girl on his arm. Still, this young woman looked unsure, even embarrassed as her eyes paraded to his captain's bars and down to the nameplate over his pocket. Red wondered if after the long war she might not be as weary as he was of soldiers and uniforms.

"My nickname's Red," he said, holding out his hand.

"Would you excuse me," she suddenly answered in English. She had a beguiling accent, and her voice was clear and sonorous. She ignored Red's outstretched hand. "I have work to finish—please?"

The cool, uninterested glance leveled at Red was mercifully brief, just enough to will him out of the room. He wasn't ready to retreat. "What kind of work are you doing?" he asked, happy at least to be speaking English. "And by the way, I'm not contagious."

Her face crimsoned again as heads turned in their direction. Red was sorry, but he couldn't help himself. He wasn't used to walking away from challenges, particularly from a woman whose beauty and sense of privacy intrigued him more by the moment.

"Would you at least tell me your name?" he pried. "Then I'll be gone."

She eyed him carefully, debating the wisdom of surrender. "Alycia Boucher."

"Alycia—that's a lovely name," he offered. He smiled cheerfully, all charm again, rocking back on his heels but hardly moving toward the door. "Now, what about dinner? Say yes and I'll really be gone."

"Non, merci," she said. He could tell she was annoyed with him.

"Please? One white lie doesn't mean I can't ever be trusted."

She went back to her drawing and wouldn't look at him. When Red didn't leave, she made her position clearer. *"C'est pas possible,"* she said.

"Everything is possible," he countered.

She laid down her pencil and gave him a firm stare. "I do not go out very much."

"Lucky for me," he exclaimed.

"I have to look after my father."

"Don't you have a brother or sister who could fill in for a night?"

"No. My father has only me."

"Then I'll be sure to bring you home early . . ."

In the end Red wore her down, as he knew he would. He gave her a small wave good-bye but she didn't seem to notice. Finishing the school tour, he returned to his hotel on the Ile de Saint Louis, showered, and changed into civilian clothes. Would she change her mind and not show up? He had wanted to pick up Alycia at her father's apartment, but she had resisted, and this time he didn't push. There was a charm to her distance. He had let her name the restaurant, a small bistro on Place San Michel, and made sure he got himself there ten minutes early.

The sky had magically cleared. In the vanishing sunlight the metal rooftops gleamed like fish bellies. Street traffic, mostly pedestrian, bustled by Red without a glance. He had mixed feelings about Paris. Its architecture and culture, resonant with history, surprised him at every turn, but like most of Europe, Paris had a certain gloom and anxiety. The city was trying to recover, yet people didn't quite trust the postwar peace, and many were still reliving the long, dark nights of German occupation. Gloom was not something Red wanted in his life.

Alycia was prompt to the minute, yet Red struggled to recognize her. In a stylish dress, without her blue smock, he simply stared. He smelled her perfume as she neared, thinking it was as elegant as her small loop earrings or the beige chiffon dress with its puffy sleeves and belted waist. Nothing was expensive, but everything about Alycia seemed right, balanced, poised.

"Bon soir," she said softly. The demure smile put a dimple in each flawless cheek.

"You look lovely," he breathed, marveling at his understatement.

"Vous ne me reconnaissez pas."

"What?" He hadn't heard a word.

"You didn't recognize me."

"No. I'm sorry."

"You look different too."

He laughed. "I don't like uniforms. They make us all look like prisoners."

Red was tempted to kiss her on the cheek, at least take her hand. Instead, awkwardly, they moved inside to a corner table. Something about Alycia intimidated him. Outside her classroom, she was a different person. As she spoke of the restaurant and its owner, whom she had known for years, Red sat spellbound, disarmed by her every word and gesture. Alycia had a sophistication that most American women lacked. But she was also a sheltered innocent—she had never been out of France, she confessed to Red. The combination made her hard for him to understand, but all the more intriguing.

Red's own charm and confidence, always reliable, came now only in spurts. He wanted to laugh. What was this spell Alycia had over him? The physical attraction he was starting to feel for her was overwhelming. He would seduce her tonight, he thought, yet he wasn't sure he could succeed. His helplessness unsettled him. How had he gone through an entire war without feeling any fear, and suddenly with every word he was almost trembling.

"Why didn't you let me pick you up at your apartment?" he asked Alycia in a moment of quiet. He wanted to know everything about her. His question surprised her, as if she thought he was being too forceful again.

"Père is very private, very proper," she answered after a pause.

"Like you?"

"Sometimes like me. My father and I are very close. He doesn't want me to have many dates, which is why I usually don't. Tonight I had to persuade him it was all right by promising to be home early."

Red smiled inquisitively. "I don't understand. You're an adult, you have your own life—"

"Of course, and I'm happy with my life. But part of that is honoring my father. He's a professor of languages at the

Sorbonne. Everyone respects him. To me it's more than that. He's very special.''

Alycia tossed her head back and looked at Red to see if he were really interested. "What about your father? What's he like?''

"I'd rather talk about you.''

She blushed. "I don't think I'm very interesting.''

"Let me decide that.''

"All right,'' she agreed, biting her lip in playful contemplation. "I'll give you a brief résumé. I speak adequate English, I love architecture, and I'll probably spend the rest of my life in Paris. How's that?''

"Tell me what you did in the war.''

She nodded, her mood turning more somber. "It's a very short history, though at the time it felt like centuries. Just before Hitler took over Paris, my mother became ill. Père had to place her in a nearby sanitarium. I think it broke his heart. Without my mother, he had only me. We became very close. Within a few months, my mother died, which was a blessing because shortly after, the Germans massacred everyone in the sanitarium. At the time, I was sixteen and felt totally lost. If not for Père I don't think I would have survived.''

"You don't have to say any more,'' Red offered, feeling her discomfort.

"It's probably good for me to talk. This isn't the kind of thing I tell my school friends. And maybe it's interesting for an American to hear. For five years Père and I lived with uncertainty. Sometimes there was food in the stores, other times people went hungry. Neighbors disappeared. Others were shot on the street. You didn't dare leave the apartment unless it was important. I was at the top of my class at the *lycée*, and then one day the German commandant took over the building for his headquarters. There was no more formal education for me—that's why I'm the oldest student in my class now. All those years were lost. Père and I spent our time reading, talking, playing chess. He always looked after me. We were very lucky—we didn't suffer like some. Père made sure there were always meat and fresh vegetables on our table, despite the risk of dealing in the black market. Books and magazines, chocolate, sometimes even a new dress came my way. And we got to know each other as well as any two people could. What's the expression? It was a silver lining for us.''

Red was too absorbed to touch his wine. "You're very philosophical about things."

"That comes naturally to Europeans. We've seen a lot more tragedy than you have."

Red had nothing to add. For his own reasons he didn't like talking about his family, and he was bored with telling war stories. Being a hero represented the past, and it was his future he was concerned about. Right now he wanted to listen to Alycia. He was surprised she barely ordered anything for dinner. He paid the check and they strolled aimlessly through narrow Left Bank streets.

"You want to do something fun?" Alycia asked, suddenly coupling her arm through Red's.

The gesture surprised him. Alycia had shed her pensive mood like an old skin. Now she was full of life.

"Some school friends are having a party," she said. "It won't be much, but they have a record player. Do you like to dance?" she asked.

"All the time," he said, though it wasn't true. He was just all right, no Fred Astaire, and after sports, in which he excelled, he had never had time or the inclination for much dancing. But all he thought about now was holding Alycia in his arms.

She led him to a musty basement apartment in Saint Germain-des-Prés. The party was in the parlor—it felt like a cattle car, wall to wall with students, smelling of cheap perfume. A few couples were dancing to a scratchy Tommy Dorsey record. Alycia took Red's hand and introduced him to friends. He knew that she was showing him off, but he liked it and felt flattered. Red was amazed because totally gone were Alycia's earlier suspicions about him. As they maneuvered through the crowded room, one young man seemed particularly eager to give Alycia a kiss. She ducked away.

"Who was that?" Red couldn't help asking as they began to dance. "He likes you."

"But I don't like him. He's different from the rest of us."

"He doesn't look different," Red said.

"His parents are rich. They left for America when the war started. Now they're back, with all their money, too."

"That's why you don't like him?"

"I don't believe in capitalism. Money divides people, don't you think? It's not a fair system."

She spoke the words with conviction, almost defiance.

"Is that what your father thinks too?" Red asked.

"Neither of us believes in a class society," she answered proudly, "but I think for myself. What do you believe?"

"I believe," Red said, taking Alycia's hand, "that we should find the bar and then keep dancing."

Red had no difficulty consuming the wine—he rarely did. Even *vin ordinaire* felt good on a warm summer night when Alycia was the only thing that mattered. Red didn't know how long they danced, or how many glasses were tippled. His capacity, legendary in college, had not diminished with the war, but he saw that Alycia was more delicate. After an hour she was almost drunk. He wondered if he should stop her. Their dancing became a case of her holding on to him and swaying back and forth. He could feel her breath in his ear. Her skin was like velvet. He held her tightly and thought again of finding a hotel.

"You do this a lot, with different men, don't you?" he whispered, suddenly jealous.

She pulled back and gave him a lopsided smile. "I told you, I almost never go out . . . and I never drink more than a glass or two . . . can't you tell?"

She let him kiss her on the lips. When someone turned off the record player, Red glanced at his watch. It was almost one.

"*Qu'est que c'est?* Alycia protested in a bleary voice when he led her outside.

"We're late."

The cool air seemed to revive her, and she understood. It took ten long minutes to reach her apartment, not far from the bistro. The squat building on Place San Michel was only four floors, shabby and unimposing inside and out. At her door, taking a breath for courage, Alycia asked Red please to leave—she would handle her father alone.

"I can't let you do that," he said. It was not just that he felt responsible for Alycia; he was curious too. Alycia claimed she couldn't leave her father because she looked after him. The truth seemed to Red that it was the professor who looked after his daughter.

Alycia fumbled her key into the lock. Red marched in behind, taking in the professor as he rose from the couch. There was more disappointment than anger in the intelligent green-flecked eyes. The man was, otherwise, extremely composed, and distinguished-looking, with wire-rim glasses and a trim beard. His thick hair had a wave of gray. A cigarette dangled from between his middle fingers. He was a good dresser too, Red observed—the white slacks looked out of a fashion page. There was gentleness in his gesture to Alycia. Obediently she moved to his side, looking contrite, which Red resented. No matter how great a man her father was, how could she be this devoted? It was as if she'd taken some vow of obedience. Wasn't she entitled to make a mistake once in a while? It was a subject Red knew all about, pleasing fathers. From the way the professor stared at him, he also knew that Alycia might be forgiven, but he was not.

"I'm sorry we're late," Red said into the silence. He thought of introducing himself, but the professor only nodded distantly.

"Good night, Alycia," Red said stubbornly, waiting till she glanced up before he marched out.

The next morning he sent Alycia flowers and a rambling letter he'd labored over endlessly. He adored her, he wrote five different times. Their night together had been more than special. He had to see her again. He could not sleep or eat. All he could think about was Alycia.

When she failed to ring or drop by his hotel, Red suspected the professor's heavy hand, or maybe Alycia distrusted his passion. Should he not have sent anything? How could he conceal what he really felt? He hated deceit and hypocrisy. Despairing, he was about to go back to her apartment—propriety and her father be damned—when, the next morning, a major in his command handed him a sealed envelope. Red returned to his room, afraid to breathe as his finger sliced it open.

My dear American soldier,

Sometimes it's easier to put in writing what one can't say out loud. I loved our evening together too! And I can't wait to see you again, Red. Thank you for *les très jolie fleurs*. You were such a great dancer—I loved your arms around me. I don't know what brought you into my life—I'm not used to happy surprises—but I hope you stay. Père and I have talked over and over about you. Yes, he's distrustful, but only because he's protective of me. Can you understand? I hope so. But I do have a mind and heart of my own—you shall see! Meet me tonight at our bistro around seven.

Love,
Alycia

At their rendezvous Alycia wrapped her arms around his
neck like a vise, as if they'd been apart for a year. Red didn't
know who was the happier. For the next week, juggling his
duties with difficulty, he was always waiting for Alycia after
her classes or evenings at her apartment. Inevitably her father
greeted him at the threshold, civil but not overly friendly,
making clear his strict standards for his daughter as well as
his general suspicion of the American. Red found the distrust
a little ironic. It was Americans like Red who'd liberated
Paris, and he was being treated like a pariah. Still, not
wanting another war, Red was careful always to have Alycia
home on time.

He would take her to the best restaurants, the Comédie
Française, the Opera, for strolls along the Seine. In the independent young woman he began to discover endless and
beguiling contradictions. Alycia was usually quiet and self-
effacing, yet he found glimmers of ambition and dreams
when she spoke of one day designing buildings and having
her own career as an architect. She was always curious about
America, inquiring about geography and the economy, but in
the end admitted she was reluctant to leave Paris. From the
class-conscious professor she'd inherited a strong distrust of
the privileged Right Bank class, though when Red bought her
the finest dresses and perfume, she adored them. When first
he'd tried to kiss her, she was docile, yet after a few days it
was Alycia who initiated the passion. Red didn't pretend to
understand the woman he was falling hopelessly in love with.
He would just look at her in unguarded moments and be
swept away.

When he couldn't be with Alycia—periods that seemed
interminable, even if they were a few hours—he turned quiet
and moody. Poker games were a distraction, just as they'd
been in the war. But now he bet heavily and recklessly and
never cared how much he lost. He wouldn't talk about Alycia,
no matter who asked for an explanation of his behavior. She
was too special, the matter too private. At Stanford he'd had
a dozen girlfriends and slept with them all. Yet he'd never
been in love, not deeply, not with certainty. With Alycia he
had no doubt at all. And with love he felt his life would
change; love would lift him out of his rut and give him new
direction—Alycia was his destiny.

One unseasonably cool afternoon as they walked down the
Champs Elysées, Alycia admitted to having been in love

before. Red knew he had no right to be surprised, but he was. The French soldier, Alycia told him, had died in an early campaign near Alsace.

"I'm sorry," Red said immediately.

"His name was Georges. After he was killed, I really hated Germans. Sometimes I'm afraid I'll always hate them."

"What was he like?" Red wanted to know.

"Sweet, charming, a gentleman. He detested the idea of fighting, but he loved his country."

Alycia bought fresh-cut daisies at a corner shop and they walked to a bus stop. "Will you come with me?" she asked.

Père-Lachaise cemetery occupied an immense hillside in the twentieth arrondissement on Paris' easternmost edge. Crippled soldiers, refugees, and beggars lined the entrance. Alycia opened her purse and spread her money among several pairs of hands.

"Why do you do that?" asked Red.

"Because they have less than I do."

"But that's the way the world is. There're always people with less than you, and more."

"That doesn't mean I have to like it. Don't you think we should all be equal?"

The question struck Red as naive and pointless, but he took it seriously. "No," he said. "People were never meant to be equal. Because they aren't."

"Someone who has money and is afraid of losing it might say that." A faint smiled played on her lips as she looked at Red. "You're wealthy, aren't you?"

"That's irrelevant."

"You always ask me to talk about myself, but you never tell me anything about you."

"You really want to know?" He dug his hands in his pockets.

"If you want to tell me."

"My father is wealthy. I'm not. And I don't want his money—I want to make it on my own, every penny."

"So you're ambitious."

He nodded. "Is that wrong?"

Red could see his response didn't please her. They'd had a disagreement, minor though it was, and it left him feeling helpless. They stepped over the fallen chestnuts and navigated among the head-high monuments, stopping at a small slab of engraved marble that bore the name GEORGES FAURE. Red couldn't help feeling jealous as Alycia laid the flowers beside the stone. Did she come here often? Was she in love with a memory? Didn't she think Red had been just as patriotic as this young man?

"Do you love your father?" Alycia suddenly asked as they started to leave.

"That may be a simple question," he said, thinking about it. "But the answer isn't. I can tell you that we don't always get along."

"Why?" she asked.

Alycia watched Red carefully. Normally he was confident and strong-willed, which she loved, only now he seemed troubled. But she liked that too, she decided. At first the handsome American had seemed so perfect, a dream coming into her life, a stroke of fate, but she was glad he had weaknesses. That made him more real. She took his hand as they walked, wanting to understand Red better.

"If you think I'm ambitious," he said with difficulty, "you should meet my father. He's not just ambitious, he's dominating and manipulative. As a child I sometimes thought of him as a ghost, this dark spirit who had the power to look into my life at any moment, to know every secret I kept, to do anything to me that he pleased. He was consumed with his business, yet he always found the right moment to intrude in my life. I was terrified of him because I knew I didn't please him. I was very nervous and physically weak as a boy . . . couldn't sleep in my room without a light on, got teased by other kids, was afraid of strangers . . . My mother tried to wean me gently from my fears, but my father had other therapy in mind."

"He wasn't understanding at all?" Alycia asked, surprised.

"Starting on my thirteenth birthday, my father hired a private tutor for me. I was made to ride horses, take long hikes in the mountains, hunt jackrabbits in the desert when it was one hundred and twenty degrees. Manly things. The more danger and hardship involved, the quicker I was supposed to find my confidence. There was never room for argument. I kept my resentment to myself, but it burned brightly and deeply, and after a while it took a strange twist. One day I decided I wanted to be good at everything my father forced me to do. Not just good, the best. And not to please my father. I wanted to spite him, to be better than he thought possible. I realized that was the only way of taking control of my life . . . and taking the power away from Father.''

"Did it work?" Alycia asked.

Red smiled philosophically. "My father never showed the slightest pleasure, no matter how well I did. He didn't even seem to notice. Which only made me furious, and also made me try even harder. When I was seventeen I stood six-feet-two and weighed two hundred and twenty pounds. I began parachuting out of planes, taking solo bike trips through South America, climbing mountains. With the Depression, money allowed me the freedom my friends only dreamed about, yet I never felt free. In high school I lettered in four sports and got straight A's. Everyone considered me talented and charming, and I enjoyed easy friendships, but I always sensed, under the surface, this immense void. Against all evidence, I still didn't believe anyone paid serious attention to me. After graduating from Stanford, I joined my father's real-estate firm. The tremendous land boom of the twenties had made him rich, and he said he would help me out if I ever needed it. He saw himself as my patron—that's what being a father meant to him. I didn't want a handout. It was risk I wanted, and success. After a year I was outhustling and outselling my father's seasoned brokers. Yet he never complimented me or showed approval. After a while, I just got disgusted. When Pearl Harbor was attacked, I was the first among my friends to attend officer-candidate school.''

Red fell into silence and Alycia didn't want to intrude. His unhappiness seemed so complicated, almost bottomless, she thought. Her own life had not been exactly easy, yet there were moments she could look back on and say, yes, I was happy then, yes, that was special. She wondered if Red could say that. She suddenly turned and kissed him hungrily. Could she make him happy? She was falling in love with him, she knew that now, and with love, anything was possible.

"I should go," she said, pulling away reluctantly. "I have exams tomorrow.''

"When will I see you?''

"Dinner tomorrow? Our bistro?''

Red kissed her again, understanding, but he had to keep himself from following her to the bus. Even for a few hours, without Alycia in his life he felt incomplete. Despite earlier doubts, it had been a relief to talk about his father—she seemed to understand, to accept Red totally. Returning to his command, he began to see the full depth and meaning of his feelings: it wasn't enough just to be in love with Alycia. He would always feel unfulfilled until he married her.

From that moment he began to plan the moment he would ask. His Paris duty was over in two days, but the bigger obstacle, of course, was Alycia's father. During the war he had been her angel, yet Alycia had to know her debt to him didn't mean never leaving home or not getting married, even to an American.

Dining with Alycia the next evening, having rehearsed his proposal fifty times, Red could barely discuss the weather. He drank his wine but didn't touch his food. Alycia seemed just as unsettled. After dinner they strolled over the Pont Neuf and watched some boys kicking a soccer ball. "You know, I'm in love with you," Red finally blurted. His eyes swung nervously to the beautiful face. His heart froze. He was afraid to ask if she loved him. What if she said no? A tear rolled down Alycia's cheek, and Red went to wipe it away.

"What's wrong?" he whispered.

"I'm in love with you too," she said, "but I know what you're going to ask."

"Alycia, I want to marry you and take you to the States. Is that so frightening? I know you'll be happy. I promise you."

"Everything's happening so fast . . ."

She drifted a few steps, troubled. Red knew better than to crowd her, yet he couldn't control his emotions. "Alycia," he said softly, "I know leaving your father won't be easy, but what about living your own life? Don't you ever think of yourself and your happiness?"

"All I think about lately is you," she said, turning back to him, "you and I, being in love, getting married maybe. All through the war I didn't know what would happen to me. I was afraid of dreams because I knew they could never come true—"

"This one will," Red swore. "I'll make it happen. Alycia, I'll give you everything you could ever want . . ." The words locked in his throat. Red felt like a hopeless adolescent, lost to his emotions, stumbling headlong without any idea where the path might take him, his voice wobbling. All he knew was, he would not leave Paris without Alycia.

Red chose the first respectable hotel he could find. He didn't ask Alycia's permission. In his desperate state he wondered what exactly he was proving—that being a great lover would convince her to marry him? He was ashamed of the childishness of the thought. Really he wanted to show his sincerity—and that he was so needy of possessing her that nothing could stop him.

In bed, too eager, they were hardly the graceful and passionate lovers Red had imagined. He was so suffused with tender impulses that it didn't matter. Afterwards he begged Alycia again to marry him. He, too, had a dream for them, he said. In Los Angeles they would work together. Alycia would design buildings for the land he developed. Together they could accomplish anything.

"I thank God for the day you came into my life," she told him, wrapping her arms around his chest. A smile lit her face with a radiance Red had never seen. "I'll tell Père tonight," she whispered. "I'll tell him I want to marry you."

Red gave a shout of joy.

"Maybe I should talk to your father," he said when he'd calmed down. This was too important to leave to chance. He had to be in control.

She laid a finger across his lips. "Don't be afraid. I've made up my mind. Nothing's going to stop us. Père understands what being in love is. You should have seen him and mother."

It was midnight when Red walked Alycia back to the Latin Quarter, long past her father's curfew. Red said again he wanted to speak for her. Alycia forbade it. The time with Père had to be private. She would meet Red tomorrow at noon, at the Hôtel de Ville, Paris' city hall. Their good-night kiss lasted forever.

Alone, Red was only filled with anxiety. He was supposed to leave Paris tomorrow. Was this cutting things too close? He stayed away from the poker game and beer at the hotel. Sleep was impossible. His thoughts swam to resigning his commission and getting married, and whether he'd rejoin his father's firm. Red loved the real-estate business, but why should he bother trying to please his father anymore? Did people ever change? He wondered what his parents would think of Alycia. His mother was a dear and would adore his bride. His father, he was afraid, would only greet Alycia with silent doubt.

In the morning, putting on fresh khakis, Red perched outside the grandiose block-long Hôtel de Ville. Noon came and went. Alycia was never late for anything. Red paced and looked at the sun and forked his fingers through his hair. One moment he was sure everything was fine, that the delay could and would be explained, but the next moment he was certain Alycia had changed her mind or her father had forbidden marriage. A little after one, a colonel reminded Red to be at the motor pool within the hour.

He hurried to the Ecole des Beaux-Arts. Alycia's seat was empty. The professor stopped Red before he ran out. Someone else had been looking for Alycia this morning.

"Who?" Red demanded. He heard the anger and frustration in his voice. "Her father?"

"Oh, no, not Professor Boucher. Someone else. A stranger."

"What did he say?"

"He was a very serious young man. Large and muscular—your size, Captain—but with a dark complexion, and very much in a hurry, very angry. He didn't say two words."

What was this all about? Red wondered as he ran to the apartment on Place San Michel. His breath came in spurts and his shirt was totally damp. The apartment door was open. His eyes skimmed over the broken furniture and littered floor. He shouted for Alycia, then looked for a note. Nothing. Every room had been torn apart. Knocks on neighbors' doors went unanswered or brought empty stares. No one knew anything.

The panic rode up to his throat. Where else could he look? Alycia had school friends, but they were all over town. He searched several cafés and the library where she studied. When he doubled back and approached the Hôtel de Ville, it was past two. He would ask his CO for permission to remain in Paris until he found Alycia. He was going to stay even if the colonel court-martialed him.

In the distance, bathed in the perpendicular shadows of city hall, Red spotted the sitting woman. Alycia looked perfectly tranquil and untroubled, as if she'd been there all along, as if the ransacked apartment he'd found was someone else's. Up close, focusing, he felt sick. Alycia stood uncertainly. Bruises darkened her arms and face. Her dress was ripped. An eye was half-shut. She had the exhausted, defeated air of a refugee.

She ran toward Red before he could speak, collapsing in his arms.

"Who did this to you?" he demanded. His calmness surprised him. He was thinking murderous thoughts.

"Please take me away from here," she whispered. The wounded voice gave him a chill.

"Alycia, what happened?"

She stood back. Her tongue brushed her lips and she squared her shoulders bravely. When she was composed, she said, "I want to marry you, Red. I want to leave here at once. That's all that's important. I want to marry you and be in love with you the rest of my life."

Red felt helplessly, gratefully in love again, yet the battered face filled him with an uneasy anger. "Alycia, I have to know—"

"No," she cut him off. "I will marry you and have your children and try to be a perfect wife and mother. But you must never ask me what happened today. Never. Please promise me."

Red could only stare. There was a part of Alycia that was private and unreachable and not to be argued with. The beating she'd suffered was his pain too—he was sure her father, angel or not, was somehow responsible—but Alycia's eyes told him that this was not his affair. It would have nothing to do with their future.

"I promise," Red said reluctantly, and took Alycia into his arms.

Upon notifying his CO that he would resign his commission, Red secured an immediate leave and arranged for a military hop to New York. At Idlewild Airport the decorated war hero and his fiancée skirted the long lines at Immigration, and at a special window Alycia had only to endure a cursory passport inspection. The lawyer friend Red had asked to facilitate their entry and Alycia's U.S.-citizenship application had also booked them the bridal suite on the top floor of the Plaza Hotel. Red wanted only the best. When he had told Alycia he would give her everything, he wanted to show he meant it.

The bellhop hefted their bags into the room, waited for his tip, and left the handsome couple to their privacy. Alycia pressed her hands together and raised them to her lips. An ice bucket with champagne stood next to the bed. Fresh flowers decorated the bureau. From a second room came a radio. When she went to explore, she found the sound wafted from some kind of small picture box.

"That's a television," explained Red, following her. "This is the only hotel in New York that has them for guests."

Alycia flicked the heavy dial, and another station crackled on. This really was a dream, she thought.

Back in the bedroom, it sounded like a gunshot when Red uncorked the champagne.

"We're not even married yet," Alycia protested half-seriously.

"A mere formality. Cheers, darling . . ."

She giggled as they raised glasses and drank by hooking their arms through each other.

"Oh, this is dry, just right," she said, finishing her glass and dropping onto the bed.

"Better be, it's French," he joked. "At twenty a bottle it ought to be perfect. Like you."

"I adore you," she whispered. She tried to pull Red onto the bed but he was moving to the door.

"Stores don't close for another hour," he called merrily.

"What do we need? We have everything."

He laughed and pulled her along.

When they crossed Fifth Avenue on a red light, running the last few meters, Alycia thought Red was crazy; then she saw that no one obeyed signal lights. The whole city seemed reckless and extravagant. Paris was restrained by a sense of order and history; New York was an old city too, by American standards, yet it was flashy and uninhibited. Buildings, side by side, towered to the clouds. The sidewalks swelled with well-dressed businessmen and society women all looking serious and purposeful. Taxis dashed in and out of their lanes like this was a derby.

"A jewelry store?" Alycia asked as Red led her through a revolving door.

"*The* jewelry store," he informed her. They snaked through aisles where the glass cases held necklaces and brooches that looked too glittering to be real. "It's called Tiffany.

"Which one do you prefer?" Red nudged her up to a display of silver and gold rings crowned with dazzling stones. "They're all three carats or more. Look at that one . . ." She followed his gaze to a clear hexagonal stone that would have stunned her father.

"I can't," she said, meaning it.

"Darling, it's your engagement ring."

"But it's not necessary."

"Alycia, the war is over," Red kidded in his sweet way. "And this is America. You have to change your thinking."

"How can you afford it?"

"I worked three years for my father before the war. What's the point of having money if you don't spend it?"

Alycia gave up resisting as Red selected the most expensive ring in the display case and wiggled it onto her finger. She faced a mirror and held up her hand. The ring somehow transformed her, she realized, but into what, she didn't know. Her glance swam to the bruises on her face and arms that were mercifully fading. Soon they would be gone, become a distant memory. The future that the ring signified would have to be better.

"Well?" Red pushed.

Like some shill, the salesman wouldn't stop admiring the ring. Alycia could only think of what her father had once told her. Save your love for people, he said, not things. Her eyes jumped to Red. He did love her; the ring was just his way of saying it. "It's so beautiful," she breathed, feeling a little overwhelmed. "I'll never take it off."

When Red had paid for the ring, they caught a taxi to Saks Fifth Avenue. Unlike jewelry, Alycia did know something about clothes—before the war, Paris had been the couture capital of Europe if not of the world—but here were more racks of dresses than she'd seen in her life. Dazzled, she picked one outfit, then another, and another. She wanted to stop, but Red, enlisting the help of two salesgirls to sort and carry the purchases, insisted she have no fewer than a dozen dresses. She was torn again between resenting extravagance and wanting to please her future husband. She saw that Red couldn't help himself. This energy of his, all this buying, was a headlong rush of love for her—what right did she have to stand in the way? Alycia held up a lacy pink evening gown to the mirror and realized she was also pleasing herself.

"You aren't tired, are you?" Red said as they left the store.

"*Pas de tout*," she lied, not wanting to disappoint him.

They had dinner at the Colony, took in a Broadway musical, *Finian's Rainbow*, and ended the night by dancing to Xavier Cugat at the Starlight Roof on top of the Waldorf. Alycia was exhausted, but she was also excited, and the next day Red hardly let up. They drank champagne in taxicabs, climbed all one thousand, five hundred and seventy-five steps of the Empire State Building, and watched construction workers starting on the new United Nations Building. Alycia felt like a stranger in her new country—curious and exhilarated—and Red was her guide and mentor. She did everything he wanted, not only because it was fun but also because Red liked being the leader. In Paris she had seen how he had to dominate and be in control. She didn't mind. Everything felt like a constant, unending surprise, like waking every morning and being told it was her birthday.

"You know something, I don't miss home at all," she confessed when they were in bed that night. Naked, she draped her arms over his muscular chest.

Without a word Red guided his hand down her belly and between her legs. His fingers manipulated and kneaded her so expertly that she was jealous. How many women had he slept with? Still, she let him play with her for what seemed forever. The pleasure began to build. When she reached out and felt his erection, she turned over, raised herself on her elbows and knees, and asked him to enter her from behind. She didn't know what possessed her. She had never done it like this. She felt her breath shorten as his thrusts came quicker and deeper, and his hands cupped her breasts with just the right amount of pressure. When Red had climaxed, she lowered herself to her belly again, flushed and happy. Then she started laughing and couldn't stop.

"It was funny?" said Red, slightly hurt.

She put her hand over her mouth. "I was thinking of a joke we used to tell in the *lycée*. Do you want to hear? If I can translate it . . ."

"I want to hear every joke you know."

She stretched her neck, trying to recall. "A priest was warning a group of young ladies about the dangers of promiscuous sex. In a grave voice he said to them, 'Dear girls, is ten minutes of pleasure worth an eternity of damnation?' One of the girls frowned and raised her hand. 'Father,' she said, 'how do you make it last ten minutes?' "

Red chuckled too. "Ours was more than ten minutes."

"I know. I loved it. I love you."

"Forever?" he asked, more serious. She saw the vulnerable side of Red again, the side she liked because she felt protective of it.

"And ever," she promised.

"Then we're getting married tomorrow."

She bit down on her lip. "Tomorrow?"

"High noon."

"Where?" She sat up in bed, breathless.

"New York City Hall."

Alycia's eyes narrowed. Was she missing something? "What about Los Angeles?"

"What about it?"

"Your friends—"

"Alycia, do you really want a formal, elaborate wedding? You wouldn't know anyone—the guests would all be friends of mine or my parents'. What's the point?"

She saw there was no room for argument as Red reached to the beside table and opened a satin jewelry box. He placed the two gold bands in her hand. Inside each were engraved the words FOREVER DARLING.

"I picked them out this morning," he announced, pleased with himself.

"They are stunning," she whispered, but she was thinking about something else.

"Then you're happy—"

"When are we leaving New York?" she asked.

"As soon as I book a hotel in Los Angeles."

Confused again, Alycia flicked her hair from her eyes. "A hotel?"

"The most luxurious in the city."

"Red, aren't we going to stay at your parents' until we find our own house? You said they practically had a mansion. Surely there's room for us . . ."

Red's smile dimmed.

"There's no rush, I suppose," Alycia caught herself. "It's just that I'd like to meet them. And I'd think they'd want to meet me." Alycia took Red's hand. "Do you think they'll like me?"

"I told you, my mother's a dear. She'll adore you."

"It's more your father I had in mind." She thought of her own father, how she'd always brought them both pleasure by doing what he wanted. She was used to being accepted and feeling close to her family. Her own family was behind her; all she had now was Red's.

"It feels funny, that's all," Alycia explained when Red stayed quiet. "Your not telling your parents about me, about us. I don't think marriages should be secrets."

"We're not a secret," Red corrected her. "We're a surprise."

"It just seems like you're sneaking me in somehow . . . that you're not proud of me."

She felt relieved to say what was bothering her, but she

saw it was Red she was upsetting now. His voice grew firmer. "The only issue, Alycia, is that I don't need my father's approval for what I do, including marrying you. Do you understand?"

"Of course I understand," she backed off, and wandered into the bathroom. Red didn't come after her. She hated the silence, and being left alone. She wondered if this constituted their first real argument. Even if it was a petty one, she wished it had never happened. She didn't want any more fights, not after what had happened to her and her father on her last day in Paris. Next time she'd know better than to question Red's judgment, especially about something personal. She and Red would be the perfect partners—in business as well as marriage—and nothing would get in the way, she swore, least of all themselves.

Their first night in Los Angeles was spent at the Beverly Hills Hotel, a hilltop pink palace festooned with billowy flags and surrounded by immaculately groomed gardens that were every color in the rainbow. Alycia found it so different from New York. Coca-Colas cost one dollar and everyone sat around the hotel pool making telephone calls. The guests were tanned and good-looking and acted very important. Red told her to ignore them, this was just Beverly Hills. Many belonged to what he called the movie colony, people who tried to cheat you when it came to money, Red swore, and were incestuously clannish and had their noses in the air. He had dealt with a few in real estate and would never make that mistake again. The most colossal blunder the city ever made was in 1910 when it allowed a fast-talking producer from New York named David Horsley to move his Nestor Film Company into a tavern on Gower and Sunset. Once the movie people had a foot in the door, Red said, there was no stopping the invasion.

The next day Red surprised Alycia with a car and driver.

"Where are we going?" she asked.

"Sightseeing. Los Angeles isn't like Manhattan. This is a city of wheels." With instructions from Red, the driver ferried them onto Sunset Boulevard. "There're only three things you need to survive in L.A.," Red said with a wink. "A gas station, a parking place, and a car wash."

Alycia was all eyes. Red took them on a crowded triple-lane highway called the Arroyo Seco Freeway that he told her was built just before the war. It stretched eight miles between Pasadena and downtown Los Angeles.

"This freeway was once a charming country wash," Red admitted. "It might have stayed that way if not for the automobile and oil industries."

"What did they do?" Alycia asked.

"In the twenties and thirties, a trolley system called the Pacific Electric was Los Angeles' main transportation system. It was damned effective, but Detroit and Standard Oil lobbied behind the scenes. The trolley system was killed off."

Alycia glanced around. "So now you have traffic jams." She thought this was almost as bad as Paris.

They took the Pasadena exit and meandered down a wide tree-lined boulevard. Red told her that every January first, this was the most famous street in the country.

"*Pourquoi*? she asked. The setting was pretty but looked quite ordinary.

"Ever hear of the Rose Bowl parade? Los Angeles is a city of never-ending promotions, and the Tournament of Roses is king. The old Pasadena Valley Hunt Club found winter to be socially barren, so it decided to host a parade. Since Southern California boasted to the country it grew flowers year-round, roses were chosen as the motif. The first parade was in 1890. Five years later, when a power schism developed in the club, the Pasadena Board of Trade took over sponsorship. Wanting to be creative, they added a football game to the agenda. That's called the Rose Bowl."

"What is football?" she asked.

Red grinned. "Just one more thing for you to learn about America."

Alycia wanted to learn. No matter what the subject, she had always been an eager and conscientious student. And this immense city, as sprawling and diverse as it appeared to be, she was determined to categorize and make sense of.

After lunch they passed through West Los Angeles, not far from the ocean, where hundreds of working oil derricks were squeezed between small, shabby homes. The air was thick with the scent of oil. "See those pitiful little homes?" Red pointed. "Don't feel too sorry for the owners. They're all millionaires living in Beverly Hills."

On Alycia's insistence Red showed her a map of the city. Mountain ranges called the San Gabriels, the San Bernardinos, the Santa Monicas, the Santa Anas, and the Palos Verdes interspersed valleys known as the San Fernando, the San Gabriel, and the Los Angeles Plain. Within that framework the city was unconscionably huge and diverse. She and Red rolled down Hollywood Boulevard, which was hardly as glamorous as she'd hoped, passed the La Brea tar pits, which Red swore still contained dinosaur bones, traveled through rustic, hilly canyons that separated Hollywood and Beverly Hills from the San Fernando Valley, and ended the afternoon on an ocean pier in Santa Monica.

"What's that?" Exhausted from the day, Alycia stared back at the city vista. "In the sky—it wasn't there this morning."

Red smiled apologetically. "A pall of hydrocarbons. Some newspaper nicknamed it 'smog.' Half-smoke, half-fog. The city just organized an air-pollution control board to study it."

Alycia rested her head on Red's shoulder. After the tallness and density of New York, her imagination had painted a large but somehow quaint city where residential and commercial blocks were interspersed with manicured parks, and the whole metropolis bled into white sand beaches and a coral-blue ocean. What she found instead was sprawl. Hadn't Red told her this was once a small Spanish pueblo? The city center today was a dark, congested downtown of shabby, unimposing buildings, their height limited for fear of earthquakes, and lacking the elegance and grandeur of midtown Manhattan. From there the city took off in all directions like pieces in a surrealistic jigsaw puzzle. Communities like Eagle Rock and Glendale and Pasadena were well-established, though none were much more than seventy-five years old, while others were being created almost by the day—in the San Fernando Valley she saw entire blocks of tract housing spring up like mushrooms. New freeways were sprouting up to connect them, as if to make the best of a mistake. The city's general disharmony was reinforced by an eclectic mix of residential neighborhoods, whose styles, shapes, and colors were never the same. Everything seemed mindless and random, without the hint of planning.

"You're being too hard," Red said when Alycia volunteered her criticism. "You've been spoiled by Paris. I don't look at these as homes or neighborhoods. I don't even look at them as real estate."

"Then what?" she asked.

"Opportunity," he clarified as his eyes swept over the

landscape. "This city is like the people who thrive best in it—spontaneous, imaginative, willing to take chances."

"But the architecture is like a series of movie sets strung together. One western, one musical, one historical—"

"All that counts," Red interrupted, "is that each week families are moving to Southern California by the thousands. They come for the climate, the economy, the recreation. This is a phenomenon of migration. The city is never going to stop growing. One day we'll be bigger than Chicago or New York."

From that moment Alycia tried hard to like her new city. Red expected that of her, and there were *some* good things. The sky was terribly blue when the wind or rain chased away the smog, the ocean magical, the climate divine. Red called Los Angeles the Promised Land.

Alycia was also impressed by how much Red accomplished every day in this disorganized city. Within a week he had found them a handsome two-story brick colonial with green shutters in an established, well-to-do community in the San Fernando Valley called Toluca Lake. He promptly put their earnest money in escrow and arranged for a twenty-year mortgage at five and one-half percent. Alycia was staggered by the thirty-thousand-dollar price, but the house was lovely, with spacious rooms that faced flagstone patios, and wainscoting that ran the full length of the stairs. The home was on the small side for Toluca Lake, but it was all they could afford, Alycia knew, though Red would never admit that their constant spending was rapidly depleting their savings.

What Red liked most was the neighborhood's prestige. Despite the disadvantage of having a movie star down the block, he said, nearby was a charming lake with ducks and geese and fish—fifty-six elegant homes backed onto the twisting half-mile-long waterway—and across the street sat a private golf club called Lakeside. Red told her he had a four handicap. Once they took title to the house, he promised, they would join the club and Alycia could learn to play.

She began to feel a glow of excitement and expectation. The home and neighborhood were more than she'd ever wanted, more than she deserved. She planned what carpets and draperies and furniture to buy, how to landscape the yard, and maybe someday, when they could afford it, they'd put in a pool. Imagine, she thought—in all of Paris she didn't know of one private swimming pool. Over lunch one day she discussed her ideas with Red. Impressed, he gave her carte blanche.

Alycia's only disappointment so far was not meeting Red's parents. Red and she had been in Los Angeles almost a month and were still at the Beverly Hills Hotel. Wasn't this a little strange? She bit her tongue every time the thought came to her, trusting her husband would schedule a visit with his parents soon.

One afternoon, in front of the hotel, Red made Alycia close her eyes and stand by the curb. A minute later she heard the smooth purr of an approaching car. The horn sounded like a deep-throated goose.

"Going my way?" Red called cheerily when she opened her eyes. The deep burgundy convertible had already drawn a small crowd. Alycia saw that Red loved the admiring stares. She only wondered how, on top of the house, they could afford a new car.

"What do you think?" he asked as she climbed in. "It's a Lincoln Continental Cabriolet."

"It is gorgeous! Is it really ours?"

"Always and forever," he said, and to impress onlookers, he lowered the rag top and roared away like the Great Gatsby.

Several miles down Sunset, Red showed her a dilapidated but quaint beach enclave called Malibu. "No one wants to live here," Red informed her. "Too many storms, and there's no sewer line. But I like it." They continued up the coast, passing for a moment the Union Pacific train that every morning left for San Francisco. At Santa Barbara, a mantle of fog hovered by the ocean's edge. Alycia insisted they stop. As they strolled through the old mission town, she fell in love with the thick-walled architecture and the hilly sightline of terra-cotta-tiled roofs.

"The town looks like it's been here for centuries," she marveled.

"Santa Barbara has been a colonial outpost for the East Coast rich since before the Civil War," Red told her, "but most buildings you see were erected no more than twenty years ago. In 1925 an earthquake leveled virtually everything. Locals considered that a blessing. Like Los Angeles, old Santa Barbara was a hodgepodge of building styles. An architectural review board was formed and an official Santa Barbara 'style' chosen—a mixture of Spanish Colonial and Mission

Revival. From that day forward, everything new had to conform to code.

"Along came an architect named George Washington Smith to carry the torch. He designed magnificent mansions for the town's wealthy, just like Stanford White had done for New York. Countless trips to Italy and Spain yielded Smith a treasure of old Florentine doors, wrough-iron grilles, shutters, chandeliers, orante tiles. His faithful rendering of the new style made the town famous. Some critics think his taste ran to the gaudy. Santa Barbarans consider the twenty-nine homes he designed to be irreplaceable treasures."

"I've studied Stanford White, but I never heard of George Washington Smith," Alycia said. "I don't think he's too gaudy. The town has such a settled, peaceful feel." She looked at Red. "Would you ever want to live here?"

Red wagged his head. "It's too snobby. There's too much old money around. The Armour family, the Mortons, the Fleischmanns, the Hammonds. A lot of foreign money too. Baron Philippe de Rothschild winters here. No matter where they're from, the old rich are clannish. Their group is led by a local grande dame named Angelica Schuyler Bryce. My father's friendly with her, but I never cared for the lady or her group at the Valley Club."

"I wouldn't care for them either," Alycia guessed. "But what's the difference between old money and new? I think no matter where it comes from, money insulates you from the real world."

It was a familiar subject between them. Alycia didn't want to revive an argument, but she wanted to know what Red thought the difference was. Was it because Red could never belong to one group that he very much wanted to be a part of the other? Was there a special distinction only for Red, and did it have to do with his father?

"The difference?" he said, pausing, as if it were not an easy answer. "One day you'll find out for yourself."

They walked for a while on the beach and stopped for drinks in the Biltmore Hotel. In a lounge overlooking the Pacific, the linen tablecloths were the color of the sunset and the starched napkins were folded in the shape of flamingos.

"A toast to our poverty," Alycia kidded. She leaned over to kiss Red on the lips and raised her glass.

"To the end of our poverty but never our love," Red retorted. He downed his Scotch and ordered a double.

Alycia angled her head back, trying to remember. *"Belle, j'auras un très grand tort,* she recited. *"Si pour votre grâce estimée, j'avais reçu l'amoureux sort, pour autre que pour vous, ma chère aimée."*

"An old French proverb?"

"A poem I had to memorize in my *lycée*. Loosely, it means that nothing will ever happen to us because we have enchanted lives."

"I propose another toast, darling. To our sexy new Lincoln. What shall we call it . . . or her . . . or him?"

"It should be something masculine," Alycia voted. "How about *Napoleon*?"

"Short men are rarely sexy. What do you think of *Alexander the Great*? Or we could name it after an architect. We could call it *Le Corbusier.*"

"Architects aren't sexy enough," Alycia said with a blush, "but developers are."

"Shall we name it, then, after my father? We can christen it the *Owen.*"

"Is your father sexy?"

"I never think of him in that category, but maybe he is. I think of him as proud and autocratic."

Her husband was getting drunk, which Alycia had never seen before, not this drunk, but Red acted perfectly pleased with himself.

"Maybe we should start for home," she suggested after a moment.

"What for? This is too much fun."

"We can drink at our pink hotel."

"I think we should stay and talk about my father. I want you to know that while he and I have our differences, in some ways I admire and respect him. You will too. He has a strict, unvarying sense of right and wrong. That's how he brought me up. Anyone that strong and inflexible, you wonder how he does it, don't you? It fascinates you, whether you approve or not."

Alycia tried to imagine what Owen Poindexter looked like.

"There's just one problem," Red went on. "Anyone who crosses him . . ."

When Red fell into silence, Alycia dropped her chin in her hand. "Go on," she coaxed.

Red finished his drink. "All right. When I was growing up, our family had a very faithful and wonderful house keeper. She was like a second mother to me. Worked twelve years for us. One day my father caught her stealing some little bric-a-brac from his study. The next day, he called her in and said he was sorry, but he had no choice but to fire her.''

"After all those years? No second chance?" Alycia spoke up. "What did your mother say?"

"My mother has always been wise enough to let my father have his way, even when she disagrees with him. There can't be two bosses in one house.''

"What did you say?"

"Nothing. Does that disappoint you? Like my mother, I knew never to confront him. He wasn't going to change. The incident became one more thing to resent about my father. I kept my distance, disgusted, yet in some ways I was fascinated by him. I wanted somehow to understand him. To get along with him. As much as I resented him, I still wanted a relationship. I wanted his love and respect. It may sound crazy, but I still do.''

Red asked the waiter for another Scotch. A smile played on his lips that Alycia couldn't read. He took a sip and put down his glass. Alycia almost laughed as he stood and tripped. "Darling, where are you going?" she called.

"To phone my parents. We're dropping over tonight.''

"But you can't," Alycia protested, shocked. This was all too sudden. "Just like that, you're going to say we're married and bring me over?''

"Why not?" he said blithely. "You've wanted to meet them since New York.''

"Red, I don't look presentable.''

"You look beautiful," he swore.

"Please, Red . . .''

"Now that I've proved myself in war and love, I think it's time to make peace on the home front.''

"Can't we talk about this?" she pleaded, but Red was already on his way to the phone.

When he sauntered back, hands dangling from his pockets, his impish smile only made her more nervous.

"Well?" she asked, suddenly wanting another drink.

"My father answered the phone. He was stunned that I was in Los Angeles. Then I told him I had just married the most beautiful and scintillating woman in the western hemisphere and would bring her over to meet everyone in, say, two hours.''

"You didn't!"

"Oh, but I did."

"What did your father say about me?" Alycia demanded, breathless.

"Not a damn thing. He didn't have a chance. My time was up and the operator disconnected us."

"Liar," she said, still on edge as she followed Red out of the hotel.

"Good thing I'm not too drunk," Red allowed with a wink as he gunned the Lincoln and shot onto the highway. Wisps of fog strayed over the road. Alycia sat rigidly as Red darted past one car after another on the single lane, the Lincoln roaring its prowess as its lights poked holes in the darkness. She was getting chilly, but Red said he was feeling too good to put up the rag top.

"At least slow down," she asked. Red barely took his foot off the accelerator. Her thoughts flicked between the danger of the highway and the prospect of meeting Red's parents in her wrinkled dress, not to mention with liquor on her breath. Alycia closed her eyes.

When they reached the city, her stomach was queasy. Negotiating the curves and hills of Westwood, she was afraid of becoming sick. Finally they glided through the wrought-iron gates of Bel Air. The elaborate homes, guarded by high walls, hugged still more steep and winding streets. Lights revealed perfectly manicured lawns and flowerbeds. Cars parked in driveways were new and expensive. She noticed, too, a huge and vast silence that dwarfed everything, as if this were a cathedral, a kingdom that sat above the rest of the world.

"Why is it called Bel Air?" she asked, trying to feel better.

"For its developer, Alfonso Bell. In the twenties, when Westwood began to grow in response to an overbuilt Beverly Hills, Bell came up here and gave people even bigger lots, plusher landscaping, views of the whole city—and cheaper prices. That was then. They're cheap no more."

"It's nice to have something named after you," Alycia offered.

"Half the towns in Los Angeles are tributes. Torrance was named for the philanthropist Jared S. Torrance, Whittier for the poet, Sherman Oaks for General M. H. Sherman, Hawthorne for Nathaniel Hawthorne, and Tarzana because it was the home of Tarzan's creator, Edgar Rice Burroughs. There's a misconception that Burbank was named for the botanist Luther Burbank; it was really for Dr. David Burbank, who once owned the whole town." Red grinned and gave an exulted honk of his horn. "Damn, do you suppose one day they'll name something after me?"

The Poindexter residence was a sprawling Mediterranean affair with rolling lawns and fountains and pieces of Greek sculpture. A mammoth greenhouse and extensive gardens dominated a lower level, which reminded Alycia of the Giverny home, outside of Paris, of Monet. Approaching the front steps, her hand in Red's, she peeked over a retainer wall to find a tennis court and kidney-shaped swimming pool. Her nerves began to unravel. In the car she had tried perfume and lipstick and combed her hair, but as she neared the mahogany front door she felt as groomed as a Gypsy.

"Mother!" Red beamed at the woman who opened the door. The willowy, graceful figure had a tan angular face in which Alycia found little resemblance to her son's, except for the eyes, which were a teal blue and a dead match. After embracing Red, she turned to Alycia.

"I'm Harriet," she said warmly, holding her daughter-in-law by the shoulders for a better look. "You're Alycia. What a gorgeous name. What a beautiful thing you are—"

"Thank you."

"Oh, this is a wonderful surprise," Harriet said. "Please come in."

Alycia liked Red's mother immediately, and for a moment she relaxed. But as she stepped into the elegant foyer with marble floors that she was sure came from Italy and an antique crystal chandelier worthy of Versailles, not to mention whole rooms whose appointments were as expensive as they were tasteful, Alycia felt anxious again. What had they been doing making a toast to poverty? When Red had told her his family was wealthy, she hadn't imagined anything this grand. She suddenly was afraid that as a simple girl from Paris she would be measured against it, that money carried a certain personality and power of its own, which would totally dwarf her. Yet she couldn't allow that. This magnificent house, and the house Red had bought for them, the car, the ring, the clothes—they were part of a world she had fallen into and would have to make peace with. If she wanted to belong, she would have to forget her views about money and class differences.

Staring at the wonderful details of the house, Alycia was oblivious of the approaching footsteps. When she finally turned and faced Red's father, she could feel her pulse beating in her neck. Alycia had imagined a much older-looking man, but Red's father, in his mid-fifties, bore the same youthful intensity as Red. He was slightly heavier, the jowls wider, hair graying at the sides, but the eyes shone and the posture was ramrod straight. Whereas Red radiated charm, Mr. Poindexter, in his dark suit and tie, seemed remote and judgmental. She watched as his hand came up to meet hers. A reserved smile creased his face. Alycia tried to be both relaxed and polite, but was sure she was perceived as nervous and confused. She was also sure those were two traits Mr. Poindexter did not like.

"So you're Alycia." He spoke in a neutral voice, the appraising eyes gliding over her but missing nothing. "I'm Owen Poindexter. I find these strange circumstances under which to meet, but here we are . . ."

Alycia forced a smile. What did he mean exactly? She wanted to say something witty and appropriate, but no words came to her, just like when she first met Red.

"May I bring you a drink?" he asked, saving her for the moment.

"No, thank you. I'm fine." She thought he'd already smelled the liquor on her breath. Her eyes swam to Red for help, but with barely a hello to his father, Red was already at the large mirrored bar off the foyer. How could he drink so much? He scarcely paid attention to anyone, much less Alycia, as if this was his triumph, his show, and she was a mere prop.

"Maybe I will have that drink," she said to Red's father.

The four sat in the formal living room. They talked about the war and Paris and what Red had been doing since fall, when he'd last visited home. The marriage was glossed over, as if its reality had not fully penetrated or nobody was sure in what context to place it. Alycia saw that Harriet doted on her son, while his father, behind the gray, judgmental eyes, sat motionless, waiting for something to happen. Alycia wondered if it was for her to disappear.

After a few minutes Mr. Poindexter stood and asked to see Red in his study. Alycia pretended everything was fine, but she sensed something was terribly wrong, something that she had precipitated. It was clear Mr. Poindexter did not care for her. Would he dismiss her like he had that errant house-keeper? She was tempted to confide in Red's mother, but as warm and understanding as Harriet appeared, Alycia was afraid she wouldn't be able to explain herself clearly. Flustered, she asked for another drink. The two talked about Alycia's and Red's new home in Toluca Lake.

"If there's any way I can help, with the house, or getting settled—anything at all—you'll let me know, won't you?" Harriet asked. "I look forward to it."

"I would love your help," Alycia promised. It occurred to her that she'd made no friends in Los Angeles and that Harriet might be the perfect start. "Things feel strange for me sometimes," she began, struggling with her English suddenly and thinking how much easier this would be in French. "A new city, I mean, and not knowing anyone, trying to feel comfortable. Red tries to help, but he has his mind on other things. Don't you think—"

"Dear, I understand perfectly," Harriet interrupted, putting Alycia at ease. "Tonight in particular must be rough on you. I apologize for Red putting you on the spot like this. It's my son's nature to be dramatic. I don't want you to worry. Things will work out."

Alycia was grateful for the candor. She screwed up her courage again. "I don't know if your husband cares for me—"

"Nonsense," Harriet answered warmly. "You're a perfectly lovely young woman—how can Owen miss that? Please understand, my husband doesn't always express himself well. But one thing is certain: I do. And I know that you and I will be fast friends, Alycia."

After fifteen minutes, Red appeared. His confident smile contrasted sharply with his father's sober countenance. Alycia rose, flushed and light-headed. At the door there were more pleasantries, and a promise from Harriet to call Alycia soon for lunch.

Alycia watched as Harriet and Red embraced and said good-bye. There were such warmth and love and mutual support between them that words didn't need to pass.

"I'm rejoining my father's firm," Red told Alycia in the car. He put the top up and was careful to take the hills slowly. She could see he'd gotten what he had come for; now he could be more relaxed.

"I'm happy everything worked out for you," she said.

"It worked better than I hoped. I was very insistent with my father, and I didn't compromise. I'll be made a full partner from the start. I'll have my own suite of offices, the right to hire my own staff—"

"Congratulations," she said quietly.

"You don't sound thrilled."

She hadn't meant to cry, or even to complain, but suddenly her shoulders trembled.

"Darling . . ."

Alycia moved away. She took a breath to compose herself. "What else did you talk about in your father's study?"

"Just business," he allowed, as if the answer were obvious.

"That's all? Didn't your father want to know anything about me? Didn't he even say if he liked me? Didn't you ask him?"

"My father's reserved in his opinions."

"His *opinions*? That sounds like I'm not a person, but a thing, an issue, a piece of real estate . . ."

Red looked perplexed. "Why are you so upset?"

"All evening I felt like I was being used. You wanted to impress him with me, or prove your independence by getting married—"

"Darling, you don't understand," Red stopped her. "I had to do things my way. On my own timetable. You had nothing to do with it. I swear."

She wanted to believe him. Instead, she was provoking another fight, the very thing she had sworn never to do.

"I also told my father you'd be working with me," Red announced in the silence.

Alycia found a handkerchief in her purse. "Really?"

"I promised you, didn't I? And I always keep my promises. We have a future together."

Alycia was suddenly sorry for her tantrum. From now on there would be no more misunderstandings between them. Her husband had not abandoned her; she just had been overanxious and imagined the worst.

Wanting forgiveness, Alycia went to kiss Red, when her stomach welled up violently. It was all she could do to scramble to her window and push her head into the cold air, where she barely missed the side of the Lincoln.

The offices of Poindexter Realty occupied the entire three stories of a nondescript stone-block building not far from the

Biltmore Hotel in the heart of downtown Los Angeles. As Red gazed up on the edifice on his first day of work, he knew the humble appearance belied the true wealth of the family business. Instead, the building reflected his father's single concession in his life to sentiment. It was the first property he'd ever owned, and he had sworn he would have it until he died.

The down payment had come from a stipend given begrudgingly to Owen by his father as a good-bye present. Against strong family wishes, Owen had deserted the banking establishment of three generations of Poindexters—a field he found too boring—to come to California in 1913 at the age of twenty-one. He knew no one there. Los Angeles enjoyed a population of 315,000, with an uncertain industrial base, and Owen's accounting degree from Princton was of little help. He rolled up his sleeves and worked as a clerk in a struggling real-estate company. He did not write home often, and when his father wrote back, it was to inquire when Owen would tire of the desert climate. The truth was, he felt like a pioneer in Los Angeles. Brave souls came from across the country with the common dream of starting their lives over, and starting big. Owen married a vivacious blond nurse named Harriet Isabel Windsor, and a year later, in 1916, they had a son. Incredibly, Red was almost five years old before the proud and private Owen told anyone on the East Coast he'd begun a family. In the same breath he announced he was also starting his own real-estate company.

With a sizable loan wrested from a skeptical banker, Owen purchased the current Poindexter Building and waited for customers to walk in. Fierce competition almost destroyed him the first year, and he barely was able to make his payments on the building. Yet he saw that Los Angeles was growing by the day. A "one-city, one-fare" trolley-car line was about to be inaugurated that would connect the entire city. If he could persevere, time was on his side. Instead of folding his tent and heading east in surrender, he sold the Poindexter Building for a small profit. By fate, the buyer, a struggling insurance company, went bankrupt within a year. Upon foreclosure, Owen bought back the building for half its original price. Similar luck and tactics, Red knew, had been his father's guiding star, starting with the twenties' land boom. In the next twenty years he absorbed whole blocks of downtown buildings as effortlessly as a shark in a tank of goldfish. Red would always give his father credit for having guts.

His first month at work, Red immersed himself in company sales histories and statistics. He wanted to know what changes had been brought by the war, what he'd missed, what new trends were being established. The more he studied, the greater his surprise and concern. Was everybody sleeping? Clearly the new and thriving market, for commercial as well as residential property, was in the suburbs. Downtown Los Angeles was at best stagnant, very possibly dying. The days of high and quick profits for his father in downtown real estate were over. Rent rolls there were declining; sales prices would be next. Historically, real estate moved in cycles, and the longer or stronger the upswing, as downtown had enjoyed, the steeper the inevitable plunge.

Red confronted his father after work one evening. He candidly suggested the firm shift its focus to the San Fernando Valley. Growth was faster there than a field of weeds. Builders couldn't keep up with demand.

"A fool's paradise," his father answered succinctly, barely glancing up from his desk. The spacious office, its walls lined with plaques from every civic organization in the city, felt musty and staid, as quaint as his father's views, thought Red.

"Fools with money," Red could only answer. "I don't see why you wouldn't consider a field office in the Valley."

Owen hunched up in his chair. The stare was familiar enough. Red had grown up with it, just like he had his baseball glove and bicycle, and it always froze him out, made him think they weren't father and son but two people who were just meeting for the first time. Then the proud mouth opened, the eyes squinted.

"Our whole country," Owen began in a lecturing tone Red knew all too well, "is reeling from a railroad strike, a coal strike, and deep-seated labor unrest. Regearing the economy from war to peace has meant massive job restructuring and declining employment. This is not a time for expansion and optimism. It's a time for pulling in horns. If what is happening in the Valley is genuine—I personally think it's a flash in the pan—there'll be time to invest later."

"I was thinking how nice it would be to get in on the ground floor."

"I've been in on a lot of ground floors," Owen said dryly. "Just as often they're false bottoms. You end up in a free-fall trying to find something to hold on to. Red, you've been away six years. You don't have the perspective on this city that I do."

Red could only turn away. It was never easy responding to his father. The man always seemed so prepared, so sure of his logic and wisdom. Answering him was like running into a brick wall.

"I should never have approached him," Red complained over a Scotch to Alycia that evening. He slipped out of his shoes and dropped onto the new sofa. The house was coming along nicely. Both had agreed that Alycia would finish the decorating before joining Red at work. "He was shaking his head before I finished. Like I was crazy."

"Can't you talk to him again? Maybe you'll change his mind," she said sympathetically.

"What can you do with a stone?"

"You're sure you're right?"

"Except for the Biltmore Hotel, some restaurants and department stores, most of downtown is becoming a morgue. Merchants are following the population shift to the suburbs. The vacuum is being filled with unemployment and crime. All you have to do is walk down the street to see."

"But your father doesn't."

"Won't. Can't. I don't know. Maybe he's just forgotten how to take risks."

Red spent the next few days driving through the San Fernando Valley. Between seven and ten miles north and west of Toluca Lake he ran into either chicken ranches or peach orchards or cow pastures, remnants of the once vast parcels owned by a Bavarian immigrant named Issac Lankershim. In 1870, with a friend, I. N. Van Nuys, Lankershim purchased sixty-thousand acres—the entire southern half of the San Fernando Valley—for $115,000, and began growing wheat and corn in the fertile soil. While towns had sprung up since throughout the Valley and even become small cities, there were still large stretches of vacant land. A residential block would abruptly dovetail into acres of nothing. Sooner than later, Red knew, the pastures and farms were flirting with extinction.

The San Fernando Valley had always been kissed by fate. In 1905 the mayor of Los Angeles, presiding over a town of 100,000 that could never grow without a source of water more reliable than the the the Los Angeles River, secretly bought options on vast land tracts in Owens Valley, a high desert community seventy miles to the east. The fertile land was tucked between two mammoth mountain ranges—the California Sierras and the Inyo Mountains—which fed the thriving Owens River. The good mayor, with the blessings of water superintendent William Mulholland, offered his city's voters a twenty-five-million-dollar bond issue for the acquisition of his Owens Valley land options and construction of an aqueduct that would ensure Los Angeles' growth for the next century. The issue passed overwhelmingly. For the next eight years the country's top engineers zigzagged a million tons of steel pipe into a gravity system that gave Los Angeles its future.

"There's your water," Mulholland was reported to have said to onlookers from Los Angeles, amid much hoopla, at the aqueduct's dedication. "Take it!"

The howls of protest from the betrayed citizens of Owens Valley did not dim for decades. Along with their water they lost a federal reclamation project that would have made them a major agricultural center in the West. The twenties brought the embittered "water wars." Hot-tempered locals tried to blow up parts of the aqueduct and reclaim their water for Owens Valley. They lost. The winners, Red remembered, were the speculators who bought San Fernando Valley land in anticipation of its being annexed by Los Angeles and the population boom that would follow. Growth had been steady and speculators had reaped huge profits, but the real growth, Red was convinced, was yet to come.

At the Bureau of Records one afternoon he obtained plats and copies of property deeds of every large parcel of land he'd driven by. That night, laying them out like puzzle pieces on his dining-room table, he quickly saw that if he combined three particular parcels he'd have 120 contiguous acres east of Woodman Street and Riverside Drive. That was the site of a new parochial high school and where residential neighborhoods currently ended—and the logical departure point for the next building development.

"What are you going to do?" Alycia asked when Red presented his discovery.

"Approach the three owners."

"What if they don't want to sell?"

"Everyone has a price."

"But how are you going to pay them? We only have fifteen thousand dollars in savings. Unless you want to go back to your father—"

"No," Red said, "I'll find my own way. I just want you to know it's going to take all our money, one way or another."

Alycia thought a moment. "I trust you," she said, pushing away her doubts, and wrapped her arms around him.

Red always considered one of his better traits the courage to admit when he didn't have an answer or a remedy. Once confessing his ignorance, he was equally good at searching till he found a solution. His first step was a visit to each of the respective owners, who he dickered with until he came away with three separate purchase agreements with an aggregate price of $310,000. For good-faith deposits he wrote checks from his savings account. When he failed to convince the owners to take back first mortgages, Red knocked on bankers' doors. Loan officers admired his war record, but it was politely pointed out that Red hardly had the business background or credit history to justify a lavish loan.

"I don't see what you're afraid of," Red said, facing his seventh loan officer at as many banks. "Look at the collateral I'm offering. This land, when subdivided, can be sold to smaller developers for four times what I'm paying. The bank's protected."

The loan officer, sliding back in his swivel chair, folded his hands over his plump middle. "Mr. Poindexter, first, we don't like to loan on raw land. Second, the land *next* to the acres you want is more chicken farms and dairies. Who wants to live next to *those?*"

"No one will have to. I'm buying them next." The banker's eyebrows shot up in dismay. "Listen," said Red, "land is a limited and scarce commodity. When demand is high, its value goes up. I promise you the bank is not at risk."

"If I ran this bank on promises and good faith, Mr. Poindexter, I wouldn't have a job."

"I already explained that I haven't had time to establish a credit history. But you know my family name."

The banker nodded at the obvious. "Then have your father take out the loan."

"This is my project," Red answered stubbornly. He was reminded again why he didn't care for bankers or lawyers or accountants. They never had any ideas of their own, never took the initiative to make capital; like parasites, they simply bled the risk-takers who did. Red started to leave. The banker dropped his chair forward.

"There is one possibility," he spoke up. "Have your father cosign. There's a chance our loan department might look on favorably."

"I'll think about it," Red said.

He thought for only a minute, over a cup of coffee at a Woolworth's down the block. His father would never sign in a million years. Red felt doomed. How would he ever make a break for himself? The answer did not sting him with fear or guilt or a sense of wrong. If he felt anything at all, it was excitement. He realized he'd never done anything seriously wrong. Fear of earning his father's wrath had seen to that. He'd never cheated on a college exam or gotten a girl pregnant or told lies to anybody. But this was different. His father's idea of navigating into the future was to look in a rearview mirror. With the cool logic and sense of invulnerability that had gotten him through five years of war, Red decided what he would do. No one would find out, and no one would be hurt, because he would start selling chunks of the land before his first payments were due. He would forge his father's signature.

"You didn't," Alycia said with disbelief when he told her what he'd done. Red was in his tux, waiting for Alycia to finish dressing for a party at Lakeside. They had joined the club even if neither had found time to step on the fairways or enjoy the pool.

"There's nothing to worry about," Red said. He resented Alycia's sober tone. She was being too cautious, as near-sighted as the bankers or his father. "I'm going to make nothing but money on this deal."

"That's not the issue."

"Oh?"

"As much as you and I disagree with your father, you don't have the right to deceive him."

"Alycia, you don't understand. This is the only way I can break out of his shadow."

"There have to be others. You are just impatient."

"What? Tell me."

"I don't know," she said, frustrated. Whenever they argued, it always seemed over Owen.

They walked the long block down Valley Spring Lane to

the club's back entrance in silence. From behind the Lakeside hedges, boisterious, intoxicated voices spilled into the fragrant evening. The club had once been known as Lushside, Red had been told, largely because of a Hollywood crowd. It had been started in the twenties by golfers who were desperate when the old Hollywood Country Club folded. Lakeside's fairways were mostly reclaimed marshland from Toluca Lake. Almost overnight the new club became another kind of watering hole. W. C. Fields' caddy carried more than golf clubs in his bag, and fresh ice cubes were ferried to the actor with the start of the back nine. In the thirties, drawn by the club's carefree spirit and its own brand of Prohibition alkie, Edgar Bergen, Buster Keaton, Harold Lloyd, and Fatty Arbuckle became regulars. No one cared that club food was inedible, the help surly, the greens poorly maintained, and the into-the-morning parties brought irate calls from neighbors. After the war, the more conservative club members made a bid for respectability. Today, movie stars were persona non grata, though the legacy of hard-drinking and partying had not totally died.

"Please don't be mad at me," Alycia finally said as she and Red navigated toward the club's large rolling lawn with a mammoth striped tent in the middle. The dance floor was crowded with elegantly dressed couples. "It's a gorgeous fall night and I'm in love with you."

"Are you?" he asked, taking her in his arms.

"How can you say that? You know I'm on your side. I adore you."

Red tried to feel better, but he was still on pins from the difficult day—and what was done was done, no matter what Alycia or anyone thought. When the music stopped, they got drinks and circulated among the guests. Red noticed how easily Alycia socialized. Something more than her French background and charming accent made her interesting and different. She had a certain presence, a grace about her. In private she worried to Red that while Los Angeles seemed like a friendly place, it might be another matter making friends. Refurbishing the house with Harriet was wonderful—the two had hit it off instantly—but Alycia had been a virtual prisoner. She had little time to meet anyone. Now she was making up for lost opportunities.

Red drifted back to the bar for another martini.

"Don't you know it's rude to drink alone?"

Red swung his glance to the smooth, finely proportioned face but for its off-center smile and receding hairline. The man had a basketball player's slope. His eyes were warm and content. Scotty Madigan managed a grin of mock pity for himself. "Especially when your pal is thirsty."

"Cheers," Red said, raising his glass as Scotty sidled up to the bar.

"When am I going to get you on the links? I hardly ever see you," Scotty complained.

"Working too hard."

"I can get you into my foursome tomorrow. Nine sharp. Just promise you won't hustle me for all my money—Electra wants a mink coat for winter."

"Nine sharp," Red said. He could use the break, he thought as he thanked Scotty.

They had known one another only casually at Stanford, and after graduation Scotty had gone to med school, finishing in time to be sent off to mend bodies in the Pacific. They had lost touch until a chance meeting in Geneva after V-E Day. Scotty was going home to Los Angeles to finish his residency. Though they had little in common and had never been close, Scotty had recently been after Red to do things together. He liked having friends, being appreciated and needed, and Red thought he was lost without a crowd. Red, though he didn't need a lot of friends, wanted to like Scotty. He was fun, he had a certain style, and everything seemed effortless for him. He combined a successful Valley neurosurgery practice with time to help local charities. And he was married to one of the sexiest women Red had ever met.

"Want to have some fun?" Red asked when he finished his third martini.

"Sounds provocative," Scotty said.

"You sure you're game? You won't chicken out on me—"

"Do I get any clues?"

"Absolutely none," Red promised, scooping several empty shot glasses into his pocket. He was light-headed as he led Scotty from the party, but the cool night sobered him a little. A lone flood light from the clubhouse silhouettted the two figures as they loped toward the darkening shadows of the first fairway.

"Anybody out here?" Red asked.

"Just the caddy shack. Sometimes a few caddies hang around at night to swill beer and play cards."

Red stopped to stare at the lanky trees at the edge of the green. The moon provided enough light to make out a lumpy figure at the bottom. Scotty nodded at the apparition.

"Must be a caddy sleeping it off," he said to Red.

"Stay here."

Scotty watched, perplexed, as Red trotted over to the dozing caddy. One of the shot glasses came out of his pocket. When he returned, he quietly pulled a silver-plated handgun from the other.

"Jesus," said Scotty.

"I carry it almost everywhere, particularly to work," Red explained. "Have you been downtown after dark lately? It's a little dangerous."

"So I've heard. Where did you get the revolver?"

"A gift from my father the day I was inducted. His father had given it to him as another going-away present, when he moved to California. I had it all through the war—a good-luck piece. It saved my life a couple times."

Scotty nodded soberly. "I know your war record."

"Trouble is," Red lamented as he checked the cylinder, spun it, and straightened the revolver in his hands, "I haven't had much time for practice."

Scotty could only stare at him. "God damn, Red, what are you doing? You're pointing—"

"I'm going to hit that shot glass." He gave Scotty a conspiratorial wink. "Then it's your turn."

Scotty squinted into the distance. "But it's on the caddy's head!"

"Don't worry, he's asleep."

"Is this a joke, or are you a little crazy?"

"Neither, just a happy, helpless drunk," Red decided.

"Jesus Christ, put that gun down!"

Scotty's voice had reached the level of shrill alarm. Red smiled coolly. "You want to try first?" he asked.

"You know this is insane."

"I won't miss," Red promised calmly.

"I can't let you do it," Scotty said. He made some vague sound in his throat as they stared together at the small glass silvered by the moon.

"Here . . . we . . . go."

The bullet made a clean, sharp whistle from the muzzle. The two watched as shards of glass exploded and sprayed up like a grenade. Scotty slumped to the ground in relief.

"Scotty, I've got a confession—"

"You could have killed him," he interrupted earnestly. He turned and gazed at the motionless caddy. Struck with fear, Scotty sprinted over.

Red couldn't stop him. He watched as Scotty approached the lumpy outline. Out of the silence came a staccato burst of laughter.

"You son of a bitch!" Scotty shouted back.

"I was trying to tell you," Red said, laughing himself as Scotty marched back. "You didn't give me a chance."

"A goddamn tree stump," said Scotty. Suddenly they were howling together. "Be on guard—next time it's my turn."

"Fair enough," Red agreed, and wrapped an arm around his new friend.

When they returned to the party Alycia looked puzzled by their disappearance but happy to see them. The four had had dinner together twice, and Alycia had warmed to both Electra and Scotty. As Scotty asked Alycia to dance, Red escorted Electra onto the floor. Like most men, he was attracted to her flowing red hair and girlish face with the cute upturned nose. The large bright eyes knew exactly when to flash on or off. She was perky and alive and always had something witty to say, or sometimes, when she'd drunk too much, off-color, which men inevitably liked and construed as flirting. Men felt wanted by her. Red knew he certainly did. One would be a fool to say no to her, if she ever asked. But for all her sexiness, she lacked mystery, Red thought as they danced and talked. Her charms were too obvious. It was easy and fun to be with Electra, but that's where Red's fascination ended.

The party began to disintegrate after midnight. Red was leading Alycia toward the gate when he spotted a photographer from the Los Angeles *Times*.

"Picture time," he declared, turning them around. "We'll be in the society section tomorrow."

"Can't we just go home?" she asked, teasing him with a kiss. "I want to make love to you."

Red didn't seem to hear. He pulled Alycia toward the photographer and they posed with a couple they barely knew.

On their way home they passed a sprawling pink-stucco mansion with a red-tile roof and high perimeter walls that looked at once inviting and forbidding. The street was lined with Cadillacs, and the house was lit up like a torch. Loud, reckless voices spilled out. Some guests were splashing in the pool in back.

"Looks like this party is just starting," Alycia said, fascinated as they lingered.

"Hollywood types," Red huffed.

"You know what Electra told me? This was once Frank Sinatra's home."

"You sound impressed."

"I'm interested, that's all. Red, we don't even know Terry Donelson. He might be very nice."

Red said nothing. Donelson was an ex-Army Air Corps hero who, through good looks and incredible luck, had crashed the inner circle of Hollywood. He turned Red's stomach. Since he and Alycia had moved into the neighborhood, the movie star had thrown no fewer than a dozen parties. Red wasn't bothered that they hadn't been invited—he wouldn't have anything to do with celebrities anyway—the sycophants who crowded around the skinny actor like he was the hottest property since Sunset and Vine. Red had been a war hero too, and he was just as good-looking; no one made a fuss over him.

"I've been waiting all night," Alycia said playfully when they finally got home and stumbled upstairs. She started to unbutton Red's shirt, but he gently pushed her away.

"Too damn drunk," he said with his charming smile. He managed to get out of his clothes and collapse on the bed.

"Then I'll have to revive you," she promised in her lilting accent.

"Sorry, darling. Could you ring for an appointment in the morning?"

She reflected a moment. "I don't think so."

She was undressed before Red could manage another protest. When his eyes skated over her figure, he found his energy again. On her knees, sitting between his legs, Alycia ran her hands down the hard, lean body, and her lips followed the blond hair that traced to his middle. With her mouth she got him hard instantly. His strong fingers began to knead her shoulders.

"Touch my breasts," she whispered.

His fingers turned sensitive and knowing. It was easy for Alycia to surrender to the spirals of pleasure. Lovemaking had come to represent their truest and deepest intimacy. Alycia felt completely at ease when she was this vulnerable, totally surrendering to Red, unafraid of anything. At night she craved the sense of helplessness as strongly as she resisted it during the day. It was a part of her that could be exposed and nourished only in the darkness. And while Red never spoke of it, she knew he was exactly the same. It was what made sex so wonderful between them. Even more than her own guarded exterior, Red's camouflaged a center of such sensitivity that she, too, was reluctant to mention it. Yet he knew that she was aware of it; this was their silent communion on the deepest level, a part of their relationship that couldn't be trusted to words. When he finally penetrated her and she climaxed, she thought not of the physical excitement but of an ineffable sweetness between them that the world could never take away.

"You're the most beautiful woman in the world," Red whispered.

"I love you in the darkness," Alycia answered.

She heard him sigh. It was more like a murmur, filled with a contentment and peace that made her wish it were those emotions, not Red's ambition, that colored his temperament. Her finger traced the curvature of his back and the muscular ridges of his thighs. She felt the soft pockets of wrinkled flesh that were his wounds from the war—one in his abdomen, another on her shoulder, two in his left thigh.

"What was the most terrifying part of the war for you?" she suddenly asked. She had never pried into those years. Normally Red acted as if they were inconsequential, as if his bravery and heroism meant nothing. Alycia knew better. Red had wanted to be recognized, and still did, yet every gesture she made to find out more was politely rebuffed. But in their bed, after making love, she could ask him anything. That was her right, and she knew he would be honest. "Maybe every moment of it was terrifying," she said for him. "It was for me."

He turned to face her. "I was never scared. I was always certain I would be fine."

"Really?" She couldn't quite believe that.

"Maybe once," Red corrected himself, thinking carefully. "Once I was scared."

"When you were in real danger?"

He shook his head. "We were mopping up after a skirmish in Lybia. I was drifting through rubble when I almost stepped on a German colonel. He'd been shot and was bleeding badly. I started to dress his wounds, but he pushed me away.

Very politely, in English, he asked me not to save him.
Rather than face the humiliation of being a prisoner of war, of
dying in disgrace, he said, he'd rather die here. The problem
was, he was too afraid to take his own life. Very calmly he
placed his revolver in my hand . . .''

Alycia sat up. ''What did you do?''

''My hand shook. The colonel begged me. His eyes burned
right through me. I wasn't sure why I was so afraid, but
somehow I understood him perfectly. I could feel his shame.
When he saw that, he knew I couldn't refuse him. 'Forgive
me,' he said. 'Forgive me for using you.' After a moment I
put the gun to his temple and squeezed the trigger.''

''How terrible,'' Alycia whispered. She recoiled as she
imagined the scene. Then her eyes moved to Red. He was
thinking about it too. She kissed him on the cheek and tried to
sleep.

''Here, let me get on the ladder,'' Harriet insisted as
Alycia struggled with the heavy drapery. Alycia grunted as
she steadied her own end and boosted the other toward a
precariously balanced Harriet. With determination and fi-
nesse, her mother-in-law placed the brass rod in its bracket.

''Hooray,'' Alycia sang. Harriet clambered down and repo-
sitioned the ladder at the other end to finish the job.

''What do you think?'' Alycia asked as they stepped back
to admire the window treatment. Her house, at last, was
almost done. Alycia had chosen a contemporary motif, just
the opposite of everything classical she'd grown up with in
Paris. This was her new home, she had decided, a new life
for her, so why not be bold and experiment? In architecture
she'd come to prefer the innovative; the same with interior
design. She didn't care what the rest of Los Angeles was
doing with its homes, Alycia wanted nothing gaudy or wild—
just simplicity and clean lines. With Harriet's help the last
three months, Alycia had picked very stark chairs with flat
cushions, functional couches in subdued tones, a neutral carpet. For color she relied on accent pieces, Chinese lamps and
lacquered tables. The house had an open, eclectic feel, a little
European in its severity, she supposed, yet it was more than
comfortable.

''I adore it,'' Harriet said. ''I have to tell you, the way you
design makes me feel young again. I think you have excep-
tional taste, Alycia.''

"I consider you my collaborator," she answered, putting an arm around Harriet. "You don't know how much you've helped."

"I'm happy if I have. My role in life seems to be in the support category."

"Then Owen's a very lucky man. Now, how about some lunch?"

"No, thank you—I'm on another diet."

"Mother, one sandwich won't do any damage, and the way you were moving around, you burned off enough calories for both of us."

"In that case," Harriet declared, following Alycia into the kitchen, "hot-fudge sundaes all around."

They laughed together. Alycia had taken to calling Harriet "Mother" because it felt comfortable, and in some ways she was not unlike Alycia's own mother—cheerful, helpful, and sensible, the kind to give good advice and be listened to. After their first shopping expedition, Alycia knew they'd work well together. Her own mother had given her a sense of style and proportion and aesthetics which, by magic or fate, Harriet understood perfectly.

But Harriet was also different. Alycia had been invited to several afternoon teas at the Poindexter home. Harriet's women friends were much like Harriet—married to wealthy husbands, active in charity and civic work, partygoers and party-givers, attractive, bright, well-read. Everyone always kept very busy. To be bored or have nothing to do was somehow socially wrong. Still, Alycia had felt a little sorry for Harriet. Almost deliberately, she seemed to leave little time for herself.

They sat over pastries in the sunny kitchen. Alycia's house was not on the lake, but from the kitchen window one could glimpse the water.

"What will you do with yourself," Harriet inquired, "now that the house is done?"

"Go to work with Red, of course," Alycia said. "I know most wives stay home in the States, but I can't wait to start, Mother. I'm restless."

"I think you're one of the few people in the world to have the energy to keep up with my son. You two will do fine together."

"Was Red always so full of energy?" Alycia asked. "He's told me a lot of things about himself, but in some areas he's reticent." Alycia hoped the question was all right. As she well knew, mothers and fathers could be possessive of their children and of what they shared about them. She and Harriet had talked candidly about their own lives—why not the rest of the family?

Harriet folded her hands, and a reminiscing smile lit her face. "As a little boy, Red was very timid—and as an adolescent, just the opposite. He never got along with his father, I'm afraid, so he gave Owen a wide berth. By college, Red was very independent, headstrong, and not a little impatient. He liked to be the leader. And take more than his share of chances."

"Yes, that's Red," Alycia acknowledged.

"He has his weaknesses, to be sure," Harriet went on, more serious. "Red can drive himself too hard, and drink too much, and lose perspective too easily. But frankly, Alycia, I can never bring myself to criticize him. Perhaps that's one of *my* weaknesses. The truth is, I always support him, whether I think he's wrong or right."

"Why?" Alycia couldn't help asking. Her parents had never been that permissive with her.

"Alycia, dear, it's because I've always doted on Red. One might blame circumstances. When I wasn't able to conceive a second child, my first became all the more precious to me. Red was a sensitive, fearful boy. Owen thought I coddled him, but I think basically my husband was jealous of the love I lavished on Red. Later, when Owen began forcing Red into physical activities I didn't approve of, I felt I had no choice but to be more supportive than ever. Red needed my unconditional love as a balance to Owen's harshness. Of course, it became a vicious circle. The more attention I gave Red, the more Owen reacted critically, and the harder he was on Red."

"That must have hurt your marriage," Alycia spoke up.

"To this day Owen believes it was my coddling that's made Red so arrogant. Owen really hasn't forgiven me. But I don't find Red arrogant at all. I only see in him confidence, and a desire to fulfill himself. Maybe I'm wrong, I don't know. Both men share the genes of ambition, yet I think it was my influence that kept Red from becoming exactly like his father. If anyone is arrogant, it's probably Owen."

"And Red has a sweet side to him," Alycia pointed out.

"I love my son very, very much. He has brought me so much joy, including by marrying you, dear."

"I want to make him happy too," Alycia said, flattered.

"And you do—he's told me."

"Thank you. Only, sometimes I feel very troubled," Alycia admitted.

Harriet looked surprised. "About what? After all you told me you survived in the war, what could possibly bother you?"

"That's what scares me," she went on, wondering how much she should tell Harriet. She had never confided this to Red. Sometimes she'd wake in the night sweaty and trembling, escaping from a nightmare she could never clearly recall. "This may sound irrational, Mother, but . . . I feel guilty for surviving the war. So many didn't. I was too lucky. Look at my life—married to Red . . . living in this beautiful home. It's like a dream. Sometimes I think I should be punished, that something terrible will happen to me—"

"That's nonsense," Harriet stopped her. "Red will take good care of you. So will I. That's for certain, dear." And Harriet wrapped her arms consolingly around the daughter she'd never had.

When the phone rang in Toluca Lake several mornings later, Alycia was sure it was either Harriet or Electra—Red was usually too busy to call—but when she picked up the receiver there was a strange pause.

"Hello?" Alycia said. "Mother, is that you?"

"Good morning, Alycia. This is Owen Poindexter."

Alycia's blood rushed to her temples. Since their first and only meeting, Alycia had kept a careful distance from Red's father. She wanted to get to know him, but at her own pace, feeling her way into the relationship. After what Harriet had told her about Owen, Alycia was still afraid her father-in-law would never totally accept her. Why was he calling? Was this just social?

"Are you free for lunch today?" Owen asked.

"I suppose I am," she answered. She resented feeling intimidated. Why couldn't she be stronger?

"Then I'll pick you up at twelve," he said, and clicked off without a clue to what he wanted.

Alycia couldn't concentrate as she tidied the house. She put away her nightgown, showered, and spent an hour trying to pick the right dress. With Red she had all the confidence in the world about her clothes; dressing for Owen, nothing seemed right. You're being silly, she told herself to calm her nerves. This was an innocent, friendly lunch date, there was no need to be defensive. If Owen had been abrupt, that was just his nature. Still, Alycia waited for him outside by the curb, afraid to let him into the house to see her decorating.

They went to the Brown Derby on Wilshire Boulevard, across from the Bullocks-Wilshire department store, "in the heart of the well-heeled," as Electra liked to tell Alycia. These were people who attended *the* charity balls and *the* debutante parties and *the* society bashes. Alycia was unsure exactly who *they* were. What little she did know about Los Angeles society she had gleaned from Electra, a walking encyclopedia on prominent local families, and hardly from the wrong side of the tracks herself. The Bishop family, of which Electra was the eldest of four children, traced its substantial fortune to railroads and utilities. Red had sworn that Electra was worth five million if a penny. Although Electra was part of the society-party circuit, and on a first-name basis with Buffy and Norman Chandler of the *Times*, she wasn't a snob. If anything, she was something of a rebel, Alycia thought. Electra and Scotty lived in a handsome Mediterranean home only a block from her and Red, but it wasn't nearly as elegant as their pocketbooks could afford. Electra refused to drive a Cadillac, and took care of her own children without the benefit of a nanny. She declined to have a television in her home.

Alycia's glance swung to the restaurant's elegantly dressed patrons. Did she belong? The outfit she'd finally chosen was one Red had bought for her in New York—a pleated forest green skirt and a pale cashmere sweater with puffy shoulders. She looked fine, she decided, but she felt self-conscious anyway. A waiter placed her napkin on her lap and took her order.

"I recommend the shrimp Louis," Owen said about five seconds after Alycia had ordered the Caesar salad. Her eyes flicked up. In the car they had barely spoken, and only on neutral subjects, each feeling out the other. Now Owen was being more forceful, as if he thought a battle of wills was necessary. Alycia found it silly. She was only trying to get along. She wondered if this was the kind of thing that Red found so impossible about his father.

She gave Owen a smile. "I'll have the shrimp Louis too," she told the waiter.

She did not want a war, did not want to make even the slightest wave. For now she would swallow her pride and get the lunch over with, and on with the rest of her day. She thought Owen was especially good-looking when he was defiant. He was, in fact, uncomfortably handsome. His mouth was slightly pouty yet decisive. The hair, silvering on the sides and swept back immaculately, revealed a broad and determined forehead. His gray-flecked eyes had the hardness of polished stones, and matched the color of his expensive suit. He dressed even better than Red, she acknowledged. Cold and remote, Owen Poindexter gave the impression of supreme self-confidence.

"I feel a talk between us is as necessary as it is overdue," Owen said when they had their drinks. "I'm a candid man by nature, so I'll come to the point."

"Please," she said with a little fear in her heart.

"Your sudden marriage to my son was, to be sure, a complete surprise to me," he began. "Being presented with a *fait accompli* took some time getting used to. Harriet has grown quite fond of you. From my point of view, whether I like you or approve of you seems irrelevant. You are part of our family whether I like it or not. What I'm determined to do is to see that you are a proper wife to my son."

"I intend to be," she said in the silence. She didn't like his bullying tone, yet she wanted to hear him out. She wanted, in fact, despite Red's rebellious feelings and her own resentment at being intimidated, to find something to like about Owen Poindexter. He was arrogant and self-righteous certainly, but she respected his intelligence and his career successes. More important, he was the leader of the family she was a part of.

"As you're aware," Owen continued in his measured voice, "I am a man of considerable wealth. After Harriet, Red is my only heir. The day will come when he will take over my assets. I want to make sure that you're not the kind of wife to take advantage of that situation."

Alycia couldn't help gulping her drink. What did he think she was? And if Owen cared so much about Red, why didn't he ever let his son know? "I don't think I am," she managed.

"How do I know that?"

"Because I just told you."

"The fact is, you've told me very little. I know absolutely nothing about you—except that Red married you three weeks after you met. Please understand, Alycia, that all my life I've believed in making determinations based on cold, hard facts, not suppositions. The more facts I know about someone or something, the more comfortable I am in my judgments. I am not an emotional person, but I like to think I am fair, and I particularly wish to be fair to you."

"Everyone has feelings," Alycia answered.

"That is not the point. Now, please, tell me about yourself."

Trying to take heart, Alycia cleared her mind and presented her past in the best light. She omitted nothing from her biography except her final day in Paris.

"You have no brothers or sisters, only your father?" Owen queried when she'd finished.

"Yes."

"Where is he now?"

Alycia hesitated. "Still in Paris. He teaches at the Sorbonne."

"What subject?"

She told him.

"Are you close?"

"Yes," came the reply, but too slowly, she was afraid.

"Does he write to you often?"

"Certainly," she lied.

"And you write to him?"

"Yes," she lied again. "May I have another glass of wine, if you please."

When the entrées arrived, Owen scarcely paused. He was very clear about his expectations for Mrs. Alfred Poindexter. Electra and Scotty Madigan were an acceptable couple for friendship, but he disapproved of the Pettyjohns and the Livingstons, who were frivolous and inconsequential people. He suggested several charities for Alycia to get involved with; Harriet could help with introductions. He instructed Alycia where to shop for her clothes, groceries, household supplies; where to have her laundry and dry cleaning done; how to find a reliable gardener and housekeeper. Last, he gave her the name of a prominent obstetrician in the Valley.

Alycia was forced to laugh. "That's one name I don't think I'll need for a while."

"My dear, you're almost twenty-five. These are your best childbearing years. Harriet had Red when she was twenty-three. We would have had several more children if not for an infertility problem."

"I'm sorry for that," she offered. "But Red and I have decided to wait. Right now I'm going to work with him in the office. I've been trained as an architect."

Owen tugged his chin up. The mouth turned down in

displeasure. "Our country is no longer at war, Alycia. Women don't work unless it is economically necessary."

"But Red told you our plans," she said, disbelieving.

"My son has never lacked for ideas. It's his wisdom that's been in short supply. I've given up trying to enlighten him, but you're someone who can be reasoned with. You'll best serve Red and your family by staying home."

She studied Owen and quickly saw that *he* could not be reasoned with. He would never back down. Red had warned her as much, and now she was seeing for herself. "I'm sorry that I don't have your approval, but I am going to work," Alycia said firmly.

"I don't think so."

"Well, you may think whatever you wish," she said, feeling anger well up. She would not be browbeaten anymore. Spending even one more minute with Owen was futile and suddenly unbearable. "I've made up my mind. Thank you for lunch. I can find a taxi to take me home." She rose from the table and started toward the door.

"Come back here, please," Owen called. The voice was strong and confident, but there was also an edge of understanding, even tenderness, to it. She considered her surprise, and for an instant turned, enough to take in Owen's handsome face and the looks from neighboring tables.

Then she proceeded out the door.

"I won't do it. I won't sit home and have babies," she told Red over dinner that night. "I want to be at the office. I want to work."

"I can't believe my father did that to you," Red said, more angry and upset than Alycia. "Didn't I warn you—he's a piece of work. If he calls you again, ignore him. He doesn't control our lives. We're going to have a great weekend, and on Monday you're starting work. My suite of offices is separate from his. You won't have to lay eyes on him."

Alycia reached across the table to wrap her hands around Red's. One of the things she loved most about her husband was that he supported her. She needed that. After her outburst at the Brown Derby, she'd felt so insecure she'd almost ordered the taxi back to the restaurant so she could either apologize to Owen or demand he apologize to her. She hated fighting. She always wanted things to be perfect, for every problem to have a solution.

"Sometimes it feels like we're at war with your father," she told Red.

"I think I've lost perspective. Over the years I've just learned to live with the tension. I have to. One can't divorce one's father."

"How does Harriet get along so well with him?"

"You haven't noticed? They lead separate lives. Oh, they get along fine—they go to parties and entertain together—but they're really not on the same level. Mother's the willing and obedient servant, although she doesn't know it anymore. That's what habit does. And the fact is, my father can be very charming if you let him into your life and do what he wants. He pays handsome dividends." He looked caringly at Alycia. "Don't let your guard down with him."

"He can't really be that much of a monster."

"He's had several mistresses over the years. Mother doesn't know. One got pregnant, and my father made her get an abortion. Does that strike you as the total gentleman?"

"An abortion?" She was shocked. "You told me he believed in a strict right and wrong—"

"That's for the rest of the world. He's a little more lenient on himself."

The next morning Alycia woke to find the bed empty and a note on Red's pillow. He was playing in a foursome with Scotty and wouldn't be home until after lunch. At the bottom there was a woeful stick cartoon character flailing at a golf ball. Alycia smiled.

She dressed in shorts and went out to her flower garden. Under the ubiquitous Southern California sun, she had developed a tan that, coupled with her tall and graceful figure, drew envious stares at the Lakeside pool. It wasn't a nasty or resentful envy, she had found. Despite some early doubts, she was starting to make some friends. Electra was her favorite, but Alycia also mingled easily at country-club functions and at parties of Red's friends. Helping Red socially with his real-estate clients and their wives was no burden. Despite her accent and mannerisms, Alycia didn't think she was perceived as a foreigner. Certainly she didn't see herself that way. With Red's encouragement, she was taking up golf and, despite her fear of freeways, learning to drive. She knew the prices of grocery items and, of course, furniture and home accessories. She liked hamburgers and chocolate-chip cookies, thought motion-picture westerns were wonderful, and had learned more history of California and the United States than Red knew. California wines, television, and most American fashion she could do without, but those were her only complaints.

She'd finished in the garden and dusted the house when Owen Poindexter announced himself.

"Red's at the club," she said automatically, standing on the other side of her front door. Why was Owen here? Maybe it was silly, but she didn't want to let him in.

"It's you I wish to speak to, Alycia. The matter won't take long, I promise. May I come in?" he asked.

He followed her into the kitchen. Alycia was sure he had known Red was away. Red had told her his father didn't act on whim or take needless chances. Everything had to be planned.

"You've done a wonderful job on the house," he offered, putting some of her anxiety at bay. "Those red Chinese lamps, the black sofa, the gray carpet—very tasteful. I didn't know you liked modern, or that you were so talented."

"Thank you. That's why I know I can help Red at work," she made a point of saying. Her eyes didn't leave Owen. After Red's warning, she found herself not trusting him. Yet he looked harmless enough in slacks and a sport shirt. Without his suit and tie, the threatening, remote air was gone, as if he'd taken off his armor. She wondered if this was a peace mission.

"What did you want to talk about?" Alycia asked when she'd fixed them coffee and they sat on the patio.

"I came to apologize for the scene at the Brown Derby."

"I'm sorry too," she said, meaning it.

"There's something else."

She waited.

"I have a proposition for you, Alycia. All I ask is that you listen carefully. You can give me your answer later."

His voice suddenly had that solicitous quality she'd heard at the restaurant as she was walking out. She didn't see how she could refuse just to listen. "Is this about me not working?" she asked.

"Indirectly."

"Red warned me you would do something like this," she said.

"I'm sure he's done his best to poison you against me from the start."

Alycia hesitated.

"What has he said about me?" Owen persisted.

Scooting back in the chair, Alycia pushed her knees up in front of her. Maybe this was a chance to clear the air. "He said you had a mistress, that you made her have an abortion—"

"Yes," he admitted, "it's all true. Does that shock you?"

"You don't have an excuse?"

"Should I need one?" he replied.

"I don't approve of abortions."

"You don't? Doesn't one have mistresses in France?"

"I suppose."

"And don't some get pregnant? When it becomes inconvenient for everyone, what else can one do? Alycia, I believe in living in the real world. Besides mistresses and abortions, what else do you find wrong with me?"

"I don't know much about you."

"What would you like to know? I have nothing to hide. I told you I always prefer candor."

Alycia smiled nervously. "It's none of my business, I suppose." She looked down to her coffee but she felt Owen's eyes on her. She wished he would leave. "Why don't we talk about what you came here for?" she said, glancing up. "What's your proposition? Did you want to offer me a bribe to stay home?"

"From yesterday's conversation, Alycia, it's obvious you are a woman of character, and that a bribe, as you put it, while tempting to me, would be offensive to you. I am here to give you something else, something better. Something for your children—when one day you decide to have them."

"My children?"

"As you know by now, Red and I have never seen eye to eye. Different temperaments, philosophies, interests. We respect one another and can work together in the firm, but there is a great emotional chasm between us. The truth is, in my own way, I love Red—he is my son, my only son. But he will never believe that, and I'm resigned to his feelings. However, I do not intend to have my grandchildren poisoned by his sentiments."

"Red wouldn't do that."

"I'm afraid that one way or another, his feelings would come through."

"But I wouldn't allow that," Alycia said honestly. "It wouldn't be fair to the children."

"You have good intentions, but I'm doubtful you would succeed."

"Why don't you confide in Red what you're telling me?" Alycia asked, frustrated. "Tell him you love him. Then none of this conversation would be necessary."

"You don't understand the nature of our relationship. Nor do you understand me."

"I'm trying."

"At any rate, we're veering from the point of my visit. Alycia, I came here to discuss only one thing with you. I have an offer . . ."

She sat back, resigned but not comfortable.

"I'm prepared to instruct my attorney to draw up trusts for each and every one of my unborn grandchildren," Owen began. "The trusts will be generously endowed, I promise you. On his first birthday, I will place one million dollars in each child's name. On his twenty-third birthday, by which time the money, prudently invested, will have grown substantially, he may withdraw that first million. On his thirtieth birthday, the rest.

"Once I put the money in the trusts, no matter what happens to me or my assets, the funds are safe. No one but you, Alycia, can invade or alter the trusts. Red has a history of recklessness and I fear he would squander the money. Only you will have discretionary powers to divert the funds to other purposes, away from your children, if, in your sole wisdom, you see fit to do so. But you must do this before their twenty-third birthdays. Otherwise, the money is entirely my grandchildren's."

Alycia finally spoke. "You're serious?"

"Very. There is one stipulation. When I give someone something, I want something back. That's only fair, I think. The stipulation is that you do not go to work with Red, but stay home to be the best mother to your children you can."

"For how long?" she asked.

"Until your last child becomes thirteen," Owen clarified, rising to leave. His eyes rested confidently on Alycia. "I know you'll want to discuss this with Red. He will accuse me of deviousness, and taking advantage of you. I assure you, no one is being exploited. There will be no hidden condicils in the trusts. It will be exactly as I have explained. You can have your own attorney review the documents."

"Is that all?" she asked.

"I'd appreciate an answer by the end of the month."

She followed Owen to the door. "I don't think you'll have to wait that long," she said coolly. "I can give you one right now. The answer is no. I won't be bought. My life is my own."

Owen looked surprised at being rejected, even hurt—it was something he wasn't used to, she thought—which only made Alycia feel certain she'd done the right thing.

"Before you make your decision final," he said, turning to her, "you might remember you're not speaking for just you and Red. It's the needs of the unborn we're talking about. And no one can predict the future, can he?"

Alycia did not go to work that Monday. Making an excuse to Red that there were still decorating details to attend to, she stayed home and mulled over Owen's words. She was sure she'd been right to refuse him. Who did he think he was? Was money supposed to bind his grandchildren to him, buy their love? Money had not bound his own son to him. Alycia understood how frustrated Red must have always felt, living under his father's arrogance and tyranny. Why did Red even bother working for the man? What was so compelling or necessary?

But as the week passed Alycia grew less sure of her position. She began to see Owen's offer in a different light. No matter what his motives, he was still being generous. And basically he had a point: Alycia had no right to be selfish about her own children. Money, if used wisely, was a shield from misfortune, a key to unlocking doors, a guarantee of advantages if something should ever happen to Red. Nobody could divine the future. The war had taught Alycia just how bad things could get. She did have her own dreams, and her pride, but morally could she put those ahead of her children's future?

A week later, one night before dinner, she poured two glasses of sherry and finally told Red about Owen's visit.

"He offered *what?*" Red cried.

In a calm voice she recited the facts again. "I want to accept the offer," she said when she'd finished, and gave her reasons in detail.

"Alycia, don't you see?" Red asked, looking at her intently. "He just wants to control you, like he does everyone else. He wants to drive a wedge between you and me. Didn't I tell you not to let your guard down? He's gotten to you."

"He has not," she said.

"Money means nothing to him. It's the power that's important. I'm sure he wants to have grandchildren, and for them to love him, but the most important thing is that he get his way. That's how he's always been."

"Forget your father for a minute," she argued back. "What about us? We were going to have children anyway, weren't we? What's wrong with now? And what's wrong with giving them a financial head start?"

"I'll provide everything they'll ever need."

"But what if something happens to you—or me? The trusts could be more than helpful. They might be necessary."

"You were coming to work with me," Red reminded her.

"Does Los Angeles really need another architect? I can find something to do around here. Look at Electra. She's got two kids and stays home—she's happy."

"I want you to work with me," Red said more strongly. "That was our agreement. We're supposed to be a team."

"We are. I want that too. But the trusts would benefit *our* children. What do you have against that? Isn't it my choice about wanting to work or not? If anyone is being deprived, it's me, and I'm willing to accept it."

"You're a fool," he declared in disgust. "You're being used and you don't even know it."

Alycia felt stung. How could Red say that? He was being as arrogant as his father. Red fell into silence and poured himself a Scotch. Finally his eyes flashed in resignation.

"Have it your way," he said. "But I promise you're going to regret this. You've made a bargain with the devil."

"You're talking about your own father!"

"I already told you: no one ever gets the upper hand over him. You may think you're different, that you've reached some kind of peace with him. You'll find otherwise."

Alycia turned away. When Red finally spoke again it was about real estate. The bank officer had called that afternoon. The loan on his 120 acres had been approved. Last Saturday Red had signed a sales contract with a developer for one-third of the acreage, to close after he got his loan, at a four-hundred-percent profit to Red.

"Congratulations," Alycia said, trying to feel better for both of them.

Red said nothing. He would probably resent what she had done with his father for a while, Alycia thought, but eventually he would understand that the benefits outweighed anything negative. She wondered briefly if Red might be right about Owen holding some spell over her—maybe he did over Red too—but she pushed the thought away. She and Red would be together no matter what Owen did. They had their love. That was the most important thing of all, and it was all they would ever need.

August 25, 1948

Dearest Père:

It feels so strange to write after the full year of silence between us. Since I haven't heard from you, I do not even know if you're still teaching, or where. I'm writing you at the Sorbonne with the hope a former colleague will have the decency to pass this letter on. I have several things to tell you, but maybe the most important is that I forgive you for what you did. It's meant deep soul-searching, but I think I understand now that what you did was out of love for me, and that it was not easy for you. I forgive you with all my heart. I have seen how my husband and his father fight so, and absolutely no good comes from standing on stubborn pride. I hope now you will write me, wherever you are, and that you've managed to make peace with your own conscience.

The other news is that I am six months pregnant! I'm so happy and excited, more so than I ever thought possible. Part of me hopes for a boy—I don't know why—but whatever it is, he or she shall be loved dearly and have a wonderful home. I will write again when I know! I love you dearly, Père, and I pray this letter finds you in good health.

Please write back!

All my love,
Alycia

BOOK TWO

BOOK TWO

Red navigated his chrome-finned white 1952 Cadillac into his parking space behind the Poindexter Building and walked inside. The oppressive, smoggy May afternoon already had his eyes and nose running, but his thoughts rested comfortably on the upcoming local Republican primary—and a chubby, bespectacled candidate with whom Red had just had lunch, Norris Poulson. The private lunch had been a thank-you for Red's generous and repeated donations. Red had written the challenger another check before they said good-bye. The straw polls leaned toward the incumbent, but Red didn't think twice about the risk he was taking. Finishing his fourth term, Fletcher Bowron was a short, curt, scholarly conservative Republican whose biggest accomplishment had been to rid the city of racketeering and prostitution. He ran Los Angeles like a church. Poulson had vowed to open the city—expand the airport, add more freeways, turn San Pedro into the greatest port after New York. Morality would take care of itself.

Achieving political power was a function of audacity and timing, and Red saw Poulson was a master of both. Two years ago, when Los Angeles had become the first metropolis in the country to abolish rent controls, the city endured a paroxysm of dislocation. Overnight, landlords jacked up rents two hundred percent. Longtime tenants were forced out in the street or into substandard housing. Protesters by the thousands paraded in front of city hall. Poulson, who also favored ending rent control, but gradually, to minimize the pain of adjustment, took the opportunity to attack Mayor Bowron for caving in to landlords and developers. The groundswell of sentiment was immediate and overwhelming. The *vox populi* declared that Norris Poulson, heretofore a congressman from Eagle Rock, run for mayor of Los Angeles.

Red had joined the Poulson bandwagon a year ago. He had begun by working after hours ringing doorbells and handing out leaflets and lapel pins. He would talk to housewives and firemen and school teachers. No detail was too insignificant for him. The military had taught him how to take orders, and he didn't mind getting his hands dirty. He could have insisted on starting higher in the organization, but as in real estate, he wanted to earn his reputation. With his brains and personality, district leaders took notice of the precinct worker, and after six months they elevated Red to strategy meetings, then to speaking engagements, and finally to introducing their candidate at high-level fund-raisers. Photos of the two together began appearing in the *Times*. Red was not so naive as to believe that Poulson didn't know the advantage of having the name Poindexter in his circle, but the fact was, Red's father was in Fletcher Bowron's camp, and Norris Poulson was as much interested in Red's political thoughts and strategy as his pocketbook.

In his office, Red sorted through his mail, answered phone messages left by his secretary, and reviewed a contract he'd written for a buyer. His suite of offices, while as dowdy as the rest of the building, were commodious enough to hold the half-dozen brokers Red had working directly under him. More than once he'd asked Alycia to come in and decorate, but she was too busy with their son. Jean, now three and a half, was a handful, and after taking care of housework, Alycia just had time to breathe.

After a while Red had forgotten aesthetics and devoted himself to business. His annual commissions, even after the split with his father, were always six figures, and each year was stronger than the last. Though his father would never credit him, Red knew he'd saved the firm from sinking into a pool of red ink. Downtown was steadily eroding, though some still couldn't see it. As one tenant or owner moved out, another dreamer would come in, lose his shirt after five or six months, then sell to the next Don Quixote. Everyone thought he knew where the bottom was, but the bottom only kept dropping, and a broker made commissions no matter what.

On balance, Red often thought, the five years in his father's firm hadn't been bad. Despite differences in philosophy and marketing, Red got along with Owen in business, and socially he and Alycia were at his parents' home once a month. Red had never made peace with the idea of Owen's trust for Jean, but he adored Alycia, and if she thought the trust best, he had to accept it. He wished, however, that just once his father could praise him for his understanding, his good will, his hard work. Why couldn't there be warmth and intimacy between them? Instead, Owen was like a statue. Everyone in the firm respected, even revered him; Red did too. As if part of him were still a little boy, he tried endlessly to be perfect, to be right, to work still harder, to accomplish more than was expected of him.

About four o'clock, Red repacked his briefcase. He had promised Alycia to be home early—Jean wanted his daddy to take him to a neighbor's birthday party—and Red was determined not to disappoint them. He was halfway out the building when his father's secretary caught up with him in the corridor. Mr. Poindexter wanted to see him right away.

"Something up?" Red asked, one eye on his watch, when he peeked into his father's office.

Behind his desk, Owen stared at him. His hands were folded calmly, but his eyes brimmed with disappointment and embarrassment. There was anger too. "Close the door, please."

"What is it?" Red said, trying to anticipate. He felt helpless in moments like this, and he hated it.

"I had a late lunch today. With a loan officer from Bank of America," Owen began, his eyes still fixed on Red, holding him there. "By coincidence, your name came up."

"Really?"

"The loan officer said he remembered you very well."

Red frowned. "I don't do any mortgages with Bank of America."

"You did one. Five years ago."

Red shook his head.

"Let me refresh your memory. I was involved too. So I was told. I cosigned the loan application. For 120 acres of farmland in the Valley."

Red stirred. His tongue skimmed his lips. The lie came out before he could control it, before he realized the mistake. "The banker's confused. That was my deal. You weren't involved."

"That's what I told him. He insisted on the correctness of his facts. After lunch I asked to see the loan application. It took some time to find it. I brought a copy back, if you'd like to see it."

Red took a breath. His glance swung to all the plaques on the walls, the images of civic responsibility and rectitude. He couldn't look at his father. "It's all ancient history," he said.

"You weren't hurt, were you? Why even bring this up? It means nothing."

"How many other times did you forge my signature?"

"None," Red said adamantly.

"Am I supposed to believe you?" Owen's voice rose an octave. "What about the future?"

"I don't lie," Red said.

"You just did."

"I mean I don't lie unless forced to—like anyone else."

"You don't tell the whole truth, either."

"Look," Red conceded, meeting his father's gaze, "I made a mistake. I'm sorry. I regret it. I was only trying to prove something to you and to me."

"I didn't raise you to be dishonest—particularly with your own father."

Red forked his fingers through his hair. He could feel the dampness under his arms. He resented that he was being grilled for this, humiliated, while his father's judgmental eyes carried not even a flicker of sympathy or mercy. "Okay. I screwed up. I guess I'm not perfect after all. Tell me," he demanded, "are you?"

Owen rose slowly. His suit looked immaculate, still holding its press, the crease in the trousers as sharp as his tongue. "You know that I can't allow you to remain with this firm," he said.

Red's lips parted. He started to laugh. "What are you talking about?"

"I think it's best for everyone if you resign."

"You can't do that. I'm a partner!"

"I'll find a way to make it legal. There's no room for deceit and dishonesty within these walls. The firm has a reputation. I have a reputation. You badly embarrassed both today."

Red felt his hands tremble. Words locked in his throat. "I'm your son," he whispered.

"That's what makes this meeting particularly painful. I'm sorry for both of us that it has to take place. But I've made up my mind."

"Just like that—you're going to throw me out?"

"I believe you did this to yourself."

"You want to make me feel like a failure—"

"No. I wish you success in whatever you do. But being

betrayed by your flesh and blood is a wound that doesn't close quickly.''

"Wound?'' Red asked in disbelief. "You want to talk about a wound? What about *my* wound—the one of being unappreciated by you!''

"This discussion is over,'' Owen said.

"You listen to me.'' Red's voice wobbled. "I want you to know something. I want you to hear it from me. All I ever wanted was for you to love me as much as I tried to love you. That's what the loan was about. The lie and the deception. So why don't you finally tell me, before you kick me out—do you love me?''

"You're distorting the issue,'' Owen answered coolly. "We're talking about trust and honesty.''

"I asked if you loved me,'' Red repeated.

"I think it's best you leave now.''

Red felt his heart knocking in his throat. "If you can't tell me, then let me make another request. Don't do this to me. Don't reject me. Show some understanding. Just this once. I want to stay on. I want to work here.''

"That's impossible now.''

Red forced the words out. "I'm begging you, Father.''

Owen fixed his eyes on his son, pitying him. "You should have considered all this five years ago.''

A silent, helpless rage swept over Red as his gaze fixed on his father, then he turned and left.

"Oh, what a handsome young man you are!'' Electra exclaimed as Jean squealed with delight and led Alycia's best friend halfway around the crowded Lakeside pool.

"You've got a birthday party to attend. Now, come along . . .'' Electra finally picked up the squirming boy and returned him to his mother.

"Jean has the same energy level as his father,'' Alycia said proudly as she toweled him off.

The chubby boy grinned and shook his head no. Laughing, Alycia half-rolled, half-slid off her chaise, her swollen belly straining against the nylon bathing suit. Five months pregnant with her second child, she didn't mind the hardships and inconveniences. If she was putting on weight or didn't look graceful or had difficulty sleeping at night, pregnancy was still the most wonderful feeling in the world. The glow of carrying another life inside her, a life that she and Red had created together, was indescribable.

"Walk on this side of the street." Electra motioned Alycia to the left as they drifted out of the club together. Electra's children scampered ahead. Jean tugged his bloated mother along like a strong man doing a good deed.

"I hear a catch in your voice," Alycia said to her friend.

Electra smiled mischievously. "I want to peek over Terry Donelson's wall. I hear he sunbathes *au naturel*."

Alycia exploded with laughter. "Toluca Lake isn't exactly Gomorrah. It's all those cheap novels you read. They give you crazy ideas."

"I like good trash. It's fun."

"And you don't really have the nerve to spy on Terry Donelson."

Electra threw her head back. "You don't know the real me."

"Rubbish," Alycia exclaimed. "I've known you five years. You're the beautiful, wealthy, scintillating hostess married to a famous neurosurgeon. You like to throw lavish parties and flirt with other women's husbands—but you always know your boundaries."

"Alycia, that sounds like an epitaph."

They both laughed. Jean, understanding nothing, clapped his hands.

"Why do men think I'm such a tease?" Electra suddenly asked. Alycia just stared. "No, tell me. I mean it."

"For starters, you have gorgeous red hair and eyes that sparkle like champagne. Do you know how many women envy you?"

"You might find this hard to believe, but I never think about what effect I have on people. Honestly. I've just always wanted to be liked and accepted, that's all." She made a small nervous laugh. "I must be insecure."

"Excuse me? How could *you* be insecure? You have everything."

"Except confidence," Electra said, gazing off. "Growing up, I thought people liked me for my family's money. I couldn't stand it. That's when I started to flirt. Later I did other little things to be different from my sisters—like using pink lipstick or not wearing a bra or going out with men twice my age. I wanted to be noticed."

"You succeeded. And look what it got you. You've been very lucky," Alycia said sincerely.

"You don't have to tell me. I have a wonderful, caring husband and two gorgeous children, and everything is perfect—but something still feels missing."

"Like spying on Terry Donelson?" Alycia could always kid Electra. It was one of the things that made them close.

"Don't you ever wish you were a movie star?" Electra asked.

"Why?"

"They have more exciting lives than we do. I think of myself as a rebel, but do I ever really take chances? I know how to buy clothes that show off my figure, what makeup to wear, how to get my hair styled. But I've never experimented. I know who to talk to at parties and what to say, who not to talk to because I'll get in arguments. I never challenge that. I know what Scotty likes me to do to him in bed, yet I'm afraid to suggest what I'd like him to do for me." She slung the beach bag onto her other arm. "Don't you see? Everything is so safe—and boring. We live in a comfort zone."

"What's wrong with being comfortable? You don't know what it is to live through a war," Alycia pointed out.

"What's wrong is that we're not making the most of our lives. We're used to a routine. When I look at movie stars, I get envious. Robert Mitchum smokes marijuana. Ingrid Bergman jumps in bed with Roberto Rossellini. Frank Sinatra gets married every few years. Margarita Cansino dyes her hair and turns into Rita Hayworth."

They howled with laughter.

"Don't you have fantasies?" Electra asked.

"Of course," Alycia said.

"So tell me."

"I'm going to disappoint you. Terry Donelson isn't part of mine. I see Red and me and the kids living away from here one day. Maybe on a New England farm, or going to London, or Africa. I love my family, and I think I'd love to travel. I guess I have simple dreams."

Standing in front of Terry Donelson's, Electra motioned Alycia down a narrow alley that led to the pool area in back. Alycia couldn't help feeling a little funny as she and Jean skirted several No Trespassing signs.

"Oh, my God," Electra whispered, straining on her tiptoes when they reached the wall by the swimming pool. Like a naughty school girl, she giggled as she ducked and turned to Alycia. "He really is nude! Guess which side he's lying on?"

"I don't believe you," Alycia said.

"Look for yourself."

"I happen to have someone with me . . ."

Electra lifted a bemused Jean from his mother.

Alycia glanced over the wall. A sleek bronzed body stirred on the warm concrete. Then Terry Donelson's head peeked up. Alycia ducked down. "He's on his back!" she said to Electra. They tried not to laugh too loudly as they hurried with Jean back to the street.

"Now, wasn't that worth it?" Electra asked.

"Maybe," Alycia said whimsically.

"Isn't he gorgeous? Believe me, Scotty is *nothing* like that. Is Red? I'll bet Terry Donelson is Superman."

They laughed some more, then promised to rendezvous at the club tomorrow. Alycia carried Jean the final half-block home. Red was due back at four-thirty, and she had to get Jean dressed for his friend's birthday party. Alycia loved Electra, and she wouldn't know what to do without her, but today what had all this been about? Maybe Electra hadn't been serious about being restless and discontent. She and Scotty lived charmed lives. They were successful, good-looking, rich, and they threw magnificent parties that raised tens of thousands of dollars for local charities; fun parties, too, where important people showed up. Everyone envied Electra and Scotty. They were the perfect couple.

By five o'clock, dressed and waiting for his father, Jean fell asleep on the living-room sofa. Alycia called Red's office. He had left more than an hour ago, a secretary informed her. Alycia debated about waking Jean and taking him to the party herself, but he had made a row about wanting his father to bring him, and Red had promised to be here. At six Alycia called the office again, then Lakeside, Scotty and Electra, and finally a restaurant Red patronized with clients. No one knew anything. Jean woke in a cranky mood. "Where's Daddy?" he asked. Alycia made an excuse, called the neighbor to say Jean wouldn't be coming, and put him back to bed.

It was after eight when the front door banged open. Alycia sat up on the couch. She started to be annoyed, but Red looked pale and upset. He gave her a trembling smile.

"Where were you? What happened?" she asked. "I was worried."

"Sorry I didn't call," he said in a strange voice after he'd poured himself the usual Scotch. "I was out looking at commercial space."

"For what?"

"My new office."

Alycia stood.

"Congratulations are in order," he announced as he met Alycia's eyes in the bar mirror. "My father fired me this afternoon. Found out about his signature being forged years ago."

Alycia drew a breath.

"I know, you told me so," he said as he faced her. "Walking out of my father's building today, I felt humiliated. Like a pariah. Like I had failed, let everybody down, including you. I even begged him not to fire me." Red flinched.

"I'm so sorry," Alycia whispered.

"Do you believe in ghosts?" Red asked.

She didn't understand.

"Remember when I told you about growing up and how scared I was?" Red continued. "It was especially true about ghosts. They lurked in corners of my room, waited for me in the schoolyard, hovered on dark streets. They plotted to do me harm. Somehow I even became convinced my father was one. I don't know why, but I thought he was going to hurt me somehow, in a way I would least expect—trick me, like ghosts did. Today, as I stood in his office, I had the same feeling. I saw someone else as I looked at him, I saw this ghost, and I had a terrible sense that I wasn't the only one he wanted to hurt. No one in my family was safe—"

"Don't say that." Alycia didn't know what to think. Red wasn't rambling. And he wasn't drunk.

"I worked my tail off for my father," he went on as he dropped into a chair. "I kept Poindexter Realty from sinking into oblivion. I'm the loyal, if not always obedient, servant. Out of some perverted instinct of filial loyalty I show kindness and respect and love to a man who has never had the decency to do the same for me . . ."

The anger was building in his voice. Alycia was afraid he'd wake Jean. "You've had disagreements before," she said, wanting to make peace. "Things will seem better in the morning."

"Not this time. This time it's over. I wouldn't go back if my father asked on hands and knees."

"Please don't be so stubborn."

"Are you taking his side?" Red asked, hurt. "This breakup should have happened centuries ago. I never want to see my father again. I feel liberated. I'll start my own firm now. I'll show him—"

"You don't have to show anybody. You don't have to prove anything," Alycia said, but Red wasn't listening. Despite what he said about being free, he didn't look it. A bright flame of pain burned just under the surface of controlled reason. Alycia knew he felt betrayed and rejected. She knew, too, he wasn't likely to discuss with her or anyone else his feelings of inadequacy. His answer was to believe he didn't have any weaknesses.

"We're supposed to go to your parents for the weekend," Alycia pointed out delicately.

"It's canceled. I already called Mother."

"What did she say?"

"She was hurt and upset, but she'll get over it."

"I want to call her too."

"I was thinking," Red continued, rising from his chair, "that we're going to start living a little better now. I won't have to split my commissions with a firm. And I'll have a couple dozen brokers working for me. We're going to buy a bigger house, throw more parties, get new cars. And new clothes for you. You deserve that."

"My clothes are fine. I don't need anything. And why do we have to throw a lot of parties? We go to enough already. In a few months we'll have a new baby to spend time with."

Red looked at her as if she didn't understand.

In the morning his resolve was only stronger. Red paused for breakfast and to bounce Jean in the air several times; otherwise he never left the phone. By noon he had negotiated a lease for a suite of offices not far from home, on Lankershim Boulevard, in the heart of the Valley. He hired a secretary and contacted important friends and associates about his move. To avoid his father, he waited till evening before removing his personal articles from the Poindexter Building.

The next day he brought Alycia to his new offices. He asked her help in ordering furniture and carpets. In contrast to his father, Red told her, he wanted to spend lavishly and fill his suite with deep sofas and cushioned chairs, plants, art, accessories. Within days he'd recruited ten associate brokers and opened his doors. His father had focused on commercial properties, but Red saw his firm's future in residential housing. His associates would service young family buyers who, impressed by the office's sumptuous appointments and helpful brokers, would become loyal and trusting clients.

"Why don't you come work with me?" he asked Alycia one morning.

"I think that would be very difficult," she said patting her belly.

"Then after the baby is born."

"Don't be silly. Who's going to take care of the children?"

"We'll find a nanny."

"Maybe," Alycia said, though she knew it was impossible. The trust agreement she'd signed with Owen would keep her home until both children were teenagers. Red knew that too. It was as if he were testing her loyalty, wanting her to break the hold Owen had over them. But there was no hold, Alycia honestly thought. The trust was the trust. It no longer had anything to do with Red's father. As for what Owen had done to Red, Alycia was still upset. It was unfair, but there was little point in getting angry. She'd spoken several times to Harriet. After Red left for the day, Alycia dropped Jean at nursery school and drove to a small park near Bel Air. Harriet was already there, waving as Alycia walked up.

"Really, I can't excuse Owen, and I don't," Harriet said when the subject soon came up, as if it could never be analyzed enough. They strolled arm in arm through a grove of magnolias. "The whole thing makes me sick. But what can I do? Remember when I said I could never bring myself to be critical of Red? The same is true about Owen. Like Red has, I've learned to give him a wide berth. It's impossible to argue with him. Perhaps it's cowardly on my part . . ."

Alycia saw that Harriet felt bad. "I hope you're not blaming yourself for this, Mother. You've had to live between two strong-willed men—that could never be easy."

"I want you to know," Harriet went on, "that Owen was a very different man when we met and fell in love. For some reason, he changed. It was slow and gradual, hard to perceive. I suppose I changed too. Through it all, despite our differences, even over Red, Owen and I have gotten along. I'm not talking about love—I'm not sure what happens to that. But I do know in marriage you learn to value coexistence and convenience." She looked at Alycia. "Can you understand?"

"I think so," Alycia sympathized, "but what are we supposed to do? Accept that Owen and Red will never reconcile? And does that mean the four of us will never get together anymore? You know how I feel about families. Meeting you secretly like this makes it seem like we're two spies."

Harriet smiled softly. "I'm not one for preaching or giving advice when it's not wanted, Alycia, but perhaps we have to wait and see. Things will work out. I've been around long enough to know that life takes strange turns. And sometimes, if we don't interfere, miracles happen on their own. We must have faith and patience. In the meantime, you and I will remain good friends, will we not?"

"Of course we will," Alycia said as she gave Harriet a reassuring hug. Owen would not come between *them*, would he? As they said good-bye, Alycia struggled with her thoughts. Harriet might be resigned to letting events take their course, but she wasn't. There had to be some other avenue to explore to get everyone back together. It was just a matter of being persistent, of wanting to make things happen.

Red's new workdays began at six and ended twelve to fourteen hours later. Alycia tried to join him for breakfast and was resigned to late dinners. Red hardly called during the day, unless it was for her to run an errand. His only time for Jean was on Sundays, squeezed around golf dates with Scotty Madigan. Alycia couldn't help but feel isolated and slightly abandoned. She wanted Red to comfort her now and then. This pregnancy wasn't easy. But Red was always running, so caught up in his own world that when they did share a private moment the topic was usually business. She told Red she was happy he was doing well, but the words felt forced. Why couldn't Red ask if she were happy? Alycia filled her days by driving Jean to nursery school or having coffee with Electra or taking walks with Harriet. Afternoons she saved for naps, or curling up with a book of baby names and explaining to Jean he would soon be a big brother.

"Well, Mother, everything under control in there?" Red kidded on Sunday as they sat on the back lawn. Alycia was pleased when he reached over and touched her belly. With a captive audience, Jean attempted a forward somersault, only to crash on his side.

Alycia clapped heartily anyway. She turned to Red. "Do you have to play golf today?"

"It's my only time all week. You're not trying to make me feel guilty—"

"No, really. I just thought we could have a picnic—you and I. Electra could watch Jean."

"Next Sunday," he promised.

"Red . . ." She saw the way he looked at her. It made her feel helpless. She knew he loved her, but she could tell she wasn't in his thoughts, not like she used to be. "I want to talk about your father. I know in his heart of hearts he wants to see you again. Maybe we could all get together for that picnic next Sunday—"

"No," he cut her off.

"Red, couldn't you just call him?"

"It's impossible."

"You have your own firm now. You're doing well. You've proved what you wanted to. What would it hurt just to talk to him?"

"Don't get caught in this, Alycia—"

"Red, I'm not taking your father's side. What he did was wrong. I'm taking the family's side."

"We have our family," Red replied. "There's you and me and Jean—and that little Poindexter you're carrying around." Red took Alycia's hand. "You have to take care of yourself. Worrying over my father doesn't help."

He gave her a kiss as Jean chased a butterfly around in the grass. Maybe Red was right, she thought. Entering her ninth month, she didn't need more anxiety or another confrontation. Her energy had to be saved for Jean and the baby.

The call from Owen the next day caught Alycia by surprise. His voice was detached and businesslike, and untroubled, as if the fight with Red had never occurred. She didn't know if that was a good sign or a bad one.

"Alycia, I need to see you."

"I don't think that's possible," she said cautiously.

"Please. I need to talk to you about Red."

"He doesn't want me to see you. We shouldn't even be on the phone."

"But what about you? Don't you want to bring us together?"

She sighed, trying to think. "You know I do. But you hurt Red. And under the circumstances, there's nothing I can do right now."

"Alycia, Red doesn't have to know we meet. I don't want to jeopardize anything for you. I just want to talk."

"I'm sorry, I really am," she said, and hung up.

Owen called the next afternoon. He asked her not to tell Red he was talking to her, and please—couldn't she meet with him for one hour? No, she said, but with more difficulty. When he called a third time, she begged him to stop. The tension was upsetting her. The baby was due anytime and she was supposed to rest.

"I just need an hour," Owen persisted. "I know a lunch spot where no one will see us. I wouldn't bother you if this wasn't important."

Alycia took Jean over to Electra's and told her where she was going. "Am I doing the right thing?"

"If you're not sure, then don't go," Electra said. "Don't show up."

"I can't do that. I don't like disappointing people. Maybe I'll just sit and listen to him."

She met Owen in a coffee shop in North Hollywood. Alycia thought he looked terrible. He was still handsome and impeccably dressed in his double-breasted suit, but the face was drawn, the eyes puffy.

"In the last week I've called Red a half-dozen times at his office," Owen confided. "Has he told you?"

"No. But everything's been so busy. We haven't had much time to talk about anything personal."

"He never returns my calls."

"He feels very strongly about what you did to him," she explained.

"That's why I want to apologize. I acted too rashly with him. I was angry when I learned about the forgery. Now I've cooled down. The mistake was mine. Will you tell him?"

"Of course," she said, feeling some hope.

"Would you also tell him I'd like him to rejoin the firm? I want to make this up to him."

"I will."

"All he has to do is call me."

They walked outside and Owen went to get Alycia's car in the lot down the street. The sun glared off the adjacent buildings. She felt exhausted suddenly as she focused on the traffic, and a little wobbly on her feet. What was taking Owen so long? Her head began to spin. She teetered toward a bus stop, but lost her footing. She felt like she was sinking

under her own weight, like she had no control at all. Trying
to stop her fall, she lurched forward into the street. One car
swerved around her. Alycia picked herself up but couldn't
make her legs move. She would be all right, she kept telling
herself, she would be just fine. And even when the blow
came and her body coiled in pain, somehow she didn't black
out.

St. Joseph's Hospital in Burbank reached Red shortly after
two. He was informed that Alycia had been struck by a car
traveling at a low speed, and had been taken to ER by her
father-in-law, who had been at the scene of the accident.
Alycia had sustained a slight concussion and some bad bruises
but no broken bones. Her obstetrician had rushed over and,
concerned about an irregular fetal heartbeat, performed a
cesarean. The baby, a seven-pound girl, seemed fine, Red
was assured on the phone. A badly shaken but now-relieved
mother was asleep in a private room.

Red breathed a sigh as he hung up, but he couldn't ignore
the fury he felt toward his father. Red's secretary told him
Owen had phoned around one, and left a message about the
accident, but Red had been out of the office. There was
nothing in the message that indicated why his father had been
with Alycia in the first place.

When Red reached the hospital he hurried down the laby-
rinthine corridors to the maternity wing. Alycia was still
sleeping. At the nursery window his eyes roved eagerly over
the bassinets and came to rest joyfully on his new daughter.
She looked so beautiful, he thought. Handsome, with high
rosy cheeks and round eyes. Transfixed, Red couldn't pull
himself away.

For the next few days he returned every morning and
afternoon to be with Alycia and the baby. Electra had taken
Jean into her house for the week. Red joked to the nurses that
maybe he should move in with his wife, he spent so much
time at the hospital. He loved watching and holding his new
baby, yet beneath the impulses of pride and love, he began to
feel a ripple of discomfort. His little girl didn't stir or cry like
the other babies in the nursery. She barely turned her head,
and the tiny red fingers seemed unable to make a real fist.

"I think something might be wrong," Red confided to the
pediatrician after a week. He walked down the hospital corridor with the jowly, curly-haired Dr. Glatzer, who tugged

absently on his dangling stethoscope like a good-luck charm. Red hadn't breathed his fears to Alycia. Recuperating from the cesarean, she was swept away in a tide of excitement and joy. The fact that the baby nursed with difficulty didn't disturb her. Nurses reassured her about what she already knew from Jean: some infants were more fussy than others.

"It's too early to tell anything," the doctor told Red. "I did learn from Dr. Kibbee, Alycia's obstetrician, that there were some difficulties at birth. The placenta had been partially separated, possibly due to abdominal trauma caused by the car accident, and consequently there was probably some oxygen deprivation to the fetus. But that may or may not have affected the baby. We can't be sure, Mr. Poindexter."

"When can you?" Red insisted painfully.

"Don't worry. I'll keep a close eye," Dr. Glatzer promised.

After ten days mother and daughter were allowed to go home. Red and Alycia named the baby Isabel, after Harriet's mother. The baby's room was ready with brightly painted furniture and stuffed animals, and Red filled their own room with roses and asters. A fidgety Jean had crayoned several creations for his baby sister, though when he finally saw the infant and how closely his mother held her, he curled his lip in displeasure.

"Isabel likes you," Alycia reassured him, putting the baby on Jean's lap. "Now, hold her carefully. See, she's not crying. Go ahead—touch her."

Jean wrapped his hand around the little fingers and squealed with delight.

A live-in nursemaid was hired so Red could go to work and Alycia regain her strength. Still, she spent as much time as possible with her baby. Isabel's appetite was hardly robust, she was sluggish, and sometimes she broke into high and prolonged fevers. Visits to Dr. Glatzer became as commonplace as trips to the grocery store. For Alycia's sake, Red pretended he found nothing unnerving, yet when alone with Isabel he held her tenderly and looked into her eyes, as if to divine something that medical science could not.

"She's three months, and she can't lift her chest when lying on her stomach. She can barely raise her head," he told Dr. Glatzer after bringing Isabel for an examination.

"You're going to drive yourself crazy, Mr. Poindexter. The *average* baby does those things at three months. That means some do it earlier, some later. Please don't be concerned."

"Then when should I be?" Red answered sharply, tired of being patronized. "When Isabel is six months, or nine months, or a year?"

"Calm down. We'll see."

Scotty and Electra were regular visitors to play with Bizzy Izzy, as Electra called the baby, bringing along an assortment of rattles and rubber ducks and mirrors. On her back, her favorite position, Isabel would stare at the colorful toys held out for her, reacting with a small but obviously pleased gurgle.

Harriet was another frequent visitor, and a great help to Alycia with diapers and bottles when the nursemaid wasn't around. Red forbade his father from even entering the house. Alycia tried to convince Red the accident had nothing to do with Owen, and since everything had turned out fine, why hold a grudge? Owen only wanted to mend fences. That's what their meeting had been about. Alycia was sorry if she'd offended Red by going, but now it was history. Red said nothing.

Isabel was seven months and still unable to raise her torso from the floor when Dr. Glatzer consulted a pediatric neurologist. After a week of thorough tests and examinations, Red was informed that the baby's slow development was cause for concern.

Red stirred uneasily in Dr. Glatzer's office. "What's wrong exactly?"

"We can't tell conclusively, but there's every indication of retardation. We can't necessarily blame the traumatic abruption from the car accident. . . ."

Red felt sick. He couldn't meet the doctor's eyes.

"I'm sorry, Mr. Poindexter."

"What's going to happen?" he forced himself to ask.

Dr. Glatzer rested his hands on his desk and pushed his fingers together, as if deciding which answer to give Red. "With brain dysfunction, I hesitate to predict. I don't know that much about the field—"

"What are you saying?" Red interrupted.

"For her first years Isabel can certainly stay at home. But as she gets older, her needs will probably demand specialized outside help. We simply don't know at this point how severe the retardation will be."

Red couldn't stand to hear any more. He wept openly in front of the doctor. At home he helped himself to two drinks before he could tell Alycia. He was amazed how calmly she took the tragedy. She was filled with sorrow, but also compassion and understanding, while Red felt only an unfocused but deepening anger.

In the weeks that followed, he drank more than usual. Just beneath his rage was an implacable wave of guilt. Why hadn't he been more insistent with Alycia that she stay in bed and rest? But he *had* been insistent. And Alycia would have done as she was supposed to if not for Owen. His father had had no right to bother her. His pestering phone calls and then the meeting were outrageous. He had taken advantage of her, gotten her tired and disoriented. Red had cut off communications and his father had known it, so Owen was doing what he always did—manipulating, interfering, getting his way.

And this time his transgression was permanent and unforgivable.

The mere resentment Red had felt toward his father before Isabel was born turned now into something darker. Not only didn't he return his father's calls, but Red told Alycia that Jean would not be allowed to visit his grandfather. Harriet could come and go freely in their house, but never his father. Red forbade his employees from having anything to do with Poindexter Realty. He refused to attend Realtor luncheons or dinners if his father would be there. He severed relations with his attorney and CPA and banker because they were also Owen's.

One night, alone in Isabel's room, Red made a final covenant with his daughter. As he stroked her cheek, he swore that somehow his father would pay for taking this precious child's normal life away. Somehow, in some way, he would pay very dearly.

On a Sunday in late October Red stood with Scotty Madigan on the par-four eighteenth hole at Lakeside. A rosy-cheeked bearded executive from Walt Disney Studios and a chubby, graying dentist from San Diego filled out their foursome. All day Red had struggled with his iron game, hacking his way through the course. Still, he was happy to be here, away from the stresses of home and work. The Lakeside course whose shades of green ran from emerald to deep reptilian and whose fairways were lined with scented eucalyptuses gave him a genuine if only temporary peace.

"I'm going to par this sucker," the Disney executive bragged as he approached the eighteenth tee. "Any takers?"

"Ah, we're fish in a barrel to you," Scotty protested. "I'll have to confer with my adviser. Hey, Manuel," Scotty called to his young Mexican caddy. The boy was only fourteen, and an illegal immigrant, but Scotty liked him so much that he pulled strings at the club to keep him around. "Would a number-two wood help my chances?"

"Ees a deef-e-colt hole," the youth reminded him diplomatically.

"Settles that. I concede defeat," Scotty declared.

"A hundred dollars okay?" Red asked the executive. The man was a scratch handicapper and ten strokes up on Red for the day. But Red liked the challenge.

"Too rich for my wallet," the executive backed off.

"Where's your conviction?" Red asked with some seriousness.

"Tell you what, friend. You say you're in real estate? You win the hole and I'll let you in on a fat little secret. I win, and I get your Ben Franklin."

"Better be some secret," Red allowed with a wink to Scotty. Red drove his ball almost three hundred yards, straight as a rail, sending it between two yawning sand traps. He felt inspired. A four iron put him on the green, and he sank his putt for a birdie.

The Disney executive finished with a bogey.

"I'm all ears," Red said as he accompanied the man toward the clubhouse.

"Nobody is supposed to know this," he began. "It's not even definite . . ." His head turned, as if somebody might be listening. "Disney—the old man himself—wants to start an amusement park."

"What kind?" Red asked.

"Something really spectacular. We're talking tens of millions. This is a lifelong dream for the old man. Some of us at the studio aren't so sure, but Walt flies by the seat of his pants."

"Sometimes that's the only way," Red said.

"We've taken an option on sixty-five acres. Orange County, of all places. You familiar with Anaheim?"

The first thing Monday, Red was in his car, negotiating the new, nearly empty freeway that took him past the Anaheim city limit. Weaving through side streets, he parked near a wide swath of untamed brush and woods. The site was almost an hour from downtown, even farther from the Valley. Houses were scattered nearby, but there were no major commercial strips. Anaheim felt almost as remote as the Mojave Desert. Red thought Walt Disney was a reckless genius—reckless to assume people would drive this far to spend their leisure dollars; genius because he probably had the imagination and resources to draw them here.

That afternoon Red researched ownership of the adjoining acres, contacted the parties, and within three weeks had tied up fifteen acres paralleling the Disney site. The owners wanted an outrageous sum, but for fifteen-thousand dollars Red got a three-month option. He nudged the Disney executive he'd met at Lakeside. Would the studio close on the land—or forfeit its option money? The executive was suddenly tight-lipped. Red wondered if he'd been suckered.

A week before Christmas, he got an early present. The lead story on the *Times*'s business page was that Disney studios was closing on a sixty-five-acre parcel in Anaheim. Red's joy was short-lived when he realized he had only two weeks to come up with $650,000 to buy his own fifteen acres outright. Without the imprimatur of his father's firm, he had no chance of borrowing a sum that large, especially on unimproved land. Yet in one day his land's resale value had been pushed into the stratosphere. Gas stations, motels, souvenir shops, shopping centers—everyone would die to be next to a Disney park.

"Sounds like an interesting investment," Scotty acknowledged the next Sunday at Lakeside. They sat at the bar, glancing between their drinks and the House Un-American Activities Committee hearings on television. "Christ, will you look who Senator Joe is nailing to the cross?" Scotty announced with fascination. "It's our neighbor!"

"So it is." Red watched as Terry Donelson squirmed behind the microphone, the perennially tanned face now white as snow. Red couldn't believe it—a war hero who went to pinko meetings. He hoped the junior senator from Wisconsin ran Terry's ass right out of Hollywood, and for that matter, Toluca Lake.

"It's more than an interesting investment," Red picked up, "it's a lead-pipe cinch. That's why I'm forming a syndicate."

Scotty squinted.

"A group of investors," Red clarified. "In this case,

thirteen shares total. Each investor puts up fifty-thousand dollars. I'm taking three shares myself to show good faith.''

"Who else have you lined up?'' Scotty asked seriously.

"Besides you?'' Red was unfazed. "Absolutely nobody.''

Scotty pushed his off-center smile another degree to the left. "You're a man on a mission.''

"We'll hold for as long as the majority desires,'' Red went on, as if the deal were already struck. "Upon closing, I take fifteen percent for putting the group together, five percent for overhead. The rest of the profit is prorated among the investors.''

"What if there is no profit? My accountant is no optimist about the economy.''

"Come on, Korea is over. Ike's in office. We're sitting pretty. Even if there's another downturn, a Disney park will be an oasis. It's a pot of gold, Scotty. I'm betting some of my own money, aren't I?''

Red, in fact, was betting everything. Without telling Alycia, to raise his $150,000 he had refinanced the house, liquidated every share in their stock portfolio, and drained his real-estate corporation so it had only enough to pay rent and the secretary's salary through January. The thought of leaving himself on the edge, with no margin for failure, was not unsettling; Red felt as high as the moon. His attorney wanted to check legalities with the IRS, but Red knew there wasn't time. Besides, he had no intention of misrepresenting anything. He had always been a man of his word.

"You want in or not?'' Red asked firmly.

Scotty mused over a small plastic card from his wallet. "Electra gave this to me,'' he said. "An astrology chart. My dear bored wife has gone over the edge. Have you heard of Ouija boards and tarot cards?'' He glanced up with a reborn smile. "You're in luck, Red. Venus is out of retrograde. I'll write you a check tomorrow. I'll tell some of my doc friends too.''

In the next two weeks Red pulled together his ten investors. It was as easy as jumping rope. Selling was a gift—it didn't matter whether the product was land or used cars— and Red had it. As he'd done with his cadre in the war, he could inspire trust, faith, enthusiasm, and sacrifice. He would not fail or desert anybody, he promised the lawyers and doctors and businessmen. He would make a profit for everybody. And this wasn't the only deal he would offer. Greater fortunes were around the corner. Red believed every word he told them.

On the fifteenth of January the *Times* carried the story of the Disney closing. A price of $2.9 million was listed, as were ambitious plans for a theme park the likes of which the world had never seen. The next day Red received a half-dozen calls from developers who'd been sleeping. The ante was jumped a dozen times within a few days. Red presented all offers to his syndicate. His recommendation was to hold, both for a higher price and favorable capital gains treatment. His investors cottoned to the idea of quick and easy money. Red kept his word and did as they wished. The fifteen acres were sold in two parcels for a total of $1.6 million, more than half of what Disney had paid for his sixty-five acres. Investors made almost one hundred percent on their money. Including his percentage for overhead and syndication, Red deposited $615,000 in the bank.

"I did it!" he exulted to Alycia that night, pouring himself a drink. "I feel like I own the whole goddamn world!" In his euphoria he almost neglected to notice Jean's mysterious grin and Alycia's own voice of joy, outshouted as she was, telling Red that she was pregnant.

A baby girl was born the first of July, exactly on Alycia's due date, in perfect health. Alycia was overjoyed. At nine pounds, three ounces, the baby ate like a horse. Her eyes flashed merrily at the world, and when she cried it was like an air-raid siren. They started to name her Felicity, then changed it to Felice because it was French, as well as out of the fear that, when older, their daughter would find their first choice too old-fashioned.

"I don't know, I still like 'Felicity,' " Alycia vacillated when they brought the baby home. "She looks like an old-fashioned baby."

"How?" said Red. Half-dressed for work, he studied the infant in Alycia's arms. "She looks pretty contemporary to me."

"Look at those large blue eyes and fat cheeks. She could be on the cover of *Saturday Evening Post*."

"I say we stick with Felice," Red voted, and kissing baby and mother good-bye, finished dressing.

When Felice was six months old, Alycia had her first party for her daughter. She invited Electra and Harriet and some

neighbors, who showered the little girl with stuffed animals
and dolls that she could barely pick up but seemed delighted
with, even when Jean sneaked one or two away for himself.
Isabel sat docilely on Alycia's lap the whole time. Red had
promised to bring a cake, but by six the party was over and
he still hadn't appeared. Alycia couldn't help but feel let
down. Was Red's work so important that he would miss his
daughter's party?

She was putting Isabel down for a nap when the front door
opened. She found Red in the entry with a bottle of champagne, shaking it playfully, a smile spread wide across his
handsome face. Before she could protest, the champagne was
uncorked. Like a trained seal, Red opened his mouth to
receive the bubbly.

"What are you doing?" Alycia demanded.

"Celebrating, darling."

"What?"

"Get some glasses. Then get in the car."

"Red—" She resisted as he took her hand.

"Come on, we're going for a ride."

"What about the children?"

"Leave them for a second. This won't take long."

"You know I can't—"

In the end she left the champagne but had to wake Isabel,
and along with a protesting Jean and crabby Felice, put
everyone in Red's Cadillac. Indifferent to the commotion,
Red drove five blocks to the other side of Toluca Lake.
Nothing was daunting his enthusiasm, Alycia saw.

The car braked in front of a breath-taking two-story Tudor
with terraced front gardens and graceful willow trees and a
winding flagstone walkway to the front door. A bird house
was visible in the upper branches of one of the willows. A
weather vane above an east bedroom turned in the gentle
breeze.

"Ready?" Red called, taking Felice in one arm and Jean
in the other.

"What are we doing?" Alycia protested.

"Darling, this is our new house."

She cocked her head at him.

"I just bought it."

Alycia didn't know what to say as she slung Isabel over her
shoulder and Red led the tour. With the possible exception of
Terry Donelson's, this was the finest home in Toluca Lake.

Alycia was in awe as she roamed through the five bedrooms. Downstairs, off the kitchen, was a walnut-paneled study for Red, a mammoth living room, and a dining room that led to several patios, all with tranquil views of the lake. A swimming pool and more gardens were on a separate level in the backyard, and from there the rolling lawn led to a boat dock. The yard seemed to Alycia as large as a football field. Red told her they could have afforded something in Beverly Hills or Westwood, but in the end he'd decided not to leave Lakeside.

"Why didn't you tell me you were looking at houses?" she asked.

"Because I wanted to surprise you. Are you surprised?"

She could only nod.

"Are you happy? Do you like it?"

"It's beautiful," she had to admit.

"I missed Felice's party, I'm sorry, but I had to be at the closing. You're not mad—"

"No." She was just overwhelmed, she thought. This was an even nicer home than Scotty's and Electra's. She wondered how much it cost. Red had just gotten a new Cadillac— what else was on his shopping list? He never discussed finances with her. That was his domain, just as raising children and looking after the house and entertaining were hers.

Moving two weeks later was such aggravation that Alycia wished Red had never bought the house. His argument was sound—with three children and live-in help they needed more space—but the real reason, she thought, was that Red saw himself moving up in the world. The new home was light and airy, but so large it wasn't easy to keep up, even with the sweet, well-meaning Mexican girl to help with the children, or for Alycia to furnish and decorate. Red was insistent on getting rid of their old furniture. He gave Alycia a budget that she thought was generous even for a hotel. Her tastes still ran to modern—if anything, they were more radical than ever—so she bought abstract-expressionist paintings and Italian leather couches and art-deco lamps imported from Paris. She worked feverishly, determined to get everything done so life could return to normal.

Alycia didn't know if the move and the ensuing chaos were harder on her or the children. Jean was now in kindergarten and very independent. As stubborn as he could be, the two girls in diapers were more taxing. It was especially painful to turn one minute from Felice, alert and playful and engaging, to Isabel, who would sit and stare out helplessly into some void. Alycia took her to a therapist several times a week. The doctor was always upbeat and hopeful, yet Alycia knew that her daughter's future was terribly limited. She wondered if her love for Isabel would be enough.

"She's such a beautiful child," Electra consoled Alycia as they pushed Isabel in her stroller. The first week of December, the days were turning chilly. The two friends took frequent walks no matter what the weather, usually with Isabel, ending up at a bridge over the lake, where the ducks and geese could be fed. Isabel would throw out bread crumbs and convulse with laughter as they got gobbled up.

"You're sweet for saying that," Alycia said.

"That's what friends are for—sticking together, sticking up for one another."

Alycia gave her a hug.

"I have a suggestion," Electra volunteered as they circled back to the house. "I'm on the board of the Sidney Green Hospital. It specializes in pediatric care for the disabled. A lot of money and talent go toward research. I know you don't have a lot of free time, but why don't you get involved with me? Isabel might be helped."

"That would be wonderful," she said, thinking about it.

"I have to do something to help you. You seem so distracted lately."

"Depressed," corrected Alycia. "And it's not because of Isabel."

"Your father-in-law?"

Alycia told her no. Owen was not part of their lives anymore. Red was insistent on that, and Alycia, while she still hoped for a reconciliation, had given up for now. "It's my own father," she told Electra after a beat.

"He's in Paris, isn't he?"

"He used to be."

"What do you mean?"

"I got a letter from him yesterday. It was the first time I've heard from him since I left France."

Electra looked astounded. "That's almost eight years. What happened? Were you two fighting?"

"No. I really can't fight with anyone. I've been trying to find Père all this time. I've written dozens of letters. Finally one got to him."

"And . . ."

"He wrote back. His letter was very disturbing. He's living in a small town near the Spanish border. No money, no friends, no hope. He supports himself doing occasional carpentry."

"You told me he's a professor."

"He was, before the war. He's an extremely bright man. And loving and giving. We were very close."

"So what happened?" Electra pressed. Her face creased with sympathy for Alycia.

"People do things, they don't mean to." Alycia didn't know what else to say. She hadn't told anyone about her father, not even Red or Harriet. There were some secrets that were too humiliating to share. But with the letter from her father, she knew she had to confide in someone. It was too much misery to bear alone. Red was so busy that Alycia doubted he would take the time to understand. And Harriet had enough worries on her shoulders.

"Père and I lived in Paris during the war," Alycia said as they walked with Isabel. "My mother had just died in a sanitarium. Life was a struggle. We were never sure what the Germans would do next, yet Père and I managed to live well. Fresh food, clothes, even some luxuries. I didn't question how Père was able to provide so much in so difficult a time. I was just thankful to be alive. Others were practically starving, but I couldn't feel for them. I was always so afraid just for us.

"The morning I was to leave Paris with Red, a young man came to my flat. He was very sullen. In an angry voice he demanded to know where my father was. I knew, but I was afraid, so I said I had no idea. He called me a liar and began ransacking our apartment—"

Electra looked shocked. "Did you run?"

"I tried, but he caught me, and then he began hitting me. I still wouldn't tell. I loved my father too much. When he finally understood that, he asked if I knew what kind of man my father was.

"I answered that he was wonderful and caring, and when he found out what this thug had done to me, he would get the police after him. The young man laughed bitterly. My father was a traitor, he said. He had collaborated with the Nazis.

"I was stunned. I denied it, of course. Then he showed me proof. Photos taken of my father with a Nazi officer. Notes written in Père's hand to the Germans, telling them where food was hidden. Nazi vouchers giving Père free supplies . . .''

"Oh, I'm so sorry," Electra whispered.

"I couldn't believe my own father had betrayed his country. I've tried to rationalize that his offenses were minor, but he's still a traitor. And I couldn't believe he hadn't been honest with me. That hurt as much as anything. I can't stand deception. The whole incident makes me feel ashamed. When I first moved here I had nightmares. It was a year before I could forgive Père. I finally realized he did what he did out of love for me.

"Electra," she said, turning to her friend, "if you were me, would you have stayed in Paris and tried to help your father? Do you think I was a coward for leaving with Red?"

"You shouldn't feel guilt at all," Electra consoled her. "What your father did was his responsibility, not yours. He had to be aware of the consequences. And you had to leave Paris. You might have been persecuted if you stayed."

"If I could just talk to Père I'd feel better about everything. I miss him."

"Can't he fly here?"

"He's not in good health."

"Then go to him."

"I don't feel right about leaving Isabel. Maybe if Red watched the children. But I know he's too busy now."

"Just go. I'll take care of your kids for a week."

Alycia smiled gratefully. "Thank you, but you do more than enough for me. Just don't tell anyone about this, will you?"

"May lightning strike me! Alycia, we're friends to the end." Electra gave her a peck on the cheek. "I have to run. Cheer up, now?"

"I will," Alycia promised. She tried her best, but returning home, she found the washing machine had overflowed, and the housekeeper thought she was coming down with the flu. Why couldn't Red be around just once? When he did return, late as always, she was half-asleep in bed. He made half a dozen business calls before turning in. He had unlimited energy, while she was always near exhaustion. As she drifted off, Alycia thought again about getting away to France.

The next day at noon Red picked up Alycia and they drove into Santa Monica for a ribbon-cutting ceremony. Still another freeway was being opened—Mayor Poulson was personally leading the festivities—and Red had been one of the players. He had sold the city a chunk of land that had helped make the project possible. The media would be covering the event, Red said happily, and he wanted Alycia by his side.

"Yours was the tract the Salvation Army had wanted," Alycia remembered.

"They couldn't come up with my price," Red said.

"Still, clothes and shelter for the needy would have been better than another freeway you can put almost anywhere."

"I'm not in the charity business, Alycia."

"What did the city pay you?"

Red smiled. "Almost nothing. Less than eminent domain."

"I don't understand."

"I practically *gave* the land to the city, as a favor to Mayor Poulson. One day I'll be repaid. That's the way the game's played."

Alycia didn't like the city politics Red was becoming increasingly involved in, but she kept her thoughts to herself.

"Is it really necessary for me to be here today?" she suddenly asked. She felt guilty for leaving the children with the sick housekeeper, and she had to get to work planning a Christmas dinner party for fifty of Red's clients.

"I'll have you home in two hours," Red said, meaning it. His glance brushed her. "What's wrong?"

Alycia gave a sigh. "I don't know. Nothing. Everything. You're never home to find out."

"Alycia, do you hold it against me that I make a good living for us?"

"You know I don't."

"You like having a beautiful house, wearing nice dresses, going to restaurants—"

"I was thinking it would also be nice if you spent more time with the children." Was she asking the impossible? Even when Red was home, she'd noticed he didn't relax easily. He almost didn't know how to play with the children, not instinctively. Being a father wasn't natural to him. She wondered if that had something to do with his own childhood.

"Alycia, I don't think you understand. Everyone else does, but you don't. In the last two years I've raised thirteen million dollars for everything from airport parking lots to marinas to hotels. I'm one of the most successful developers in the city. And it's made us a lot of money. Do you have any idea of our net worth—do you care?"

"I do," she insisted, but she knew she didn't care as much as Red. He had that hurt look now, as if he didn't think she appreciated him enough. She dropped her head back on the seat. She did appreciate him; it just wasn't always for the things he wanted to be appreciated for.

"Alycia, my investors count on me," he continued, determined to make her understand. "It's a point of honor that I don't let them down. No one has ever lost a penny with me—and never will."

"What about me and the children?" she asked. "Don't we count too? Red, you never catch your breath. You complete one deal, and no matter how spectacular, it's never enough. It just makes you hungrier for another. Maybe there're other things in life for us . . ."

If she couldn't understand his reasoning, neither could he see hers. Alycia waited, hoping Red would open himself, but a silence descended on the car and nothing could lift it. There was no point mentioning her wanting to go to France. At the ribbon-cutting ceremony, she posed with Red for the media, all smiles, and shook hands with the mayor and everyone important. The perfect wife, exactly as Red wanted her, exactly as she'd once thought she wanted to be.

The evening of the Christmas party Electra arrived an hour early to help Alycia. "I resent it," she said, helpless, as caterers scurried around them in the kitchen. "Alycia, you're more efficient than I am. There's nothing for me to do."

"Relax and have a good time. That's what guests are supposed to do. By the way, I love your dress!" It was wonderfully outrageous, vintage Electra—turquoise with red sequins, low-cut, slinky, tight, sleek. Dressing wildly had become one of Electra's antidotes for boredom, Alycia knew. To Scotty's discomfort, Electra was lately on one binge after another. Besides her work at the Sidney Green Hospital, she raised money for antivivisectionists, wrote her congressman about the plight of Negroes in Arkansas, and campaigned for the preservation of the old Victorian mansions on Bunker Hill.

"Come here—quickly," Electra called from the den to Alycia. On the television they took in a terribly pale and somber Terry Donelson. A newscaster prattled about the politics of Hollywood. Blacklisted and unable to find work, the actor had declared bankruptcy. "Can you believe it?" Electra asked. "Of all the outrageous things. Don't you feel sorry for him? What did Terry Donelson do to hurt anyone?"

"It's wrong," Alycia said, just as angry as Electra. No matter what his political views, the actor was a victim of a witch hunt. Alycia couldn't help thinking of her father as she moved to the backyard. Across the way, on the other side of the lake, the Donelson house was totally dark.

She pulled her thoughts back to her party. The flickering lights of the tiki torches outlined the perimeter of the lake. A dance floor and mammoth tent occupied the flat part of the lawn. Everything was in order, but in some way the evening felt lonely. It was Christmas Eve and the temperature was sixty degrees. It never snowed in Los Angeles. She remembered all her Christmases in Paris, making a snowman in the street, skating at the Tuileries, sipping *vin chaud* with her parents.

The band arrived and set up by the dance floor. Alycia took a final walk around. The role of hostess was something she'd grown into. Her first parties had been trial-and-error, but with support from Electra, who threw the best parties in the Valley, Alycia had improved. She enjoyed entertaining. It was her only escape from domestic responsibilities, and more important, gave her a chance to develop another side of herself. Nights like this, she didn't see herself as Red's appendage. She was her own person, and she was as determined to please her guests socially as Red was never to disappoint a client in business. Creating an imaginative menu was something she had an instinct for. Growing up in Paris, she'd never dined at Right Bank restaurants, yet in her mother's kitchen she'd sampled the best food in Paris. Her father had, like most French fathers, instilled in his child an appreciation of wine. Those were gifts she'd been given; in turn, now she gave them to her guests.

She loved dressing up, too, keeping in touch with fashion. She'd bought tonight's dress from a small Beverly Hills store that carried Paris clothes exclusively. The outfit wasn't outrageous or irreverent like Electra's, but it was still bold, and very classy—an asymmetrical pink satin bodice over a black lace chemise. The design reflected the biomorphic movement, which most Americans had never heard of. In Europe, Jean Arp and Max Ernst and Miró had made it famous in the art world. Alycia was determined to use her dress to make a fashion statement in a city she found hopelessly unfashionable.

As the first wave of guests arrived, the band began playing some velvety number and Alycia moved into the house. Some of the guests she'd entertained at her other parties, but many faces were new. Mayor Poulson and his wife arrived, followed by Norman Chandler and his wife, Buffy. Alycia danced with a young city councilman who complimented her on her taste in art. Jackson Pollock was an old friend, he bragged. He pulled Alycia closer and told her he found her appealing. Flattered, she turned the discussion back to art.

Alycia knew that certain men were attracted to her. Not the kind who liked Electra, of course—they were more flashy. The two women had kidded each other about affairs more than once. Electra swore she'd never strayed—flirting was just a game. Alycia replied that she didn't believe in affairs— marriage should be sacred and forever. Still, Alycia knew what she liked in men. Sincerity and intelligence, having a passion for something; then charm and looks.

Alycia excused herself from the councillor and strolled toward the pool. Lifting a glass of champagne from a caterer's tray, she picked out Red in his new silk suit, looking handsome and confident as he spoke with a client. Her eyes traveled a short distance, to the other end of the pool, and took in the trim, tanned man in a dark suit and silver tie. He was talking with Norman Chandler as if old and trusted friends. Alycia felt a bubble rise in her stomach. For a moment her composure crumbled. Red was now looking straight at the man too. Alycia wondered if she'd done the right thing. Even from this distance she could make out Red's face, pinched in anger.

When Red found Alycia, he walked her into his study and shut the door. His hands were shaking.

"My father's here," he said.

"And your mother," she pointed out. "They just arrived."

"How the hell—"

"I invited them," Alycia admitted after a beat.

His face grew crimson. "You had no right—"

"I'm sorry I didn't have the courage to tell you," she explained. "I didn't want us to argue. I thought it was something I could decide alone. At Christmas this should be a house of peace and forgiveness."

His hands rose to his forehead in disbelief. "Why are you ruining this evening for me?"

"I think it's wrong there's bad blood between you and your father. Your mother can come and go freely here, but Owen can't. It's not fair. It's not what I want for us—"

"What about what I want?" Red demanded.

"You're a wonderful, giving man. Why can't you be generous about this?"

"My father is out there talking to Norman Chandler, *my* guest of honor. He'll take over the whole party if I let him!"

"I was hoping for a reconciliation," she persisted. "Is there something wrong with a last chance? Despite all that your father's done to you, I think he still loves you—"

"If he does," Red interrupted, "then his love is the most lethal thing about him."

She had never seen Red like this. His rage brimmed just under the surface, and it seemed to control him. For a moment she was afraid he'd storm out of his own party, but he went back to his friends, though hardly himself. Harriet was aware of her son's agitation and made Owen leave early. Alycia felt terrible for them. Even when they were gone, Red didn't look appeased. By the time the last guests had said their good-byes, she found him sitting by the boat dock, gloriously, embarrassingly drunk, looking haunted as he stared out at Terry Donelson's darkened house.

It was the caterers, finally, who had to help him upstairs to bed.

The day after the party, Sunday, Red left the house before anyone stirred, even before Felice, who usually was the first to wake. He had slept off his liquor and wakened to a sense of something pressing on his chest, robbing him of breath. A cold sweat covered him like a sheet over a grave. He had showered and dressed but still couldn't escape the suffocating presence of an invisible enemy. Red knew it all too well. He had been trying forever to chase away this ghost, but it was more stubborn and pernicious than ever. And now he had to conquer it before it conquered him.

At his office he made a call and waited. Farley Gibbons showed up a little before eight, sleepy-eyed but functioning. The bright, personable UCLA-business-school grad had been hired to help with syndications, and was the most loyal employee Red had.

"Is the money in place for the Long Beach mall?" Red asked after he offered Farley some coffee.

"You bet," the young man said in his cheerful way, loving

to deliver good news, though he didn't see why this couldn't have waited till Monday. "That's a very sweet deal for the investors. All cash, no financing, an eighteen-percent return if you include depreciation—"

"We're not going to buy that mall," Red broke in.

Farley gave a bemused smile, wondering if he'd screwed up somehow. "Something wrong with the deal?"

"I want the money for something else. Something downtown."

The young man's smile faded. "Unless you're talking Wilshire Boulevard on the Santa Monica side, there's nothing for sale that won't lose you money."

"There's a large warehouse on Fifth and Spring. Far from Wilshire. It's on the market for two million."

Farley squinted back, waiting for the punch line.

"It's next to a very handsome office building," Red continued. "One my father owns. Twelve stories, one hundred and thirty thousand square feet. Right now it's worth maybe seven, eight million. It's his biggest asset—the only one that's bucked the tide of declining values."

"I still don't understand."

"Just tell the investors we're raising another half-million and buying the Fifth-and-Spring warehouse."

"I should point out," Farley replied with a tremor in his voice, "that there might be resistance. Everyone knows downtown isn't Long Beach—"

"All my investors trust me," Red stopped him. "I have a perfect track record. I could tell them I was buying in Antarctica and they'd keep writing checks."

"I know that, sir, but I was just wondering," Farley said, measuring his words carefully, "how you're going to give them a decent return. Is the warehouse fully rented?"

"The building is half-empty. Rents are falling. That's why it's for sale. When we take over, we're going to evict the remaining tenants. There's no return at all short-term."

Not to annoy his employer further, Farley nodded as if he understood clearly, when in fact he wondered if this wasn't April Fool's Day.

Red closed on his warehouse the third week in January. He assured jittery investors that downtown values, while in retreat for the moment, would one day rebound and the building would be worth twice what they were paying. For now the syndication would benefit from depreciation write-offs. Red realized the risk he was taking. But downtown was a place of geographical and historical uniqueness. That alone gave it value. And as confidant to the mayor, Red was privy to something that made his gamble not so extravagant. Mayor Poulson would shortly approach the city council and request that the height law for buildings, now limited to thirteen stories or 150 feet, be abolished. New building materials and construction methods made earthquakes less fearful. Red could already imagine a future skyline of high-rises, maybe not as grandiose as Manhattan's, but the new law would forever alter the dynamics of downtown real estate.

It was the short term, however, that dominated Red's thoughts, and his plan had nothing to do with investors or real-estate values. By the middle of February he had successfully evicted his last tenant, from his own pocket paying a stubborn wholesaler five thousand dollars to vacate. Doors were boarded with plywood, but that was no deterrent to the itinerants and whores, who were delighted with free rent, even if they had to cohabit with a rodent colony the size of Poland. Walls inside and out grew scarred with graffiti. Police came and went to settle fights and answer false alarms. Soon the sidewalks were clogged with panhandlers who waylaid secretaries and executives trying to enter Owen Poindexter's building. Muggings and holdups became commonplace.

By April, his father's tenants began moving out, even breaking leases to escape the filth and danger. Owen's lawyers threatened to sue Red, but he knew he'd broken no laws. Every week he drove to the site to see the deterioration feeding on itself. By October Owen's building stood at fifteen-percent occupancy. With debt service, utilities, taxes, and insurance, Red estimated his father's losses at twenty thousand dollars a month.

Red was not surprised when, working late one evening, his mother arrived at his office. He rose and walked over to embrace her.

"Mother, what brings you here?"

"I need to talk to you, dear, if you have the time."

"Of course I have the time. Maybe you can come to dinner tonight—"

"Thank you, I appreciate that, but I wanted us to speak in private."

He pulled up a chair for her. "Speak—please."

Harriet knew what she wanted to say, but it wouldn't be

easy. Confronting her son was something she'd never done, not in a critical way. Yet it was time; it was necessary. She had been waiting too patiently and too long for Owen and Red to reconcile. The miracle had not occurred. Alycia's Christmas party, while well-intended, had done more damage than good—had pushed Red in a direction that, for the first time, made Harriet think she no longer understood her son. That was the most frightening thing of all.

"You haven't called me lately," she began.

"You're right," he apologized. "Business is crazy."

"It's not something else?"

"What else would it be?"

"Red, dear, you know that I've never interfered in your life. You mean more to me than anyone in the world, and I would do anything for you. I'm extremely proud of you, of everything you've done—but now something is bothering me."

"What is it?" he asked calmly.

"You already know, dear. You and your father . . . This war cannot go on any longer. I forbid it. You must forget the past and forgive each other."

"What war?"

Harriet drew a breath. "I know that Owen has been manipulative and unfair to you, and I've admired you for your strength and perseverance. But what you're doing now—taking revenge—is more than a little cruel. It's full of hatred, Red, and I know you're not a hateful person. It's hurting Owen, and it's hurting me."

Red leaned back in his sumptuous chair, pondering his mother. "Did he ask you to come and talk to me?"

"He did not. This is my idea."

Red said nothing.

"I know," Harriet continued, "that your feelings about your father run deep, and we don't need to discuss them if you don't want to. But you and I have always communicated on a very special level, a level where words are not necessary. As your mother I think I understand you better than anyone else, even Alycia." She leaned forward to reinforce her point. "I want you to make peace with your father. For your own sake. That's what I'm asking. If you don't do it now, I'm afraid it will never happen. And something else . . ."

"What?" Red asked quietly.

"I'm afraid of losing you, dear. Something has come over

you. I feel it. I don't know what it is, but it scares me. Over the years I've lost my relationship with my husband. I will not lose you.''

It seemed forever before Red's face showed the slightest ripple of emotion. Harriet thought it was disbelief, but she saw love too. ''Mother,'' he said, his voice suddenly filled with pain, ''I will never, *never* do anything to hurt you. If it's your wish I make amends with my father, I'll do it. But you must understand it will have to be done a certain way, on my timetable. There are many things you don't understand, but I respect your wishes. I know you've always been supportive of me. I know how much I owe you—''

''Please don't do this for me, Red. I want this to make you happy too.''

''Mother, you don't have to be concerned. Everything will be fine.''

''Can I count on all of you at our house for Thanksgiving? Just our two families.''

''We'll be there. I promise.''

She gave him a strong hug before leaving. Levering herself into her car, for the first time in several years Harriet allowed herself to feel genuine hope. Unlike last year, maybe this would be a holiday season of peace and happiness.

Red watched from his window as his mother's car pulled away. He went back to his desk and called Farley in.

''You know the Poindexter Building?'' he asked.

Farley didn't have to think. His boss had spoken often of it. ''Your father's office. His pride and joy.''

Red pushed back in his chair. ''I want to buy it.''

Farley cocked his head. ''Didn't you tell me, more than once, that your father would never part with it for love or money?''

''I want you to get me a full abstract on the property. Then I want a complete and thorough title search. Thirty years ago, after my father acquired the building, he lost it. When the new owner defaulted to the bank, he got his building back, but not everything may have been kosher in the transition. Knowing my father, I imagine he took a shortcut or two. If you need help at City Hall . . . the mayor and I are comfortable.''

Farley bit his tongue and turned away.

''One more thing,'' Red called after him. ''This must be

done discreetly. I don't want my father to find out until I'm ready to act. Nor my mother. Is that perfectly clear?''

"Yes, sir.''

The next week, Red called his mother and told her he wouldn't be able to come for Thanksgiving after all. He was deeply sorry and hoped he wasn't disappointing her too much. Unexpected business was pulling him to New York that week, and he wanted to take the kids as a treat.

When he hung up he sat quietly in his office, his gaze equally still and hollow. Forgive me, Mother, he finally thought. I don't know what I'm doing.

Between Christmas and New Year's Red found himself official caretaker for three small children. Alycia was visiting her father in France, and Red, knowing the holiday week meant a business hiatus, agreed to stay home. He had hoped the housekeeper would be able to shoulder the load, freeing him at least to work in his study, but the children were continually at his heels, giggling, quarreling, showing off, running the house like a private fiefdom.

Jean was now seven. He was tall for his age, and lanky, with a sweet, animated moon face and a full head of very blond hair. He had declared himself the incarnation of Hopalong Cassidy, except when he sometimes donned a mask and forgot his loyalty, whereupon he decided that Isabel was Tonto and made her watch as the Lone Ranger rode an imaginary Silver up and down the stairs. Red marveled at the boy's energy. His attention was scattered, but he was obviously bright, the way he picked up on things. Nothing scared or fazed him. While he could get angry with Isabel when she took one of his toys, he understood that she was special and different, and he never abused her or took advantage. He was equally understanding with Felice, who sat restlessly in her crib, holding on to the bars and drooling excitedly at the life that passed around her.

The more Red observed his son, he was struck by how different a child Jean was from himself. That brought him great relief. Perhaps being a big brother helped, but Jean wouldn't have been a lonely child even if he'd had no siblings. The boy was continually inventing games, putting his nose into others' business, with his unflagging curiosity seeking out the world. He was more interested in adults than in his peers. If clients and friends came to the house, Jean would come in from playing with Electra's children and hang around the adults. He especially loved Harriet, and often asked why Grandfather never came to visit.

Red was careful not to speak harshly of his father—Jean was told that Grandfather was very busy and didn't have time to visit—but eventually the truth would have to come out. Red didn't look forward to the day. He wondered how he would explain it, and if Jean would understand, or if somehow he might take his Grandfather's side. Jean would never do that, Red thought. Still, he feared it. He adored Jean, and felt admiration in return, yet Red fumbled when he tried to be close to the boy. He came on forcefully in business, but ever mindful of his father's overbearing ways, with Jean he was always soft and low-key. Jean seemed to know this wasn't his real father, and he would twist his head up at Red, waiting for something to happen or change or come to light.

"Want to go shopping?" Red asked Jean one afternoon while the girls took naps.

"Where?" His eyes lit up.

"Anywhere you want."

"Mommy doesn't let me do that."

"I guess I'm a pushover."

"What's a pushover, Daddy?"

Red only laughed. "Come on."

Jean took his father's hand as they strolled through the toy department of the Valley Sears. Red wasn't trying to spoil him or buy his love; he only wanted to treat Jean in a way Owen had never treated him. Jean was very businesslike as he filled the shopping cart with tin soldiers and trucks and a six-shooter, as if he thought his father expected decorous behavior. "Thank you, Daddy," he kept saying.

"Jean, you don't have to tell me that."

Jean looked at him uncertainly.

"I know we don't spend that much time together," Red offered gently, "but I'm your father, not some visiting uncle."

Jean nodded as if he understood, but Red saw doubt in his face. When they got home, Red resisted turning Jean over to the housekeeper, instead parking himself determinedly in the boy's room. Together they began building a castle out of blocks.

After a few minutes the housekeeper called up the stairs. There was a phone call.

"Aren't we going to finish this?" Jean asked as Red stood.

"Of course we are. Wait for me, will you?"

"Are you going to be long?"

"No," Red promised, tousling the boy's hair.

In his study, Red juggled the phone on his shoulder and grabbed a pencil. The mayor's voice was pitched with urgency. He was about to do Red the biggest favor of his business life, Poulson said, if Red could come up with an answer or two. Red started scribbling dates, names, times. He had known the mayor was actively recruiting a major-league baseball team to the city. When it came to sports franchises, Los Angeles was a city of blanks waiting to be filled in. First the Rams had come from Cleveland. Then the Lakers from Minneapolis. Now negotiations were at a flash point for a baseball team. Walter O'Malley, owner of the Dodgers, after much wooing from Poulson, had decided to move his team to Los Angeles. About a mile north of downtown Los Angeles, a stone's throw from Chinatown, sat a neglected neighborhood known as Elysian Park. In its midst were three hundred barren acres of a city-owned trash dump called Chavez Ravine. Money had been donated privately to Poulson from a backroom player—reputed to be Howard Hughes—to survey the site and estimate building costs. This had all been done without the knowledge of the city council. Poulson was afraid certain councillors would wreck the deal because of politics. The mayor would make everything public as soon as he had something concrete to put on the table. The problem was, O'Malley wanted the city to "donate" Chavez Ravine to the Dodgers—and the city charter forbade the mayor from giving anything free to a private corporation.

"I'm stuck," Poulson said to Red. "We're so close . . ."

Red tried to think. "What about some kind of swap?"

"Such as?"

"Does O'Malley own anything here?"

"Nothing substantial."

"Then have him buy something," Red suggested.

"Just tell me what," Poulson said, "and you can make the deal."

Red hung up and pulled out a map of the city. All he could think was baseball. The Los Angeles Angels, a minor-league team, played in a small stadium called Wrigley Field, which, like its sister in the Windy City, was owned by the Chicago Cubs. If O'Malley could somehow buy that on the cheap—

and still make it look like a legitimate deal—then trade it to the city for Chavez Ravine, wouldn't everyone be happy?

Red hardly ate or slept the next three days. By the time he finished, he had brought together representatives of the Cubs and Dodgers, who agreed on a price for the Angels' stadium. Poulson jumped through hoops to make sure everyone was content. The Dodgers would rent the Los Angeles Coliseum for their first year, until the Chavez Ravine stadium was completed, and the city would contribute several million to the new ballpark. It would take months for details to be worked out, and the city council would argue vehemently before stamping its approval, but Red knew Los Angeles, a city that had grown to almost six million people, would finally have major-league baseball. For brokering the Wrigley Field sale, Red would receive four hundred thousand dollars.

"Come on, let's pick Mommy up at the airport," a weary Red told Jean that evening. He crouched down to straighten his son's sweater.

The boy looked at him with misty eyes.

"What's the matter, son?"

"You know."

Red tried to think. "No, tell me."

"You forgot something."

"What's that?"

The boy sniffled as he ran his hand under his nose. "The castle we were building."

Red was amazed. If Alycia had been the one to abandon Jean like this, the boy would have howled in an instant. But with his father he was more circumspect. He rarely argued with Red; instead, like now, he was inclined to keep his hurt inside, even for days, as if he forbade anything to come between him and his father. Red didn't want anything to come between them either.

"I'm sorry," Red apologized, giving his son a hug. "I got so busy."

"We could finish the castle now," he said carefully.

"Then we'll be late for Mommy's plane. Don't worry, we'll finish it soon, I promise. Will that be all right?"

Red heard the sigh of resignation. Jean wasn't going to argue.

"I won't disappoint you," Red swore, and he took Jean's hand as they went out the door.

*   *   *

"Please don't be so down. Things will get better," Alycia
tried to cheer Scotty as they meandered through the Bullocks-
Wilshire furniture department. The early-summer sale was a
perfect excuse for Scotty to ask Alycia for help in redecorat-
ing his medical offices. Still, she could see she wasn't helping him where it mattered most. "One affair is not the end of
the world," she finally consoled him.

"But why Terry Donelson?"

"I think Electra felt sorry for him. The man did lose
virtually everything, even his house." Alycia had felt for the
actor too, though she didn't tell Scotty. He would think she
was on Electra's side. The truth was, Alycia didn't know
what to think. After their candid exchange on the subject of
affairs, Alycia had been surprised that Electra had gotten
involved—and more surprised she'd never confided the ro-
mance to Alycia. The first she'd heard about it was when
Scotty called. Alycia had been a little hurt. Weren't she and
Electra best friends?

The lack of candor had made Alycia think of her father,
how he had once concealed the truth from her too. At least
those troubled times had been put to rest. Over Christmas
she'd had a wonderful visit to France. Though his health was
failing, Père and she had never enjoyed one another's company more, and had made complete peace with the past. She
was glad now she'd gone. Three months after the visit, she'd
received a call from a friend of her father's. Père had passed
away, quietly and without pain, talking proudly of his daughter until the end. She had asked if she should fly back for the
burial, but the friend had taken care of everything.

"It's not just Electra's affair that upsets me," Scotty went
on as they finished shopping. "I think it's only a symptom.
The bottom line is she doesn't want to be with me anymore."

"How can you say that?" Alycia asked.

"Because she's never around. She's always off to some
reading group, or by herself to the beach, or just disappearing
for days, like now. Did you know she's writing a novel?"

"Yes, she told me. Scotty, don't be too hard on her."

"People are talking about us, that's what bothers me. They
say we're just staying together for the kids."

"The ones who talk aren't your real friends."

"Alycia, I know you're close to Electra—I'm not asking
you to take sides—but what do you think is wrong?"

Alycia hesitated. Electra had confided to her the last few

months how restless she was. She wanted a distance from Scotty, wanted time for herself to pursue new interests. Alycia tried to be supportive—Electra had been more than that to her—but like Scotty, she also felt unsettled by the changes in her friend. When Scotty and Electra had stopped giving their famous parties and didn't even venture out in public together, it felt like the end of an era.

"I don't think anything is *wrong*," Alycia said. "Electra is just restless. Maybe she's always been that way and got good at covering it up."

"She's groping."

"Sometimes you have to get lost before you find your way. I still believe in you two as a couple," Alycia said.

She felt sad about Scotty as they said good-bye and she drove home alone. He was painfully sensitive and hopelessly in love with his wife. Electra was not making it easy for him. He was lost without the crowd that Electra did more than her share to attract, and Alycia wouldn't bet, despite the encouragement she'd just given Scotty, that they'd get back together soon.

Maybe it really was the end of an era. The magic and aura of her friends had faded like a vibrant painting held up too long to harsh light. And taking their place, whether Alycia liked it or not, she and Red were suddenly the handsome young society couple who always got their picture in the paper and in whose presence it was chic and important to be seen. Alycia was considered elegant and gracious and the perfect hostess. Red's burgeoning real-estate empire moved like an impressive war machine, exhibiting the power and success people gravitated to. If fame was sometimes perishable, Alycia had found out, it was also highly infectious.

Sometimes it felt like their lives had taken a momentum and direction she couldn't control. Electra was always saying that about her own life. Still, Alycia tried to keep a perspective; she tried to keep her private life separate from the public. She didn't want what had happened to Electra and Scotty to happen to her and Red. As busy as Red was, as isolated as Alycia sometimes felt, she had faith that somehow the future would take care of itself.

BOOK THREE

As the air trembled, Brother Andrew forced one eye open, then the other. Levering himself forward in bed, he peered up through the palm thatches of the roof. The plane roared overhead in the pink dawn, dipped into silence, and a minute later approached the river to land. Over the years the monk had trained his ear to recognize every missionary or supply or government plane, but this one gave him pause, as did the early arrival hour. He slipped into his habit and scurried down the ladder of his house, his bare feet landing in the soft mud.

Since Alycia had vanished two weeks ago, Brother Andrew had not been himself. He had slept poorly, his concentration had wandered helplessly, and a medical dispensary he was building had gone neglected. And he was continually visited with premonitions which, like whispers from the dead, warned him of disaster. Yet his days had passed without event. He thought often of Alycia, and was determined to find her, if only he had a clue and his restless mind could settle on a plan. But each day of procrastination seemed to sap his energy and make resolve more difficult.

The children were already mushrooming around the narrow quay as he approached the river. Heads bobbed for a view as hands waved gaily at the bright silver bird squatting in the dark waters. Brother Andrew had never seen so new a plane, nor did he recognize the call letters on its rudder. Someone important, he thought. Edging in front of the children, he watched as a welcoming village dugout weaved inexorably toward the visitor.

The sun exploded off the plane door, making it difficult to identify the passenger until he was seated in the dugout, had straightened himself, and his eyes bore ahead back to the quay. When their gazes locked, Andrew felt total shock. Wearing a simple clerical suit with collar, the stocky, rotund visitor looked far different than Andrew remembered him. The face was more jowly, the hair whiter, the dark hooded eyes more contemplative and burdened. Andrew's memory struggled to establish how long ago their paths had crossed—seven or eight years, he decided—and he wondered if the archbishop had any chance of remembering a faceless monk like himself. The responsibility of overseeing the New England diocese had never allowed Archbishop Rationi abundant time to visit the small Trappist monastery, but when he had come and eaten with the brothers, Andrew had been impressed. The archbishop was a formidable servant of God, known for his erudition, sophistication, articulateness, and political skill. The latter talent was a necessity in dealing with the outside world, not to mention the higher echelons of church power, and while it was not a gift that Andrew enjoyed, he had the wisdom and perspective to admire it in others.

The monk also understood that an archbishop's visit to a tiny forsaken jungle outpost five thousand miles from home was not merely a gesture of goodwill.

The august visitor was helped by several eager villagers onto the quay, where Andrew knelt and kissed his ring. The pleased and honored onlookers answered with applause.

"Come, there's no need for formality here," the archbishop chided the monk good-naturedly, beckoning him to rise.

"I am honored by this unexpected visit," Andrew said. "Perhaps you don't remember, but years ago you came to my monastery. You and I talked at some length . . ."

The archbishop looked contrite. "Forgive me for my poor memory, but I compliment you on yours." Rationi paused to take in the vast jungle and, in the dirt clearing, the hundred homes on their stilts, crowded and tottering together like clusters of mushrooms. The archbishop looped his arms around two children, and with more following, paraded behind Andrew into the village.

The monk proudly showed his special guest the chapel the villagers had built, their extensive vegetable gardens, a schoolhouse, a generator-powered refrigerated storeroom, and the medical dispensary that he now chided himself out loud for not having completed. Under a portico by the school, they sat alone, taking refuge from the already blinding sun, as Rationi gave the monk snippets of news from home. Andrew listened, absorbed. Occasionally he received news from the monastery or from friends in the States, but only now did he realize how much he had missed.

"Will you be celebrating a special Eucharist with us?" Andrew asked when a silence finally intruded.

"I'm afraid I won't have time."

"Then Penance—"

"No, not that either." Distracted, Rationi let his gaze swim around the village again. "You are a man of remarkable energy and resourcefulness, Brother Andrew, not to say leadership."

"I have done my best," Andrew answered modestly, "but I could not have done all this alone. I had help."

"From God?"

"Yes, of course, but also from a friend. A woman. She left here only recently."

Rationi smiled reflexively.

Andrew gazed at his superior in disappointment. Did the archbishop lack the courage to admit why he was here? Andrew didn't like being coy—it wasn't his nature—and now his anxiety was ready to spill over. "Her name is Alycia Poindexter. But I think you already know that."

Rationi's brow shot up at the monk's temerity.

"Can you tell me where she is," Andrew went on, "and if she's all right?" He couldn't disguise the register of concern in his voice. "And who took her from here—it must have been her son, Jean, was it not?"

Rationi raised a hand. The hooded eyes blinked somberly. "You are prescient as well as industrious, Brother Andrew. I compliment you on that too. But please understand, this visit is not particularly easy for me. I would rather be tending my own garden than taking up the affairs of Rome."

Andrew's stomach tightened at the mention of the Vatican. This was every bit as serious as he'd feared.

"Your friend Alycia is in a hospital in the States, receiving the finest care. I would tell you more, but Jean Poindexter has solicited my confidence."

The monk felt a pang, not so much because he was being excluded from information he felt entitled to as because he missed Alycia. He thanked God that at least she was all right. Andrew squared his shoulders and waited for what was to come.

"Brother Andrew," Rationi said earnestly, "I need to know everything about Alycia Poindexter."

"What do you know already?" Andrew temporized.

"Very little. That's why I came: Her son complained bitterly to the Church. He has not painted you in a very favorable light. He's implicated you in a scandal that involves a rather staggering sum of money. Now, I need to hear your story."

Andrew did not swing his eyes away from his visitor, but inside he was trembling. Jean had never liked or accepted the monk in his mother's life. Now, somehow, he must have learned the secrets that Alycia had tried so hard to keep from him. But there was so much more Jean couldn't know. Andrew was torn. He could hardly lie to an archbishop—he could not bring himself to lie to anyone—yet he knew that the truth might confuse more than illuminate, and could well be used against him.

"I would prefer if you started from the beginning," Rationi urged, making himself as comfortable as possible in the crude chair. "I have plenty of time."

"The beginning?"

"When you first met Mrs. Poindexter."

The monk was silent.

"Brother Andrew, I am not here to judge you or to take Jean Poindexter's side. Please don't be intimidated. My mission is to learn the facts and bring them to my superiors. You must trust me, just as I trust you to tell the complete truth."

Andrew let his memory drift. The process was like sorting through earlier and earlier photographs to find the very first. Finally he seized on Alycia in a stunning ball gown. "I believe we first met in the summer of 1961," he spoke up. "I was thirty-two years old. Alycia was around thirty-eight. The occasion was a charity ball in Los Angeles . . ."

Andrew stopped himself. Sweat beaded on his forehead, and he felt the knot tighten in his stomach. The archbishop leaned forward and took the monk's hands in his own. "Remember your vows of obedience to the Church, Father," he said softly.

Andrew slowly liberated his hands, sat back, and studied the slanted patterns of light from the portico on the ground. He did not need to be reminded of anything.

"How did you arrive in Los Angeles?" the archbishop prodded. "You were not yet a monk—"

"I was," Andrew corrected.

"But as a Trappist you were secluded from the outside world— "

"Not exactly," he replied. "Not in that instance. The circumstances were very special. Did my abbot not tell you?"

"I have not spoken with Brother Manning in any depth."

"I was sent to Los Angeles from desperation," Andrew explained. "Our monastery needed money. Traditional sources for donations were drying up. We had no funds for continuing our projects near home, much less around the world. I was supposed to be a spokesman, an ambassador, for our cause."

"And what qualified you for that?" Rationi frowned.

"I recall very clearly when Brother Manning approached me, how shocked I was, just like you now. The idea was so unorthodox. To avoid temptation, and dedicate our lives entirely to God, we had deliberately separated ourselves from the secular world, except to work among the poor—and here I was being asked to seek out wealthy individuals who could help us! The abbot knew of some of these people. People disposed to charity, he said, particularly to the Catholic faith. All he needed was an emissary. Someone with wit and intelligence and charm. I suggested the abbot himself go, but he insisted, knowing my background, that I was the best candidate. As I had taken a vow of obedience, I had no choice.

"There would be another fund-raising trip for me five years later, but on this maiden journey I was away three months. Washington, D.C., Chicago, Dallas, Denver, Seattle, San Francisco, Los Angeles. I traveled very simply, staying at the cheapest motels, bringing canned food to my room, living only in my habit and sandals. I drew more than my share of stares. But I knew vanity and self-indulgence were sins, and I strove to live humbly.

"That proved impossible, however. Too often I was invited to sumptuous meals at expensive homes and restaurants. I sat in smoke-filled rooms with some of the most powerful men in the country and listened to their opinions. I remember one asked me whether I thought God ever intended for black men to be the equal of whites. I was embarrassed but I answered as wisely and truthfully as I could, without offending him. It was not easy. And in the back of my mind I couldn't help feeling guilty. God had never intended me for this role, I kept thinking, but I was doing as my abbot bade, and performing successfully. I found that people knew nothing of the Trappists, and when I explained what our work was about, the money flowed quite freely.

"By the time I reached Los Angeles, on the last leg of my journey, I was weary. I only wanted to return to the monastery. But I had an invitation to a Red Cross ball, whose hostess was Alycia Poindexter. She was also, I learned later, involved with several other large charities. She was an important society figure who sat on boards and councils and every year raised hundreds of thousands of dollars. I did not relish going to a black-tie ball, but I did, out of duty, and in my simple habit I found myself again a center of attention.

"I arrived on the late side that evening, and after half an hour of mingling with guests, I was introduced to Alycia. She was extremely beautiful, but no less sensitive and intuitive. She took me aside for what seemed forever. She said she understood how difficult this fund-raising must be for me, that being a monk I was from a totally different world, so she was surprised how well I mixed with her friends. I answered that a black-tie ball was not entirely foreign to me. My abbot had known that when he selected me for this task. Before I entered the monastery on my twenty-first birthday, I informed her, I was from a world exactly like her own. My father was a wealthy businessman, and my mother's family traced its roots to a prominent colonial family. I had attended private schools all my life, ending up at Harvard. My friends were as rich and carefree and pampered as I, including my fiancée. I was considered gifted athletically and played football in college. I could also play the piano, had a good tenor voice, and knew by heart every opera ever written in Italian.

"Alycia listened to me, totally absorbed, before I realized I had revealed far too much. I had forgotten my vow of humility. I asked that she please excuse me, but she would not. She said she would be very sorry if she let me disappear now. 'Someone so gifted, so much a part of this world,' she asked, 'why did you ever join a monastery?' I did not want to tell her, but Alycia had a way about her, a grace, a sincerity, that was irresistible. My mother had died suddenly after my junior year at Harvard, I explained. The death devastated me. She and I had been so close, yet I had taken the relationship for granted. I began to think about the rest of my life, my values, goals, feelings, and I came to realize that something was wrong. As relatively happy as I was, I felt hollow. There was always a sense of strife and uncertainty at the periphery. I wasn't in control. A spiritual peace was absent. I had camouflaged my needs by keeping busy, but I saw then that I was only deceiving myself.

"Alycia listened very carefully, as if my life somehow held relevance to her own. She was also upset about something that had happened that evening, before I arrived. I could just tell. She looked like she wanted to find the same peace that I was after. I told her how during school weekends in my senior year I attended retreats at the nearby Trappist monastery. They only strengthened my sense that I was floundering, that I needed something, an anchor, a God, in my life. I finally decided I would enter the order as a novitiate.

"My father, of course, was stunned. He tried to talk me out of it, as did my fiancée. They were certain I would tire of this novelty. The Trappists were particularly self-denying in those days. Meals consisted of meatless soup, bread, and water. One could own only a cloak, one pair of sandals, and one pair of underwear. The order was governed by the Holy Rules of St. Benedict, and speech was strictly forbidden except at the request of the abbot. There was no contact at all with the outside world. Yet in the atmosphere of severe discipline and celibacy my spirit and love for God flourished. Oh, there were moments of uncertainty, but I did not quit. For the first time in my life I could see everything clearly, what was important and what was not, and that there was a place for me in this universe. . . .

"When I finished my history, Alycia smiled at me. She said that there was such a down-to-earth warmth and love about me that I made everyone else at this charity event, including her, look less than sincere. I was uneasy with the compliment, but intrigued by the woman who spoke it. It was my turn to be sorry when she drifted back to her guests."

Brother Andrew suddenly stopped himself. He wondered if the archbishop was hearing him. He had not seemed to move throughout the recitation, the hooded eyes fixed soberly on the monk.

"Do you wish me to continue?" Andrew asked.

"Indeed," Rationi said, for the first time shifting his weight in the chair. "Did Alycia Poindexter give you money for your cause?"

Andrew decided that his superior had missed nothing. "The next day, a check for twenty thousand dollars was dropped off at my motel. It was the most I had received from anyone, by far."

"And what did you think?"

"Think?"

"Didn't you wonder why she was so generous?"

"I thought nothing at the time," Andrew said honestly, "except that she had a very giving heart."

"But what do you think now, looking back?"

Andrew was quiet.

"Brother Andrew, I must be candid. Jean Poindexter has told me that you fell in love with his mother. Is that true?"

"I did not see Alycia Poindexter again for another five years," he answered evasively.

"But what happened in between?" Rationi inquired.

"To me, very little."

"And to Mrs. Poindexter?"

"It's a very long story. I'm afraid a great deal happened to her."

"Then please proceed," the archbishop said, as one of the villagers, an older woman with a beautiful smile, brought the monk and his honored guest some coffee.

Andrew let his gaze drift to the river, wishing he might be on some boat taking him to the woman he missed so much, but he summoned his courage and resumed the narrative.

The limousine glided off Sunset and navigated the incline to the entrance of the Beverly Hills Hotel like a sleek black torpedo. Ahead, motors purring, a dozen more limousines lined the curb. The impatient efficiency of the doorman notwithstanding, the black-tie guests moved in slow motion as they stepped into the balmy June evening. The hotel gardens yielded the sweet scents of hyacinth and crocus and honeysuckle. Red only gazed out his window, preoccupied by something he couldn't identify. When their turn came to enter the hotel, Alycia drew admiring stares in her navy-blue satin gown and long white suede gloves. Her hair was in a wave, and around her neck was a birthday present from Red—a discreet string of small diamonds he had bought in Europe. Her cheeks had only a touch of blush. A trace of perfume mingled with the scent of the flowers. Alycia had always had a gift for subtlety and detail, Red thought, and he only wished he had more time to appreciate it.

Entering the crowded ballroom, Red found his hand swinging out repeatedly to greet people whose names he sometimes had to feign. The annual Red Cross Ball was filled with his wife's many good friends, yet just as many guests wanted to talk to him. The number of people in his life had become overwhelming. New clients, associates, and sycophants appeared by the day. In five years Red had built his brokerage firm into the city's largest. Seventeen field offices, seven hundred employees, more than $100 million in annual sales. Next year he would expand into Orange County and San Diego. He had dreams of a national franchise. Why not— what were the limits? He loved to be creative. His imagination was his strong suit, the edge he enjoyed over his competition.

What he didn't like about his business was the encumbering machinery of success. Success required bankers, accountants, business managers, and attorneys, who were all forever notifying Red of important meetings he had to attend. Invariably he sat at one end of a long table and listened to everyone else worry about his assets and investments and tax liabilities, then ritually affixed his signature to countless pages he had no time or inclination to read. He had civic meetings to attend, public-relations appearances at local businesses, ground-breaking ceremonies for new buildings, endless parties. Half his life was spent in airports and strange hotels and taxicabs. He was always in motion, fighting time, promising himself that tomorrow would bring a chance to breathe.

When he did manage a free weekend or afternoon, he tried to spend it with the kids. Disneyland was a favorite destination, especially for Isabel. The two would march hand in hand down Main Street, Isabel's eyes and mouth open wide at this universe that perfectly matched her ideal for the world. Here she fitted in, and she knew it. Frontier Land, Adventure Land, Fantasy Land—everyone was happy, everyone was equal, and no one had problems. Why, she seemed to wonder, couldn't the real world be this way?

"Daddy," she had said during their last trip in her slow, deliberate way, turning her pretty face to Red, "do we have to go now?"

"It's late, sugar. Almost six. Mommy wants us home for dinner."

"Do . . . do we have to?" she whined.

"Yes, sugar."

"Daddy, I want to live in."

"What?"

"I want to live in here."

"You can't. No one lives in Disneyland. It closes every night."

She stopped, angry now as she faced him, holding both of Red's hands in her own. "You make me one, Daddy."

"Make you a Disneyland?"

"Yes," she said, believing it was possible, believing her father, who she knew worked with big buildings, could do anything.

"You promise, Daddy?"

He kissed her on the cheek. "I promise, sugar."

In the end he felt only pity for Isabel, yet something had nagged at him about the conversation. Red knew he made too many promises to everyone. He didn't like to disappoint investors and partners, much less his family, but he couldn't stop promising. He wanted everyone to expect great things from him as surely as he wanted to deliver them. No challenge was too great. And Red knew that with each success the praise and adulation built on itself. Newspapers, journals, even the TV networks had done features on him. His quick thinking with Disneyland and the Dodgers were legendary. Even his detractors, who found him too flashy, conceded he had a Midas touch. He could go almost anywhere in Los Angeles and be recognized. People asked his opinions on Khrushchev, birth control, civil rights, Snoopy—he was supposed to be an expert on everything. At a recent reunion of his military battalion, enlisted men and officers alike knew everything that had happened to him. He was the toast of the evening. He had become a god, as big as any movie star. Good-looking, charming, rich, married to a beautiful woman— for that, people loved and worshiped you.

In public Red pretended that the hosannas meant little, but in fact they meant everything. No one—not even Alycia— knew that celebrity was his addiction. He was amused when some people called him overly ambitious and consumed by money madness. Money wasn't the issue. He owned several houses, a vineyard, a yacht, a fleet of cars, and could do anything he pleased. It was recognition he lived for. The thought of living without it was chilling. To be somehow an unknown, an anonymous face, a lost soul, was a kind of death. He remembered how, in high-school, he would run for a hundred yards and score three touchdowns, but in the deafening cheers Red only felt, against all evidence, that he had let himself down. He always had to do more, better, reach the next rung on the ladder. That's when he would finally believe the cheers were for real. Now he was forty-four years old and nothing had changed inside him—the ladder always had an extra rung, and he couldn't afford to stop for fear he would fall.

"Are you all right?" Alycia asked as they danced the first dance. "You look preoccupied. You promised you'd relax and enjoy yourself." Her lips brushed his cheek.

"I was thinking," Red said, "that the last time we were here was fourteen years ago. Before we bought our first house. We had the Lincoln ragtop, remember? We drove to Santa Barbara . . ."

"Sometimes I wish you'd never sold it," she said. "You looked like the Great Gatsby. You were wonderful."

"Let's do it again," Red suggested suddenly. "We'll start by booking the bridal suite. Tonight. What do you say?"

Alycia pulled back. "Is this really you? You're sounding almost sentimental."

"The housekeeper will take care of the kids. You always say I don't spend any time with you."

"I didn't bring my nightgown."

He winked. "That's what's so great about my idea."

She kissed him on the lips. "You have a deal, Mr. Poindexter."

Red wanted to keep dancing, but at a tap on his shoulder he departed gracefully. This was really Alycia's show—she'd worked months planning the ball—and everyone would want to dance with her. Red was drifting through the crowd when he spotted a tall, slinky woman in a shiny lavender gown. Her gloves were a soft pink. Even before she turned, Red knew it was Electra. He waved back, but not enthusiastically. Electra looked incredibly young— no more than twenty-five. Her date was a trim, self-important man with a deep Mexican tan and silver hair. If the guy wasn't attached to some Hollywood studio, Red bet, he'd give up gin martinis.

"Hi, Red."

He turned and took in Scotty Madigan's pinched face, which looked at once sad and hopeful. His friend's hands dug self-consciously into his tuxedo pockets.

"What are you doing here?" Red asked, surprised. "You brought a date—"

"No," he answered, and at the same moment Scotty spotted Electra.

"Hey, let's go somewhere we can talk," Red suggested.

"I'm fine," Scotty said stubbornly. He kept his gaze on the woman that Red knew he was still in love with.

When their divorce was finalized two years ago, Scotty had taken the textbook plunge. Red remembered painfully the stints at two clinics that were supposed to dry him out. A week later Scotty had shown up at the operating table too sodden to hold a scalpel. His surgical privileges were suspended for a month, but Scotty didn't get the message. He couldn't stay sober. Malpractice suits followed, along with his embarrassing denials. His partners forced him out of a flourishing practice. Now he was a staff physician at a city clinic in Glendale, treating clap and inoculating babies and senior citizens. He lived like a hermit in a North Hollywood apartment and had dropped his Lakeside membership. Red was always asking him out for lunch or dinner, but Scotty rarely accepted.

"Scotty, why are you here?"

"I came for Electra," he said with total seriousness.

Red saw Scotty wasn't drunk, but he might as well have been. "I thought that was history," he said diplomatically.

Red could never quite forgive Electra for what she'd done. She knew Scotty still carried a torch for her, yet she'd never shown one measure of sympathy or mercy. Part of the problem was her writing career. Her novel about a wealthy young socialite who had been misunderstood by her friends and gone to Europe to find herself had actually been published. Red refused to read it, but Alycia loved the story, and she wasn't alone. The book had sold well enough to be optioned for a movie. Now Electra was filled with the idea that the world waited with its tongue out for a second novel.

"Scotty," Red said more firmly, "this is futile. Let me get you out of here . . ."

Scotty's face sagged. "You're the only friend I have left, and you're asking me to give up? I need Electra back in my life. I haven't had a drink in ages."

"Drinking isn't the point," Red said, "Electra is, and right or wrong, she doesn't want you."

"You know what it is to have an obsession about someone? It means you have to have that person. You must have her. You can't live without her."

Red knew. He remembered how he'd pursued Alycia in Paris. He also knew how much courage it had taken Scotty to show up tonight, and he needed every reinforcement to approach Electra. But he wanted the impossible. Red wanted to tell him that Electra wasn't worth it.

"I know how painful everything has been," Red said carefully. "You've been degraded and embarrassed by the woman. Somehow you've forgiven her. But if you get close again, the damage is going to be twice as bad.''

"Red, she won't let me near the house. The court gave her total custody of the kids. This is my only chance. I want her to see me sober—okay?''

Red kept close as Scotty approached the dance floor. Electra saw him right away and stopped dancing.

"You look gorgeous,'' Scotty announced, standing there bravely. Around them couples kept dancing, but it felt to Red like the whole world was watching. Electra's silver-haired date gave Scotty a distant smile.

"I'd like to talk to you,'' Scotty said, undaunted.

Electra lavished a long second look at Scotty. Red thought that beneath her surprise there was sympathy; she was touched that he'd had the courage to come and see her. Red wondered if he'd been wrong about Scotty's tactics.

"Could I have the next dance?'' Scotty asked.

Electra started to say yes, but her boyfriend moved closer. His smile had faded.

"Just one dance,'' Scotty clarified. "We used to be great dancers together.''

"I remember.''

"Electra, things have changed for me. I've gotten better. I mean it.''

She nodded, as if wanting to believe him, but her eyes said she couldn't. She seemed afraid suddenly.

Mr. Studio stepped in. "I think you're bothering the lady.''

"We're just going to have a dance,'' Scotty replied.

"Maybe some other night.''

"You don't understand,'' he said patiently, his eyes still on Electra. "We're old friends.''

"Then write her a letter.''

Scotty's face darkened with pain. "It's not going to bother you, is it?'' he asked, facing the man.

"I mind.''

"I don't see why.''

"Do I have to make this any clearer?''

Scotty ignored him and reached for Electra's hand.

Mr. Studio was a head taller and twenty pounds heavier than Scotty. Red just watched the first shove, which propelled Scotty a few steps back without serious damage. But the second landed him hard on the floor. It was enough to stop the music. Red got behind Scotty and hoisted him up.

"You made your point," Red said, angling his head to the bully. "My friend's leaving now."

"Tell him not to come back."

"I'll tell him," Red promised, controlling himself. He was close enough to smell the man's cologne and notice the perfect white teeth against the deep tan. The symmetry of his face was perfect, the skin youthful. The plastic surgeon had done an amazing job. Red couldn't even tell how old he was.

"If he's your friend, I don't think I want to know you either," the man added.

"Please," Electra whispered.

Red's eyes narrowed. This guy didn't even know who he was.

"Well?" the man said. "What are you staring at?"

Red felt Scotty's arm tugging on his own.

"A jerk," Red said.

Red would have been willing to call it a draw, but a fist suddenly floated toward him. Even if it had connected, a bee sting would have hurt more, he thought. Red's own blow landed efficiently. The spurting blood from the man's nose hit three bystanders as he fell.

Electra dropped on her knees to see to her wounded boyfriend. Red turned and strolled to the bar after he noticed Scotty had vanished. The music resumed, but Red knew that tongues would be wagging long after it stopped.

"What was that all about?" Alycia asked as she hurried over to Red. She looked embarrassed.

"Sorry," he whispered, and he was, for Alycia. This was her night.

"Why did you do it?"

"I believe in sticking up for my friends."

"Do you know who that is?"

"Alycia, I don't care—"

"Walter Mandrake. The producer and director. He's the one interested in Electra's novel. And he's supposed to be the next president of Livingston Studios."

"I didn't start the fight," Red reminded her, unimpressed with the résumé. "Like a drink?"

"What I'd like is for you to apologize," Alycia said. "Please? Before the ambulance comes? Red, you really hurt him. Electra thinks you broke his nose."

"Forget it," he said quietly.

"Do you want to make an enemy? Walter Mandrake is supposed to be a powerful man."

Red put down his drink. "Alycia, do I look frightened? I'm powerful too. That Hollywood jerk deserved what he got. End of discussion."

Red wanted to tell her more. But it would come down to their difference of opinion about Scotty and Electra. Scotty's fall from grace had pained Red more than Alycia or anyone else knew. If he'd been humiliated like that, Red thought, he would have been destroyed. Alycia couldn't understand that kind of pride. And whenever Red criticized Electra, she automatically took her friend's side. Why are you so blind? Red had asked. Here was this full-blown eccentric who did exactly as she pleased, living by her impulses, speaking whatever came into her mind, not caring whom she hurt or offended. The truth was, Electra was totally spoiled. All that money and no idea what it meant to earn it. Alycia had once asked him the difference between old money and new. People who had inherited wealth thought it was a birthright that made them superior. They trusted it more than they did their friendships. That was the difference. But when Red told Alycia, she didn't seem to understand.

Red watched now as Alycia, resigned, wandered back to the ball. He was sorry she was upset, but he was even sorrier to be left alone. He was always so busy that suddenly to be in a corner by himself was unsettling. The bartender was ordered to line up three martinis. Red studied Alycia as she danced. He saw the way men looked at his wife, moved their arms subtly around her, giving her a message. She smiled back at them, as if to say she didn't mind innocent affection. It wasn't innocent, he wanted to tell her. Or did Alycia know? Red wondered what he should do. He had so much power, there were so many people he controlled, but with his wife he felt helpless. At the start of the evening there had been a flicker of hope and renewal in their relationship. Maybe they could find it again.

Red started from his chair and dodged around clusters of guests. Walter Mandrake had been taken to the hospital. For the moment the incident seemed forgotten. Alycia was in a corner, not far from the band, but Red stopped halfway. His wife was talking animatedly to a tall, strapping man in a brown habit. A monk. Red was startled. She seemed almost spellbound by the stranger.

"Who was your friend?" he asked, stepping up when the monk finally departed. Red was feeling the martinis.

"His name's Brother Andrew. He's raising money for his monastery. I'd like to give him something."

"Really?"

"He just seems purer than most people. I know that's an old-fashioned word, but he reminds me of certain priests I knew in Paris. They were very devoted men, very caring. But Brother Andrew is different too. He doesn't seem as conflicted as the priests I knew. Maybe that's because he lives mostly in a monastery. I told him it was a shame that someone so conscientious and loving wasn't more involved in the real world . . . he could do so much good."

"I doubt it," Red said with a cynical smile. "He'd just be corrupted like the rest of us."

Red resented the tone of adoration in Alycia. A small spark of jealousy flared in him, which he found amusing. This was a monk, after all. Red let his arm drop over Alycia. He didn't want any more arguments. He went to kiss her, but she resisted, as if still thinking of the fight with Walter Mandrake, or disapproving of how much Red had been drinking.

"Shall I see if our bridal suite is ready?" he asked, unfazed.

"We can't leave the party now."

"Then when?" He meant to be charming.

"We'll see," she said.

Red nodded that he understood, but he was filled with anxiety. His sudden longing for Alycia was as strong as when they had been in Paris. The party lasted another three hours, and Alycia hung around until the last guests. She was so tired, she said when they were finally alone, would Red mind terribly if they went straight home?

I do mind, he thought. I won't let you go. But Alycia almost crumpled in his arms from fatigue, and in the end they climbed into their limousine for home.

Of all her wealthy society friends, Alycia got along best with a striking, outspoken divorcée named Countess Carmine Angela Bradbury. The tall, rangy, fortyish brunette collected homes around the country like some women collected recipes, but her flagship residence was a four-acre Westwood estate not far from UCLA. Alycia arrived every Wednesday morning for bridge—two tables were set for the regulars, sometimes a third for out-of-town friends—a ritual she found fun and enlightening. With her sandpaper wit, the countess had no shortage of gossip and commentary, especially about men. She had marched to the altar four times. No marriage had lasted more than a few years. Her title resulted not from matrimony but from a very substantial donation to the Vatican, which rewarded her with the title of papal countess and an unlimited number of private audiences with the pope. Carmine, whose only link to Catholicism was through her first husband, said all her title really proved was how badly the Church needed money.

Carmine's great-aunt had been the wife of the wealthiest man in the history of Los Angeles. Edward Doheny, for whom two streets in Beverly Hills were named, had been the West Coast John D. Rockefeller. Alycia had heard Carmine tell the story more than once. In 1892 the young, rough-tempered gold prospector arrived in this lazy, restless city of eighty thousand and noticed a farmer hauling several barrels of a black, gooey tar called *brea*. Doheny was informed that the mysterious substance oozed and bubbled from a pit at the edge of town, where poor families collected it for fuel. The pit was in Hancock Park, and *brea*, Doheny discovered, was crude oil. He quickly leased the land from the city but hadn't a penny left for a rig. With a pick and shovel, he managed to extend a four-by-six foot shaft to a depth of 460 feet, where he promptly hit California's first gusher. Within five years the city skyline was dominated by the silhouette of Doheny's oil rigs.

He next ventured into Mexico, leasing a million acres for exploration just off the gulf, and struck it rich with his Mexican Petroleum Company. By 1925 Doheny claimed a net worth of $100 million. At the same time, the man who had once been a mule driver, a fruit packer, and a gunslinger began sporting a walrus mustache, monocle, and British-tailored silk suits. He was the toast of Los Angeles—a man who thumbed his nose at East Coast traditions and said folks in L.A. could be just as rich and important. Even when Doheny became imbroiled in the Elks Hill scandal under Warren Harding's administration, and was indicted for bribing his friend, Secretary of the Interior Albert Fall, the city still loved him.

Doheny's eccentric attitudes and behavior became typical of Los Angeles high society. This was a city of outspoken mavericks. Mrs. William Astor of New York City had de-

cided who was who in East Coast society by seeing how
many friends she could squeeze into her private ballroom.
Her social arbiter, William McAllister, took the names of the
guests and created the famous New York Four Hundred, a list
of old-wealth families that would be an impossibility for Los
Angeles. Here, most money had a history of no more than
thirty or forty years. Carmine thought Mrs. Astor's approach
was bunk. The mere accumulation of money was not enough
to qualify for social status. Even being rich and knowing how
to translate French, use a finger bowl, and recite passages
from *La Bohème* was not enough, Carmine said. Wealth was
a privilege, and it demanded a social conscience. One had to
give his or her money away. One had to be truly generous.
One had to want to help.

Carmine did as she preached, Alycia knew. Except for her
love of houses, she had no great extravagances and managed
to live almost frugally. She had only one car, did her own
cooking, and tended her own investments and business affairs. Every year she gave away, to a wide spectrum of
cultural and social causes, no less than two million dollars.
She was very popular among the needy, yet she would suddenly abandon one beneficiary and jump to another. She
never gave any reason. Alycia thought Carmine didn't want
to be taken for granted. She was a strong woman with strong
opinions, and she wanted her voice heard.

Trust was not her friend's long suit, Alycia had decided.
Carmine refused interviews, never gave parties and seldom
attended any, turned away even the most clever suitors, and
could not make herself be nice to anyone she considered
hypocritical. She had liked Alycia from the moment they met.
Delighted, Alycia had been on guard about Carmine's fickle-
ness, but the friendship had run a smooth course.

Alycia parked in the long, circular drive behind the other
Cadillacs and marched up the flagstone steps to one of the
few houses in Los Angeles she respected architecturally.
Designed about 1905 by brothers Charles Sumner Greene and
Henry Mather Greene, who'd had an early influence on the
Prairie School and Frank Lloyd Wright, Carmine's home was
a sophisticated bungalow with Oriental influence, strong hori-
zontal lines, and warmth and integrity in its large open rooms.
"Taste" was not a word Alycia found easy to use in Los
Angeles. In a city of castles, chalets, pagodas, mosques,
miniature Tudors, Mediterranean villas, and Samoan huts,

where Coca-Cola had built a bottling plant that looked like an ocean liner, and a tire manufacturer occupied a factory that was a replica of an ancient Assyrian palace, it was comforting to find real style and grace.

Entering the house, Alycia saw she was the last to arrive, gave and received quick hellos, and took her spot at the second table. She had learned bridge only two years ago. She knew she'd never be proficient because she wasn't clever or patient enough, not like Carmine or some of the women who played almost every day. Carmine set strict and inflexible rules: the bridge lasted only until twelve-thirty, not a minute longer; the hostess supplied coffee and tea but guests brought their own sweet rolls; no liquor was served or consumed, not even in the coffee; no betting was permitted; there was no smoking; and no gossip or anecdote could exceed two minutes. The women were mostly older than Alycia, bright, well-educated, secure, their children grown. Some looked elegant, others dowdy; none was really snobbish. A few had inherited their money, but most were married to extremely successful husbands: owners of supermarket chains, art dealers, contractors, manufacturers, exporters.

Initially Alycia had felt little in common with the group, but with time she'd warmed to her Wednesday friends. The truth was, she had begun to feel more comfortable with the world of money. She believed in philanthropy—that was her link to Carmine—but spending on herself and her children was pleasurable too. Excepting Carmine, all the women in the group were great spenders. Alycia listened to them talk matter-of-factly about closetfuls of fur coats and garages with new cars. By comparison Alycia thought she lived on cookies-and-milk money, yet it felt more than ample. She loved clothes, shoes, jewelry if it wasn't too ostentatious, fine restaurants, collecting porcelain china—and parties. She adored parties, especially her own. Even more than Electra had when they'd first met, Alycia loved dressing up for an evening and thinking that every moment was magical, wanting to make her guests happy. She knew she was beautiful, she had a handsome and successful husband, and she could cook, dance, and always knew what to say to her guests. With her children and charity work, her days were crowded and often strained; parties were a reprieve, the time she felt most free, most herself.

"Alycia, I have a proposition for you," Carmine suddenly

announced from the other table. Eyes skated with anticipation to the hostess, to Alycia, then back to the cards.

"I want you to think about taking the vacant board seat on the Helen Mayer Foundation," Carmine said. "The board thinks it needs another man, but I don't agree."

Alycia tried to hide her surprise. She was flattered. The Helen Mayer Foundation controlled more charity dollars than any other organization in California. A lot of her wealthy friends had spoken enviously of the chance to sit on a board with that much cachet and power. With the backing of Carmine, Alycia knew she'd have better than a decent chance. But did she really want it? Her days were busy already. Yet this was an honor. It didn't matter if she was a woman; at least gender wasn't the most pressing requirement. Money was. Not just how much one had, but how much one gave away. Board members of any charity were expected to be generous. The more prestigious the board, the more one was expected to give.

Alycia knew Red couldn't match Carmine's annual total. Still, he made a lot of money, and he gave Alycia free rein in writing checks. How much would she be expected to donate to Helen Mayer? Carmine would let her know. These things were discreet, often unspoken among the wealthy, but somehow communicated. Alycia didn't feel totally comfortable with the idea of "buying" her way onto the board, but that was the way the charity world worked. For many of the rich, giving to charity was a way of buying into an entire social circle. It meant social acceptance and prestige that was otherwise unobtainable if one wasn't an alumnus of the right college, or born into the right family, or didn't have the right friends. Alycia knew a handful of women who she was sure would demand a divorce if their husbands cut off their charity allowance.

"Thank you for the vote of confidence," Alycia answered modestly, "but I'm already involved with the Red Cross, Carmine, and Dorothy Chandler runs Helen Mayer."

"Exactly my point," Carmine said, breasting her cards to turn her full attention to Alycia. "I know you're friends with Buffy, but the dear woman does not devote enough time to the foundation. I know that you would."

"Carmine," one of her friends cautioned, "you don't want to step on the toes of the most powerful woman in Los Angeles."

"Pecking order be damned," huffed Carmine. "I don't care for Dorothy Chandler, period. I don't like the way she and her husband—and now their son, Otis—run the *Times*. Look at whom they endorsed last year for President—Mr. Checkers."

"That's *Nixon*," she was corrected.

"I don't care what his name is. That dreary little fool has never drawn an honest breath in his life. He's a pox on civilization."

"You're happy with a *Catholic* for President?" the friend inquired with surprise.

"Times are changing. We can no longer afford to be too cautious. That's sometimes the most dangerous thing of all. My point is that a woman is sorely needed on the foundation. It's bad enough that men in this state earn, spend, and control most of the money, including our biggest foundations. Alycia, please consider my idea."

"Thank you. I will."

Alycia half-hoped Carmine would let the matter die—her days really were crowded—but the next week Carmine called to nudge Alycia again. Reluctantly, Carmine admitted, she had spoken to Dorothy Chandler and asked her wisdom about filling the board seat. "Your name came up, dear," Carmine told Alycia. "We all want you now."

Alycia realized she had to accept. She was flattered, and she thought she really could provide some leadership. She'd done it with the Red Cross. The Helen Mayer Foundation simply meant dealing with more dollars. It was true that California money was predominantly a male domain, and Alycia agreed with Carmine that there should be nothing wrong with letting a capable woman into the club.

"Are you happy?" Electra asked.

"What's that mean?" Alycia answered evasively.

"You heard me! Are you happy?"

They were having some laughs as they finished up two bowls of steaming chili at Chasen's. Electra had ordered for them, and provided a running commentary on how the famous chili was so favored by Liz Taylor that the actress had it flown to her by the Beverly Hills restaurant wherever she happened to be—which, at the moment, the fall of 1962, Electra would bet was in some bed with Richard Burton. Electra lately told so many Hollywood stories that Alycia didn't know whether to believe them. Alycia did know that

Chasen's was very obliging to its clientele. The restaurant drew heavily from the movie colony, with which Electra, whose current beau and housemate was Walter Mandrake, liked being associated. Walter was making her first novel into a movie—shooting had already started—and Electra was on pins and needles.

"I don't care for the chili," Alycia ribbed her friend. "I don't care about Liz Taylor or Richard Burton either."

"Burton is a dream and you know it!" Electra shot back.

"And I think I'm quite happy," Alycia added, more seriously. It was a question she hadn't really asked herself, not the way her friend apparently did. Electra looked in the mirror every morning and had now filled two novels with what she found. For Alycia, with the children and the charity work and her social world, she was mostly just busy, and keeping occupied was a kind of contentment. She knew she was supposed to be happy. Even if Red was away much of the time and she had her hands full on the home front, she and Red looked upon themselves as everyone else looked on them: they might have their differences, but they were committed to one another.

"You know, I'm envious of you," Electra said as if reading Alycia's thoughts.

Alycia started to laugh. "I don't believe you."

"I am. You have something I don't."

"What's that?"

"I wish I knew exactly."

"Will you stop it?"

"I don't mean just a nice marriage, though I miss that sometimes. It's something else about you—your calm, consistent way of looking at the world."

"It's not as interesting as yours," Alycia couldn't help throwing in. "I love your new novel. Is the man supposed to be Walter? He's really wicked!"

Electra dropped her voice. "Of course it's Walter. I always draw my characters from life. Only the real Walter is so egotistical he can't believe that's him in the book. He thinks my character's a wimp!" Electra burst out with a laugh, drawing stares.

"Are *you* happy?" Alycia turned the tables.

Electra pulled out her lipstick and engrossed herself in her compact mirror. "I wouldn't tell this to anyone but you. For now, it's a lark—Walter showers me with gifts—but tomorrow, who knows? Walter and I won't last forever. He's impossible to live with. The man wants to rule the western hemisphere. And he collects grudges like my son does stamps and coins. Poor Red. Walter *loathes* him. Even after plastic surgery, his nose isn't quite right—''

"What Red did was wrong, and I'm sorry, but can't Walter forgive and forget? I would.''

"That's why I envy you, Alycia. There's something very strong about you. Some people can never forgive.''

"You're strong too," Alycia offered. "Look how much you've gone through.''

"Alycia, why do you always deflect the conversation to me? You shouldn't be so modest. It makes me think you're hiding something.''

"Maybe I am,'' she admitted, suddenly feeling the need to talk. "Maybe I don't have the confidence you'd like to think I do.''

Electra put down her compact. "What's the matter?''

"I've been having a lot of problems with Jean lately.''

Electra's face creased with sympathy. "Jean? You're kidding.''

"He's more of a handful than Isabel. At fourteen, the hormones are running like a waterfall. He gets in fights at school, won't do his homework, can't make friends. When he comes home, all he wants is to plop in front of the television or take a boat out on the lake. Except when Red gets home. Then Jean is the model teenager. He adores his father.''

"Isn't that a positive note?''

"Maybe, but it also creates a discipline problem. Jean resents me when I get tough with him. And Red can't see why I ever want to punish him. If there's a problem, Red has an excuse for Jean. Part of it's guilt because he's not around enough, but mostly he wants to be the supportive father that Owen never was to him.''

"Don't you two talk about it?''

"Of course, but it's hard for Red to accept. He's so stubborn. Maybe it shouldn't surprise me that Jean is the same way.''

"I think all men are. At least the ones I run into. Stubborn and handsome. I keep wondering why I'm so attracted to that type.''

"It's also funny the way I see Red and Jean being so much alike," Alycia said. "Red likes to think they're very different.''

Electra insisted on charging the lunch to Walter's account. "Please stop worrying about Jean," she said as they walked out. "All kids go through phases. Mine did. Jean's got so much going for him—he's bright, has the same good looks as his father, and I've seen how personable and charming he can be around adults. Maybe he's one of those kids who don't relate to their peers. Don't give up."

"I won't," Alycia said, appreciating the support. Electra kissed her on the cheek and promised to call. Alycia hoped it would be soon. Since selling her Toluca Lake house and moving with her children into Walter's, Electra wasn't around often.

Alycia took the freeway home, hoping she'd be in time for Jean. She'd insisted he come straight from school to start his homework. No matter how bright he might be, he was practically failing English and getting D's in algebra. She didn't look forward to what she was afraid would be a confrontation. It was more pleasant to dwell on her lunch with Electra, though that, too, had left her feeling uncomfortable. It was ironic that Electra should be envious of her, because lately Alycia had wished she could live her friend's life. Alycia did know herself and her values—growing up in the middle of a war had seen to that. But, oh, all that freedom Electra enjoyed! Alycia only felt tied down. The Helen Mayer Foundation demanded her time almost every day. And with Dorothy Chandler, who almost single-handedly had rescued the Hollywood Bowl from extinction, Alycia had helped raise twenty million dollars for a new downtown music center and theater. All that felt good—Alycia knew that she made a difference—but something was lacking. She never had time for herself.

She wondered what she would do if she did. She knew others had ideas for her. At the Sidney Greene Hospital, where for years she'd taken Isabel for therapy, a tall, young pediatric neurologist had lately joined the staff. Dr. Richard Hiller was now Isabel's primary physician, and Alycia quickly saw he was equally interested in her. After almost every therapy session there was an invitation for coffee. She was torn when she had to tell him no. He was blond, with crinkly blue eyes and a warm smile, and Alycia couldn't deny there was a spark or two between them.

And there were others—husbands of the women she worked with on charity boards, clients of Red's, strangers she would meet at parties. There were a lot of attractive women in her circle. Was she being singled out more or less than the others? Alycia had never focused on what made her so desirable. She supposed that being European had something to do with it, having a certain grace and sense of herself, a distance from the world—maybe that's what Electra had been telling her. But it was that very distance that Alycia yearned to erase. She suddenly wanted to be involved with someone or something, wanted to fill a void she was growing more conscious of by the day.

She looked to Red to understand and satisfy her, but his thoughts were elsewhere, and not just on business. Six months ago Owen had suffered a minor stroke. With typical bravado, he was soon back at work. A month later he had had a second, more damaging stroke. Now he mostly stayed at home, partially paralyzed and unable to walk without a cane. His brokerage business had been in decline even before his illness; lately it was flirting with extinction. Harriet had persuaded Red to drop the suit challenging his father's ownership of the Poindexter Building. Still, despite her pleas, he would not come to the Bel Air house to see his father. "Do you expect me just to snap my fingers and make the past disappear?" he had asked Alycia. As much as he regretted hurting his mother, he was still full of anger, and sick or not, Red didn't trust Owen not to exploit him in some new way. Alycia had learned her lesson and knew to steer clear of the private war.

Arriving home, Alycia was greeted by frantic shouts from the backyard. Through a window she saw her Mexican housekeeper by the pool, fluttering her arms like a bird trying to fly. Alycia rushed out to take in Jean's lanky, handsome figure in the middle of the upper lawn. He was in jeans and a T-shirt. A silvery object flashed in his hand.

"Jean, give me that gun," Alycia said, startled.

"It's not yours." His voice was as calm as the waters of the lake. "It's Dad's. I found it in his study."

Ignoring his mother, he turned and leveled the weapon on the row of soda cans stacked on a nearby two-by-four.

"In any case, it doesn't belong to you. Now, please put it down."

"No," he said, not even looking at her.

She'd never seen him this defiant.

"Jean—"

The gun exploded against the still air, jerking up in the

boy's hand. One of the cans flew off the board. A smile creased Jean's lips.

Alycia caught her breath and tried to stay calm. The housekeeper had fled into the house. "Jean, what you're doing is very dangerous, you know."

"Why?" His gaze stayed on the cans.

"You could hurt yourself. And maybe an innocent bystander. The neighbors—"

"I don't care," he said sullenly. He turned to Alycia, his look accusing her of never understanding him.

"But you should."

"Maybe I want to hurt myself."

"Now, what does that mean?"

"I don't know."

She kept her eye on the gun as it dangled by his side. Was he just wanting attention, maybe trying to get out of doing his homework, or was he legitimately upset about something?

"Was school all right today?" she asked.

"No."

"What happened?"

"You don't care."

"Yes, I do."

He glanced back to his targets, not believing her.

"Jean, if you don't put down that gun right now, I'm going to take it away from you," she said.

He took a step back, taunting her, ready to run. Or maybe he wouldn't. The revolver firmed in his hand.

Alycia refused to be intimidated. As she stalked forward, their eyes met.

"Stop!" he commanded when she was a few yards away.

The gun levered up at Alycia and trembled in his hand. She froze. Jean's finger coaxed back the fat trigger.

The hollow click filled the air like an explosion. Alycia's terror gave way to relief, then outright fury. With one hand she seized the weapon, and the other dragged Jean into the house.

"I only put one bullet in the cylinder!" he tried to exonerate himself, as if she was being too hard on him again. Alycia marched him up to his room. It pained her to do this but she felt she had no choice. "I want you to stand in that corner," she said, pointing. "For one hour. Don't cry. Just think about what you did. Do you understand?" Jean started to cry anyway.

When Alycia told Red that evening, his face squinched in disbelief. "Come on—"

"He pointed the gun at me! I didn't know if it was loaded or not!"

"But he told you there was only one bullet, and he'd already discharged it."

"He told me *after* he pulled the trigger. Red, I was terrified."

"I'll speak to him," he allowed.

"You'll do more than that. You have to punish him. And please lock up that gun."

"I will," he promised to both requests, and started up the stairs to Jean's bedroom.

Alycia strolled back to the kitchen. The place mats and settings were already arranged. Felice was patiently standing on a stool over the stove, stirring the vegetables.

"Thank you. You're a sweetheart," Alycia gave her nine-year-old a kiss and a hug. The string bean of a girl with the dark, wise eyes and legs that seemed as long as Alycia's was always helping around the house, yet she didn't make a show of being good. Felice did things because she wanted to. A private, undemonstrative child, she rarely asked for help, and went about her life with confidence. She made time for her school friends, household chores, Brownie troop, swimming lessons, homework, hobbies of collecting dolls and stamps, play with Isabel—and seldom wanted to watch television. Everything had a place and time for her. She listened more than she spoke. She showed a proud and stubborn side, but very seldom were there arguments, and never a tantrum. Jean was the only one to challenge her quiet, strong will. When he bullied her, she retreated to her room and without a word closed the door on him. Jean seemed to know not to go any further.

When dinner was ready, Alycia called upstairs to Red. There was no answer.

"I'll get Dad," Felice volunteered.

"No, sit down, sweetie."

At the top of the stairs Alycia put her ear to Jean's door. She had expected a lecture at the least, but there hadn't been even a squawk from Jean. She listened to the low, intimate voices, comfortable with one another, and the shared laughter that seemed to exclude the world. Like he was Audie Murphy, Red was telling war stories! He rarely talked about the war with her. Suddenly he was lost behind enemy lines, surrounded by two dozen Germans, and all he had to defend himself with was a bent fork.

On a damp, windy Thanksgiving afternoon that most of Los Angeles ignored by gathering around a fire or something alcoholic, Harriet drove alone up the quiet streets of Bel Air and swung into her drive. Her back seat was packed with groceries she'd just purchased, none of them essential. The turkey and all the trimmings were already cooked and ready to serve. It was Owen who had sent her out, unwilling to wait for their housekeeper tomorrow, as if everything were a matter of life and death. She knew he'd always run the show, but until his stroke he'd also given her a great deal of freedom she came to assume was her right. Now, housebound and frustrated, Owen was more demanding. On a moment's notice Harriet had to write his letters, make appointments, run errands, answer phones, and attend to a thousand and one details, most of which she found onerous and unimportant but over which she had no veto power. Owen persevered in the illusion he was still an important business and civic leader, and the world waited for his every move. The reality was that his real-estate empire had dwindled to all of three buildings. Sometimes Harriet thought she saw a glimmer of understanding in his eyes. But if Owen realized his impotence, it only made him more dictatorial.

For the first time in years they would have no company for Thanksgiving. The void left by Alycia and Red had been filled for a while by old friends, but they, too, had drifted away. Harriet was afraid to think about the future. The chances of a medical recovery for Owen bordered on the miraculous, which meant a continuing prison sentence for her too. Harriet fought off her frustration as she pulled the first two bags of groceries from the car. Somehow she would endure. After nearly five decades of marriage, and the fighting between Owen and Red, she was used to silent suffering; what was required now was to dig deeper and find more patience. Lately she had wondered if the effort was worth it. Part of her had begun to feel old.

Harriet did not see the car pull up across the street, nor hear the approaching footsteps. Only when a gentle hand fell on her shoulder did she turn with a start.

"You need some help," Red said cheerfully, kissing his mother as he handled the bags.

It felt like ages since a real smile had come to her lips. The burden lifted from her was more than the weight of the groceries. She couldn't remember the last time Red had been to the house—years.

"Happy Thanksgiving, Mother."

"It's good to see you," she said, studying the handsome face she loved so much.

"You look wonderful," Red said.

"No, I don't, but I don't care."

"You always look wonderful to me."

"Why are you here?" she had to ask.

His head angled toward the front door, and he hesitated. "I came to see my father. I know this is very late in coming, but I decided it was time to have a talk."

Harriet absorbed the words along with Red's smile of contrition. She had never expected this. What better Thanksgiving present? she thought. But something stirred inside her. The uncomfortable silence weighed down as she sifted through her feelings.

"This wasn't easy for me," Red confessed, "but here I am."

"No," Harriet said quietly. She forced the words out. "You don't have to see your father. Not now, anyway. I don't want you to."

Red looked uncomprehending. "Mother, it's you who've been after me. I finally forget the past and get up the nerve—"

"I know what I've always asked you," she said, "and I appreciate your coming. Your courage and love are the most important things of all."

"Then why?"

"Because seeing your father won't accomplish anything. It hurts me to say this—and I didn't realize it until I saw you now—but it won't mend fences, or make the future better, or cause Owen to change. I'm afraid he's beyond that. Since his stroke, there's no light at all in his heart. Why should I subject you to more disappointment? I love you, Red, and your life with Owen has been difficult enough. So has mine."

"Are you all right?" he asked, suddenly concerned.

"No one has to worry about me."

"I don't like the sound of that. Why don't you come to Toluca Lake for a while? I'll find a nurse to fill in for you for Dad. You need a break."

"No, my place is right here," she said stubbornly, "and

you don't have to worry about your father either. Everything will work out.''

"Mother, you're sure—"

"Quite," she asserted. Part of her would always want to bring her son and husband together, Harriet thought. She wanted hope, something to hold on to and give her strength, but this wasn't the answer. Owen, wounded and in decline, would only resent seeing Red now. Any grace and remorse he once possessed had been vanquished by something darker.

Red kissed his mother good-bye. "Come see the kids soon. They miss you," he said.

"I will. I miss them."

She took the groceries back and studied her son as he turned and left. She thought she'd feel an ache, but her spirits were suddenly lifted. Red, she realized, was all the hope she ever needed.

"Oh, he is *such* a shit—I can't begin to tell you . . ." Electra hissed out her words as she strode with Alycia down the quiet streets of Toluca Lake. Isabel walked between them, oblivious of the conversation, singing a nursery rhyme. Her features were plain but not distorted or dim like many of the retarded, and the eleven-year-old's dark eyes almost sparkled, as lovely a feature, Alycia liked to think, as the black shoulder-length hair Isabel proudly combed herself every morning. As the three approached a pedestrian bridge spanning the still, greenish waters of the lake, one of Isabel's hands was in her mother's, together with a bag of bread crumbs, the other in Electra's.

"I don't think I've ever seen you so put-out," Alycia said to Electra. "You're taking this too seriously, especially on a sunny spring morning." The two hadn't laid eyes on one another for six months—Electra had been hopping between Los Angeles and London, trailing Walter Mandrake and his movie crew—and then an hour ago Electra had appeared at her front door.

"What did Walter do, exactly?" Alycia asked.

"Besides kicking me and the children out of the house, taking away the Mercedes and diamond ring he gave me, and confiscating my charge cards?"

"You said yourself the relationship wouldn't last forever."

"But I never said it would end by Walter dropping the atom bomb on me."

"It's not like you're destitute, with all your family money—"

"It's the humiliation," Electra interrupted. "All of Hollywood knows. Walter finds some twenty-year-old bimbo he thinks is the next Marilyn Monroe, and whoosh, out I go."

"I'm sorry."

"The real burn is, Walter claims this is *my* fault because *I* didn't make him happy in bed. I swear, Alycia, I did everything but let him tie me in chains. The man is the devil himself. He points the finger of blame at anyone if it serves him. Whatever happened to conscience? You know what I think? Only women have consciences."

They stopped in the middle of the bridge, where Isabel carefully opened her brown bag. Her eyes lit up as a cluster of ducks swarmed toward their free meal. Though the ducks looked alike to Alycia, Isabel yelled out a different name for each, drawing a throaty response or the quiver of a head, upon which Isabel hurled a crumb to its deserving recipient. Alycia smiled down on her daughter.

The two made this same journey every week. On the advice of Dr. Hiller, Isabel's life was structured almost to the hour—a brightly colored calendar was affixed above her bed and Isabel could read enough words to know exactly what to look forward to. Her sense of order and organization was her strongest instinct, and within her limited range she took pride in what she mastered. With Felice's patient coaching, Isabel could recite the names of some of the Presidents. Whenever she finished, Red would break into applause and Isabel would blush and giggle.

"I want to tell you one final Walter story," Electra offered as they drifted over the bridge and dropped onto a swatch of grass. Alycia turned an eye back to Isabel as she leaned over the rail to her hungry menagerie.

"Sweetheart, be careful," she called out.

"Mama?"

"Yes, darling?"

Isabel beamed at her mother. "I be good."

Alycia turned back to Electra. "You swear this really happened?" she asked as she lounged back. The sun beat on her pale face and made her legs tingle.

"On all the Girl Scout oaths of the world," Electra said, holding up her right hand. "I didn't read this in *National Enquirer*."

Alycia grinned.

"Two months ago, Walter and I were invited to a big Hollywood anybody-who-is-somebody party at Harry Bigelow's winter palace in Beverly Hills. Walter envies the hell out of Harry. Walter's feelings aren't unique—Harry is the biggest producer in town—but not a day goes by that Walter doesn't wish Harry a fatal cardiac arrest. Harry couldn't find his ass if he had a bell on it, Walter likes to say. Of course, when they're together, Walter kisses that ass till his lips are numb.

"Midway through his party, Harry starts banging on his champagne glass with a gold-plated fork. He has finally chosen a director for his new, eagerly awaited movie, he announces to the gathered cognoscenti. This is a role Walter has drooled and lusted over for six months. He thinks he has the inside track. When Walter lost out for head of Livingston Studios, Harry promised this plum as consolation prize.

"Harry pauses as his eyes circle the room—all that's missing is a drumroll—then he clears his throat and says he's giving the directing job to Sterling Kaufman, a brilliant up-and-comer. Walter just stands there grinning and nodding as if he couldn't be happier for Sterling. He walks up to Harry and compliments him on his wise choice. He pumps Sterling's hand a dozen times. Inside, of course, Walter is going berserk. He is *liv-id*. We leave the party early. Walter is silent in the car. His eyes have sparks. I know better than to say a word. When we get home, he doesn't come to bed. Little wheels are turning in his finely tuned brain. I don't know whether he's planning to poison Sterling or Harry.

"The next day, at the studio, Walter makes a lunch date with Harry's twentyish secretary, with whom, Walter knows, Harry is having a little affair. Walter introduces the secretary to an extremely handsome stud who, unbeknownst to the secretary, is a fledgling porno star. Also unknown to the poor girl, but not to Walter, our stud has an outrageous case of the clap. The two have a tumble in the hay. To make a long story short, boy infects girl, girl infects Harry, Harry infects Harry's wife, Harry's wife infects Sterling Kaufman, with whom *she's* having an affair. 'Two birds with one stone,' Walter says to me proudly one evening over dinner."

Alycia couldn't stop laughing. "Electra, you got off lucky—you only got kicked out of the house and lost the car."

"Walter is still getting reamed in my new book. I'm going to have him kidnapped, held for ransom, and nobody is willing to pay. Even the terrorists can't stand him. He ends up in a tank of piranhas."

"You're as bad as Walter! Since when did you become so vengeful?"

Electra sighed. "I don't know. Maybe you're right. I don't want to become a shit. Hollywood's doing this to me."

"Your crowd sounds like a bunch of spoiled, insecure brats."

"Maybe that's what I have in common with them."

"Come on. You sound almost resigned to that," Alycia scolded.

Electra looked lost. "You know I'm not. It's just that I feel trapped."

"Then change."

"Into what?"

"I like the way you used to be. When you lived nearby and I saw you every day and we had fun together. I'm not asking you to go back to Scotty necessarily, but you could settle down, have more time with your kids, throw some of your spectacular partics again. Maybe we could throw one together!"

Electra was startled. "You mean become a *society* woman again? Are you kidding? All those people—they're not my crowd anymore."

"They're not so bad. Carmine Bradbury is a very strong woman, don't you think?"

"We always got along, I guess." She waited for her thoughts to come together, then looked at Alycia. "It's just that I feel like an outsider. You and Red are loved by the world. Yesterday I saw a photo in the *Times* of your whole family at church. Everything's so perfect for you."

"That's not the point—"

"Look," she interrupted, "your crowd wouldn't take me back after my Hollywood escapades. Too many sordid scandals. Not to mention kiss-and-tell novels. Those people are so judgmental—I know them—and I'm a threat."

"Those people have plenty of their own scandals, I'm sure. Everyone has a few skeletons in the closet."

"But mine are out in the open."

"I wouldn't worry about it," Alycia said. "With all your millions you could be Lady Godiva and it wouldn't matter. They need your money. They'd court you like you were Lady Astor. They'd even let you write your scandalous novels—

they'd just label you quaint or eccentric or something. Money heals all wounds."

"Let me be totally honest. I'm thinking of giving up writing too."

"I won't let you!" Alycia swore. "I love your novels—really. They're funny and witty, and something unexpected always happens."

Electra held her hand. "You're a real dear for your support."

"You've done the same for me," Alycia said, and casually swung her head back to the bridge. She looked again. It was empty.

Alycia brushed off her skirt as she rose. "Isabel?"

The ducks quacked back impatiently.

"Isabel!"

On the bridge Alycia let her eyes skate down the deserted street. Sometimes Isabel drifted off, but never far, or she made a game of hiding from her mother, though rarely for long—and she'd been only fifteen yards away. Alycia hadn't heard anything, but she knew with a sinking feeling that she should have been watching more carefully.

"I'll go this way," Electra said quickly, darting down the street.

Alycia peered over the railing to the bevy of ducks treading water. One swam in a rough circle, shaking its beak, trying to spit something out. Alycia's stomach tightened as she refocused on the water. What was left of Isabel's bread bag dotted the serene lake in dark little patches.

She threw off her shoes. The cool, murky waters folded around her as she sank to a depth of seven or eight feet. There was no visibility. Her arms and legs flailed, hoping to touch something, but all the time she told herself Isabel had not fallen in the water, that everything was fine, that she was a ridiculous figure thrashing about with her clothes on. When she came up for air she shouted futilely for Isabel. Should she run to the golf club, or a neighbor's house? Instead she plunged down again. As she maneuvered blindly, she swallowed the dirty water, spit it out, and suddenly felt so much fear and frustration she wanted to cry.

It was ten minutes before she discovered Isabel under a foot of water by the adjoining bank. Alycia struggled to carry her out. This wasn't happening, she thought, couldn't be. She watched from a third eye as she laid her daughter on the grass. The sparkling eyes were closed tight, the forehead bloodied. Alycia pressed her lips against the cold, lifeless mouth and blew in. *Please, please, please, God* . . . When she felt Electra fluttering behind her, Alycia told her to go for help. Alycia kept blowing into the small mouth. *Please, God, let my baby live.* . . .

An ambulance arrived but Alycia knew it was too late. She sobbed in Electra's arms as they rode to the hospital and then sat in the emergency room. How could this have happened to Isabel? Her sweet little innocent girl was defenseless. She'd been born into a world where pleasures were so limited, and even the pleasures were full of danger. But the accident wasn't Isabel's fault, it was my fault, she thought. A child like Isabel only knew to trust.

A young doctor confirmed the death and expressed condolence. Alycia couldn't make herself call Red. She couldn't do anything. Electra did it for her, then drove Alycia home. She poured two glasses of whiskey.

"Drink this," Electra said.

Alycia didn't touch her glass. "I'd like to be alone," she whispered.

"You're sure? Alycia, I can stay till Red comes—"

"I'll be all right," she managed, though she wasn't at all sure. In her mind's eye she watched as Isabel, unable to reach her ducks from the bridge, walked to the embankment to feed her skittish charges. Had she just slipped, or silently stepped into the water, maybe even knelt, only to bang her head on a rock? Had she had no time to yell, or to realize the danger she was in? There had not been a sound, not a witness. And in the two minutes it took Electra to tell her story, Alycia knew her own life had changed forever.

Jean and Felice arrived from school around noon, before Red. Tears welled up in Felice's eyes as she wrapped her arms around Alycia's waist. Jean paled for a moment, but he deliberately kept himself from crying and in the end went to ride his bike. Felice stayed near her mother.

Alycia embraced Red when he came home, and started crying again. "It was my fault," she told him.

Red didn't seem to hear. She wanted him to say something, perhaps that it wasn't her fault, but he looked exhausted and in shock. He fixed himself a drink. Like Jean, he felt grief and pain, but something kept him from displaying them. Red would mourn for a while, Alycia thought, watching him, and then life would go on for him.

It would never go on for her. Red had his work, but she had struggled with Isabel every day, feeling hope one moment, sadness the next—but always a special love and understanding. Now she didn't know what she felt. Was love diminished by death? Were memories ever a substitute, even an approximation, of the joy of the present? She felt empty and alone, and nothing, she thought, not her friendship and support from Electra or Harriet, not her love for Jean and Felice, was going to heal that feeling. There was an anger inside her too, but she didn't understand it.

A graveside service for family and close friends was held on an overcast afternoon at nearby Forest Lawn, on a grassy knoll overlooking the Valley. Harriet came without Owen. Exhausted from sleepless nights, Alycia was going through the motions of receiving everyone when she looked up into the warm blue eyes of Dr. Hiller. The young pediatric neurologist laid a bouquet of daisies on the grave.

"Thank you for coming," Alycia managed.

"Isabel was a very special child. She was honestly my very favorite patient. I always wanted to tell her that. I'm sorry now I didn't."

"I'm glad you're telling me. It makes a difference. Isabel certainly cared for you," Alycia said, remembering all the visits to the pediatric wing at Sidney Greene Hospital. For the first time in days she allowed herself a smile. Isabel had loved her doctor. Intuitive and sympathetic, the soft-spoken Dr. Hiller had never let them down.

"If there's anything I can do, Alycia, you'll let me know, won't you?" he said sincerely.

She was comforted by the way he spoke her name, and the warmth of his hands around hers. She watched him trail away alone; then she took Red's arm and with Jean and Felice returned to the car.

"Do you think we could go away for a while?" she asked Red that night when the children were asleep. "I mean all of us. The entire family."

Red looked up from his papers. "Where?"

"I always wanted us to live on a New England farm. Or take an exotic trip—"

"Alycia, I don't think I have the time," he answered sympathetically.

"Couldn't you make it, for me? I went up just now and looked at Isabel's room. It was so painful—"

"It would be more painful to leave and have nothing to do but think of Isabel. Alycia, I have to keep busy."

"Then just a short trip."

"Let me see what I can do," he said.

At the end of the week Red told her he had too many obligations and appointments to extricate himself. He was sorry. He had tried, but it was impossible. Why didn't Alycia and the children travel somewhere? Felice was more than eager for adventure, she found out, but Jean said he wanted no part of tramping around on foreign soil and he'd miss his father. Alycia knew she'd miss Red too. The purpose of a trip was to bring everyone closer. Didn't anyone want that except her? Was she the only one who felt starved and isolated?

Alycia settled for lunches with Electra and Harriet, but they were no cure. The daily void without Isabel to care for was immeasurable. Alycia realized she missed not just her daughter but also the responsibility of watching over her. One day she was okay, the next a basket case. She had only two children now. How was that possible?

She tried to keep busy. There were only so many parties she could host, charities to rally behind. She never had learned to like golf. Felice was a loving but self-contained child, while Jean, cold and suspicious, didn't like his mother meddling in his life. As always, Red was rarely home. One morning she walked to Lakeside and plunged into the Olympic-size pool. There were no lifeguards or sunbathers—the season didn't start until June—and the water wasn't even heated. She swam twenty laps, rested, then twenty more. She stretched out and let the pale sun warm her and bring a tint of color to her face.

The next day she was at the club again. After her laps she dried herself in the sun, and swam some more. She repeated the ritual every day. Felice asked how she was getting so tan. Alycia waited to tire of the swimming, for something to pull her away, but the water never lost its fascination. She liked being bundled in its silence, separated from the world.

After two weeks she was able to swim a hundred laps a day. Her body always throbbed and burned toward the end, but she forced herself to drag one arm through the water, then the other, accepting the pain. Sometimes she thought she blacked out, because she would suddenly find herself sinking and then thrash her way back to the surface.

Dr. Hiller called her the last week in May. In the back of a drawer he'd discovered some drawings Isabel had crayoned. He wanted to keep one or two, but would Alycia like the rest?

She met him in hospital reception the next day at noon. The boyish-faced doctor now sported a crew cut and looked even younger. "Hi, stranger," he said, flashing Alycia his warm smile. He handed over the folder of drawings.

"Thank you very much," she whispered, fighting off a wave of sadness.

"How are you getting along?" he inquired.

"Much better, thank you." She had decided just to take the pictures and run. "I'm keeping busy."

"You seem tense."

"No, I'm fine."

"And you've lost weight," he noticed.

"Really?"

"Let me fatten you up on a nice lunch. My treat—"

"I don't think so. Not today. Maybe a rain check," she suggested, folding her arms nervously.

"I don't believe in rain checks, not with you. You're like a phantom. Now or never," he said firmly.

"Dr. Hiller, I really have to be going—"

"Richard."

"Richard." She sighed, feeling her face warm, "You're very sweet, and I appreciate everything you've done for us—"

"Break your appointment and I'll take you to the best Arabic restaurant in the city. Then I'll show you an art exhibit that'll turn your head around. Ever heard of Claes Oldenburg?"

"No," she said.

He took her hand and there was no more argument. What was she doing? Alycia wondered. Whatever it was, it was fun. Richard had a battered Chevy convertible that was so undoctorlike she had to smile. He couldn't be poor, but he didn't seem to care about acquisitions or status. He turned on the radio and they listened to a rock-and-roll station.

"What's so funny?" he said.

"I'm not laughing."

"Inside you are. I can tell."

"You're a mind reader?"

"I have intuitive powers," he boasted.

"It's nothing. Maybe just this car. Most doctors drive Cadillacs."

"I'm not into the doctor game, thank you. You can stuff all your tax shelters and stock portfolios. I'm not the ambitious sort. My career is mostly academic. And when I'm not teaching at UCLA, I do clinic work at Sidney Greene or Children's Hospital."

"That's refreshing," she said.

"Tu es, aussi," he answered.

"You speak French?"

"Let's say I try. I trained in a Paris hospital for two years. That was a trip. French doctors are *très sérieux*. I was always loose and informal—they didn't know what to make of me. You grew up in Paris, didn't you?"

"Did I tell you that?"

"No, Isabel did, but I thought you were French. Your accent—"

They toasted the culture of Europe over a bottle of Bordeaux. The last time she'd had Arabic food was when she'd visited her father, she told Richard, but this was better. "Don't get me drunk," she said when they finished the bottle and ordered another, but she didn't protest strenuously. She felt somehow she was on holiday, and because no one knew her here, she could do whatever she wanted. Maybe she felt a little naughty, but there was no guilt. She didn't have to be responsible all the time, did she?

It was almost three before they reached the art gallery. Forgetting time, Alycia wandered in awe among the oversize soft vinyl tennis shoes, plaster-of-paris chocolate éclairs, and drawings of colossal teapots.

"I love modern art," she said. "It's a special universe here. You don't need words. You just want to touch everything."

"Isabel would have enjoyed this, wouldn't she?"

"Yes," Alycia agreed.

"It's the kind of world that makes you forget reality."

Outside, Richard brushed his hand against her cheek. She felt his eyes bore into her. "You know how wonderful you are?" he asked.

I don't know, she thought, but you could tell me. I need to hear someone say it. He slipped his arms around her. When she kissed him back it was with even more passion. In the car she told herself this was wrong. She was not in total control, but somehow she didn't care.

Richard's house was close to UCLA, in Beverly Glen Canyon, a small rustic cabin that sat on a cul-de-sac. There was nothing pretentious or expensive about it, except for his art—lithographs of powerful abstract artists she wanted to know more about—and a book collection he showed her with pride. He was totally different from Red, she thought as he led her to the bedroom—was that why she trusted him so much? Sitting on his bed, she let him unbutton her blouse. He took off her clothes carefully, laying them in a neat pile, as if everything about her were special. When it was her turn, she undressed him. Richard was not as muscular as Red, but his body seemed perfectly proportioned, and when the long arms wrapped around her they were warm and protective.

"Let me look at you," he whispered. She was thrilled by the adulation in his voice. Lately she had felt only sad and confused. She listened as he described the way she dressed, looked at people, laughed, held a wineglass—observations that were so thoughtful and detailed that it felt like he was already making love to her. Then his lips moved gently down her neck to her breasts.

She scooted back on the bed and allowed his hands to glide over her flesh. It was easier than she had thought to forget Red. She was suddenly flushed and aroused, the warmth spreading through her in quiet waves. No part of her was neglected by her young and thorough lover. His lips brushed against her breasts, then her belly, and finally moved between her legs. She opened them wider. She wanted to feel as open and vulnerable as possible. She wanted him to devour her, she thought as her breath shortened. He clearly adored her, would give her pleasure without asking for anything in return. His tongue brought her to her first climax. Her back arched and she begged him not to stop. Disobeying, he raised himself and lay beside her, forcing his tongue into her mouth. She let his warm, dry breath fill her lungs, then she pulled the full weight of him on top of her. She refused to release him even when he'd climaxed.

"I want to make love again," she said, teary-eyed.

"Why are you crying?"

"Because it was so wonderful, and I don't want it to end."

"What would you like me to do?"

She ran her hand through his matted hair and then touched her open palm to his lips. "Anything you want."

He lowered his head between her legs and made her belly tremble. Her legs wrapped hungrily around his neck and shoulders. She arched her buttocks toward him and could feel his tongue push deeper. After a while he put his fingers into her. Finally she turned on her side, facing him, and they made love again with a slow, steady rhythm.

They slept, entwined in each other's arms. Alycia woke to the aroma of coffee. On the tray Richard had also brought in a single red rose.

"Can I see you again?" he asked.

"Richard, this was wonderful," she said honestly, "but I'm married, I have a family—"

"Are you afraid of me?"

She blushed. "No, that's not it. If anything, I want to thank you for helping me. You made me feel good about myself again."

"Alycia, I'd make love to you day and night if you'd let me. I'd do anything for you."

"But you don't really know me. You're just infatuated."

"What do I need to know? You're beautiful, you're kind, you respect yourself, but not enough. You take chances when you make love, that's what makes you a wonderful lover, but you need to take more with the rest of your life."

A knowing smile lit her face. "You *are* infatuated."

"I believe in passion. That's all infatuation is, isn't it?"

"You're a nice man," she said, and kissed him.

"That's all? Just a nice man?"

She turned away.

"What are you upset about?" he pressed.

She told him she had always been faithful to Red. Did Richard care? Did it matter if he did? He listened to her in a way that made her think he did care, but that somehow, if she really needed him, he would be there and everything would be all right.

Alycia didn't reach home until after five. Walking in the door, she expected to be greeted with suspicious stares and demands to know where she'd been. She'd already rehearsed her answers. Now she was disappointed. No one seemed to know she'd been away. Red, home early for once, was in his study. Outside, Jean shot baskets. Felice was doing homework. The housekeeper had already started dinner. Alycia took her place in the routine, setting the table and making tomorrow's shopping list. She felt her anger building and tried to deny it. What was eating at her? It was more than being taken for granted, she knew. Something deeper, something she couldn't quite reach. Only when she thought of Richard could she push away her anxiety. Whatever was wrong with her, Richard would make the anger and pain go away.

They met every day, always at noon, always at Richard's house, but the assignations were never the same. A different way of making love, a different thing to do afterward. Lunch, or just wine, his classical guitar, anecdotes about med school, stories of friends. Richard was thirty-two and had never married. He had a dry sense of humor and loved to talk about his ideals. In some ways he was stubborn and immature—an old-fashioned romantic—but always gentle, always sincere. One day she told him about her compulsive swimming, but now that she had him, she was giving it up.

"Then I must make you happy," he said.

"Yes."

"But you're still holding something back from me."

She talked about Red and Jean and Felice, and Electra—and Isabel. Alycia hoped that one of those was the knot inside her, and that Richard would help loosen it, set her free. She should not feel guilty for the drowning, he assured her. It could have happened to anyone, and of the hundreds of burdened mothers he saw every year in his practice, Alycia had been the most collected, the most conscientious. Nor should she blame Red for being unsupportive, or gone so often, because there were things about him she did love, and she had no choice but to live with the rest of him. Nor should she be so demanding on herself and expect an instant recovery. Grief had to work itself out.

Next morning, opening her mail, Alycia lingered over an envelope from Bank of America. She automatically left all financial statements on Red's desk, regardless of whose account, because she had no patience for balancing checkbooks or keeping figures straight. This one was addressed "Alycia Poindexter, Trustee for minors Jean, Isabel, and Felice Poindexter."

She'd forgotten to notify the bank about Isabel. Would it ever be possible to completely extricate herself from her daughter? Should she want to? Alycia had begun to feel caught in some net, watched by some pair of eyes, judging her, waiting for something to happen. Were they Isabel's eyes, or someone else's?

Alycia opened the bank statement out of curiosity. Isabel's share of the trust would have to be dealt with. Her eyes skimmed the column of numbers in amazement. Jean now had over three million dollars. Isabel, almost three quarters of that. What should she do with it? There were a dozen worthy charities she supported—divvy it up? Or parcel the money between Jean and Felice? As trustee she had the right to do what she thought best, including abolishing the trusts. Alycia pushed back in her chair. Red earned more money than they could possibly ever need. The trusts had been set up in less certain times. She wished now she hadn't accepted them. She wished she'd gone to work with Red. Wouldn't that have made the future different? But Owen had talked her into the trusts.

She drove to Bel Air before noon. Owen took forever to answer the door. Alycia almost didn't recognize him. How many years had it been? He was bent over his cane, his face sunken and lined. His hair was receding. His cheeks had no color. It was painful to think of him as the handsome, powerful man she'd met fifteen years ago. He looked crossly at Alycia. Harriet was running errands, he said, and started to turn away. Alycia asked if she could come in. It was not Harriet she wanted to see, it was him.

"I'm occupied. I have a business to run," he informed her in his arrogant way.

"This is important."

"I'm sorry—"

"I insist," she said, and moved past him before he could shut the door.

They sat across from one another in the cavernous living room. As poor as was his health, his voice had lost none of its authority. Alycia let her eyes wander. The furniture was musty and unkempt. The gardens looked neglected too. She did not feel pity. There was only anger in her.

"I'll come right to the point," she said. "You like directness and candor, if I remember."

"Go on."

"I want to abolish the children's trusts."

"You mean Isabel's."

"No. I mean all of them," Alycia made clear.

His brow arched in surprise. "I disapprove, but why come to me? You have the right to act unilaterally."

"Because I want you to know why I'm doing this."

"My dear, you're being rash. You're upset about Isabel's death. Felice and Jean still have a future you must oversee."

"That's why I'm here. Red and I will mind their futures. Not you or your trusts. I don't want you interfering in our lives anymore, not even indirectly."

"I don't think I understand."

"I blame you for what happened to Isabel," she said, saying it more calmly than she had anticipated.

Owen's face tightened. "Your daughter's death was not my fault!"

"Not her death. Not specifically. And not even the car accident when I was pregnant. Red blamed you, but I forgave you because at least I had a child, damaged or not. But now she's gone, and I have this feeling that won't go away. You're responsible—"

"Preposterous," he bellowed.

"You're responsible," she insisted. "Red told me once, but I never understood what he meant, not until Isabel died. You're this presence, this spirit, that hovers over us and has never left us alone. For so many years I wanted to be your friend, just be accepted by you, but that was too hard for you. You can't accept anybody, not unless there are strings attached. By setting up those trusts you almost *knew* I'd have difficulty with my children, you made it happen that way, you wanted it to happen—and my deepest fear is that the worst is still to come."

Owen straightened in his chair, his waxy face rigid with anger. "Your deepest *irrational* fear," he corrected her. "You're a grieving, out-of-control woman—"

"And you're a predator. You're a curse."

"You had best leave now."

"Or what?"

"Go, Alycia!"

The cold, sharp voice intimidated her, but she wasn't walking out until she had said it all. "I'm giving you back the trust money. Every last penny."

He stared at her, digesting the words. A crooked smile appeared.

"It's mine to do as I please," Alycia reminded him. "You can't change that."

Owen's smile widened. "I have no intention of taking the money."

"Are you too proud? I know you could use it. So could poor Harriet. She hasn't bought any new clothes—"

"Who told you that?" he demanded.

"Who do you think?"

"My wife has no business talking to you about private matters!"

"You can't control people," Alycia shot back, "not if you really love them. You always told me you loved Red, but I don't believe it."

"Stay out of our lives, Alycia."

"*Our* lives?" she said, astonished. "You think you still control Red?"

"He's my son."

"He's my husband!"

Owen's pale eyes shone on Alycia, as if to hold her there, as if he thought he owned her too.

"I really can't stand you anymore," she said, feeling a shiver. She was eager to leave now. "I don't want to see you again. If you won't accept the money, I'll give it to somebody else."

"That will be harder than you think."

"Somehow I doubt that," she said, turning toward the door.

"You know so little about money, Alycia. But what could I expect from an ignorant middle-class girl from Paris?" The cold, condescending voice pulled her back.

"Really?"

"People who don't have money think it's hard to come by and easy to get rid of. But those who have it know the truth. You just can't give it away. It dominates and changes you. It changes the way people think about you, what they expect of you—what you expect of yourself."

"Is that what happened to you?" she asked abruptly.

"It changes the heart—"

"Of which you know absolutely nothing," she answered, wanting to feel superior. But as she left the house her whole body trembled, and she was afraid that Owen knew exactly what he was talking about.

*   *   *

When Alycia told Richard about her confrontation with Owen, he was hardly agitated. "You should feel good," he encouraged her. "You found out what was making you angry, and you responded to it."

"But when I left him I was shaken again. I still am."

"Alycia, you're letting the man under your skin. I don't doubt that's where he wants to be, but if you're strong, and you are, you can keep him out."

"What about the trust monies? I'm still not sure what to do."

"Don't rush it. A solution will come."

"You're right, it's all up to me," she agreed, feeling better. Yet she wondered if she would have reached the same realization, or believed it as much, without Richard's reinforcement. She leaned on him more than she wanted, and she was getting used to it. Every noon hour was a fix, an injection of support and hope that sustained her for the next twenty-four hours. Sometimes, when Felice and Jean were asleep and Red was out of town, she didn't wait. Richard was always home to take her calls. He swore he was dying to call *her*, but they'd established strict and prudent rules to avoid involving Red or the children. Had she just gotten lucky with this sweet, caring man, she wondered whenever she hung up, or one evening would someone else answer the phone at Richard's house?

She found herself buying him little presents—cufflinks, a tie, socks—wondering if her thoughtfulness was more from insecurity than love. He always adored the gifts. "You've got great taste," he said one afternoon, sitting her on his lap, "and so do I—at least in women." She smiled back, but too slowly.

"What?" he asked, surprised. "You're not jealous—"

"Should I be?" she asked.

"You're the only one," he swore, stroking her cheek. "You're the only woman who's interesting enough to keep me hooked."

But the next morning he called to beg off from their noontime tryst. A neurosurgeon had asked him to assist in OR, and the complicated procedure promised to take hours. "That's okay, I understand," Alycia breathed, but she got off the phone quickly. She gardened, ran errands, worked on the

summer Red Cross Ball. Her imagination wouldn't shut off.
When she called Electra early in the afternoon, the words
perched on her tongue, ready to tumble out. She needed help,
a perspective. Instead, her tongue stayed tied. Now she understood why Electra hadn't been able to tell her about Terry
Donelson. Even between friends there had to be secrets sometimes. The doorbell put an end to the aimless conversation.
When she opened the door, Richard was suddenly there, in the
flesh, the tan, slender arms folded awkwardly.

"I'm sorry, rules or no rules, I had to come here,"
he apologized. "I thought you were mad at me this
morning . . ."

She put her arms around him and kissed him deliriously.
"Oh, I missed you! Thank you for coming. Thank you for
reading my mind again," she said, and led him upstairs. The
housekeeper was off for the day. Jean's school bus wouldn't
arrive until after three-thirty, and Felice had Girl Scouts.

Upstairs, Richard pulled the blinds closed and felt his way
to the bed, half out of his trousers already. His lovemaking
was even more desperate and reckless than hers. "I love
you," he whispered as he thrust into her. Were they both
falling in love? Afterward, lying in the crook of his arm as
Richard dozed, Alycia wondered if she'd ever been more
fulfilled. She watched, mesmerized, as his chest rose and fell,
the short, staccato breaths that kept a rhythm with her own.

Alycia lurched up and her eyes swam through the darkness.
Had she been dozing? Light spilled through the half-open
door. Something stirred in the room. As she focused on the
intruder, shame lodged in her belly like a hard, cold stone.

"Jean," she whispered. She looked down at Richard, as if
for help, but he was still sleeping. The fluorescent clock
hands read a quarter to four.

The boy didn't move. His unfaltering gaze locked on his
mother.

"Jean, please go."

He edged a step closer, as if to be sure for himself.

"Jean," she whispered louder, angry. He waited deliberately before he turned and closed the door behind him. She
roused Richard and they dressed quickly, but it seemed forever before he was out of the house.

She fixed herself coffee and tried to think. She heard Jean

moving upstairs. Red's plane from New York would arrive at five-thirty. She had promised to pick him up, but her mind raced in so many directions she wondered if she could drive. She puttered around in the kitchen, waiting for Jean to come down. She remembered that Felice would be home soon too. She called Richard but there was no answer. Folding her arms, she marched upstairs and knocked on Jean's door.

"Go away," ordered the estranged voice.

Alycia opened the door anyway. The room was not in its usual disheveled state. She couldn't believe Jean had cleaned it up since this morning. This was a first. What was going through his mind? Once the room had been filled with model battleships and war planes, but two years ago he had transformed it into a sports mecca—pennants, souvenirs, memorabilia —for the Lakers, Dodgers, and Rams.

"Can we talk?" Alycia began.

Jean turned at his desk. The hurt, angry eyes snapped at her. "About what?" he said sarcastically.

"I think you know." She walked up and knelt beside him.

"Oh, you mean your boyfriend?"

"Jean, you don't understand—"

"I understand," he shot back coldly, "that you don't love Dad."

"That's not true!"

"Then why did you do that? Who is he? This wasn't the first time, was it? Bobby Franklin's mother screws anybody—"

"Stop it, Jean!" She raised her hand. He flinched and drew back, starting to cry.

Alycia drew a breath. What had come over her? "Jean, I love you. I love your father. But there are some things you're too young to understand."

"Do you know how embarrassing this is? How humiliating?"

"Jean, I'm your mother, but I'm also your friend. I want you to trust and like me. It seems like you and I only end up butting heads. I know you're closer to your father, but you have to understand my feelings too."

She wondered if she was making any sense, or getting through to him. His foggy eyes drifted in and out of focus.

"You mean you don't want me to tell Dad about this afternoon, is that it?" he said.

She thought a moment. "No, I don't want you to tell him."

"Will you?" His voice suddenly hardened.

"I don't know," she said honestly.

"Bull. You're not going to tell him, ever."

"I said I don't know."

"I don't want you to see that man again," he ordered, as if he were his father's keeper. He suddenly looked stronger, bigger, more confident. More like Red.

"Jean, this is my life. I don't interfere with your happiness—"

"I don't care," he stopped her. "You're not to see him again. Is that clear?" His eyes had dried, filmed over, and now blazed into her.

She pulled back. Her heart rode into her throat.

"Is that clear?" he demanded.

She wanted to shake him by the shoulders, to make him realize he was insolent and unloving and selfish, nothing more than a bully, but she felt a wave of pity for him, and for herself. She understood, too, that there was no way out.

The words rose reluctantly from her throat. "Yes, I understand."

Jean's eyes swept away and he turned back to his desk, as if satisfied their relationship was not quite the same as it had been even minutes ago, and that he was the one better off for it.

Alycia was too shaken to drive to the airport. Red eventually arrived by cab, too ebullient over events in New York to be disappointed at being stood up. He had just purchased his first building in Manhattan, and the Los Angeles media already knew about it. He had presents for everyone, and over dinner, stories that riveted Jean and made him smile. Everything suddenly felt normal again, Alycia thought. Normal and empty.

When everyone was asleep, she called Richard. "I can't see you anymore," she said, letting him hear the sadness in her voice. She explained about Jean.

"I understand," he finally allowed, hanging on the line. The silence felt unjust and wrong, but for once Richard didn't have an answer. Love had nothing to do with this impasse, she knew, and was also powerless to overcome it. Alycia told Richard again how much he had helped her, how much she would miss him, and then they said good-bye.

The round, handsome face in the mirror squinted back in approval as Jean straightened his tie, rebuttoned his tweed jacket, and with a comb parted his fine strawberry-blond hair in the middle. Classes had already started so he had the upstairs boys' john at the Harvard School to himself. A residue of cigarette smoke from someone else irritated his nose and eyes, but he didn't want to leave. If he could kill ten more minutes here, another ten putting his books in his locker, then his father would arrive to pick him up for the father-son Chamber of Commerce luncheon.

Jean couldn't decide which he dreaded more—this snobby prep school for Los Angeles lawyers' and doctors' sons or the idea of disappointing his father by asking if he could transfer out. He was aware that as a sophomore he had to endure the baiting of upperclassmen, but he also knew that in a million years he'd never grow to like the rigid academic institution. His father wanted him to be a good student and end up at Stanford—that was pie in the sky. Jean knew he was quick and imaginative, but school had always felt like a prison. Bored and restless, he could never make himself focus.

He splashed water on his face and turned to go, when the door creaked open. The two seniors blocking his way wore blue-and-gold armbands.

"I've got a pass," Jean spoke up before they could hassle him. He pulled the piece of paper righteously from his pocket.

The taller boy, with wide green eyes and sandy hair that flopped over a narrow forehead, looked pained as he read. *"Jean Poindexter is excused at eleven-thirty, October 11, 1963, to attend a special luncheon with his father—"*

"Congratulations, you can read. Now give it back," Jean ordered.

"Hey, worm, it's not even eleven-fifteen. You're supposed to be in class," the other boy chimed in. He was the school's starting fullback and as wide as a bank-vault door. His nose suddenly twitched in the air. "Been smoking too? You're in deep shit, worm."

"That wasn't me—"

"And you're violating the Harvard School Honor Code, worm. Cutting class—"

"Bullshit," Jean said.

The tall one beamed at the smart-mouthed sophomore and slowly ripped up the pass. Jean looked on helplessly as the other boy pulled back his leg and punted Jean's books into a urinal.

"You think you're special, worm? Just because your dad donates a lot of money to this school? You think he can take you out of here whenever he wants—"

"You better shut up," Jean warned, feeling the anger rise in him.

"*What?*" the football player said with mock astonishment.

"Leave my dad out of this."

"Your dad's a prick," he continued, moving closer. "He's nothing but a publicity hound. Likes to be in all the papers. Real pretty boy. My folks can't stand him."

"You better take that back," Jean said, trembling.

"Oh, my, I'm getting scared."

"Take it back!"

"You mean *apologize?*"

Jean was quick enough to land the first punch, but it barely made a dent in the slab of beef. Suddenly he was in the air, being hurled into the mirror. The glass shattered against his cheek. His temples pounded like a drum, and blood dribbled from his nose. Jean heaved his chest and charged again.

"Don't you ever say that about my father—"

The second assault was no more successful, and this time he landed on the floor. The two boys gave up out of pity, sprinkling his pass on his head like confetti as they left. Jean picked himself up slowly. By the time he'd cleaned up and put his books in his locker, his father was waiting.

In the car Red surveyed his son's shiny cheek and bruised nose. He was alarmed, but he kept his voice calm. "You run into a bus, son?"

Jean's eyes bored straight ahead.

"Don't you want to talk about it?"

"I just want out of that school. I hate it."

Red paused. "Then what would happen? I'd put you in another school—and wouldn't you hate that too? You and institutes of higher learning don't get along."

"It's not my fault," Jean huffed.

"You have to give the school a chance, Jean."

"Why can't I just quit?"

"Quit?"

"I could go to work for you," he found the courage to say.

"Jean—"

"You know how well I get along with your business friends. I like them, and they like me."

True enough, Red thought as he drove. Sometimes Jean

was mature and sophisticated. He was a good listener, and a persuasive speaker.

"I could learn from you," Jean went on. "I've learned a lot already. Ask me anything about real estate. Go on . . . please . . ."

Red smiled reflexively. "Jean, you're fifteen years old—"

"I know how much land is worth on Wilshire Boulevard. I know what it's costing to build the Music Center. I know how many Negroes and Mexicans live in Los Angeles. I know about the Watts Towers. I know Mayor Yorty came from the Midwest. I know who's important at the Los Angeles *Times* . . ."

Watching the surprise cross his father's face, Jean knew he'd made an impression.

"I'll make you a deal," Red finally spoke. "You stick it out at the Harvard School, and I'll let you help me in the afternoons at work. Weekends too, if you want. And I'll pay you."

Jean, intrigued, bit his lip. "Doing what?"

"Research."

"What kind of research?"

"First, is it a deal?"

Jean knew the compromise was worth accepting. He could put up with the local Neanderthals if he had something to look forward to. And it was a foot in the door with his father. He extended his hand.

"You've heard about Century City?" Red asked.

"Sure, who hasn't?" Jean said. The development was continually in the papers. Just southwest of Beverly Hills, off Santa Monica Boulevard, one hundred and eighty acres of what had once been the Tom Mix movie ranch and later a back lot for Twentieth Century-Fox, had been sold to Alcoa. The aluminum company was developing the land. The Century Plaza Hotel was already up, and more buildings were under way, all using aluminum as their basic building component. The project would be as ritzy as anything on Wilshire Boulevard, Jean had read, or what was going on over at Bunker Hill. There, one hundred and thirty-six acres that represented the city's highest elevation had once boasted the Victorian mansions of the city's wealthy, but had now deteriorated to run-down housing for the poor. After years of debate, the city council had ordered everything be torn down for a new civic center. Work had already started. With the old height restrictions removed, soon there'd be a new acropolis of towering office buildings, apartments, parking garages, shopping malls. Downtown Los Angeles was in a building boom.

"Well, I happen to have my own project in mind," Red announced.

"Your own?" Jean felt a flush of excitement. "Like Century City or Bunker Hill?"

"I think so. I think it can be bigger."

"Where?"

"It's a secret."

"You can trust me," Jean said eagerly, and he meant it. He remembered his mother's secret, though he wasn't proud to keep that. He was staying quiet only to protect his father's feelings. Like those two morons at school, what they'd called his father—Jean would never reveal that either.

"We'll talk about it soon," Red promised.

The Chamber of Commerce luncheon was held not far from his father's new offices on Wilshire Boulevard. The room was crowded with faceless pairs but Jean felt the revering eyes as he and his father sat on the dais. After the meal he listened raptly to the speaker, an ex-Army pilot named Phil Anthony. One day in 1947, on a lark, Mr. Anthony said, he decided to put a swimming pool in his small home in east Pasadena. He operated a masonry-and-cement-contracting business, so he had the materials, and he persuaded two of his four brothers to help him dig the hole. Neighbors laughed. A swimming pool? Sure, hotels and motels had them, so did fancy homes in the East—but a little frame-stucco home like the Anthonys'?

When Phil finished on a sweltering July afternoon, and the cynics watched as his family frolicked in the cool azure water, the laughter died. One neighbor asked Phil to build a pool for him. It had never been the carpenter's son's intention to get into the swimming-pool business, but the right climate, a growing population, high disposable income, and a willingness to spend on the good life made the opportunity irresistible. Phil Anthony wasn't afraid to work hard or take chances—it was the American way. Today, Anthony Pools, Inc. was the largest builder of swimming pools in the world.

Jean applauded wildly. His imagination, which at school

roamed helplessly in all directions, took off on another journey. Why couldn't he do something like this? Los Angeles was growing faster than ever. What did people need? He knew for sure that a college education wasn't required to make a bundle of money—it was imagination and work that made the difference, just like Mr. Anthony had said. The real world was the best classroom of all.

"I'm going to make a million before I'm twenty-one," Jean proclaimed boldly as he sauntered out of the luncheon with Red.

Red smiled. "Really?"

"You'd be proud of me, wouldn't you?" he asked.

"I'm always proud of you."

"But I mean, making money, isn't that what you'd expect me to do?"

Red hadn't given much thought to Jean's future, other than to his receiving a good education and, one day, Red hoped, joining his real-estate firm. He liked that his son was ambitious, but Jean's impulsiveness needed to be channeled and harnessed, his awareness of the world widened. Red remembered his own impatience when he was younger, and Owen's arrogance, so he told himself to be understanding. But he also feared that without structure Jean would have difficulties. Working together after school was a way to teach him.

"I just want you to be happy," Red finally said.

Jean frowned. "What's that mean?"

"It means what it says."

Jean was still puzzled. "Being a millionaire will make me happy. It made you happy."

Red thought of the yacht he'd bought, anchored off Newport Beach, that he was lucky if he used once a year, and the mountain cabin in Sun Valley, which he'd purchased sight unseen and had never visited, and a vineyard in Napa Valley that he ran as a tax write-off. That's what his money had been good for, buying things he didn't need or couldn't enjoy. Suddenly he thought of Isabel and what money could never do.

"Hey, Dad, what's the matter?" Jean asked, staring at the solemn face.

Red recovered and forced a smile. "Let's go to my office before I drive you back to school. I want to show you my idea."

In his penthouse suite of the new Bank of America Building, Red led Jean around the four-by-six-foot scale model of greater Los Angeles that perched next to his desk. Red's army of properties were identified with miniature blue flags; those he wanted but had yet to acquire, a number almost equal to the blue, had green flags. Together, they flanked every freeway and were parceled almost evenly between strategic residential and commercial pockets, as if this were a mock battlefield and the enemy was anything still unconquered. Red fixed his gaze on a solitary red flag that adorned the corner of Lankershim, just off the Hollywood freeway.

"What's there?" Jean asked, following his father's stare. The location wasn't far from Toluca Lake.

"Trans-Universal Studios. It's mostly back lot and offices and storage. Four hundred and twenty-seven prime acres in the San Fernando Valley, ten minutes from Hollywood."

"You want to buy it, don't you?" Jean said with a knowing smile.

"Trans-Universal is in as bad shape fiscally as was Twentieth Century-Fox when it had to sell to Alcoa."

"What would you do with the land?"

"Something very special."

"Like a hotel?"

"Remember how much you liked Disneyland? I took you and Felice and Isabel there enough times."

"You mean when I was a little kid," Jean clarified.

"I'm going to start another one," Red said.

Jean's soft face squinched in confusion.

"Not a Disneyland exactly. But an amusement park," Red said. "I don't know what the theme will be, something for kids. Right in the heart of the city." He turned to his son. "What do you think?"

Jean digested the idea and tried to make up his mind. He knew it didn't matter if he or anyone else thought the idea was too wild or that his father should stick with brokering instead of developing. His father's face now had that look of determination that meant he truly wanted something.

"How much does the land cost?" Jean asked.

"It's not for sale."

"Then how can you buy it?"

"Because it will be for sale." Jean's eyes shined with incomprehension again. "You'll see," Red said. "You can help me."

Driving his son back to school, Red wondered if he really needed the Trans-Universal property. Developing an amusement park was expensive and ambitious, and there weren't enough hours in the day already. But he wasn't doing this one just for himself or the applause. When he told Jean the project would be special, he could never forget his last trip to Disneyland with Isabel, what she'd asked of him, and what he'd promised. Maybe this was all a dream, but he believed in it—and in Los Angeles anything was possible.

There was something else. Mighty, self-aggrandizing Hollywood was awash in a sea of red ink, floundering after a couple years of extravagant budgets for movies that had died at the box office. No matter how polished their smoke-and-mirror tricks, or what they wanted the world to think, Red knew the industry was hurting. He intended to be its savior whether he was wanted or not. He would start by buying the land from Trans-Universal, and he wanted the whole world to watch.

On the cool, overcast morning of November 22, Red breakfasted at the Los Angeles Country Club off Wilshire Boulevard. The most exclusive golf club in the city had a waiting list a country mile long, but Red, relying on friends, had been inducted quickly, though he had little time for his favorite sport even at Lakeside. The Los Angeles Country Club, however, was an ideal venue for doing business. Half his investors were members. His guest this morning was a square-shouldered man whose face had the cast of a patrician Caesar and who sported a custom-tailored silk suit and one-hundred-dollar wing tips. Burt Galton, whose savings-and-loan empire had a near-stranglehold on Los Angeles and an asset value of almost one billion dollars, liked to describe himself as an artist whose medium was money. He was usually brazen, loud, full of manic energy, and inclined to talk about his personal friendships with Baron Edmund de Rothschild, and the Russian composer Shostakovich. At the moment, however, he was the listener. As the two men sipped coffee in the hushed dining room overlooking the first tee, Red commented on the strict, unforgiving fairways, comparing them favorably to Hillcrest, the swank all-Jewish club where memberships were inherited and working oil wells interspersed the fairways. Burt Galton, a lapsed golfer like Red, chuckled along.

The two were good and trusting friends. Their companies had done business together for years.

Burt enjoyed flaunting his considerable wealth and influence, Red knew. He was proud of what he'd accomplished, and if he knew you appreciated that, as Red did, he was your friend for life and would do you endless favors. His success story, a by-product of the city's financial subculture, could have happened only in Los Angeles. As late as 1950, the man didn't have two nickels to rub together, and knew as much about high finance as walking on the moon. He was a committed but struggling screenwriter for RKO, out of work more than in, and in Hollywood it was easy to be branded a wash-up.

Bitter and broke, Burt parted ways with Tinsel Town and moved to Nevada, joining his aunt in her small mortgage business. To his surprise, he found he was good at managing money. Within a few years he opened his own mortgage company in Las Vegas at the time the federal government was chartering institutions known as savings-and-loans. Burt grabbed a couple of charters for Nevada. He might as well have been in the casino trade, because overnight his business soared. Flush with cash, he moved back to Los Angeles. First on the agenda was the purchase of the largest S&L in the growing San Fernando Valley, which he renamed Galton S&L. His timing was impeccable. The housing wave had just hit the Valley, and in ten years, as Red knew well, it had never ebbed. What Red appreciated even more was that the Hollywood crowd who had once spurned Burt Galton now kissed his butt. Producers came to him for backing, stars wanted to be seen at his flamboyant parties, executives even asked for rights to his old screenplays.

"So how go my negotiations?" Red got around to asking.

"Tough going," Burt announced in his flat voice. "Red, I wish we could be throwing a party, but instead it feels like a wake."

Red hunched forward uncomfortably.

"The boys at Trans-Universal want forty-five million."

"Come on—"

"God's truth."

"For four hundred and twenty-seven acres of unimproved land?" Red was too furious to speak. When he'd first asked Burt to help negotiate the sale, the studio response was unequivocal: the land between Barham and Lankershim was not for sale. Without Red pushing, Burt got a second call within a few days. Correction, the land *was* on the market— for thirty-eight million. Red had laughed but not walked away. He countered with twenty million, or the appraised value, whichever was higher. The studio tentatively accepted, but wanted the appraisal from someone they chose. Red balked and demanded an independent. The studio declined. Just when the deal appeared dead, Burt was called again. Forget the appraisal; if Red could come up with thirty-five million cash, it was his. Red countered with twenty-three million. To his surprise, the studio said it was amenable. A purchase-agreement was drawn up and approved by lawyers on both sides. The afternoon Red was to sign and write an earnest-money check, the studio called Burt. The board had reconsidered and wanted more money.

"They're playing with me again," Red said.

"It's what the boys do best."

Red didn't like the term "the boys"—it sounded too much like a secret fraternity—but Burt, a reinstated member, used it often. "This is not like Trans-Universal and I are making some movie together," Red complained. "This is a business deal. Do they know who I am?"

"Of course."

"Then why do they take me for an idiot?"

"Red, may I speak as candidly as a friend is entitled? If the negotiations are a pain, bow out. No one's got a gun at your head."

"I want the property. But I want to stop being treated like I'm one of the seven dwarfs. Maybe I should talk to them myself."

"Go ahead. See Walter Mandrake."

Red wondered if the surprise and disgust showed on his face. "Since when is Walter Mandrake with Trans-Universal?"

"Joined their board two weeks ago. You know Hollywood, it's musical chairs. Walter's protégée and current sweetheart, Lindsey Macintosh, is Trans-Universal's big star. They think she's another Marilyn. Walter was just calling in some markers. He personally asked the rest of the board if he could handle these negotiations alone."

Red slouched in his chair. "Walter and I don't get along. But a deal should be a deal."

"All right, I'll go back, one last time. Give me your best shot."

"Tell them forty million. Final and best offer. I'm crazy, but I want that land. I also want an answer within forty-eight hours."

Burt gave his best Hollywood smile. For a disturbing moment it reminded Red of Walter Mandrake's very white teeth. The two friends shook hands and parted. Charitably, Red knew, the land was worth nineteen to twenty-one million dollars. He was being played for a chump. And where was he going to come up with forty million dollars? Banks usually didn't lend on raw land. He had an unsecured three-million-dollar line of credit, but that was only a drop in the pond. He could sell some of his properties, but that seemed like compromise or retreat, and in this rising market he'd be a fool to give up anything. Besides, what equity he enjoyed was relatively small; all his buildings were either syndicated or highly leveraged.

For the rest of the morning he sequestered himself in his office with strict orders to his secretary not to be disturbed. Red was confident the forty-million offer would yield a contract. Walter Mandrake wasn't that stupid or vengeful. When the first deal had been ready to sign, Red had had enough cash and collateral to handle the debt. Now he needed outside help. The investors he began calling were mostly positive, but a few thought he was paying too much. Red had never been more persuasive. In the long run, he promised, escalating Valley prices and inflation would make forty million dollars seem like loose change. Just like Disneyland had, his amusement park would pay for itself in a couple of years. Red reminded any doubters of the deteriorating warehouse he'd purchased next to his father's office building years ago—everyone had quadrupled his money when Red sold the property to an Arab prince eager to start a downtown hotel.

By noon he had verbal commitments totaling thirty million. The ease of the effort astonished him. To retain control for himself, Red promised, as the sole general partner, that no limited partner was at risk. In the event the investment soured, everyone would get his money back. His own lawyers advised against giving guarantees, but in this case Red was positive. He made a mental note to call friends at the Los Angeles *Times*, the *Herald-Examiner*, and the network affili-

ates. Once Walter Mandrake came back with a contract, Red
wanted the media to cover every chapter of how he built his
amusement park.

The door burst open without a knock. Red was annoyed
until he focused on Jean, pale and upset but curiously elated.
"School got out early," he said, answering Red's unasked
question. The deep blue eyes squinted at his father. "Don't
you know?" he finally said.

Red pushed his chin up.

"The President is dead."

"What?" Red felt his body go limp.

"President Kennedy was assassinated in Dallas. Some kook
named Oswald shot him from a book depository."

Jean transformed his long arms into an imaginary rifle and
aimed out the window. Red tried to gather his thoughts as he
checked with others in the office. Everyone already knew of
the tragedy—but Red had asked not to be disturbed.

Jean was put to work in his usual after-school role—filing
news clippings, reading staff reports about market trends,
learning everything he could about amusement parks, particularly Disneyland. Red let most of the staff leave early. In a
stupor he flicked on the radio in his office. He kept asking the
same question as most of the country: How could fate be so
whimsical and unjust? Anger seemed like the wrong emotion—
too tiny, too futile. He remembered how he had survived the
war, arrogant and unafraid, knowing he would live because
there was some purpose for him. Now he wondered if there
was any purpose for anyone. Several calls to Alycia went
unanswered. Where was she, anyway? Red fixed himself a
Scotch, but it still felt like the earth had split under his
feet.

"What are you thinking about, Dad?" Jean peeked out
from a file cabinet.

"Nothing. Let's get out of here." Red stood and grabbed
his jacket.

"You bet." He grinned. "Man, this is like a holiday. No
homework."

The choked freeways took forever to navigate. When they
arrived home, Alycia and Felice stared at them distantly from
the couch, as if the two men were intruding on something.
Red thought they might be watching the news, but the television was off. He went to kiss them both. Alycia held back.

"Red, sit down," she said, upset.

"I'll just get a drink. Some shock."

"Please come here," she called to him at the bar. Red saw a tear roll from Felice's eye. Her fist quickly blotted it out.

He looked at his daughter with concern. "What is it?"

"Your father's dead," Alycia whispered.

Red squared his shoulders and squinted, as if confronting something he couldn't see. "My father?"

"I tried to call you, but you'd left. I'm so sorry."

"My father?" he said, still disbelieving. His stomach softened. "You mean Kennedy—"

Alycia shook her head. "No."

"When—"

"About an hour ago, at the house. Another stroke. There was nothing Harriet could do. She called an ambulance but Owen couldn't be revived. I told her I'd stay here until you came, then we'd all go over."

"Of course," Red breathed, dropping into a chair. He still couldn't focus. "How's Mother?"

"She said she'd be all right, but I'm not sure. We should go right now."

Red tried to rise, but he was wobbly. Jean came over and stood beside him. Then he got his father's car keys. On the ride to Bel Air Red took refuge in the uncomfortable silence. He kept wondering how he felt after the shock—sad or relieved or just indifferent? It was just like Owen to try to upstage history—dying on the same day as the President, stealing the show anyway he could. At least his father was consistent; Red gave him that. He searched himself for a purely benign emotion, but cold honesty intruded—the two had never gotten along, and no amount of sentiment or guilt could camouflage it. He was sorry now he hadn't made a final visit, but he doubted his father would have cared one way or the other.

When they arrived at the house, Harriet cried in Red's arms as they sat alone in the living room. She told him stories about Owen when he was younger and impulsive, funny stories that brought a smile to Red because they seemed so far in the past, about parties they'd thrown in the great house, how they'd raised Red—memories he'd tossed away but was glad his mother had remembered. They talked for hours. The whole house suddenly seemed alive with its dust-covered history. Red saw how strongly his mother loved her place in it, and he knew that no matter how huge and dwarfing for one woman, the house was not something she'd give up. He would not try to dissuade her. His father's finances had been pinched, but there was enough money for her and the upkeep.

"Mother, whatever you want or need, you'll let me know, won't you?"

"I love you, Red." Her hand trembled in his.

"At least for a few weeks, until things get settled, come stay with us," he said. "Your house will be fine. I'll make sure."

"No, dear. I think I'll stay here. I'll be more comfortable. You'll come visit—"

"Of course, starting tomorrow."

Handling funeral arrangements and the details of his father's estate kept Red occupied the next week. At the private graveside service, he had kept waiting to feel something, a final and firm peace, the end of Owen's era. Instead he was agitated. He could still see his father's cold, judgmental eyes and hear the scorn in his voice. Would Owen always be alive to him? It wasn't right. What would it take to finally chase his father from his life?

Leaving the cemetery, he channeled his thoughts to business. Neither Walter Mandrake nor Burt Galton had called all week. Red excused the omission because Burt was out of the country, and Mandrake would have read his father's prominent obituary in the papers. But by the end of the following week the long silence nettled him. He called Burt's office, only to be told by an impressed secretary that Mr. Galton was in Europe as the guest of the Spanish artist Mr. Picasso, and could not be reached. Red called Trans-Universal himself. Walter Mandrake phoned back in fifteen minutes.

"Hello, Red, how are you?" The voice was casual and easy with itself, as if they'd never had a misunderstanding. "Sorry for the delay in responding—I know you had a deadline—but I thought with your father's death you'd want to slow things down. We've lent serious consideration to your offer, I promise you, and we have a response—" A hand slipped over the phone and Mandrake's sultry whisper went out to whoever was in his office.

"What's happened, Red, to be honest," he picked up, "is there's another player at the table. It's a group, actually, a syndicate made up of friends of the studio. I can't tell you more than that, except it doesn't involve me—I'm staying neutral to help negotiate this—but they've put together an offer. Forty-three million, cash on the barrel head. That leaves you in second place."

Mandrake's dramatic pause was a hook Red was supposed to take, but he countered with a pause of his own. "Well, best of luck to you, Walter." And he clicked off.

The joy of one-upmanship lasted all of an hour. Red stared vacantly from his penthouse window to the panorama of a city that was growing like a field of riotous weeds. He *had* to have the Trans-Universal land. He knew he was negotiating with a bunch of cannibals—how could he feign surprise that they'd used his offer to fashion their own? He was also sure Walter was part of the other syndicate. If Red came back and offered forty-four million, would the opposition keep bidding, only to drop out when Red reached fifty million and was crowned chump of the year? Or did they really covet the land? Maybe they had their own plan; maybe their high bid was a way to force him out of the picture so they could end up grabbing the parcel for twenty million.

Red threw the dice one more time. If his dream was sound, did it matter what he paid? After a few days he called Mandrake and casually upped the bid to forty-five million. The voice on the other end sighed, with surprise or disappointment, Red wasn't sure. Hollywood specialized in ambiguity. Red hated it. Mandrake asked if he could call back. By the end of the day the bidding war had escalated to forty-seven million. Red responded in the morning with forty-nine million. Fish or cut bait, he said, and meant it.

"I'm getting sick of this myself," Mandrake echoed wearily. "I'll be back to you tomorrow. Ten sharp."

That night, after visiting with his mother, Red sat with Alycia in their living room over two glasses of wine. He was on edge and the drink didn't help.

"Why do you want the land so badly?" Alycia asked.

"We've been over this. It's for Isabel."

"I think it's really for you."

Red shook his head. "You don't want me to do this project, do you?"

"Everything feels out of control. You're paying way too much."

"So what?" Red said defensively. "Price isn't the issue."

"Beating Walter Mandrake is?"

"You've never understood business," he said, growing more annoyed.

"Outsmarting Walter Mandrake is like beating the tar baby. You get one fist stuck, then the other—"

"I can handle him."

"Red, you don't know the kind of man you're dealing with. He's not smarter or more clever or harder working than you—he can't hold a candle to you—but he is vindictive. You know what Electra told me?"

"I don't want to hear more gossip," he cut her off, starting toward his study.

"Don't leave," she begged.

He twisted his head back impatiently.

"Red, let's go upstairs. Please?" She walked over and put her arms around him. "I'm tired of being a stranger to you. You don't even know me anymore. But I still know you. The part of you I fell in love with, the sweet, vulnerable side, the honest side, the sharing side—I know it's still there. We're an enchanted couple, remember?"

She was suddenly teary and couldn't stop. Red was right, she didn't understand the business world. She didn't want to. She despised it because over the years it had turned Red into something she thought that even he didn't want to be.

"I want you to forget the Trans-Universal land," she said one last time. Her voice had turned firmer. "I have this feeling. It's about your father."

"He's gone," Red said succinctly, as if that were all that needed to be said.

"No, he's not. He still controls us. You still want to prove something to him. I'm only telling you what you told me when we were first married. I wouldn't believe you then. But it's you who won't believe it now."

Red felt himself melting a little. When he kissed Alycia there was a spark, a warmth he knew he'd shut himself off from. Was it because of his father? He thought how much he'd neglected Alycia. "I don't want you to worry," he said, kissing her again. "Forget my father. My instincts have never been wrong about real estate."

Alycia took a breath. "Do you want to make me happy?"

"You know I do."

"Then quit."

He was amused. "What are you talking about?"

"Quit everything. We have more money than we'll ever need. You don't have to prove yourself anymore. You've never had to prove yourself to me. How much success do you need?" She wrapped her arms around him fiercely.

"Alycia, please—"

"Think about it tonight. Really think about it. We'd have all the time and freedom in the world. We could do anything we wanted!"

Alycia pulled back. Red's eyes were deliberating. She knew she'd made an impression. "I love you," she whispered, and they went upstairs to bed.

The next morning, Red was in his office early, but he couldn't focus on anything but Alycia. Maybe it was time, if not to quit, at least to slow down. Why hadn't she told him sooner? She probably had. He never listened. Red walked to the window and gazed out on a city he treated like his personal empire. After he made the Trans-Universal deal he would call a stop to his acquisition binge. If he paid more attention to his wife and children, got from them the gratification he was always trying to win from business triumphs, maybe he wouldn't feel unfulfilled. Maybe he would finally have some peace.

Mandrake called promptly at ten. His voice was so unbearably cheerful that Red could see the teeth bright and shiny as piano keys. Good news and congratulations. The other group had backed out. The property was Red's—if he were serious about performing. Red was suddenly sure his chump theory had been correct, but did it matter? The Trans-Universal attorneys would draft a contract by close of business tomorrow. No more bullshit, Mandrake promised as he said good-bye.

When the thirty-page document arrived the next day, Red flipped past the boilerplate language. Closing on or about January 15. All cash, Trans-Universal would not take back any paper. No financing or other contingencies except for a boundary survey, which had to be approved and signed off within twenty days. Earnest money would be ten million dollars, and it was nonrefundable if Red or his partners walked before closing. No more bullshit? The terms were pathetically one-sided. Red had the contract promptly delivered to his attorneys. Let the hundred-dollar-an-hour soldiers fight it out in the trenches. The results would be academic. He could live with the contract. As his spirits brightened the rest of the day, the first calls he made were not to his investors but to his contacts in the media.

The house was alive with the kind of frenzied, unsynchronized Christmas Eve energy that Alycia always liked. Jean had a record blaring from his room—a new English group called the Beatles—Harriet wrapped last-minute presents under the silvered evergreen in the living room, Electra and her children, having moved back to Toluca Lake, had dropped over to share a bottle of Dom Perignon, and Alycia and Felice, expecting Red at any moment, were in control in the kitchen. It was really Felice who was in charge, Alycia knew. The pretty, willowy ten-year-old had insisted on orchestrating the entire dinner.

Alycia watched as her daughter opened the oven and gave the turkey a final basting, wondering again what made a child so efficient and capable. Alycia tried to be objective, but even her friends commented on Felice's remarkable competence and maturity. It was hard not doting on her daughter. After Isabel's death, Alycia found herself spending more and more time with Felice, as if her constant, hovering presence would somehow insulate her last little girl against harm. Felice sensed her mother's insecurity and didn't like the overattentiveness, but she didn't protest out loud, as if she knew she could steer her way around it. Lately, Alycia had given her a wider berth, and sometimes she wished that Felice were not quite so perfect, even if her daughter never made a show of it. Inadvertently she put pressure on her brother. Jean deeply resented his sister's golden glow. Goody Two Shoes, he called Felice.

"Turkey's ready, Mom," Felice announced, staring at the huge plump bird with satisfaction. "Where's Dad? It's almost five. I mean, how long do office parties *take*?"

"When people drink, they forget about time," Alycia advised.

"He promised to be here," she said, not wanting to be disappointed.

"Then he will. Your father almost always keeps his word. Don't you know that by now?"

There was an office party, Alycia knew, but she doubted Red had spent five minutes there. She imagined him secreting himself in a quiet room with charts and graphs and tables. The media were already treating his amusement park as a *fait accompli*. Kids had written asking about the rides. Alycia was still worried. Red had promised her he was slowing down, but the publicity and hype were blinding. She hadn't seen him so consumed since he'd bought his first acreage in the Valley. Maybe he wanted to make his last deal his best.

The front door swung open. Red, beaming his charming smile, had his arms loaded with presents. He dropped everything under the tree and embraced everyone, even Electra, whom he still hadn't forgiven for the way she'd treated Scotty. His buoyant mood brought everyone together, took the disparate energy and made it whole, and pushed Alycia's doubts away. They gathered around the tree, and Red insisted on passing out one present to everybody before they ate. Into Alycia's hands he thrust a tiny velvet box. She cracked it open, gasped, and gingerly took out a cluster diamond ring. "It's gorgeous," she breathed as Felice and Electra craned their necks to see.

After the dinner, when the children were in bed and Harriet and Electra had said good night, Alycia linked arms with Red and marched him upstairs. She had not needed another piece of jewelry, but Red's sweetness and thoughtfulness were the best surprise of all. The drought of affection had seemed interminable, she thought as he laid her gently on the bed and unbuttoned her blouse. His lips moved down her neck and breasts and made her forget. Flushed, she circled her arms around his shoulders. "I love you, Alycia Poindexter," Red whispered. She stretched out naked on the cool sheets and watched Red undress. His body was almost as taut and firm as when they'd married. Lying beside her, he moved his hand deftly over her thighs. His skill as a lover had not diminished either.

After they made love they dozed and woke in one another's arms. The bedside clock read midnight. "That was wonderful," Alycia said as she traced her finger over his chin. "I want us to do this every night. I want us to be close again." She wondered if she had the courage to tell him about Richard, if it was even necessary. The past had nothing to do with their future. With a murmur Red spread his fingers through her thick hair and gently pushed himself between her legs. Alycia wanted the night to go on forever.

The Monday of the second week of January was the clearest day Red had ever seen in Los Angeles. A tropical weekend storm had cleansed the city and brought it into focus under a powder-blue sky. He stood for a long minute at his office window like a soldier on sentry duty, his eyes skimming from building to building, knowing the owner and history of every property. His mind was jammed with facts and statistics, but all the knowledge in the world couldn't help him over his impasse with Trans-Universal. He had gone to contract, paid the earnest money by taking a personal loan and recollateralizing several properties, called investors and waxed eloquent on his dream—and still had come up $6.5 million short.

Despite his track record, heartfelt promises, and his own money in the deal, the forty-nine-million-dollar price tag made cowards out of the normally fearless. People who had made nothing but money from Red were suddenly counting their loose change, chipping in half of what they normally invested. Others balked on general uncertainty over the economy. A President had just been assassinated, and no one was in love with the man with a twangy Texas accent and funny ears and even funnier fiscal policies. Only Scotty, his good friend, who could least afford it, had antied up without a prod. Red returned to his desk and looked again at the escrow statement. In ten short days the purchase-agreement would be enforced. The possibility of walking and losing ten million dollars would make him a laughingstock. He had to dig deeper.

Burt Galton called a little before noon. The swaggering voice was full of apology for being out of the country. Red listened to a long-winded anecdote about Princess Grace of Monaco before he could interject a word about his deal with Trans-Universal. Burt already knew. Walter and the boys, he said, were pissing and moaning that Red was stealing their land.

"Burt, I'm having some trouble," Red confessed. The words felt awkward and unfamiliar on his lips. "Investors are a little tight right now."

"Then they're fools," Burt said. "This property is one of a kind."

"I'm looking for some new leads."

"You know I'd jump in, Red, but all my money is in my own stock. You ought to buy some too. Galton S&L. We're going places in a hurry, friend."

Burt offered several names, but when Red called, he encountered more polite resistance. Walter Mandrake phoned for a progress report and Red gave no hint of trouble. He began to think of selling a couple of his buildings, but he couldn't close in time to meet the Trans-Universal deadline. There was no recourse but to stay on the phone and wait for his luck to change. It had never been down for long.

"Making any progress?" Burt asked when he called the next afternoon.

"Some," Red said, uninspired.

"How much did you say you had in escrow?"

"Universal's holding my ten. I've got a little shy of thirty-three million in mine."

"Let me give you some help," Burt put in good-naturedly. "No one's tape-recording this, I hope," he added with a little laugh.

"Am I supposed to take this seriously?"

"I don't know. How serious is your situation?"

Red decided to listen. He was on the edge financially and out of tricks. As much as it had hurt, he'd instructed his attorneys to call Mandrake and ask if Trans-Universal would carry paper for a short term. Sorry, said the studio. Red's second request was for an extension of the closing. No again.

"Red, I think we're going to the moon," Burt said with his trademark enthusiasm.

Red smirked. "Maybe I'll go with you."

"I'm talking about my stock, Red. We're at seven now. Twelve is around the corner, and that's just a start. I have it on good authority that some pension and insurance companies are about to act. Get in on the ride."

"I'm low on risk capital, thanks."

"No risk, friend."

"I'm short on capital, period."

"Didn't I just hear the figure thirty-three million?"

"That's escrow money. I can't touch it."

"Red, read my lips. You're several million shy of making your dream come true. This is a business decision, not a legal or moral question. A couple hundred thousand shares of stock only has to go up a few bucks.''

"The money is in escrow, Burt," Red repeated firmly.

"Did I ever suggest taking it out? Good heavens me. I can't even give you a stock tip—that's insider trading." He paused. "Red, the big buyers are jumping in on Monday," he said, and hung up.

Burt was always a little full of himself, but in matters of finance the man rarely jeopardized a nickel for himself or his friends. Red called his broker. Galton S&L had been trading for weeks in a narrow range of seven to seven and one-half. A good solid-growth company, the broker reported, but he had no wind of a spectacular earnings quarter or anything that might light a fire under the stock. Red kept thinking. What was the worst scenario? He could put in a stop-loss on any order to prevent a downside. As for moving the money out of escrow and into the market, it might be illegal but not undoable. The officer at Bank of America overseeing the funds was a friend who didn't ask questions. Investors wouldn't find out. He would play the market until Monday, and if there was no jump in price, bail out and find another strategy. As Burt had said, this was a business decision.

The next morning he purchased one hundred thousand shares of Galton S&L at between seven and one-quarter and seven and one-half. His order alone bumped the stock up to eight. On Wednesday the price dropped a half-point on profit-taking. Red bought another one hundred thousand shares. By Friday he owned a total of half a million, along with one hundred thousand "call" options, which would make money for every tick up in the stock. The weekend he played with numbers. If Galton rocketed to twelve as Burt predicted, Red would be up five million dollars, counting the value of his "calls"; at fifteen, well over seven million. The numbers began to sound like notes in a symphony.

"How's the deal going?" Jean asked with adult intimacy as they tossed a baseball Sunday afternoon.

Red had given him a few details, educating him on the art of deal-making, but not about the stock play. No one knew about that.

"We close a week from tomorrow."

Jean nodded his approval. "You know Mom still doesn't like it."

"I know."

"She asked me to talk to you about it."

Red smiled. "You mean talk me out of it."

"I guess so. Is it a good idea? Are you paying too much?"

"Everything's fine, Jean. Trust me."

Jean's arm levered back and he catapulted the ball high in the air above his head. It floated forever before he centered himself underneath and it thudded into the web of his mitt. "You know I do," he said.

Red was at his office at six Monday morning, nine New York time, for the market opening. Galton S&L began climbing and never took a breather. By closing it was up a point and a quarter. An ebullient Red called Burt to thank him. "All my friends are making money, except Mandrake," he confided. "Mr. Good-Tan doesn't trust me or the market. Maybe that's okay, because I don't trust him anymore."

"What's the matter?"

"I just found out the sneaky little bastard is using you, Red. There was no syndicate bidding against you for the land. It was all a fabrication. Walter Mandrake's brainstorm. The boys wanted top dollar, and promised Walter a cut if he got you up."

Red was quiet.

"I feel bad, Red. I think you've got grounds to get out of the contract."

"Don't worry about it." Red expected to be furious but he wasn't. He'd already figured on Mandrake's deviousness. The last laugh would be his when he developed the land. On Tuesday, Galton S&L ratcheted up to nine and a half on almost half a million shares. The extraordinary volume earned a small article in the *Times*'s business section the next morning; analysts from several major brokerage houses were now recommending the stock. Red almost gloated as he watched the shares continue climbing Wednesday, closing at ten and seven-eights.

Another article on Galton S&L appeared in the Thursday *Times*, but Red didn't see it until late in the day. At the opening bell the stock began to drop. Red, assuming profit-taking, didn't worry until it had fallen two ticks. It was only noon New York time. An hour later, shares had plunged another two points and rested at seven.

Red couldn't get Burt on the phone. Red's broker took his call with little sympathy. He was surprised Red didn't know. It was in all the media. The SEC was investigating Burt Galton on insider-trading charges.

"Sell my shares, the calls, everything," Red said quickly. He pushed back in his chair and felt his world caving in. How could he have been so stupid? A well-meaning Burt had blabbered his tips to everyone in the world—that was how he made and kept friends. And ruined them. By the time Red's sell order was executed he'd lost more than two million dollars. The stock had collapsed so quickly the price had jumped below his stop-loss orders.

Red tried reaching Burt again. After a dozen rings he knew. His friend was already signing his confession for the SEC. It didn't matter what he told them, a paper trail would lead investigators to Red's doorstep anyway. How long would it take the dominoes to fall? The invested money would be traced to the violated escrow fund. Betrayed investors would be outraged. Lawsuits would start and take years to settle. His deal with Trans-Universal was over, his ten million dollars gone. His career as a developer, which had taken two decades to build, was finished too. He had committed at least two felonies, maybe more. How much time would he have to serve?

The media would have a field day. Some would look at him with pity, but the final judgment would be one of greed and recklessness and stupidity. Then he thought of Alycia and Jean and Felice and Harriet.

Red sat immobilized for a long minute before pulling two sheets of blank paper from his desk. When he was finished writing he was exhausted. He phoned Scotty at his city clinic and asked if they could meet at a bar in the Valley.

"It's three in the afternoon, not the morning," Scotty replied. "And I'm on the wagon, Red."

"Then this will test you, because I'm going to drink like a fish."

"Celebrating something?"

"Our friendship. You can't turn that down."

"Give me an hour," Scotty said.

"I'll have a head start on you."

Approaching Red's table through the shadows of the bar, Scotty looked tanned and rested. He brimmed with a confidence Red hadn't seen when they last met. Red rose and offered his sweaty hand. He wondered if Scotty noticed.

"Willpower," Scotty complimented himself as he sat and ordered a ginger ale.

"I'm impressed, no kidding."

"I'm a new man—and it's going to last," Scotty swore. "I just got a staff appointment at Kaiser Hospital. Who would have guessed that Dr. Scott L. Madigan, fervid opponent of socialized medicine, would work for the enemy? But it's a respectable start for me, and I've even got a girlfriend these days."

"To Scotty," Red said, raising his glass, "and to all brave men of the Second World War."

"To heroes. To you," echoed Scotty. He gave Red an admiring wink.

"When I'm done drinking, you can shoot this glass off my head," Red said cavalierly.

"What?"

"The glass. Don't you remember that night at Lakeside? We were quite a pair." Red finished his drink and ordered another. "I had you, Scotty. Admit it."

Scotty's eyes lit with mischief. "Completely. It was damn funny of you."

"What we need in this life is more imagination and humor. Puts everything in perspective. Especially the persistent pain of living."

"That sounds grave. You all right?"

Red stared off. When his eyes swam back to the table they tried to appear calm and in focus.

"I've got something for you," Red said, pulling an envelope from his jacket.

Scotty slid the check out. "Did I win the Irish sweepstakes?"

"It's your money. The Trans-Universal deal isn't going to work. Just as well—a pain in the butt. I guaranteed all investors their principal."

"What should I do with it?"

"Spend it on your girlfriend. Do me a favor, Scotty?"

"Sure. You never ask for anything."

Red gave a sad, half-throated laugh. "Forgive me."

"Red, I think you're drunk."

"You're probably right. Help me home, will you?"

Jean used his key to enter the empty house. Thursdays his mother took Felice to ballet, and the housekeeper was off, but he'd hoped to find his father. He had shown up at the office as usual after school, only to be told his dad had left half an hour before. Lakeside, he figured. Jean thought of running over. His father rarely had time for golf anymore, but last summer he'd taught Jean the game, and now he played as often as he could.

Jean helped himself to leftovers from the fridge. Then he put his Beatles record on the living-room stereo and settled on a lounge on the back patio. The music drifted through the screen door and made him feel lazy enough to give up the thought of tracking down his father. The sun shimmered off the lake. He loved this view, loved the entire house, he thought not for the first time. His father had had a sharp eye when he bought the Toluca Lake property—it had shot up dramatically in value over the years—but then, his father rarely made mistakes in real estate. He had once confided to Jean that he'd forged Grandfather Owen's signature to buy his first parcel of Valley land, but was that really a mistake? Jean knew his father and grandfather had never gotten along. His father had tried to hide the schism, but Jean had read between the lines, and he didn't even care. All that counted was making things happen for yourself. If you never took chances, you never accomplished anything.

Jean drifted upstairs and opened his algebra text. *If three men can dig a ditch in four hours, how long will it take two men to dig the same ditch* . . . Someone had crossed out "men" and penciled in "women," but Jean didn't see the humor. He finished the problem without difficulty. He was doing better in school and had pushed his average to a B. The bargain he'd made with his father to stay at the Harvard School was one he intended to keep, though when he graduated he was sure there'd be another disagreement. College held no interest for him. He wanted to work for his father, fulltime, as soon as possible. The knack of selling and the imagination to dream were his born gifts. He just had to prove it to everyone, starting with his father.

And he would. All those properties his father had accumulated, a kingdom that spanned the width and breadth of metropolitan Los Angeles, one day would belong to him. Without anyone making promises, Jean knew this was his birthright.

He heard the front door open. Rough, carefree voices spilled in. Jean leaned back in his chair, listening. Dr. Madigan was politely trying to say good-bye but his father wouldn't let him. Jean moved to the top of the stairs at the very moment the two friends drifted outside. He just had time to glimpse the familiar silver-plated revolver in his father's hand. Puzzled, he crossed the hall to the window that looked out on the large rolling lawn. On the lake, brightly plumed mallards paraded in formation without a care. Jean rapped his knuckles on the window, but no one glanced up. He watched as his father placed a shot glass on his head and knelt in the grass, grinning. The gun had changed hands. What was going on?

"Go ahead—shoot it off my head!" his father challenged Dr. Madigan.

"Red, be serious—"

"Don't worry. The chambers are empty."

"Then how can the gun fire?"

"It can't. Consider this a dress rehearsal."

"What are you talking about?"

"Scotty, I want you to practice your aim."

"For what?"

"A joke."

"On whom?"

"A man named Walter Mandrake."

"Red, this is making no sense—"

"You remember dear Walter, don't you?"

"I hate him," Scotty said.

"Then pull the trigger!" his father commanded.

The window turned foggy with Jean's breath, and his fingers stuck to the glass. "Dad . . ." he said, but his voice didn't carry.

Dr. Madigan steadied the revolver in two hands.

"Dad!"

His father flinched, as if he'd heard Jean, but not enough to disturb the shot glass. The explosion was as sudden and puny as a firecracker. His father's head snapped back and he fell softly into the grass, on his side, the muscular neck angled out. Dr. Madigan darted over and shook him roughly. That was all Jean remembered, except for the rush of blood through his heart as he sank under his own weight.

Felice knew she would always remember that everyone wore black, the women with veils that hung like spiderwebs over their faces, the men somber and grim as soldiers. They hovered around her like giants as she perched on a couch next to her mother and brother, swooping down to kiss her on the cheek or to say how sorry they were or what a great man her father had been. She smiled politely and tried to appear brave. But her heart thudded so loudly she was afraid the entire room would hear.

In the kitchen Electra and Carmine Bradbury warmed casseroles and opened bottles of liquor. Grandmother Harriet was secluded in a corner, knowing even fewer people than Felice did. Last night, sharing the same bedroom, Felice had crawled into her grandmother's bed when she'd heard her crying. Her body felt bony and rough and cold. Felice snuggled her arms around her and they'd cried together. No one had slept. When she'd closed her eyes, Felice had seen her father dressed in his dark blue suit, and the red suspenders she'd given him for a birthday present. He was floating in the clouds. She thought it must be heaven. He looked asleep but he seemed to be smiling too. He was very happy, and he knew Felice was watching him. She could almost reach up and touch him.

Before dawn her grandmother was snoring roughly. Felice slipped into Jean's room. He was still sleeping. The room was picked up now, but she could still see signs of damage. Two days ago, after the accident, Jean had destroyed nearly everything. Bookshelves had come down, old model airplanes had crashed against walls, windows had been broken with his bare hands. A doctor had come and given him something to calm him down. She had never seen her brother like that. He'd always had a temper and liked to pout, but this time he'd gone crazy, frightening everyone. At this morning's funeral service he was better, but he still refused to talk to anyone, as if he blamed the whole world for what had happened to his father. Felice said nothing, but she was resentful. What right did her brother have to feel singled out? What about the rest of the family—didn't he care how they felt? Were they only supposed to feel sorry for Jean? He had always thought he was special, that he was closest to their father. Felice wondered if that's what she really resented.

She fidgeted on the couch and gripped her mother's hand more tightly. It was her mother she loved the most and felt the sorriest for. Her mother had always been her favorite person in the world. She was beautiful and full of life, but when Isabel had died she'd changed. Felice had pretended to everyone that she didn't notice and that everything would be fine again. That would be impossible now.

Before going to bed last night, she'd heard her mother stirring in her father's study, rummaging among papers, opening desk drawers. Suddenly there was a deep and surprised silence. Then her mother had begun to cry.

"Mom, are you all right?" Felice had called from the top of the stairs, suddenly afraid. "Mom? Mom!"

"Go to bed, darling," came the tired, sad voice.

Felice had done as she was told, but she knew something was wrong.

She rose now from the couch and drifted unnoticed into her father's study. A group of men stood awkwardly talking about Scotty Madigan. The shooting was an accident, they said, a prank that had gotten out of control. The police, after talking to Scotty and Jean, who had seen it happen, said the same thing. Felice didn't blame her father's best friend. She was sorry for him. Her mother said Scotty had taken a trip somewhere to rest.

The men began talking about real estate. Felice didn't know anything about the deal her father had been working on. She listened carefully but still didn't understand, except they were saying her father had done something wrong. She didn't want to believe it—Jean would never accept that, she thought—but maybe her mother would tell her. Maybe it was true.

Her head turned as a stranger peeked into the study. The deeply tanned face was framed by gray, well-groomed hair. He was handsome, and he smiled at Felice, but when he moved closer she turned away. She didn't like the smile. It was how a wolf might look at you, she thought. She watched as he strolled into the living room and approached the couch. Her mother stood with an effort and her eyes narrowed. Her hand came up and struck the man across the face. The room turned quiet.

"Get out of my house, Mr. Mandrake," her mother ordered.

"Mrs. Poindexter, I came to say how sorry I am."

"Get out!" Her voice filled with cold fury. Felice had never seen her like this.

Electra appeared and slipped her arm comfortingly around her mother, and the man, his smile fading, turned quietly and left.

"Why were you so upset by him? Who was he?" Felice asked after everyone had gone home. "Please tell me."

"I can't explain it to you, darling."

"Why not? I'll understand. I promise."

"Maybe someday."

"When?" Felice demanded. She didn't like being left out, and she wanted to help her mother.

"Someday." Her mother hugged her.

Jean was on the back lawn, gazing at the lake. He hadn't moved for half an hour. Felice wondered what he was thinking, and if the world would ever be the same for any of them again.

BOOK FOUR

The twenty-fifth-floor lobby of Galbraith Life and Casualty Company was a blend of chrome and glass and marble, a seamless flow of abstract, sensuous shapes bathed in filtered light and suggestive shadows. The low-slung leather chairs looked too immaculate to sit in, the tables and ashtrays dusted every hour. The visitor, uncomfortable in the elegant setting, found himself drifting to a window and the vista of downtown Los Angeles, a view that extended no more than several miles, where a wall of pollution rose up intransigently. Closer in were several modern high-rises where five years ago had stood squat, flat-roofed buildings. The growth and change of the entire city had not gone unnoticed by the visitor. It was 1966 but it felt like the year 2000. The distant future was here. Under a blinding summer sun the man watched as scurrying miniature figures darted into gleaming buildings and streamlined automobiles—no one stayed outside for long. This was an air-conditioned city.

The visitor's glance jumped back to the wall of smog. It was not just smog, he saw now; there was smoke too. Driving here, he had heard the plaintive wail of sirens, a cacophony of pitches that suggested fire trucks, police cars, and ambulances, and now he could see actual flames spidering up into the gray sky. The belching smoke seemed to climb from the canyons separating the San Fernando Valley from Hollywood and Beverly Hills. The sky was assuming an orange cast that suggested the inferno was building, not diminishing. It had a beguiling beauty. The visitor had heard of the city's legendary brushfires that could destroy thousands of acres in one swoop, and the earthquakes, and the violent rains that washed houses into the ocean. He was relieved to be here only as a visitor. To live in this city, he thought, would be to get used to such calamities.

Brother Andrew turned when the receptionist called his name.

As he walked in his simple habit toward the president's office, secretaries gave him furtive glances and the monk smiled back softly. At over six feet and solidly built, and with his rugged, angular face, he had to look strange in a monk's garb. He accepted being a curiosity figure, though he would never feel comfortable being the center of attention—that position belonged only to God. Brother Andrew was merely his reluctant emissary. In 1961, after his first fund-raising effort, his abbot had thrown his arms around Andrew and with the entire monastery congratulated him on his success. He alone had raised almost half a million dollars, and for the next five years the Cistercians' work among the poor had flourished. But now money was running low. Andrew had been dispatched once more into the world of wealthy, influential laymen and a privileged social universe that, even though he knew it well and could carry on a conversation with even the most knowledgeable host, left him uneasy. He was and always would be a monk who had taken vows that separated him from worldly wealth and its temptations. His interactions now were but temporary, justified for the ultimate and necessary end of doing God's work. Having traveled hard for months, inhabiting cheap motels and renting cars that broke down whenever he was in a hurry, the monk looked forward to returning to his New England monastery.

"Brother Andrew, you look as fit and youthful as ever." The president, whose name was Evan Chambers, rose from behind his gleaming desk and reached for the monk's hand. Andrew received it warmly. He remembered the heavyset, hawk-faced executive as shrewd and political. He'd let his hair grow over his ears and even sported a mustache—like half the men in the country, it seemed—but there was no disguising the cleverness mirrored in his steady dark eyes. The monk's appearance had changed a little too—he had a neatly trimmed beard, which lately had shown spots of gray.

"And how do you find Los Angeles, Father?" the executive inquired. "You managed to stay away from our big barbecue?"

"How long will the fire go on?"

"That depends on the winds. It won't last forever. The city will survive. It always does."

"I don't know," Andrew opined as he sat. "Yesterday I took it on myself to walk through Watts—"

"That was brave of you."

"I was fine, really. But most of the stores were still boarded up. The riots must have been terrible. Is anything being done?"

"There's some relief, but it's entangled in city bureaucracy. And the Negroes—excuse me, the *blacks*—are very hostile. They want help, but it has to be on their terms. Everyone's fighting. Frankly, it's a pretty ugly time, Father."

"I don't care for confrontations either, but they are inevitable, and one can't run from them. Like any repressed people, the blacks feel great rage, centuries of it, that must be addressed. Don't you think so, Mr. Chambers?"

The executive nodded, but with neither sympathy nor great interest. He had a business to run, and Andrew knew he was trespassing on his time.

"It's certainly not ugly here," Andrew continued, "not downtown. Everything looks new and busy and successful. Like two different worlds."

Chambers smiled disarmingly. "Success is a most transient judgment, Father. With heavy debt service and inflation, a corporation has to check its balance sheet every day to know if it's still in business."

Andrew returned the smile, but felt a familiar discomfort and helplessness. He'd heard the same story almost everywhere this trip. Companies were cutting out the fat, tightening their belts.

"I'd like to tell you what the Trappists have done in the last five years, work that would have been impossible without your generous help . . ." Andrew spoke eloquently of projects in Appalachia, in Africa, Mexico, South America. Chambers' eyes registered approval but hardly burning enthusiasm.

"What did we donate last time?" he finally asked.

"Fifteen thousand dollars. Today, with inflation—"

"Father, I'm afraid the best we can do is one-third of that. I'm sorry to disappoint you. It's not just the uncertain times, or maybe it is. I sit on several foundations and charity boards—everyone wants more, but people are giving less."

Andrew knew he should be grateful for receiving anything. As hard as he tried, as many sources as he tapped, his pledges were well below what he'd collected five years ago. He had begun to feel like a failure.

"Thank you for your support," Andrew said gracefully as he rose to leave. At the door he hesitated. "Could you perhaps tell me one thing, Mr. Chambers," he asked, his face

pinched in curiosity. "When I was last here I attended the
Red Cross Ball. I met a woman, Alycia Poindexter. Perhaps
you know her?"

"Yes, I do, Father."

"She was very generous. I was hoping to approach her
again."

"To be honest, I don't think you should. The woman has
had several tragedies."

"Oh, dear," Andrew said, startled.

"One of her children, a retarded girl, died in a drowning
accident. Two years ago, her husband was killed in a bizarre
prank. Worse, there were some serious financial improprieties
that still haven't been sorted out. Alycia has been placed in
some compromising positions. I like and respect the woman,
but I don't think she's handled herself properly. We sit on the
same board—the Helen Mayer Foundation . . ." He cut himself short as a secretary drifted in.

"I'm very sorry to hear that," Andrew spoke, still upset.
He remembered well Alycia talking about her daughter, Isabel, and how proud she was of the girl's progress. The monk
was impelled by his natural curiosity to push for more details,
but discretion told him it was time to slip away.

Alycia drifted through the crowded Renaissance room of
the Los Angeles Museum of Fine Arts, waiting for Carmine
Bradbury. Without success she tried to focus on the dark,
richly colored works of the Masters. She was reminded of
countless trips to the Louvre as a schoolgirl—in more innocent times. Her thoughts kept jumping now to her just-
completed strategy meeting with her attorneys. Except for
Scotty, every one of Red's Trans-Universal investors was
suing his estate. They didn't want just their money back, they
wanted punitive damages too. Part of Alycia understood, but
part of her resented their greed. What about all the good
things Red had done—the investors had made money from
him in the past, lots of it, more than they'd lost on this deal.
And who was supposed to be punished now—her? She had
decided to fight back.

"Sorry I'm late, dear."

Alycia turned and gave Carmine a kiss on the cheek.
"Thank you for meeting me on so short notice," Alycia said.
She had called her friend only this morning. What was weigh-

ing on Alycia's mind was not yet urgent, but it would soon reach that stage.

"I need to know your thoughts about my place on Helen Mayer," Alycia began as they found a bench in the corner. "My term comes up pretty soon."

"I'm aware," Carmine said candidly.

"Then you're also aware that certain board members—certain men—want me to step down."

"Yes, I am." Carmine's voice was all business.

"I don't intend to do that. My record speaks for itself. Revenues are flat, but more community causes are benefiting, and long-terms goals for the foundation have never been clearer . . ."

Carmine stared off at one of the paintings, a Uccello with bold, pure geometric lines. "I know your record, Alycia. Your accomplishments are admirable. Even the men on the board recognize that."

"Then why do they want me off?"

The tall, pretty countess cocked her head at Alycia. "But you already know, Alycia. The shadow of your husband's legacy seems to grow longer, not shorter. One reason is, you won't let it go away. You keep fighting the lawsuits and prolonging everyone's memory of a most embarrassing situation. Evan Chambers feels your stubbornness is increasingly hurting the foundation. Certain benefactors will not contribute to an organization steered by someone whose past they find . . . unwholesome."

"And there are others who like me and my work and wouldn't care if I'd been married to Al Capone."

"My dear, you miss the point. We're talking about the individual as a standard-bearer, an example, a paragon."

Alycia was startled. "I thought we women were supposed to stick together. That's what you've always said. You sound like you're on Evan Chambers' side."

"I am decidedly not, Alycia. You know I've always tried to stand up to the men. But I also want what's best for the foundation. That's why I put you on the board originally. Have you forgotten?"

"No," Alycia said, backing down.

"Then consider the greater good."

"Maybe you don't understand," Alycia said, "I don't excuse Red for what he did. It's because I feel some responsibility for his actions that I want to stay on the board—I want to make up for his mistakes. But I need your support."

"Then please make it easy for me by dropping those lawsuits that always get in the papers."

"Carmine, those people are behaving like scavengers and parasites. I respect my husband and his memory. You and the rest of the world might think of Red in light of his scandal, but I remember him as loving, generous, and truthful."

"You're taking this much too personally, Alycia," Carmine warned. "It's just business."

"What you mean to say is, it comes down to money. Money's a way of settling scores and correcting imbalances and earning forgiveness. It repairs the damage, but it also causes it. Money divides people and turns them against one another. I think that's wrong."

"My dear, to hear you talk, it sounds like you're making a show of your virtue."

"I don't mean to," Alycia clarified. "I don't want to be considered a martyr just because I want to do what's right. But I'm not stepping down from the board. If people don't like that, they can vote me out."

"I would hope it never comes to that," Carmine said, and with a hug for Alycia, went on her way.

Driving home, Alycia wondered if she'd said the right things. There was a simple answer to her problems: write the foundation a very fat check and she'd have her board seat for another term. Alycia had the money. Despite her considerable legal expenses, she had reaped huge profits from selling Red's buildings and liquidating his business. Jean had opposed her—at the tender age of sixteen he'd wanted to take over his father's corporation—and they'd argued endlessly. "Those are mine. Dad was going to give them to me," he would say when she began selling the buildings. Then he would slam the door to his room and not speak to her for days. Alycia was sorry—she was sorry for Jean—but she was finished with the business world and what it had done to her family.

No, she would not write the foundation a special check, she decided, nor was she going to beg anyone to let her stay. She hated politics as much as she did business. Carmine was supposed to be an ally, but Alycia had begun to see that the countess wasn't someone to rely on. She seemed to have principles, yet they didn't run very deep.

Alycia found her house empty. Depressed, she settled with a glass of wine on the patio. Jean had graduated from the Harvard School in May and now had a summer job, so he wouldn't be home until six. Felice was with Harriet for the day. It was at times like this that Alycia wanted to sell the house. Without Red it was the emptiest place on earth, and the painful memories didn't fade fast enough. Immediately after the death there had been so many hands to hold, so many details to look after, that Alycia hardly had time to mourn or be alone. As difficult as Jean was at first, and still could be, he was relatively on track. Felice, however, had only become more troubled. Despite Alycia's efforts to help, her daughter's gift of efficiency and cheerful organization had vanished. Her once impeccable schoolwork suffered. Friends seemed hard to come by. Nothing made her happy or proud of herself. Alycia tried to remember that Felice was only twelve, not an easy age under any circumstances, but she worried a lot for her daughter.

This was no time to sell the house and destabilize anyone further, Alycia knew. Maybe when Jean settled in college or a career, and Felice was stronger.

When the doorbell sounded Alycia hoped it was Electra. They saw one another often now. Her friend had given up writing, to Alycia's disappointment, and had settled into the social circle into which she'd been born. Electra never offered an explanation other than she was tired of being a maverick. It was ironic, because the rest of the country was caught up in a flurry of social change, while Electra was suddenly becoming more conservative. Maybe it was a function of her age, thought Alycia, but whatever anger or discontent had once been in her friend now seemed purged. Electra was embarrassed by references to the past ten years, her escapades with Water Mandrake in particular, so the two friends' conversations stayed in the present. Electra had hosted the Red Cross Ball last year and would be in command again this summer. She had a new boyfriend of the old guard named Randolph Fitzhugh—he was fifteen years her senior and twice as rich as she, the sort of courtly gentleman she could respect and who was more than pleased to have a young and attractive society woman on his arm. Alycia was happy for Electra. She missed the rebel in her friend, but Electra had turned her life around.

When Alycia opened the door her eyes jumped to a tall,

muscular figure in a coarse brown habit who stood so still he didn't seem real. The sun washed over the pale, handsome face, highlighting the angles of his nose and cheeks, and a neatly trimmed salt-and-pepper beard. His eyes shone with warmth and understanding. Alycia could only stare. The monk responded with the slightest of bows and a blush of shyness.

"I hope this is not an intrusion," he said, standing ever more erect. "My name is Brother Andrew . . ."

The monk extended a hand but saw that Alycia Poindexter was slow to accept it. He wondered if he should be here. When he'd heard from Evan Chambers of Alycia's difficulties, his deep sympathies had compelled a visit. The search for meaning, for an understanding of God's hand in letting any of his creatures suffer, made Andrew feel inadequate. He, the interpreter of God's will, had no explanation for tragedy, only a wellspring of sympathy and love for the sufferer. Yet from experience he knew that some preferred to keep their grief private, resenting even the most well-meaning heart. Andrew took a step back.

"We met five years ago at a charity benefit, a Red Cross Ball," he explained. "Just yesterday I learned how difficult these last few years have been for you. I wanted to say that if I can help in any way, you have only to ask."

Andrew clasped his hands patiently in front of him. He saw Alycia's face soften, as if her memory finally had made the association. Still, he didn't think she wanted him here.

"Yes, I remember," she said, studying him. Alycia wondered if she sounded or looked too distant, too inconvenienced. She was just surprised. The monk had impressed her the first time they met with his thoughtfulness and wit, and here he was, just as warm and gracious, out of nowhere.

"And Jean and Felice?" Andrew continued. "How are they?"

"You remember my children's names?"

He smiled apologetically. "I have one of those undiscriminating memories that picks up everything and lets go of nothing. Are they well?"

"Thank you, yes," she said. "And you?"

"I dare not complain. God gives me health and the opportunity to serve him in many ways. I consider myself a fortunate man."

"Are you fund-raising for your abbey again?" she asked.

"That is my mission," he said, his smile fading a degree,

"but I've not been nearly as successful as on my last trip. I hope it's not my cause, but people seem more reluctant to give . . ." Andrew stopped himself, his face prickling in embarrassment. "Please, forgive me, I didn't come to talk about that." He extended his hands and wrapped them consolingly around Alycia's. "I must be going. Accept my deepest sympathies—you and your loved ones will be in my prayers."

He turned to leave, but Alycia's voice stopped him. He had not heard what she said, but when he spun back, she was asking if he wanted coffee. The door had opened wider.

"Father, you do drink coffee, don't you?" she said.

"Yes, of course."

It was Alycia's turn to blush. "I'm sorry, you probably have an appointment somewhere . . ."

The monk wondered if he was rude to want to leave so precipitately. Perhaps Alycia did need to talk, to share her feelings. He was here to help, wasn't he? He had no appointments. His business in Los Angeles, as unsuccessful as it had been, was finished. Tomorrow he returned to his abbey to less than a hero's welcome.

"I'd be happy to accept your invitation," Andrew replied graciously.

The coffee was put on and they settled in the living room. Alycia spoke about the changes in Los Angeles the last five years, local politics, what was happening in Vietnam. After ten minutes Andrew straightened impatiently. What was he listening to? Did even Alycia know what she was saying? He saw such frustration and pain in this poor woman.

"Forgive me," Andrew interrupted when he could not bear the masquerade any longer. "I don't mean to be impertinent, but I know something is troubling you. I assure you that you may speak freely. I will not betray any confidences, and I may be able to help you . . . if you let me."

Alycia's hand trembled slightly, and there was no disguise for her look of surprise. The silence closed around them as she met the monk's unwavering eyes.

"Alycia, you must trust me," he continued, levering forward in his chair. "There is nothing to fear. We are in God's presence. There are no secrets from him."

Alycia took a deliberative breath. Why was she so uncomfortable? This monk might be kind and full of sympathy, but he was also a stranger. What did he really know about her?

And how could he help? But Alycia realized she needed *someone* to talk to. The monk certainly didn't feel like a stranger . . . he felt like someone she had known for a long time. In some ways it seemed they were carrying on the conversation they had started five years ago.

"Are you sure you want to hear what I have to say?" she asked, bringing two cups of coffee from the kitchen. "If I start telling you my problems—"

"I am sure. You may tell me anything and everything. And take as long as you wish. I am not here to judge you, Alycia, I am here only to understand and to help."

There was something magical about the monk, she thought. Her self-consciousness vanished. Feelings that had rankled inside her for years began to bubble out, raw and unvarnished, and the monk listened with patience and concern. She confided about Owen and Isabel, her affair with Richard, Red's death and the financial scandal, the trying times with her charity-board friends, the difficulties with Jean. For two hours she scarcely paused. At the end she found the courage to mention two letters Red had left in his study desk the day he died. One was to her, she told Andrew, the other to Jean.

"What did they say?" Andrew pressed gently.

Exhausted, Alycia rubbed her temples.

"Confession is painful, but it's nourishment for the soul," the monk encouraged her. "There is nothing you've done that God will not forgive you for and that you should not forgive yourself for."

Alycia nodded, but her eyes resisted.

"Please," Andrew said more firmly.

"You wouldn't understand. Not as a member of the clergy."

"Let me decide that. I'm also human."

Alycia pressed her hands together, fingertips extended, and rested them under her chin. She forced out the words: "My husband committed suicide."

The monk's face furrowed in doubt. "But you just told me his friend had shot him accidentally."

Alycia began slowly, trying to recall the words exactly as they had been written. "In his letter to me, Red said he loved me dearly but he saw no choice but to find a way to kill himself without bringing more embarrassment on the family. He said he was going to dupe Scotty. He asked that I never tell Scotty the truth, and he hoped he wouldn't have to rot in hell for the deception. He told me to give Felice a hug and

kiss for him, and to say how much he loved her. He mentioned Walter Mandrake too, what he'd done to Red on the
land transaction. But Red said he didn't want revenge. He
just wanted to be left in peace. He mentioned the word
'peace' several times. I never realized that's what he wanted
most from life, at least at the end. Now I want to give it to
him. That's why I destroyed the letter.''

"I'm so sorry," Andrew said in the silence. "I understand
your anguish now. But you must not feel guilty, Alycia. You
tried to warn Red to give up the transaction. For his own
reasons, he did not listen. You did everything you could. You
were not responsible.''

"I tell myself that, but I don't always believe it.''

"In time you will. Your wound will heal. You must believe that.''

"I'll try," she said, grateful for the support. Already she
was feeling stronger.

"Did you tell Red's mother?" Andrew asked.

"I thought Harriet had suffered enough. I haven't told
anyone.''

"And the letter to Jean?''

"I read it that same night. Red revealed everything to
Jean that he revealed to me. I was tempted to destroy it, but
in the end I just hid the letter.''

"Do you have that right?" Andrew asked delicately. "The
letter was written to Jean.''

"Would you want your son to know his father had killed
himself? Jean can be so destructive as it is. And there was
something else in his letter I didn't want him to know.''

Andrew sat back, crossing his arms with interest.

"When each of his grandchildren was born, Owen established a trust—in the amount of one million dollars. The
children were never told. Only Red, Harriet, and I knew. I
was in charge of administering the trusts. Over the years, as I
got to know Owen better, I began to despise the money. It
represented his damning grip on our family. It was a hold he
never really relinquished, even when he died. In Red's letter
to Jean he mentions his trust, all the money he'll receive one
day. It was Red's way of asking for forgiveness, I think,
letting Jean know how much he loved him. But there's so
much hypocrisy in this. Red never wanted me to accept the
trusts in the first place. He also didn't think it was good for
people to inherit too much money—he said if they did, they

never understood its value or meaning. And it's my choice whether Jean and Felice are to have any money at all. The truth is, I don't want them to have it. After everything that's happened, it feels like blood money."

"How much money is it?" Andrew felt compelled to ask.

"When Isabel died, I divided her share between Jean and Felice. The money has been invested wisely over the years. When they're twenty-three—that's the age when the money becomes theirs—Jean and Felice should each have ten million dollars."

Andrew's words lodged hopelessly in his throat.

"So much money would only twist and cloud their judgments," Alycia continued, "as surely as it did their grandfather's and father's. The trusts are a curse, and legally I can end them anytime, before the children turn twenty-three."

"But how?" Andrew couldn't help asking.

"By giving the money away."

The monk straightened slowly. Doubt creased his face. "Do you feel entirely comfortable with that decision? Won't you first consult Jean and Felice?"

"I'm torn, I admit it. It's not unlike Red's letter to Jean. Someday Jean should see it, yet I don't know when. I'm not absolutely sure about denying my children their trust money, either, but the decision is mine to make. Morally as well as legally. Jean and Felice are my children. I have a responsibility to do what I think is right for them. I intend to pay for their education and leave them enough to get started with their lives. But I will not blithely hand over a fortune and simply hope it won't affect them. I want them to find something in life to pursue that's not tied to money."

Alycia was suddenly uncertain, even afraid, as she studied the monk. "You don't think I'm doing the right thing, do you?"

"I'm not sure what I think," he admitted. "I'm not the wisest counsel about money. I grew up with it flowing like water. Today I live virtually free of it. Like you, I feel it means endless temptations for abuse. Yet it's the oil that runs the wheels of society. I seek it out to help with our work among the poor. I can't deny its importance. Jesus said to render under Caesar what is Caesar's, but that is too metaphorical, too simple. Perhaps you should ask yourself what your children would do if you gave the money away. What would they think of you?"

"Felice wouldn't care, I'm sure. She trusts my judgment. And money has never seemed to interest her."

"And Jean?"

"He would probably despise me. He already may. He feels cheated by his father's death. He doesn't really trust anyone now. Yet his bitterness hasn't dulled his ambition. It's only sharpened it. He graduated from his prep school with honors, which surprised me, because he hated the school. But he'd made a promise to his father. He can do great things when he makes up his mind—he has tremendous drive and willpower. Right now he just has to blame someone for his unhappiness."

"Let me guess," Andrew said. "One day he wants to be a real-estate developer."

"Of course. And he's said more than once he won't go to college. Should I be surprised? Jean can't wait to prove himself to everyone, just like his father and grandfather. I intend to do everything in my power to persuade him he doesn't have to."

"Someday I'd very much like to meet Jean. Your daughter too. I think you're a very conscientious mother, Alycia. Your road has not been easy."

Andrew rose to leave, but with difficulty. Something about Alycia held him. His emotions caught him by surprise. He had come here as an emissary of God to dispense sympathy and understanding, yet Alycia's story had touched him more deeply than he had anticipated. Not so much her suffering— the monk had seen much of that in this world—but her reaction to it. Hers was a courage and tenacity he found so rarely, and which he admired so much. They were qualities he tried to embody in his own life, yet he'd never been tested like Alycia.

"I'm afraid it's growing late," Andrew allowed, approaching and taking Alycia's hands in his own. "I will pray for you. The wisdom to decide what to do with the trusts will come from God."

The warmth of the monk's hands matched the kindness in his eyes, Alycia thought as she held Brother Andrew in her gaze. She was sorry when he pulled away. As they walked to the door, she was exhausted from her long confession, but somehow refreshed. For the first time since Red's death she felt a stirring of hope. She recalled how she had thought what a pity that someone like Andrew was sequestered in a monastery. He was so strong and sure of himself, the good he could do if he were part of society would be immeasurable. But she also understood his wanting to separate himself from the

politics and temptations of the world. She was tired of them
herself.

"You're leaving tomorrow?" Alycia asked outside the door.

"My abbot is expecting me."

"I was hoping to invite you for dinner. You've been so
kind to me."

"You have nothing to repay," he said assuredly.

"But I want to." Hearing the stubbornness in her voice,
she felt her face warm. "Couldn't you postpone your trip a
day? I promise you, I'm a wonderful cook. You'll never be
fed any better."

A self-effacing smile broke on the monk's face. "Knowing
my normal fare, I'm quite sure you're right."

Andrew watched as Alycia's head tilted away. The late-
afternoon sun washed over her subtle features. It was a
European face—the broad forehead and full mouth, the high
cheeks, the delicate nose. She had a certain poise, a classical
kind of beauty. Andrew realized he was staring, and made
himself turn and take in the young man coming up the drive.
Andrew had seen Red's picture in the living room. Jean had
his mother's steel-blue eyes but otherwise he was the image
of his father. His soft, poutty face was handsome, and he
walked tall and straight, with an air of authority.

"Hello, Jean, I'm Brother Andrew." The monk extended
his hand as the young man approached. Jean returned his
stare but ignored the outstretched hand. He darted a glance to
his mother, nodded almost indifferently, and moved around
them into the house.

"Jean, wait a minute," Alycia called.

"I'm tired," he answered, his eyes dimming impatiently as
he turned.

"I want you to say hello to Brother Andrew."

He looked the monk over. "I don't know you."

"We've never met."

"Were you a friend of my father's?"

"Not exactly. But from what I know of him I think I would
have enjoyed his company. I would have liked to be his
friend." He saw Jean wasn't convinced of his sincerity. The
boy's stubbornness was like a wall. No one was going to get
in. Andrew wondered if this young man would ever get out.
Then he remembered his own stubborn and petulant adoles-
cence, and tried to be understanding.

"How do you know my mother?" Jean asked.

"We met at a charity ball."

"I can't stand those things," Jean volunteered. "How do you?"

"I believe in charity."

"I guess somebody has to."

Andrew ignored the sarcasm, but his heart went out to Alycia. "Your mother tells me you're interested in real estate."

"I really have to go. It was nice meeting you," he said, and went inside.

Alycia folded her arms in frustration. Her road was tougher than the monk had imagined. "Is he like this often?" Andrew inquired, breaking the tension.

"He is to me. Sometimes I think I've lost control of him."

"It may seem like it, but I don't believe you have. You must never give up. If you do, Jean will see that, and he'll give up on himself."

The look of defeat didn't leave Alycia's face.

"Can I change my mind?" Andrew suddenly brightened.

Alycia looked perplexed.

"When I think about it, I'm sure my abbot can wait another day or two. I'd like to have that dinner with you."

She smiled gratefully at the monk. "I look forward to it," Alycia said. "The day after tomorrow, seven o'clock?"

Andrew waved and was gone.

Jean lounged on his bed with an issue of *Golf Digest*. He couldn't believe what he'd just overheard. Was his mother inviting a monk to dinner? Was it a joke? Jean didn't like anyone who acted righteous and superior, who pretended to be close to God—Jean didn't even think there was a God. He'd given up church after his father had died and he couldn't imagine anything that would bring him back. Religion had no more to do with the reality of making a living than did the charity work and society hobnobbing his mother wasted her time on. Jean had expected that by now his mother would have given up her society routine, maybe remarried, but she didn't even date much. The monk was the first single man she'd invited into the house in centuries. Jean got a good laugh. Big society news, he thought. Maybe the Los Angeles *Times* would cover the evening.

Jean was embarrassed every time his mother's picture or name *did* get into the society section. Why couldn't she just butt out of the limelight? Hadn't it been bad enough living

through the endless coverage of the Trans-Universal deal and
the stock manipulation? He would never forget the way the
media had crucified his father. The irony was that in the end
Trans-Universal Studios had decided to develop the land itself
into a small city of banks, hotels, restaurants, office buildings—
and a movie-set tour for tourists. That had really blown Jean's
mind. His father's dream of an amusement park had been
essentially right. Still, people would remember Red Poindexter
not as a visionary but as a villain.

Jean cursed his father's enemies one and all. Those
phonies—he wanted them out of his life forever. All except
one, he thought. Jean had put together the pieces without
anyone pointing an actual finger. He knew Walter Mandrake
was to blame. He wasn't sure how, but he also knew that one
day he'd get even.

Jean showered and dressed, debating whether to go down
for dinner. His mother would wait for Felice to come home,
but Jean doubted even then he'd be hungry, and he didn't
want to sit around for another mindless conversation about
what everyone did today and wasn't the weather terrific and
how about that governor's wife, Mrs. Ronald Reagan, who
had to leave Sacramento every weekend to fly to Beverly
Hills because she said "no one in Sacramento can do hair."

Jean wondered what it would be like to have Mrs. Reagan
for a mother. Maybe he was lucky to be who he was, but he
still couldn't get along at home. How could he forgive his
mother for selling his father's properties? She'd had no right,
not without Jean's consent, not without giving him and Felice
some of the profit. Now he'd have to start his real-estate career
from scratch. His mother's incredible selfishness aside, he didn't
mind that challenge. His father hadn't really relied on Grandfather Owen, he had made it himself. So will I, Jean thought.

The father of a friend from the Harvard School had gotten
Jean a summer job in the real-estate department of the Irvine
Company. Every morning he drove an hour from the Valley
to an Orange County office building. His work involved
mostly research, but it was a foot in the door of a company
that sat on one of the most valuable pieces of undeveloped
land in the country, the old Irvine Ranch. With miles of
coastline, the property was worth no less than four hundred
million dollars, and its value increased by the day. Private
developers were clamoring for some of the action, but the
Irvine management was caught in internal conflict that made

decisions difficult. The history of the company was almost as impressive as its price tag. The more Jean studied both, the more he was convinced this was the kind of company to build his future on. It was just a matter of impressing the right people with his ingenuity and drive.

He skipped dinner and stayed in his room. From his desk drawer he pulled voluminous sheets of carefully calculated numbers and neat, handsome sketches that he'd worked over endlessly—cost studies and scale drawings of residential enclaves, shopping malls, a marina with restaurants, and high-fashion shops, with parks and landscaping—his interpretation of an 82,000-acre development for part of the Irvine land. Tomorrow, after weeks of wangling, Jean finally had an appointment with the marketing vice-president.

In the morning, before his mother or Felice stirred, Jean had read the *Wall Street Journal* front to back. He dressed in his most conservative suit and combed back his short hair, despite the fashion trend to the contrary. Orange County was the citadel of conservatism. His father had taught him that preparation was the key to success, so in his car he rehearsed again and again what he would say. Orange County airport was already the sixth-busiest in the nation. What had happened to the San Fernando Valley after the war was now happening here. There was a fortune to be made.

In the vice-president's outer office Jean held his thick folder of drawings, drumming his foot nervously. After half an hour he followed a secretary into musty dark quarters that hadn't been redecorated since the forties. The vice-president, a short balding man, shook Jean's hand impatiently and asked how he could help.

"I have some ideas I'd like to share, sir," he began, holding the executive's gaze. "I know outside developers approach you all the time, but I work for the company—"

"You just started, I believe."

"Yes, sir," he said, undaunted by the put-down, "but let me show you what I've prepared on my own time." Proudly Jean placed his folder in front of the surprised eyes. The vice-president flipped through one or two pages and pulled his glance back to Jean.

"Young man, I see you're a hard worker, but you're only a summer intern—I don't think it's possible for you to really understand this company."

"I think I know as much as you, sir," he answered boldly.

He could hear the arrogance in his voice as he watched the executive stiffen, but Jean would not retreat or soften his tone. "I know that the original Irvine Ranch was purchased in 1875 by James Irvine Sr. for one hundred and fifty thousand dollars. It comprised one hundred and thirty-eight square *miles* and was passed on to his son, James Irvine Jr. J.I., as he was called, was eccentric and rough-tempered, but he dearly loved his land. At the turn of the century he built a thirty-eight-room mansion for just him and his new bride twenty miles from their nearest neighbor. He began planting the largest Valencia orange grove in the world—over one hundred thousand acres. That's how the county got its name.

"As the land became more valuable, J.I. fought off poachers, squatters, and the United States government, which finally took two thousand of his prime acres for the El Toro Marine Base. After his wife and two children died, J.I. turned over his empire to his only surviving but least-favorite child, Mike Irvine. The son preferred art and music to business, but he gave up his San Francisco mansion to live in his father's house and manage the ranch. It was disaster. J.I. reappraised the situation and formed the Irvine Company to hold title to the ranch. He asked four close associates to join his son on the board of directors of the James Irvine Foundation, which was the Irvine Company's major stockholder."

Jean caught his breath. The executive looked spellbound. Jean couldn't help feel pleased. "When you think about the opportunity Mike Irvine had, sir, it's incredible," Jean interjected. "Can you imagine wasting a chance like that? He was a wimp. In 1947, eighty-one-year-old J.I. was found floating facedown in a Montana river. The only witness was his fishing companion, who was also his ranch foreman, Brad Hellis. The death was ruled accidental. After the funeral, the foundation board informed Mike Irvine it was turning over the ranch to Mr. Hellis. Do you know what Mike Irvine did? Absolutely nothing! He gave up without a fight. Ten years later Joan Irvine, the twenty-four-year-old granddaughter of J.I.'s, presented evidence that Mr. Hellis, just before the fatal fishing trip, had asked her grandfather for a two-hundred-thousand-dollar loan and had been refused. Under the threat of an investigation, Hellis left the ranch. That's when Joan Irvine started to try to take over. . . ."

Jean knew to stop. The antics of Joan Irvine were a subject not openly discussed in corporate headquarters. The woman was still warring with the James Irvine Foundation and was considered the enemy. Jean couldn't help admiring her. She had some guts.

"Well?" Jean asked brightly, smiling at the executive. He folded his hands in front of him and rocked back on his heels.

"Young man," the vice-president said as he rose, "how old are you?"

"Eighteen, sir."

"Eighteen."

"Yes, sir."

"Son, I see you have a lot of balls. Maybe you've got some talent too. But you really don't know anything about this company, or real estate. Take my advice, go to college. When you've got your degree, come back and we'll talk."

Jean didn't shake the executive's hand. He barely controlled his fury as he turned and stalked out. What the hell was happening? He had spent weeks on his drawings, and this asshole acted like they were something scribbled on the back of a cocktail napkin. He had barely glanced at them! If you had great ideas, what difference did it make how old you were or if you had a college degree? The only thing that counted, Jean was starting to see, was power, and he didn't have a lick of that. A goddamn summer intern was the lowest of the low, and it would take thirty years to crawl up the ladder to respectability. No, thank you. He couldn't wait that long.

That night he pulled down the atlas from his bookshelf, thumbed to the middle, and dropped his index finger on a thin, squiggly purple landmass that, a few years ago, ninety-nine percent of America had never heard of.

"Dinner, Jean."

He turned, annoyed by the intrusion. The lacy white dress showed off his sister's summer tan and bright blue eyes. Tall, with a delicate nose and high forehead, Felice looked more like their mother every day.

"I'm not hungry," he said, turning back to his atlas.

"You didn't eat last night either. It would make Mom happy if you at least came down and sat with us."

"All you ever think about is Mom. Don't you care about pleasing yourself?"

"What's that supposed to mean?"

"You're a carbon copy of Mom. You know: noble, selfless, a do-gooder. I think you should be yourself."

Jean was still focused on his map, but he could feel his sister's face redden. He knew she couldn't stand him, but Felice prided herself on staying cool.

"Do me a favor," Jean spoke up. "Get lost."

"With pleasure," she said icily.

"And next time, knock before you come in."

He could hear his sister's breathing. He angled his head back. Felice's face had swollen like a blowfish.

"Your attitude is really terrible," she blurted out.

"Hey, history is made! Miss Repressed speaks her mind. Anything else you want to tell me?"

"You're incredible. Don't you know how the rest of the world looks at you? Selfish, vain, angry—"

"Better than being a pathetic little excuse for protoplasm like you."

"Shut up!"

"Oh, my, I see a temper. This is doing you good, you know. You should thank me."

"I wish you weren't living in this house anymore. I wish you were out of my life forever."

"Don't worry, I'm moving soon."

"Where?"

He knew she didn't believe him. "Overseas."

"Where?"

"Ever heard of Vietnam?"

She wanted to say she had, but she couldn't, Jean saw, and his smile of superiority widened.

"It's in Southeast Asia. We're fighting a war there—in case you haven't read the papers. I'm going to join the Army."

The red dissipated from her cheeks, as if she suddenly felt sorry for him. Jean wondered if it was him she was worried for, or their mother. "I don't believe you," she said.

"Yes, you do. I always do what I say. I keep my promises. I'm going to a recruiter this week. I'll be in basic training by fall."

"So what's that supposed to prove?" Felice demanded.

"War is going to make me a hero," he said without a doubt in his voice. "People will finally know who I am."

Felice wagged her head in pity. "You're crazy."

Jean gave a smirk. "What if I am? What's so terrible about that? I feel sorry for people who're always in control, who don't know what they want in life. Like you."

Felice's lips pressed together in rage. "You think you're just like Dad."

"I don't *think* it," he replied coolly.

Felice spun away and headed toward the stairs, but not before Jean got off the last volley. "Sorry to disappoint you, but I'm coming back alive!"

Alycia dropped Felice at Harriet's for the evening and returned to finish her four-course dinner for Andrew. Her spirits were so low she wondered if the monk would find her much company. Her fight with Jean this evening had ended with him storming from the house and jumping into his car with a promise never to return. Alycia half-believed him. She had pointed out all the reasons why the Army, not to mention a war, might hurt him, not help, but Jean had stubbornly cited history as his precedent: his father had served his country, why shouldn't he? Patiently Alycia had outlined the differences—to begin with, the Vietnamese had never bombed Pearl Harbor—but Jean heard only the urging of an inner voice. He was eighteen and could enlist without parental consent. When Alycia began to cry, he'd blown up in disgust.

Andrew arrived precisely at seven. Alycia made an attempt at looking happy, but she was a poor actress, and she knew the monk could see through any disguise. They sat in the living room and she told the truth. Andrew listened patiently. It was what she liked most about him—she could be herself in front of him, she could tell him anything.

"Maybe the Army will do him good," Andrew suggested when they moved to the dining table.

"But you told me never to give up on him."

"That's not necessarily the same as not letting him do what he wants. He has so much anger in him that perhaps the Army will be a way to exorcise it. And Jean has so much to learn about himself and life. Think back to when you were his age. Weren't you headstrong and convinced that society was incredibly stupid? You were the only enlightened one?"

"But what about Vietnam? Jean wants to be in the infantry. Surely you don't approve of killing—"

"I don't approve of it, no, and I speak against wars," Andrew said thoughtfully, "but I also know I can't stop them. Just as I can't stop Jean from enlisting, or killing, any more than you can stop him. But I can and will pray that he comes home alive, and that he learns that killing is wrong."

"I'm afraid of war," Alycia said. "I've seen it firsthand. I hate it. And I don't want anything to happen to my son. I've lost a husband and a daughter. That's enough."

They ate in silence before Andrew finally spoke. "Forgive me, but I think I'd look like Friar Tuck if you had me here for a week," he said with a wink. "Where did you learn to cook like this? And how did you know I was a lover of sweet, succulent lamb?"

"There aren't many things I do well, but cooking is one. I used to give a lot of parties."

"Ah, when you and Red were active in society. But you're active still. I read your name in the paper this morning. You had some things to say about the Helen Mayer Foundation."

"I was interviewed yesterday," Alycia said. "I haven't seen the article."

"You were quoted as saying the foundation was in danger of losing sight of its objectives."

A smile framed Alycia's face as she remembered the interview with the *Times*. The writer, focusing on why and how much the city's wealthy donate to charity, had interviewed a dozen of Alycia's friends. Alycia knew her comments were probably the most outspoken. It had been a relief to get out some of her feelings. "I was critical of the amount of money that goes to overhead," she explained to Andrew. "As a board member I've watched our budget increase every year for parties, celebrity appearances, hiring outside firms to help with the fund-raising. But I wasn't that critical. I didn't say what was really on my mind. Raising money has become not just an extravagant expense, it's mostly a social event. People want to be seen at the right party. How much money comes in is incidental."

Her curiosity piqued, Alycia looked at Andrew. "What about your monastery, the money you raise?"

"It's very simple. We have no overhead, except for me." He smiled sheepishly. "And I keep getting fed delicious meals like this! Our expenses are minimal. Almost every penny raised goes directly to the poor."

"I wish you'd tell my friends and fellow board members that," Alycia said.

"Why? How do they feel?"

"They think everything they do is perfect and that I should keep my mouth shut. The common view is that since Red died, I've become a contrarian." She sighed. "Are they right?"

"You must never believe that," Andrew admonished. "You're only speaking your conscience. You have an obligation to speak out. Silence in the face of something wrong is cowardly and shameful."

"It wouldn't bother you to stand against the world?"

"When I chose to become a monk, I asked myself the same question. I was certainly an oddity—I still am—but I'm convinced that what I'm doing is right for me. Alycia, I know it's easier to talk about courage than to demonstrate it, but if we don't act on our principles, if we instead listen to society all the time, we would think it's the individual who is always in error."

Andrew's words made her feel better, but even more, it was the way he spoke them, or maybe it was Andrew himself. She didn't care if he were a monk, she decided, she just liked him as a person. She felt an affinity toward him she couldn't quite define, but it was very strong and very special.

"You know, I barely know you," she said as they finished dinner, "yet I think I understand you. I'll miss you when you're gone." She left the table and with a faint smile skirted past her guest to Red's study.

Andrew watched as Alycia drifted from his sight. He was surprised by her words. What exactly was there to understand about him? He did not see himself as a complex philosopher. His desire to do good in the world was motivated by a love for God that he tried to keep pure. If anything, he was a simple person, far more so than Alycia, whom he considered not just courageous but also full of contradictory impulses. Her acts of rebellion, he decided, conflicted with an instinct to have a normal place in society, to be accepted and appreciated. But was that not also a little true of him? There were times when he wished he led a normal life. Maybe he and Alycia were alike. Andrew suddenly realized that as much as Alycia would miss him, he would feel the same toward her.

He rose from the table, ready to leave. The innocent thought of missing Alycia began to trouble him. What were his real feelings? Was it just her mind and spirit he found so engaging? Alycia's physical beauty was a warm, suffusing glow that would hold any man, monk or not, he thought, so why would he not be attracted to her? Still, he did not want to admit it. Temptations of the flesh were something he'd abandoned with his youth. The world was full of enough other hazards. His passion had to be saved for God. He had no choice but to return to his monastery and put his relationship with Alycia behind him.

His heart conflicted, he turned as Alycia approached.

"I know you're going to resist, but I want you to have this," she said.

Andrew handled the check as delicately as he would a butterfly. He studied the numbers, shocked, and wagged his head. "You're right. I cannot accept this."

"You have to. I insist. This is my gift to your monastery. I'd rather give it to you than to any of the charities here."

"But fifty thousand dollars—"

"Now you won't have a shortfall."

Andrew drew an uneasy breath as he focused on Alycia. Her loveliness was like a beautiful flower. His hands trembled. "Thank you," he said. "My abbot will be most grateful."

"Can I visit you at the monastery?" she suddenly asked.

"Visit me?"

"I don't know if I will, but if I feel like it . . . if the opportunity comes . . ."

"Alycia, I'm afraid that is not possible." He felt his face warm. "Women are usually not allowed within our walls."

"Can I at least write to you, then?"

Andrew let the silence build around them. He resolved to say no, it was an idea as foolish as wanting to visit him, but he was paralyzed.

"I don't see what harm . . ." she said.

"Nor do I," he found himself saying.

"Then I will write to you."

He met Alycia's gaze, and started to tremble again. "I'd like that very much," he admitted.

"Will you write back?"

"Yes," he promised, and Andrew turned to go before any more words he could not control poured from his heart.

From her living-room couch Harriet watched the dusky, smudged sunset with the benign detachment of someone who'd had too much to drink. Yet she wasn't drunk—since Red's death she hadn't even sipped an after-dinner liqueur—it was only a vacuous stupor with those same desired qualities of amnesia. She stared out toward the Pacific almost every evening like a lone supplicant in the great cathedral of a house that she rarely set foot out of. The housekeeper brought in groceries and ran errands—after all her years of servitude, she had told herself, let someone else do the work—and Harriet contented herself with television or books or sometimes inviting Alycia and the grandchildren over. Time was uneventful and innocuous. At her age she didn't expect to find a new hobby or be filled with a sudden passion. Life was a routine, a game of waiting, and only Harriet knew for what.

Of course, she knew, no one worried about what a widowed septuagenarian was waiting for. She cared more about the world than it cared about her. Because she'd lost both her husband and son, she was viewed by society with some sympathy, but mostly she felt forgotten. The logic of that wasn't lost on Harriet—she had wanted to forget too—but something in her resisted. Time for her wasn't entirely innocuous. She was not ready to die, not yet.

A car horn sounded from the drive. Harriet rose with an effort. She wore a pink silk gown she hadn't put on since Owen had taken her to a country-club Valentine's dance. She watched herself from a third eye, amused by the crinkly, swishing sound the gown made and the thought of a recluse going out on the town. Alycia had insisted she come to the Red Cross Ball. "I'm not inviting you just to get you out and circulating, Mother," Alycia had said with a faint smile, "I'm doing it for me. You're my date." They had laughed together and finally Harriet had agreed to go. She wouldn't know many people, but she was more fond of Alycia than ever, and they'd have a chance to visit.

"Mother, you look gorgeous." Alycia opened the car door for her. "And I love your perfume."

"Flattery will get you everywhere."

"Thank you again for doing this." Alycia guided her Cadillac onto the street and gave Harriet another glance. "You look ten years younger. See what going out does?"

"I still don't understand why you couldn't get a *real* date. A woman as good-looking and wealthy as you . . . Even *I* have men calling me occasionally."

"I'm going tonight for Electra. It's her show. I just want to be supportive."

"You've always been a good friend, dear. Certainly to me." She reached over and patted Alycia's hand. "Now, go ahead and indulge me—tell me about my grandchildren."

"Which one first?" Alycia said after a moment.

Alycia's procrastinating tone was almost predictable, Harriet thought. It came whenever there was trouble, and there was plenty of that lately. Alycia had only the best intentions, but she tried to hide from Harriet the ongoing problems of the lawsuits, not to say the invariable crises with Jean, as if to protect a woman in old age who had been hurt enough. But it was Alycia whom Harriet felt sorry for, not herself. Her daughter-in-law carried too many burdens, and she was too proud to ask for help.

What concerned Harriet most was Alycia's fights with Jean. Watching her grandson mature, Harriet knew Jean had rough edges but she also felt he had great potential. She felt close to him even if he didn't visit as often as Felice, and she knew that Jean trusted and liked her. As difficult as he was, as much travail as he caused Alycia, Harriet was confident that one day her grandson would surprise a lot of people.

That was why she wanted to live on. She would live to see Jean fulfill the potential Red always believed in. Red had been troubled and distant at eighteen too, and Harriet believed, unshakably, that when Jean finally made peace with the world he would be like a star shining in the heavens. He would be everything that Red had been, and more.

"Tell me about Jean," Harriet said.

"He's fine."

"No, he's not."

"Mother—"

"Dear, I want to help, not be kept in the dark."

Alycia surrendered with a sigh. "All right. He's enlisted in the Army. He reports for basic training in a month. I'm sick about it." Her eyes darted to Harriet. "I tried to talk him out of it. He wouldn't listen."

"Why are you so worried?"

"How can you ask that? How could any mother not be worried? There's a war going on—"

"Jean will be all right."

"What gives you such faith?"

"The boy knows how to take care of himself. I saw the same quality in Red at that age. It wasn't easy for me to see Red off to war either, but since I knew I couldn't stop him, I just told him I was proud of him. I let him know he had my complete faith. And when I said that, when I surrendered total control, I *knew* he would be all right."

Harriet wondered if her explanation would sound like a rebuke. She didn't mean it to be. Jean was Alycia's child, and

Harriet was not interfering. She was simply trying to put Alycia at ease.

"I still worry," Alycia confessed.

"All I mean," Harriet explained, "is you have to learn to let go. You can't control people. Especially those you love."

Alycia's lips formed a contemplative smile. "It's funny, Mother, but you sound like someone else."

"Who?" Harriet inquired.

"A Trappist monk. His name is Brother Andrew. He told me it would be good for Jean to become a soldier, and that I shouldn't interfere or worry."

"How do you know a Trappist monk?"

"I first met him five years ago when he was fund-raising here. Out of the blue he came to visit again last month. I find him so different, so refreshing. He's the most sincere person I've ever met. I like him," she allowed herself to say.

Harriet cocked her head. "It sounds as if you more than like him."

Alycia was caught off guard. "It does?"

"Yes, dear."

"Then maybe there is more."

"I have no right to interfere," Harriet admitted, laying a gentle hand on Alycia. "You're an independent woman. You always have been, and I know you're an excellent judge of character. But what are you going to do with a monk?"

"I don't know, Mother. Does it matter? I only know what I feel."

The only things glittering brighter than the chandeliers in the ballroom of the Beverly Hills Hotel were the pale, exposed necks weighted down with the latest creations from Van Cleef and Arpels, and fingers with rocks the size of lollipops. Alycia and Harriet drifted through the maze of elegantly dressed couples to their table, but not without feeling the flicker of cold eyes. The society crowd considered her comments in the *Times* in bad taste at the least, Electra had already warned her. Alycia was relieved when a few old friends came up to her table, but Carmine Bradbury and her group stayed away. Alycia knew not to be surprised, yet she felt hurt; after their meeting at the museum she had expected Carmine at least to call, maybe invite her back to the bridge games she'd abandoned after Red died. But the only one who'd lent any support was Electra. "Don't pay attention to the fuddy-duddies," she had chirped merrily.

Alycia watched as Electra swished through the room from table to table, the perfect hostess who knew whom to be serious with, whom to touch delicately on the wrist or buss on the cheek or whisper discreetly to. The cavernous room glowed with prominence—the mayor, half the city council, industrialists, developers, media people. The faces all seemed to have a patina, Alycia thought, just like their money. She wondered if she wasn't a little jealous. She couldn't help thinking of when she and Red had owned this evening. Now it was Electra's turn. She wore a three-thousand-dollar designer gown and a priceless smile. She was no longer the reckless, irreverent adventurer who had peeked over Terry Donelson's wall one afternoon long ago. When she darted up to Harriet and Alycia, she was almost out of breath.

"Hello, Mrs. Poindexter," she said, taking Harriet's hand. "You look ravishing." Then she leaned toward Alycia. "I am *so* nervous," she whispered.

"Why? Everything looks wonderful," Alycia assured her. "And you're an old hand at this. Where's your beau?"

"Randolph is off flirting. He loves parties. I'm sure he'll find his way to you."

"Good. I need a dance partner."

"I can do better than that, I can get you a husband," Electra said with a wink. "I don't mean Randolph," she amended, "he's mine. But there are some eligible men around."

"Define your terms," Alycia said mischievously.

"We'll talk again when you're drunk."

"I haven't been that in ages."

Electra bestowed a kiss. "Then start tonight. See ya!" She vanished into the mushrooming crowd just as the band began to play.

Alycia got drinks for herself and Harriet and returned to her table. As happy as she was for Electra, she was becoming bored and uncomfortable here. She promised herself to leave early, when a hand graced her bare shoulder. Alycia stared into a pale countenance with eyes as dark as stones. A charming smile suddenly broke over the sober face.

"Hello, Evan," she said.

"Alycia, would you like to dance?"

Not just yet, she thought, but like a good sport she rose and followed. She was sure Evan Chambers would be as hopeless as a cow on the dance floor. She was wrong. He was surprisingly agile as he took her in his arms. "My wife doesn't like to dance," he admitted.

"Then how did you get so good?"

"Arthur Murray. I took lessons for a year," he said. "And you're a natural," he complimented her.

"I'm afraid I'm rusty."

"That's your fault, Alycia. I'll dance with you anytime."

One arm slid to her bare back and he pulled her closer. Alycia stifled a laugh. She had never thought Evan Chambers a flirt. At Helen Mayer meetings he was mirthless, analytical, evasive. Now his grip was strong and insistent.

"I want to talk to you," he broke the silence, whispering in her ear.

"About?"

"I think you know."

She was quiet, expecting an offer to go to bed. Part of her was enjoying this. "Why don't you tell me?"

"Maybe we could meet somewhere this weekend."

"That sounds intriguing. Why don't you give me a clue?"

"I never discuss business before pleasure."

"And I always do," she said.

Evan Chambers looked disappointed. "All right. We might spend a minute discussing your board seat."

Alycia stopped dancing and looked at him. "What about it?"

"You still haven't resigned," he pointed out.

"No, I haven't. And I don't want to talk about it."

The executive's wooden smile was not much of an apology. They began dancing again, but neither was enjoying it. "A lot of us are disappointed," Evan said. "You've become something of an embarrassment, Alycia."

"To whom?" she asked coolly.

"Us."

"*Us*?"

"Don't act surprised. I'm only trying to be a friend. I just want to make you happy." His tone was suddenly fatherly. She tried to break from his grip but he wouldn't release her. What was he thinking—that if he seduced her she would be convinced of her errant ways? And this *us* business—as if there was an unspoken oath of allegiance among the givers of money.

"Just suppose, Alycia," he continued, "that you were offered another board, another committee. A position could be created just for you."

"Something ceremonial?" she interpreted. "Something without real power? If I just resigned the Helen Mayer seat?"

"Why not?"

"And the other boards I sit on—abandon them too?"

"At least for now."

"I won't do that."

His face turned harder. "Why are you being so stubborn? You have everything to lose, nothing to gain." He suddenly sighed, and his grip loosened. "You misunderstand me, Alycia. I like and respect you, but I don't think you know how many people you've upset. Maybe you don't care, but this is a small, clannish group, many of whose families have been giving to charity for decades. They do not like to be told, in your words, 'If the poor did not exist, the wealthy would invent them.' "

"I was only defining *noblesse oblige*."

"These people are just being proper."

"Proper people who have only one way of doing things, who are afraid of criticism," Alycia interjected.

"Criticism is fine if it's kept in the family. But one doesn't blab to a newspaper. I'm talking about etiquette. You insulted them."

Alycia drew a breath. She would contain herself. "I'd like to sit down, Evan."

"Will you think about this?" he asked, escorting her back to her table. He was suddenly charming and full of sincerity again. Alycia ordered another drink. She was beginning to feel like a heel. Maybe Evan had a point. Why was she such a rebel? She did believe in etiquette and a social order. Kids today were flip and surly and disrespectful, like Jean, and she couldn't stand that. And were her principles and sense of outrage so important that she had to sacrifice old friends? Did she really want to start a war?

By her fourth drink she just wanted to go home. She danced for a while with Randolph Fitzhugh, who was fun and full of comforting wit. He had the bearing and looks of a Confederate general—his thick hair and trim mustache were the color of corn silk—but what Alycia noticed most was his heavily lined face. She thought of the lines as battle scars, harsh marks of servitude, but no matter what story of woe they told, Randolph was a cheery survivor. Maybe she should be more like that.

Electra was suddenly hovering over their shoulders, swaying

with them to the music as she beamed impishly. She looked like she would explode. "Shall we tell her, Randolph?" she asked. "Alycia deserves to be the first to know. She's my best friend."

"Whatever you want, darling."

"Tell me what?" Alycia demanded.

"We're engaged!"

"That's wonderful! What a surprise! I'm so happy for both of you," Alycia exclaimed, and gave kisses all around. After a moment Electra seized her friend by the wrist and led her to an empty powder room.

"Am I doing the right thing?" she asked, deadly serious.

Alycia fought off a laugh. "You're asking *me*? I don't know. It's your life. Randolph seems very sweet, charming, accommodating. Do you love him?"

"What?"

"Are you in love with him?"

Electra dropped on a stool in front of the mirror. She looked up to the reflection of Alycia. "I don't think that's relevant. I want a steady, dependable companion. Randolph is right for me. Love only complicates things."

"I could never do that," Alycia admitted, "marry someone I don't feel deeply for."

"Then I'm more practical than you," Electra said, pleased with herself.

The smug tone unsettled Alycia. "Well, congratulations," she managed, "if you go through with it."

Electra's smile was as big as the moon. "I think I will."

Alycia wanted to feel happy for her friend, but it was envy that suddenly burned inside her. When she wished it away, it only grew brighter and made her face color in shame. Electra seemed to get stronger as she got weaker. Everything was going Electra's way. Alycia had a sense she was falling off some precipice.

"Evan Chambers approached me tonight," Alycia said uneasily. "He asked me to resign my board seat. If I did, he promised I'd be a lot happier. Isn't that crazy?"

Electra stared into the mirror and teased her hair, as if she hadn't heard a word.

"Isn't it crazy?" Alycia repeated. "He doesn't know me at all. Not like you do."

"Take the offer," Electra said suddenly, turning around. She looked sad and pained for Alycia. "It's just like Randolph asking me to marry him. I can't turn him down. If I do, there's just more uncertainty and anxiety for me. Maybe no one else will come along. You shouldn't turn down your offer either.''

Alycia was stunned. ''I can't believe you saying that about Randolph—an offer? Like this is just business. And I don't see any connection with my predicament.''

''Alycia, resigning the board seat is for your own good. If you don't, you'll be kicked off. That'll mean more anxiety and pain and isolation for you. You don't realize how you've lost touch with everyone since Red died. Maybe you're just bitter about the lawsuits, or a little confused, or it's been difficult raising kids alone, but you've become much harder and more distant.''

''That's ridiculous.''

''Everyone talks about it. You just don't listen. Tell me, do you enjoy playing the apostate?''

''That's what you were once,'' Alycia shot back, hurt.

''And I thank God that period's over.''

''What about doing what's right?''

''Please, spare me. What's right is living as comfortable a life as you can make for yourself.''

''I don't agree. And I don't need a lot of friends. I have Harriet, I have you—''

''That's not enough.''

''What's that mean?''

''It means you can't count on anything, including friends. Nothing lasts.''

''You mean one day I won't have you either? You're not taking my side on this? What about all those fuddy-duddies you talked about—'' Alycia was so upset she had to force her words out.

''A lot of them *are* fuddy-duddies. That's not the issue. You have to get along with people, Alycia. You've been hurt and you've reacted defensively. Well, I've been hurt too, but I learned my lesson. I want things to go easy for me. Why do you think I'm getting married? Why do you think I'm hosting this ball?''

''I don't understand. You're a bright, energetic, independent woman. You can do whatever you want—''

''I'm also forty-four years old and not getting younger,'' she said honestly. ''Alycia, don't find fault with me for accepting my own weaknesses. I'm finally to the point where I can be realistic about myself. You should be too. Don't turn against your friends.''

"None of these people tonight are my friends," she answered stubbornly.

"Jesus, you're proud."

"I don't think I'm proud at all."

"Then you're a fool."

"Electra, will you stop it!" Alycia was almost in tears. Maybe she was just drunk, but she hated the harsh words, the fighting. They had never fought in their lives.

"I've got to get back to my party," Electra whispered, embarrassed herself by the confrontation.

Alycia lowered her eyes and let her friend pass.

After school, Felice sat alone on the patio, her leggy frame sprawled over two chairs. She liked the late-afternoon quiet of the lake. The calm, silvery waters were disturbed only by a rowboat gliding along the far embankment, and the voices of two boys she didn't know competing with the throaty cry of mallards. Felice dropped her sketchpad and picked up the postcard from today's mail. The handwriting was sloppy, ink stains everywhere, the message barely readable.

Jean had probably written home because his drill sergeant had made him, she decided as she read the card again. He bragged he was the best in his basic-training company—squad leader, sharpshooter, the captain's favorite trainee. As different as they were, Felice understood her brother's ambition. He burned with a passion which she knew largely by its absence in her own personality. Jean was afraid of nothing, and welcomed all adversity as a challenge. The month before he was inducted, he had read everything he could on Vietnam. He'd also trained like he was going to the Olympics— push-ups, sit-ups, weight lifting, dawn and sunset runs near the lake. He would take over for General Westmoreland if the Army allowed. With Jean sloshing through the rice fields, eyes alert and rifle ready, the United States would beat down its yellow enemy.

Felice was relieved that Jean was out of the house. When he came back from Vietnam she prayed he wouldn't return here. A great and comfortable silence had descended on her and her mother the day he'd departed. Uneasy with himself, her brother was always at war with other people's happiness. He had a genius for smelling out weaknesses, knew how to get anyone's goat with a few choice words. He could bully and cajole, or simply sting with his silence. The first time he'd made Felice aware of her lack of courage was when he'd caught a frog in the lake. Jean had placed it, squirming and bug-eyed, on the kitchen table. "Hey, Miss Efficient," he goaded when she walked by, "you think you can do anything—okay, you wanna be a surgeon?" and he handed up a steak knife. When she drew back, Jean promptly sliced open the tight gray belly and the slimy intestines oozed into his hand.

She was afraid not so much of the frog, Felice had decided later, as of cruelty, and of her brother, which she often thought of as the same thing. No one could anticipate what Jean would do next. What upset Felice most was that she had no defense except to turn away and pretend her brother didn't exist. Like some tempest, she once told her mother, Jean had the power and fury to strike down anything in his path, and not care about the consequences. Her brother symbolized the world to her—noisy, difficult, full of treachery. After her father died she'd retreated willingly into a private universe of diaries and sketching pads. There was safety and calm there. She saw herself as an observer of the small details that others were in too much of a hurry to notice. The way a duck paddled through water, switching its rump, was not unlike a woman climbing stairs; when someone was talking to a group, and no one was really listening, the speaker raised his voice; trees were usually at war with insects, but flowers were not. Felice felt comfortable with her imagination and its quirky associations. If she was bored with schoolwork or having gossiping girlfriends or joining the chess club, she did care deeply about understanding everything around her and her place in the world.

"Happy birthday, sweetie—"

Felice swung around to take in the flat box in her mother's outstretched hands. "Chocolate?" she asked, perking up.

"Of course. Don't you think I know after all these years?"

"You'd better," she said, delighted. She opened the cardboard top and took a swipe of the icing. "Let's have two pieces right now," Felice insisted.

"I thought you were going to have friends over this evening. I mean, you can't celebrate alone. A thirteenth birthday is big-time."

Felice only shrugged. "I thought about it. Then I didn't want to do it. Mom, I don't like parties."

"You're sure?" Her mother looked concerned.

"Positively, absolutely, one hundred percent . . ." She gave her mom a hug. "Thanks for doing this. Now, sit down. I'll get some milk and plates."

She dashed into the kitchen, but not without feeling guilty. Her mother really wanted her to have the party. She wanted to know her daughter was well-liked and happy, because that was exactly what her mother was not, and it was exactly what she was afraid would somehow happen to Felice. Felice continually had to assure her that she was, in her own way, quite content, even if it was not totally true. What was true was, Felice was afraid of hurting or disappointing her mother, who had been hurt enough. It was painful, losing the Helen Mayer seat, but when Electra had been named to replace her—that was somehow devastating. Whenever her mother talked with Electra now, the conversations were strained and unnatural, as if each was holding something back. Felice couldn't define exactly what, but she knew what the tension did to her mother.

"Here, the big piece is for you," Felice said when she returned with two glasses of milk and cut the cake. "I almost forgot," she added lightly, nodding to the table, "something came in the mail."

She took a bite nervously and watched her mother's eyes parade down Jean's postcard. The same worry she spent on Felice now mirrored in her face over Jean.

"*Il est un soldat magnifique,*" Felice said with a perfect accent. She had insisted her mother teach her some French last year.

"*J'espère,* Felice," her mother answered slowly, still deliberating the meaning of the postcard.

"He even says he likes the food," Felice pointed out. "I mean, Army food? Jean has to love being a soldier."

"He says he thinks most trainees are stupid and lazy . . ."

Her mother had found the only negative line in the postcard. "Jean means compared to him, no doubt," Felice explained.

"He's so intolerant, isn't he?" Her mother shook her head. "Maybe he gets that from me."

"Mom, will you stop it? Jean is who he is, and he'll be fine. Quit worrying and eat the cake. It's terrific."

"Happy birthday, sweetie," she said, recovering. The two laughed as they clinked glasses. "Are you going to change, now that you're a teenager?"

"In what way?"

"I don't know. That's what teenagers do. Suddenly they become very independent. I like you the way you are."

"I can't stay thirteen forever."

"Of course not, but don't ever lose that special quality of yours."

Felice let her mother kiss her. "What special quality?" As capable as Felice was at analyzing and understanding others, she was sometimes blind to her own character.

"You're a very kind, giving person. I think I'm a lucky mother."

"No, I'm a lucky daughter," she corrected, meaning it.

They swapped stories as they ate their cake, but her mother's spirits didn't stay up for long. When they drifted into the house she dropped quietly into a chair with the latest memos from her lawyers. She suddenly looked tired and restless. Felice wished she could help, but there were things about her mother she did not understand, things she was afraid for. What made her feel better finally was when her mother, not knowing Felice was watching, returned to the mail and pulled out another letter. Felice had glanced at the postmark and known instantly. She could only wonder what Brother Andrew had written, and what her mother would write back.

Specialist Fourth Class Jean Poindexter arrived in Saigon on January 29, 1967, hauling a duffel bag on his shoulder and wondering if this was the same planet from which he'd taken off fifteen hours earlier. As soon as he stepped from the plane a driving rain leached into his combat boots and saturated his clothes. Inside a dank Quonset hut, he spit water from his lips and studied the two hundred other arrivals as they milled around, looking like lost, sad puppies. Jean plopped in a chair and studied his soggy papers. "Poindexter, Jean. 387 770989 sp4 S45Y2T USARV TRANS DET APO SF 96384." More gibberish, he thought, when he endured a staff sergeant's two-hour lecture on hygiene, Saigon's black market, MACV procedures, how to requisition pillows and sheets, and what to do if you couldn't tell a VC from an RVN regular (using the chain of command, ask your CO!). Jean groaned out loud. What the hell did this have to do with *war?* Where the hell was the fighting, anyway? He had spent sixteen long weeks in infantry training, doing both his basic and AIT at

Fort Ord, and taken a brief leave to say good-bye to his mother and sister. Now he was ready to kick some ass.

Around him pasty-faced kids, their hair as short as putting-green grass, sat in frozen attention. The pudgy sergeant droned on about the nasty goings-on at Nha Trang, Qui Nhon, Chu Lai, Tuy Hoa, Da Nang, and Quang Tri. There were no sanctuaries in this war, came the message. What do you want me to do, shit fear? Jean thought. He didn't care which hellhole they dumped him in. Just get him there in a hurry. This goddamn military bureaucracy was amazing—he would bet his father never had to endure it. No wonder the United States wasn't winning this war. Too many people were in Saigon pushing papers when they should be in the field pulling triggers.

In the next seven days Jean's medical records were twice misplaced; a sergeant major whose IQ was lower than the temperature tried to assign him to a graves-registration unit; the company of the 101st Airborne Division, to which he was supposed to be attached, was for the moment topheavy with grunts; and a fifty-year-old captain in charge of new arrivals only wanted to play poker. Jean politely declined the card games. Marooned, he began hanging out at GI bars, drinking warm beer and listening to horror stories about booby traps and Claymore mines that had blown hands and feet off in opposite directions. Charlie was one mean, vicious, American-hating son of a bitch, everyone swore. The conversation would jump to the eternal hunt for the best pussy in Southeast Asia, narratives conveyed in the same obsessive, charged, ready-to-do-violence voices as the war stories.

Jean had to smirk. He wasn't here to hunt pussy; he wanted nothing to do with the Vietnamese except to put as many bullets as he could between their squinty eyes, get himself declared a blue-ribbon hero, and head the hell home.

As days passed, Jean only grew more impatient. This was a land of loonies and lost souls. Americans, Vietnamese, they were all zombies. Did he really belong here? Jean slowly intuited what no one was willing to speak out loud—that even if he and any other Audie Murphy each killed a thousand of the little yellow suckers, the VC and North Vietnamese were tough and stubborn and not inclined to wave white flags. They'd been beaten on by the French, and now the Americans, and were so pissed off that unless LBJ decided to nuke them, this war was going on forever.

On the twelfth of February Jean was finally flown, courtesy

of a ten-thousand-pound assault helicopter, to a distant out-post about twenty kilometers from Tay Ninh City, near the Cambodian border. The entire flight, Jean perched recklessly on the edge of the chopper with the door open. The gunner beside him wore a cowboy hat and looked like he wanted to talk, but the engine noise made anything but chewing gum impossible. There was a languid beauty to the squares of flooded rice paddies, blocked out as they were like a chess-board. The symmetry was interrupted by jagged craters made by B-52 bombs, holes so desolate and sterile that nothing, Jean figured, would grow there for a hundred years. The chopper finally landed in the middle of nowhere on a small flat-top hill, its blades kicking up dust that the waiting soldiers grimaced at and then ignored as they glided stiffly toward the helicopter to unload supplies. What a sorry place, Jean thought. He surveyed the blank, bored faces and the compound of tents and sandbag-reinforced trenches and the ubiquitous perimeter defense rolls of concertina wire. The Seabees had come in at one time and built a permanent mess hall and CO quarters, and maybe once this place had held a full company, but Jean saw there were no more than fifty men now. The compound was called Hill 642, for its metric height. Around it sat a thick, endless carpet of brush and jungle where the heat rose in shimmering waves.

After a couple of days he knew his first impressions had been correct. Hill 642 was full of pot-smoking, paranoid, acid-rock-loving kids who hated being in Nam, did as much as they could, with the collusion of their CO, First Lieutenant Marvin Harp, to avoid engaging the enemy, and whose favor-ite activity was marking off days on short-timer calendars. It was one big happy family of sloth and indifference. Lieuten-ant Harp, fresh from OCS, blond, blue-eyed, had a face full of moles and a streak of fear as wide as a freeway. He *had* to send out two patrols a day—a major from Tay Ninh would fly in unannounced to check on things—but the patrols never ventured very far, and otherwise Hill 642 hardly considered itself part of the war. There hadn't been a genuine firefight in six months, Harp bragged to Jean, because this pissant little compound meant nothing to the VC, which only proved how intelligent the enemy was. The lieutenant couldn't even tell Jean why the United States Army occupied it, except for observation and intelligence gathering, and there was precious little of that to pass on to MACV. That was the way things went in this odd little war, Lieutenant Harp added in a self-congratulatory tone, and no one wanted to mess with fate.

Jean immediately asked for a transfer.

"What's your problem, soldier?" Harp demanded, amused, as he slouched back in his chair.

"I'd like a chance to fight, sir."

The lieutenant gave a twisted smile. "I think I can help you. We have a shrink who flies in once a month."

"Sir, I enlisted for a reason. I'm not wasting my or my country's time getting stoned or just standing guard duty or doing KP—"

"Soldier," Harp interceded kindly, "I have to point out that this is not the sands of Iwo Jima. It's not now, nor ever will be a John Wayne war. I think your expectations are a tad high."

"The only reason this isn't a real war is that everyone is too chickenshit to fight one."

"Boy, you should have joined the Marines."

"Is it too late?"

"Would you like a drink?" Harp asked, opening an ice chest and holding up a wet beer. It was clear he thought Jean had a death wish. It had given the lieutenant something to do, trying to talk the young specialist out of his mood, and now he would change his ploy to one of appeasement. The glistening brown bottle was opened—Harp took his first swallow with exaggerated pleasure—and a second beer was offered to Jean. His eyes swam from the bottle to the lieutenant and back to the beer. His fatigues were totally damp. The dry season in Nam was a furnace chamber twenty-four hours a day. The sky baked to a glossy enamel blue at six in the morning and never saw a cloud.

"No, thank you, sir."

Harp looked disappointed. "I'll see what I can do about getting you to a real war, Poindexter. Here you're only going to be bad for morale."

Jean didn't share the lieutenant's easy laughter. He just wanted out. But over the next weeks Harp did nothing but make excuses about paperwork and how hard it was to transfer anyone anywhere, except in a body bag, which he said he was proud that he had never done once as a commander. Jean was forced to go through the motions of being a soldier. He volunteered for at least one search-and-destroy patrol every day, and asked the lieutenant to consider a third daily excursion, at least stage drills for the compound because no one was combat-ready. Jean had listened to the intelligence reports that came in on the radio—the VC were massing along the Cambodian border. Harp gave Jean's suggestions as much credence as he did the alarmists squawking on the radio. The damn war was out *there* somewhere, and that was the way the lieutenant would bet it stayed. As for the piece of real estate known as Hill 642, he seriously doubted the gooks would want it even if it were wrapped up in ribbons for Christmas and the lieutenant said *please*.

Bullshit, Jean thought. The war was a lot closer than that. He was the only one who didn't sleep through guard duty at night, his eyes straining against the darkness for signs of enemy life. Twice one stint he fired off flares, annoying Harp no end and earning the derision of his fellow EM's. They began to look upon him as a ward case, and a threat to their way of life. That he actually polished his boots and brass and cleaned his M-16 every evening while they were partying to the Doors or Mothers of Invention only added to their keen dislike. They began calling him "Marine." Jean didn't care. They were all assholes who stood a good chance of waking up dead one morning.

But he didn't really want that. He wanted to save their lily-white asses in a huge firefight and have them grovel around him afterward in supplication and gratitude. As the days grew hotter and filled with dust, he would sit alone on a dike of sandbags, staring out hollowly into the jungle, knowing that those grimy little VC were just outside the perimeter, reproducing and growing like mushrooms, waiting for the right moment to overrun the Americans and cut off their balls to string up on trees or tie them to their waists in the name of high fashion, Vietnamese style. They wanted to have their own little party.

After six months in-country Jean had endured two hundred patrols and fired his weapon exactly five times. No enemy had ever been found, alive or dead. "Body count" was not part of the working vocabulary of the men of Hill 642. Instead of VC, Jean had been attacked by insects and leeches, dehydrated by dysentery, emaciated by the heat, and strung out on sleepless nights. His throat was always dry and his eyeballs squeaked and his tongue felt like rubber. The dust was almost worse than the heat. It crept into his soap dish, his toothpaste, his shaving cream; he found it in his food, his socks, his hair, and his underwear; it clogged his rifle chamber and jeep engines and the typewriter he used to write letters home. Staying clean, even for a few hours, was impossible, and for reasons he didn't understand, that little failure troubled him deeply, brought him almost to the edge of despair. He wanted to be ready to engage the enemy at all times, to be able to think clearly, but all he thought about was the damn heat and dirt and insects and how unhappy they made him, how little he could do to stop them.

Something was happening to his mind, Jean realized one night when he couldn't sleep. For the first time since he'd arrived in Vietnam, he began to be afraid. This whole country was twisted and deceiving and vengeful. It was a land of abiding meanness. A sense of chaos and paranoia burrowed into Jean's brain, festered there, and altered his thinking. The enemy was anything he couldn't touch, hear, smell, or see, a ubiquitous, forbidding silence that trailed him like a shadow. The silence was clever and persistent and played tricks. On the way to the mess hall or walking the perimeter, Jean would hear surly whispers behind his back, only to turn and stare at thin air. Late one night, buck naked in the latrine, he was ambushed by a vision so powerful his knees quaked—he was going to die in a firestorm that sucked the oxygen right out of his lungs. He tried to stay calm but his heart rose to his throat. What was happening to him? In Saigon he had thought he could stay above the madness—it was the others who were lost souls—but now he felt doomed.

He returned to his tent, slept lightly, and was wakened by whispers again. He shot up in the darkness, making out the contorted figures of sleeping comrades. Their snoring crescendoed and ebbed like a lullaby. Jean settled back, but sleep was impossible. From his fatigues he pulled his latest letter from home and let a flashlight dance over the words.

June 10, 1967

Dear Jean,

Is everything all right? Felice and I worry whenever a week goes by and we don't hear from you. Did you get our care package of cookies and candy bars? I know you must be starved for a good meal—I promise to fix you one the day you come home! What else do you need? Is the weather still hot, no rain? I never told you, but I know something about Vietnam. My uncle fought there when the French occupied the country—he thought it was *très diabolique,* and it's probably no different for you and your friends. I only hope time goes quickly. The antiwar movement is building by the day here—there are campus demonstrations across the country. The war is folly, like all wars, and it must stop. Jean, I'm enclosing some snapshots of Felice and me at the county fair. You said someone in your group has a Polaroid—please send something of you back to us. Each day you're away I say a prayer. Your grandmother tells me not to worry. I know she writes you once a week—she misses you as much as we do.

> We love you,
> Mom

Jean crumpled the letter and tossed it on the ground. If his mother loved and missed him so much, why didn't she get him the hell out of here? Jesus, she wrote all these sweet words but didn't do anything. No one did. What did anyone know about this fucking war in which no one had fired a shot at him but something told Jean he was dying anyway?

From that moment he decided to stop writing home, stop talking to anyone, even keep his distance from the amiable Lieutenant Harp, who in a week was due to be shipped back to the States and was suddenly cheerful and forgiving of deviants like Jean. Jean could not forgive himself. What had made him volunteer for the draft while others were pulling tricks to stay in college or join the National Guard or flee to Canada? He *was* a ward case. In the evenings Jean gave up polishing his brass and cleaning his rifle. He didn't volunteer for patrols or guard duty. They stopped calling him "Marine." Whenever he could, he slept, but his dreams were populated with whole battalions of grim-faced VC armed with grenades and Russian rifles. Like in an arcade shooting gallery, when Jean fired at a figure it would drop for a moment only to pop back up. He would scream, but no one would hear, and when he woke, drenched in sweat, his eyelids hot and heavy, he wondered again if he wasn't already dead.

He began to smoke pot. The men of Hill 642 were geniuses at that. There was never a problem obtaining marijuana—besides local gardens, grass came in with the food on the Tay Ninh choppers—but finding novel ways to ingest it into one's bloodstream took on the highest forms of creativity. The

EM's made their own pipes, invented water-suction devices, blew the grass through their M-16's, fashioned it into incense sticks, fanned it through the mess hall, mixed it in with crunched-up M&M's. Grass was the religion of oblivion and survival. Jean took a hit in the morning, again at ten, noon, three, and the inevitable nightcap. Pot increased his tolerance for pain and took away his dreams, if he were lucky, and turned time into a pleasant, meandering river. It even made the gunk they called food mildly tolerable. But when he wasn't stoned, the darkness swirled around him in ever-present shadows. It didn't matter whether his eyes were open or not. He could feel the jungle through his pores, as if he were submerged in it, an interchangeable part of it, swimming through the undergrowth, lost—and always afraid of who would find him.

One night Tay Ninh City, twenty clicks to the east, lit up like Mount Vesuvius. Jean and everyone else jumped on top of the sandbag bunkers for a display of fireworks unlike any ever seen back home. "Goddamn, will you look at that," Harp kept saying, incredulous, as he peeked through his binoculars, then ran to his radio to find out what was happening. Everyone knew it was the VC, including Harp, but he was angry about this inconvenience, especially since he was about to fly home. Stoned, Jean regarded the pyrotechnics as a thing of rare and privileged beauty, but Harp was disturbed enough to put the compound on twenty-four-hour alert. The hysterical major on the Tay Ninh radio said he was holding back a flood of VC. Within half an hour came the air strikes around Tay Ninh, the bright bursts of napalm dumped by U.S. pilots on the invisible enemy, and the artillery pounding away until the earth shook and the sky lit in unholy brilliance.

Whattaya know, Jean thought dimly as he continued sitting on the sandbags, the laughter building in his throat. I'm finally seeing a fucking war!

He was too stoned that night to volunteer for guard duty. In bed he fell asleep despite the noise and new tension, relaxed as a baby. He dreamed about his father, the time they were going to built a castle out of blocks in Jean's room—how old was he? How could he remember something he had entirely forgotten? This time they really finished the building, a high, dramatic structure with turrets and knights with gleaming swords.

The first incoming round dropped a few yards from Jean's

tent, crashing into his dream like an ocean wave on fire.
When he struggled up he heard low, strangulated breathing
and sharp howls that sounded close to laughter. His eyes
opened. The heat was so intense that he was sure the earth
had split open, its molten core rising like a sun to roast
everything in its path. There was a black kid with a hawkish
face named Skeeter across from him. His clothes were on
fire, and he was gyrating on his bed, trying to say something,
patting the flames on his stomach like it was a game of Simon
Says. Jean dragged him to the floor. The entire tent was in
flames. He hauled Skeeter into the open compound, where he
somehow thought there would be safety. The sky was a
theater of iridescent flares and exploding mortar rounds and
dancing shadows. Men whom Jean knew only as lazy and
cocky now zigzagged through the sulfurous mists screaming
at each other, panic choking their voices, half-mad, holding
up their M-16's and dashing toward the black holes of bunkers. A swath large enough for a jeep had been punched
through the concertina wire. Jean watched as a rush of dark-
clothed figures—they were like fish leaping up a stream—
scrambled through it and into his compound. Lieutenant Harp
was silhouetted in the lit doorway of headquarters, watching
the siege of Hill 642 with his patented look of angry wonder.
Defiant, he suddenly pinwheeled his arm back, launching a
grenade that looped haplessly into a nearby bunker and within
seconds blew permanent holes in three of his own men.

Jean almost tripped over the M-16 that lay beside Skeeter.
As he dropped on the weapon, a mortar round whistled over
his shoulder and sailed into the pile of gasoline drums in a
corner of the compound. The explosion lit up anew the arena
of combat, an illumination so fierce and unrelenting, but also
somehow personal, that it had the feel of stage lights. Lieutenant Harp was revealed standing in the middle of the compound, his face creased with worry and a sense of embarrassment.
He seemed to understand that leadership was called for and
that he was this compound's designated leader. He trotted
ahead, toward the hole in the fence, .45 held high—Jean
thought: This *is* John Wayne—when something bounced off
the lieutenant's chest. He scooped up the troublesome missile,
debating where to send it, but it detonated and sent a thousand
tiny fragments into every region of his disbelieving body.

"Shit," moaned Skeeter as he cringed next to Jean. "Git
me outta here, man."

"Right," Jean agreed, but he wondered where the hell they could go.

His chin jutted up for surveillance, only to find himself staring into the frightened, morose eyes of a kid no more than fifteen. Jean's M-16 was, by some miracle, pointed in the right direction. His finger glided back on the trigger. The boy crumpled without a sound.

"Nice," breathed Skeeter in gratitude. He was still smiling when a bullet slammed into his neck.

Jean hugged the ground. He stared at his comrade. Skeeter's eyes rolled back and Jean couldn't hear him breathing. He whispered Skeeter's name. *Jesus H. Christ . . . get me the hell out of here.* On elbows and knees, Jean slithered off. He didn't feel a spark of pity for the dead, nor an obligation to save the living. The only emotion he knew was fear. Wild, unbridled, frenzied fear that took control of his pot-stupored brain and filled him with the blackest dread.

He was a few feet from a bunker when a bullet rudely struck his leg. A second punctured the small of his back. He pushed himself forward anyway, into the hole, and curled up in a fetal ball. *Please . . . please . . . just go away.* Whenever the flares subsided, pitching everything into darkness, he thought maybe the battle was over, but then came a new wave of flares, and gunfire rattled through his consciousness, counterpointed by the thudding of boots and squeals of pain. *Oh, God, please, save me . . . save my ass.* Jean felt the molasses quality of his dreams, that everyone was pinned down here by a special unrelenting gravity; escape was possible only by dying.

A silence abruptly dropped over the compound. Jean had no idea at what point it came, or if it would be permanent, but it was a welcome peace that wrapped around the night. Accompanied by total blackness, it made him aware of both his exhaustion and his exhilaration. He had been shot and was bleeding and he was in pain, but he was alive. He resisted shouting out. Maybe the VC were being quiet on purpose, so he would be quiet too. Maybe he was deaf from the gunfire, maybe that's why there was silence. His mouth was filled with dirt, and the acrid smell of burned bodies made him gag. His whole body shook. He was suddenly terrified. He couldn't stop himself from remembering what General Westmoreland was telling the whole world: the light was at the end of the tunnel. Oh yeah, oh yeah. What the hell did Westmoreland know? His five stars and too many years padding a linoleum floor in the Pentagon blinded him to what war was all about. Had the general ever been in a firefight like *this?* The truth was, there was no fucking light *anywhere*.

Jean woke stiffly to the dawn heat and the blades of a chopper. When the medics turned him over gingerly, he took in their surprised eyes and answered with a defiant smile. "Hey, this one's alive," a dour-faced corpsman said, patting Jean on the shoulder. They put him on a litter, which was when he saw the gook lying no more than four feet away, a neat round hole between his brooding eyes. Had Jean shot the sorry mother? When he gazed around, he saw that Hill 642 was a morgue. The maze of bodies was an obstacle course as he was carried to the chopper. The VC hadn't taken the compound after all, he finally realized. Jean was surprised by his pride, then overwhelmed by it; suddenly he loved the war and his role in it. And, goddammit, he was alive! Skeeter had somehow survived too, and was already waiting in the chopper. So had a burly E-6 sergeant named Hodges, who was dragging on a cigarette with his one good hand like this was a World War Two movie. Everyone else, a corpsman said, was body-bag material.

"God damn you, Harp," Jean whispered.

He got airvacked to a U.S. hospital in Okinawa, where he had three operations to remove shrapnel and repair organ damage. His prognosis was for a complete recovery. When a pasty-faced full-bird colonel from the Public-Information Office showed up in Jean's room, he looked the other way. He never wanted to see another fucking officer in his life.

"I think your father would be proud of you," the colonel began, his hand jumping out to wrap around Jean's.

Jean wondered if that was a figure of speech, or maybe the colonel had actually known his father. "Sir?" he said, confused.

"It's my privilege to inform you, Specialist Poindexter, that for your role in repelling the enemy assault on the night of August 8, 1967, you've been awarded a Distinguished Service Cross. You've also been recommended for the Congressional Medal of Honor."

Jean gazed back numbly. No, wait a minute. He'd killed one, maybe two VC. Most of the time he'd been cowering in a bunker. The colonel was mistaken—some poor other dumbfuck had been the hero, only he'd gotten wiped out before he could claim credit. But before Jean could open his mouth, the colonel was filling the air with his praises. According to Specialist Jordan "Skeeter" Washington, Jean had turned back the enemy almost single-handedly. When Jean felt strong enough, *Stars and Stripes* was waiting to interview him. His grit and integrity were an example to every American who put on combat fatigues. Hill 642 had been saved for the proud people of the Republic of Vietnam and freedom-cherishing nations everywhere.

Jean was dumbfounded. Until the VC siege, you couldn't have given away that pissant mountain—just ask Lieutenant Harp. But Jean also understood he had become, for one night's unwanted adventure, a badly needed morale booster for the kind of lost, misguided fool who'd died on Hill 642 and in dozens of other outposts just like it, and would keep on dying. Jean represented hope. A false hope in a war of ever-bolder lies, he thought, but even if he was a counterfeit hero, he was still a hero. All those negatives somehow added up to a positive. He wasn't going to call the colonel a liar. And goddamn if it didn't feel nice to be wanted for a change. Fate was bestowing on him the very opportunity he'd always coveted.

"Thank you, sir," Jean said, "very much."

Jean did interviews for *Stars and Stripes,* the New York *Times,* the Los Angeles *Times,* and *Newsweek.* Besides his mother and sister, his congressman and both senators called. Telegrams arrived from General Westmoreland, the Pentagon, and the State Department. Around the hospital, basking in revering eyes, Jean walked with a bounce in his step. He lost track of how many times he'd recounted the all-night battle in which he'd kicked so many VC asses they couldn't all be found. It didn't matter, he thought, because the story just got better and better. For sure it was a lot better than the truth.

On a windy, overcast morning, when the clouds scudding overhead loomed like warships heading back to Nam, Jean stood on a tarmac waiting for a plane to take him to Germany. He had another eight months to serve before his discharge, but soon the name Poindexter was going to mean something again to the good citizens of Los Angeles. The crowning of a new war hero would wipe away the unjust stigma that had destroyed his father. And Jean would have the currency to walk into any real-estate firm in the city and name his job.

God damn, he thought, turning and blowing Asia a kiss good-bye, his future was finally here.

August 20, 1967

Dear Andrew,

Forgive me if I don't make sense today. Jean was wounded and has been evacuated to a hospital in Okinawa. He's supposed to be fine, and will finish his tour as a desk clerk in Germany, but I'm still on pins and needles. I've come to hate this war more than the one I lived through. When I gave Jean a good-bye hug seven months ago, I caught my reflection in the brass insignia of his hat and it was impossible not to see myself twenty years earlier, in Paris, when I first met Red. Jean, with his soft, handsome face, so proud, *was* Red. I prayed then that he got out of his war whatever it was that he wanted, just as Red got what he wanted from his war. Now maybe Jean has. The Pentagon sergeant I spoke to said my son was a hero and had saved dozens of lives. We'll see what that does to him. My hope is he'll settle down and go to college.

Andrew, I'm sorry if I ramble on too much about Jean. I don't think anyone occupies my thoughts as much as he, except maybe for you. I owe you so much. It has been a long and lonely year with Jean in constant danger and me doing battle with the high and the mighty of the charity world. I still have difficulty seeing the future, not knowing what I should do with my life. But I know I wouldn't have survived so far without your letters. They always fill me with hope and strength—you write with eloquence and passion. And there is such warmth and light in you that I know I have to see you again. Is that ever going to happen? I've asked you before, but you never give me a firm answer. It feels like you're in prison, shut behind those silent walls. It frustrates me. You always write me about the importance of holding out hope in my life. I can't let myself believe that we won't see each other again.

Please write soon and keep me in your prayers. I miss you very much.

Love,
Alycia

She sealed and stamped the envelope and carried it to her mailbox on the front porch. The more unreachable Andrew made himself, the more forbidden, the more he was part of her fantasies, the more she wanted to see him. She had never told Andrew she was falling in love with him, but didn't he have to know? She liked to imagine him opening and reading her letters. What was he feeling? Sometimes she fantasized about Andrew as a young man, before he joined the monastery. Young and rich and reckless—would she have fallen in love with him then too? There was nothing comfortable about falling in love for Alycia. As Harriet had discreetly said, how could she have chosen a monk? Alycia didn't think that quite fair. How did one ever control one's heart? The real question was, if Alycia was falling in love, what was she going to do about it?

She was turning to go back into the house when a powder-blue Cadillac convertible rolled up to the curb and honked with urgency.

"Alycia, I need you," Electra said before she was half out of the car. She looked agitated. "Right now. I mean, if you can spare an hour or two."

"For what?" Alycia asked, a little startled. She hadn't seen Electra in several months.

"I'm supposed to speak at this luncheon. I haven't prepared at all. Just having a friend around will make it easier for me, and maybe you can give me some hints on the way. You always have this presence . . ."

Married to Randolph now, Electra was a different woman. She had put weight on her hips and face, totally losing her girlish glow. Her personality had faded with it. What filled her now was not mischief and daring but a sense of self-importance that was almost an imitation of Carmine Bradbury's. Getting older meant growing up to Electra. She defined that as winning the respect of everyone she ran into, because respect was something she'd never had much of before. For a while Alycia had been jealous of the ease of her friend's life, the breaks Electra got and the way she always compromised herself out of trouble. Finally, with the perspective of Andrew's advice, she'd accepted they were two different people, two separate lives.

The trust and empathy the two women had once shared were badly eroded. The deterioration had begun with their argument at the Red Cross Ball and accelerated when Electra was named to the Helen Mayer board seat. Electra had to be aware of everything, Alycia thought, but she pretended that nothing had changed between them, simply that Alycia, under stress, had behaved badly with the old crowd, and it was only a matter of time before she'd reform and everything would be back to normal.

Alycia did nothing to correct the impression. The night of the ball she'd learned how painful a confrontation with a best friend could be. She decided that the two would see less and less of each other, a relatively painless process that would end with each finally disappearing from the other's life. It was the best way, she thought.

"I don't think I can get free right now," Alycia said as pleasantly as she could, walking up to the car. The sun blazed on the nape of her neck.

"The luncheon won't take very long, I swear."

"I just can't, not today. If you'd given me more notice—"

"Alycia, I *need* you. How can you turn me down? If you needed me, I'd be there. You know I would."

"I'm not dressed," she tried.

"You look wonderful. Now, are you coming or not?"

Electra's face had turned so plaintive and helpless that Alycia surrendered. Maybe a small part of her still wished they could be friends. But in the car Alycia only felt trapped and wished she wasn't doing this.

In the luncheon room of the new Century City Plaza Hotel, Alycia sat at a table with women she didn't know, and watched as Electra circulated like a butterfly. A woman society reporter from the *Times* scribbled names. When it was time to speak, Electra glanced to Alycia for assurance. She started slowly but gained confidence and her delivery was fine. Describing a recent gala ball for cancer research, Electra informed everyone that of the $425,000 raised, more than eighty percent had gone directly to National Cancer Institute laboratories. A middle-aged doctor with twinkling blue eyes rose from his dais chair to acknowledge the money. The women at the tables applauded. When Electra announced the next fund-raiser, everyone wanted to help.

"Tell me something," Alycia said when she and Electra were walking alone to the car afterward. She had told herself to keep silent, but she couldn't. "Why did you say those things? Eighty percent of what you raised went to research? I know the people who ran the event. They always keep half for expenses.''

Electra shrugged, as if she didn't hear or it wasn't important. "You have to tell me how I was as a speaker. Did my voice carry?''

The silence pushed down on them. Alycia wished she were somewhere else. "Electra—"

"Here you go again," she said, disbelieving.

"You lied.''

"I exaggerated," she corrected.

"And the doctor went along with your lie. Or maybe he isn't a doctor—"

"Of course he's a doctor," Electra said, dismayed.

"How could he agree with you?''

Electra's eyes jumped to Alycia and they were shooting sparks. "Haven't you heard that the end justifies the means? It was my job to stir interest today, to broaden our base of support. The doctor said he would cooperate in any way he could. He didn't know the exact numbers anyway.''

"Electra, you can't lead people on like that—"

"Who says I can't? Are you writing the rules?''

"No, but maybe somebody should.''

"The cause is a good one and you know it.''

Alycia bit her tongue. What was she doing? Hadn't she told herself to let her relationship with Electra die in peace? The cause *was* good. Alycia didn't totally dismiss the way society had been raising money since Victorian times. People weren't perfect—there would always be some hypocrisy—and maybe she was speaking more for herself. But what she objected to was a lack of self-awareness in people like Electra, the sense that their way was the only way, so perfect it could never be improved on.

"All I want to say," Alycia said calmly, "is that you might be more honest with your audience. People respect honesty. You're still going to raise money—maybe even more by not being phony.''

"My God," Electra said, stopping Alycia in the parking lot, "you really don't give up, do you? I try to patch things up between us and you pay me back by attacking me. Everyone warned me you were hopeless. What is your problem? Are you jealous of me? Are you bitter about your life?''

"My life is fine," Alycia responded, though Electra had hit a nerve.

"You know what I think?" Electra said. "I think you need a man so badly it's pathetic."

Alycia struggled to control herself. "My private life is my own business."

"And so is mine. Please keep your nose out of it. I don't need your criticism."

"I don't like hypocrisy," Alycia said.

"You're acting like you don't like me. You've totally isolated yourself from everyone. You don't know how to make friends anymore, or keep them."

"Please don't say that."

"Christ, you don't know how furious you make me, Alycia. You're so foolish and pigheaded it's embarrassing. Let's not see each other anymore. You can find a way home, can't you?"

An agitated Electra levered herself into the convertible and roared off. Left behind, Alycia trembled, and she felt tears coming. Why did this hurt so much? She had been the one to want to keep a distance from Electra, but to have Electra say it first, and so brutally . . . No one understands me at all, Alycia thought. But how could she expect old friends to understand or be sympathetic after she had rejected them? It wasn't realistic to expect anything like that. Maybe Electra was right—she had purposely isolated herself, and her loneliness was her own fault.

But she hadn't willed any of this, Alycia thought as she found a taxi to take her home. Her husband had been broken by a scandal that had tarred the entire family. Red had taken his own life and left Alycia to pick up the pieces. She had tried to understand and to forgive him, but if he really had loved her, how could he have left her like this? It had taken time to bury her anger. Gradually, her circumstances had made her more sensitive to the plight of others in need. That was one reason she bristled at Electra and the countess and their friends—women who thought they understood the suffering of the world and gallantly set out to relieve it. They understood very little. They had never really suffered themselves.

And the money—they didn't understand that either, Alycia considered. Or was it she who had never understood? Despite all her money, her hopes and expectations, Alycia wasn't very happy. For people like Electra and the countess, money meant power and cachet, and they never seemed to feel any guilt. Their charity work took care of that. Whatever their secret, they had a contentment that had eluded Alycia. She wasn't envious. She wished them all the happiness in the world. She just wondered if they understood how lucky they were.

At home, a glass of wine did little to chase Alycia's pain. In the morning she glanced at the *Times* write-up on the luncheon. Alycia had been noted as one of the prominent guests. She stiffened when she read Electra's rosy speech and the lies about budgets. Everyone who read the article would think glowingly of Electra and her world. Alycia folded the paper in disgust. Just once, she thought, wouldn't it be nice to set the record straight?

She sat at Red's typewriter and composed a two-page letter to the *Times*'s society editor. One by one, she refuted Electra's points. She challenged the motive of the wealthy for giving to charity. Was it really from the heart, or the desire to belong to the right social circle? Alycia signed her name. She doubted the letter would see the light of print, but just sending it made her feel better.

The next Sunday the letter appeared verbatim in the society section under the headline "War Among the Wealthy." Underneath was a photograph of Alycia and Red from a Lakeside party years ago. For an instant Alycia didn't recognize the young, attractive woman, and she suddenly missed Red. But it was her own words that jumped out at her the most. Not because she sounded spiteful—she didn't—but because they were clear and obvious. They were also a threat, she knew, the sound of a gauntlet being thrown down. Suddenly she could see the future. If before she had been merely ostracized, now she would be sent into exile, an expatriated socialite whose name and reputation would be unmentionable in Los Angeles' rarefied circles.

Alycia expected an angry phone call from Electra or Carmine or Evan Chambers. Instead, a puzzling silence descended, as if none of her adversaries cared. Maybe they were plotting in secret. Alycia began to feel paranoid. She had never been comfortable with uncertainty or ambiguity, the rustling in the shadows.

The following Sunday the *Times* carried another letter to the editor. The pen of Carmine Bradbury had the same barb and wit as her tongue. Alycia Poindexter made a Fourth of July celebration of idealism and righteousness, her former friend wrote, but her actions did not support her sermons; she was a virtual recluse who shunned the poor as well as the rich because she couldn't get along with anybody.

Alycia had no choice but to write back. Her rebuttal was succinct. She would very much *like* to stand behind her sermons, she informed the *Times*'s readership, except that the self-appointed leaders of the charity world had labeled her *persona non grata*, kicking her off every board on which she had ever worked because she'd criticized those in power.

The next week it was Evan Chambers' turn. While Alycia Poindexter might be a well-intentioned human being, he wrote the *Times*, she had succumbed to a grandiose and distorted view of herself and the importance of her board work. The truth was, the term of her board seat had expired and someone else was being given a chance to hold the reins. There was nothing personal, he concluded.

Incredulous, the next Sunday Alycia treated the city of Los Angeles to the confidences Evan Chambers had whispered in her ear at the ball—every promise, plea, and proposition. Signing her letter, she knew she had escalated the battle. When Evan Chambers responded the following Sunday, denying every allegation, the paper burned in Alycia's hands.

The *Times* was enjoying the fray. Accompanying Evan Chambers' latest letter was a photo a reporter had dug up from the ball. The executive was shown dancing cheek to cheek with Alycia. Television and magazine reporters began to call. Was it true Alycia had had an affair with Mr. Chambers? A bitter falling out with her best friend, Electra Fitzhugh? Was Alycia trying to protect someone or some secret? The web of gossip left almost no one untouched. After a while Alycia refused to talk to reporters, but she didn't stop writing her letters, which the *Times* gratefully accepted, and were inevitably answered by various denizens of the charity world, until the whole city looked forward to the weekend revelations and the glimpses into the closed, privileged world of the wealthy.

Since they had parted ways at the luncheon, Alycia had not heard a word from Electra. She had not written a letter to the *Times*, or phoned or visited, as if she'd suddenly left the city, or for reasons no one understood, was staying out of the fracas. Maybe Electra finally felt some compassion for her, Alycia dared to hope; maybe she was silently rooting for Alycia but hadn't the courage to confront her new friends.

As letters continued being exchanged, to Alycia's chagrin

she found more and more references to Red and the stock scandal. Lawsuits against her husband were still pending, pointed out a wealthy attorney who happened to represent Evan Chambers' company, because Alycia Poindexter loved to create causes and not let them die. In a time when the youth of America were burning flags, bras, and draft cards, smoking pot, and joining the Communist party, an irresponsible gadfly who should know better was not what this country needed.

It was at that point that Alycia stopped reading newspapers.

February 14, 1968

Dearest Andrew,

I haven't heard from you in several weeks and am getting very worried. Are you sick? Has something happened? Please let me know. My spirits have been so low lately. The latest news is, on the advice of my attorneys, I'm suing for libel some of the people who've written letters about me in the *Times*. I'm not doing it for revenge or justice, but to put an end to this messy and endless bickering that I'm sorry I ever started. It's worn me down. It's not that I don't believe in fighting, but I just know I'm not going to win. The *Times* gets flooded with letters from outsiders, and a lot of people are in my corner, yet the powerful ones aren't. You've encouraged me to follow my conscience and not give up, but what can I possibly gain from all this? I need more than your advice, Andrew, I need to see you. I don't know why I haven't been more forthright. Maybe it takes adversity to make me totally honest and forget my prideful independence. I love you. I'm *in* love with you. We've been writing each other for a year and my feelings have grown too strong to pretend they'll pass away. They never will. I pray this doesn't shock or embarrass you, and I'm well aware of our compromised position because of what you are, but I have to be honest. Please answer me soon!

All my love,
Alycia

Weeks passed and there was no reply from the monastery. One day the head of the Lakeside membership committee called Alycia. He politely suggested, for the good of a club that did not take kindly to members whose names were repeatedly in the media, that she resign. Alycia couldn't believe it. Controlling herself, she told him she didn't like being in the papers either, and she wasn't resigning. She began to feel like a pariah. Even at church she found herself at the mercy of roving eyes. Felice, normally unflappable, came home from school one day in tears. Girls who had once kept their teasing to whispers were picking on her openly. Furious, Alycia went straight to the faculty and demanded they be more protective of her daughter. She received assurances they would, but in some teachers' eyes she saw rebuke for being an irresponsible parent.

A letter from Andrew finally arrived early in June. Alycia carried it in her purse all day, afraid to open it, and even in bed that night she wasn't sure what to do. She had written a half-dozen times without a reply. She could understand if Andrew had been taken aback by her declarations of love, but she had a right to be angry too. He'd deserted her when she'd needed him most. Didn't he care enough about her to write back?

Opening the envelope, she focused on the neat, measured writing, a hand so steady and confident that it immediately put her fear and anger at bay.

May 29, 1968

My dearest Alycia,

Forgive me for what must seem an inexcusably long delay. Just yesterday I returned from three months in the Amazon basin. The Trappists, with the help of your money, are starting a resettlement project for Indians who've lost their homes and land to the government. In Rio, the economics of minerals and timber are deemed more important than the rights of indigenous peoples. I was put in charge of getting the project off the ground, organizing labor and securing building materials, but I barely made a dent and at some point must go back. When I returned to the monastery I had never felt so exhausted, but then my abbot handed me your sheaf of letters and my spirit rebounded. I don't quite know what he thought of so much correspondence from one person—he is a dutiful but somewhat suspicious man—but I explained you were merely concerned with how your money was being put to use.

I read your letters immediately and in private, of course. Alycia, forgive me for not finding the time to write you from the jungle. I had no idea how wearing your enemies could be. You were in my prayers always, but I realize that prayers are sometimes not enough. I can only tell you that you must be strong, Alycia. You must not be discouraged, no matter how overwhelming the forces of your enemy. Righteousness is a gleaming sword that will slay deceit and hypocrisy.

I have read and reread your words about you and me a dozen times. I don't know how to answer. Perhaps cautiously is best. I suppose I did know all along how you felt about me, but I didn't want to admit it for all the troubling questions that your feelings raise. Now you have brought the matter squarely in front of us, confronted me, and I have nowhere to run. I also no longer have an excuse to pretend my own feelings do not matter. I wonder if God has singled me out for some purpose in having me fall in love with you. My heart has not sung like this, in such defenseless innocence, in my longest memory. To make such an admission seems heretical for someone who has taken vows of not only carnal but also spiritual chastity, vows to serve only the bride of Christ. But I cannot believe I have been betrayed by a starved and vulnerable heart for the sake of sin. There is something in our bond, Alycia, that means more than you and I can know at this time. It is faith that carries me to this judgment . . . yet I am also afraid. What is happening to me is so radical that I have nothing to compare it with. Do we not need, both you and I, more time together to understand what we are embarking on? I do miss you more than I can utter. When will I see you? I cannot leave the monastery. Please come at once.

> With my overflowing heart,
> Andrew

Felice, out of school but not yet in summer camp, peeked in her mother's bedroom the next morning to catch her packing a suitcase.

"What are you doing, Mom?"

Alycia felt her face warm as she turned. The pretty, long-legged girl in cut-off jeans stared back expectantly. Her breasts were budding under a T-shirt and the face seemed more mature every day. Alycia knew she had to be honest, but she thought Felice was smart and observant enough to guess.

"I'm taking a trip. I don't think I'll be gone long, but I don't know. I've asked Harriet to come stay with you. Is that all right?"

"You're visiting someone?" Felice asked disingenuously as she dropped onto the bed.

"Yes. Someone special."

"Brother Andrew?"

Alycia took Felice's hand and gave it a squeeze. "You know everything, don't you?"

"What did he write you? I saw the envelope—"

"That he loves me."

"And you're in love with him, aren't you?"

"Very much." Alycia hesitated. "Do you think that's somehow wrong?"

"I think it's wonderful!" Felice beamed. Then her face squinched in deliberation. "How can being in love be wrong? Because Andrew's a monk? I think it's kind of neat. I mean, who cares? It's your life, and his. Anyway, you've never done things the easy way, Mom."

Alycia dropped beside Felice and pulled her closer. "You say that as if you're proud of me."

"Shouldn't I be? The kind of grief everyone gives you, I don't think I could handle it. But you—"

"I don't know if I'm handling it either. I just do my best. And don't ever sell yourself short, Felice. You never know what you're capable of until something is demanded of you."

"But it's so painful, what you're going through, especially with Electra. I don't like pain. I don't understand why you and Electra can't get back together, if you both really want to."

"Darling, it's more complicated than that. Sometimes people drift apart even when they don't mean to." Alycia mussed the hair from Felice's eyes. "I don't want you to worry about anything. I'll take care of that department for both of us. Promise you'll let me do that."

"But that's not fair to you."

"Promise me," Alycia said.

"What about school this fall? Are you still going to worry for me then?"

"We'll cross that bridge later."

"I want to go away, you know that. The art education at Oakley Academy is better than anything in California."

"We'll see," Alycia answered evasively. She thought how miserable she'd be without her daughter. But Felice was becoming more independent by the day—in some ways she was as headstrong as her mother—and Alycia knew Felice could handle herself. She was in love with art history. Every free moment, she was at the library delving into the glories of Chartres or the Renaissance or the Byzantine Empire. She begged constantly to be taken to Europe, and until then, that her mother tell her everything about the art museums of Paris. Alycia couldn't help but feel proud, yet she knew there was a second reason Felice wanted to leave home. Her brother was due back in a month. Alycia couldn't wait, but Felice sensed disaster. To her, Jean would always be a bully. Alycia prayed that Vietnam and being a hero had changed him for the better, but she knew she couldn't talk Felice out of her feelings.

On a blustery afternoon when the Boston sky blackened and swelled with rain, Alycia flew into Logan International Airport, rented a car, and drove two hours on drenched roads to the Trappist monastery. She was too nervous to hold a thought. Maybe she was too afraid to think of the future. What would she tell Andrew other than that she loved him so much she couldn't stay away? Then what would happen?

The monastery was almost impossible to find. Just inside the New Hampshire border, a series of stone-and-stucco buildings sat in the middle of an isolated, bucolic field. The rain had eased to a drizzle when she drove up. Several monks moved quietly through the flowered grounds, but none returned her gaze, and after a moment they vanished into different buildings. What did they do all day? Didn't they wish once in a while for outside company?

A simple pine door was marked "Office." There were no other signs or directions. Alycia knocked several times, heard nothing, and pushed her head in. She shivered as she stepped inside. The room was unheated and cold from the rain. The simple plaster walls were unadorned, and the entire room, while ample in size, held only one chair and a desk. Resting on top, undusted, was an old-fashioned school bell.

Alycia picked up the implement, just as a monk with a gentle face entered the room through an interior door.

"I'm Brother Manning," he said in a reedy voice, approaching. Alycia thought the abbot to be about fifty, very average-looking, except for his hands, which he held solemnly, passively in front of him, so large and white and beautiful that it was easy to imagine them in a position of prayer, fingers straight and pressed together, like the saints carved on the doors of cathedrals. The abbot's eyes searched her without ceremony, which for a moment turned the gentle face into a mask of suspicion.

"May I help you with something?" he inquired.

"I'm Alycia Poindexter. I came to speak to Brother Andrew."

The abbot did not look surprised, as if he'd been expecting her. "So you are Mrs. Poindexter. This is a great honor. I want to thank you for your generosity. All of us are very grateful." The words came without much feeling.

"It's really Brother Andrew you should thank." She forced a smile. "He's a very persuasive speaker. If you let him, I think he could raise more money than you'd know what to do with." Dispelling the abbot's seriousness was as impossible as banishing the cold from the room. Alycia's heart rose to her throat. "Would it be possible to speak to him, please?"

"I'm very sorry, Brother Andrew is away."

Alycia's eyes rounded. "Away?"

"Yes."

"How long?" she asked.

The bands of gray above the abbot's eyes lifted apologetically. "For quite some time, I'm afraid."

"Are you sure?"

"Quite." He smiled modestly. "I know everything that happens here. Brother Andrew is on church business."

"Is he fund-raising, did he go back to the Amazon—"

"He is on church business," Brother Manning repeated softly.

Alycia's eyes bore into the stubborn man. It was hard keeping her anger down. "Did he leave any message for me?"

"None that I'm aware of."

"But it's not possible," she protested. "He was expecting me."

"I'm very sorry you're disappointed, Mrs. Poindexter. If there's anything I can do . . ."

"You must know how long he'll be gone."

"I cannot say, really. Would you like to leave a note?"

The abbot rummaged thoughtfully through a drawer for paper and a pencil.

"Tell him I was here, please," Alycia finally whispered.

She tried to stay in control, but in the car her hands shook on the steering wheel and she couldn't focus on the road. What had happened to Andrew? Why was the abbot turning her away? She was suddenly so angry she had to stop the car. Why would Andrew be part of a deception like this? It wasn't possible. She thought of turning around and waiting at the monastery until Andrew returned or she was told the truth. Had he changed his mind about wanting to see her? The thought stung deeply.

When Alycia arrived in Los Angeles she brushed aside Harriet's and Felice's inquiries about her quick trip as nonchalantly as she could, sorted through her mail with more disappointment, and tried to sleep. In the middle of the night she warmed some milk and sat in the kitchen leafing idly through back copies of the *Times*. Her eyes stopped at the bottom of the Sunday society section. The letter to the editor ran two columns. Her temples pounded, and she felt her skin stretch tightly over her forehead.

. . . unknown to her many friends, the art of masquerade and deception has been practiced by Alycia Poindexter ever since she arrived in the United States after World War II. Evoking pity for a life of hardship in Nazi-occupied Paris, she neglected to tell anyone the real facts. She and her father lived a privileged life where there was never a shortage of food or clothes or winter heat. The other fact she's failed to mention is she was hounded out of Paris by Jewish groups who uncovered indisputable evidence that her father had collaborated with the Germans. Professor Boucher fled to the south of France and changed his identity. Alycia married a wealthy American captain named Red Poindexter and never cared to look back. This is a woman who purports to want to help the oppressed and downtrodden, who has the arrogance to call others hypocrites . . .

Alycia didn't need to read further to find who had authored the letter. She was too furious and hurt to believe it. She remembered why she had given up reading newspapers. But now, so she'd never forget, she cut out the page, folded it into an envelope, and stored it in a safe place.

*   *   *

With the triumph of a hero Jean paraded off his plane in San Francisco on a chilly July afternoon in 1968. He wasn't expecting a marching band, but he thought someone might at least shake his hand and escort him through the ritual maze of paperwork that would free him from Uncle Sam. Instead, he was herded with a hundred other vets into a bus to Fort Ord. Mustering out entailed a week of hurry-up-and-wait, getting his severance pay, mess food that Jean was afraid would kill him, and a barracks of pot smokers who kept losing their paperwork because they had no desire to go anywhere. They looked at Jean with his Distinguished Service Cross breasted on his dress greens as if *he* were the deviant.

When Jean reached Los Angeles, he only wanted to crash. His mother threw her arms around him so tightly that he wondered if she hadn't given him up for dead. Drifting through the familiar house, glimpsing his old room, it did feel great to be home. He suddenly saw what his father had seen when he bought the Toluca Lake property—the quiet, charming neighborhood wedged between a golf course and a lake, an elegant house, the huge rolling lawn. Everything felt safe. No VC was going to lob a mortar round into this home. The best news of all was that little sister was off at summer camp, and in the fall she'd be going east to prep school. Jean would have the run of the house.

"I have a present for you," Alycia got around to saying after dinner. They sat at the patio table, fanned by a lake breeze. She suddenly held up a bright silver key festooned with a ribbon. "You always wanted this. After all you've been through, you deserve it."

"Jesus H. Christ, a Corvette?" Jean whispered, reading the key. He examined it as if it were gold. "This is fantastic, I mean it. Thanks, really . . ." He leaned over and gave his mother a kiss.

"It's in the garage, tank full. You can drive it over to your grandmother's tomorrow."

"How is she?"

"She's fine, but she really missed you."

"I missed her too. Sitting in those bunkers, I missed a lot of things."

"Did you think at all about college?" Alycia asked.

Jean cut himself another piece of pie. His mother sure

could cook. "Yeah. It would be a waste for me. I want to go to work."

"What kind of job can you get without a degree?"

"You'll see," he promised.

"I don't want you to set your expectations too high," she cautioned.

"Because you think I'll be disappointed? I can handle it, Mom."

Jean looked away. His mother meant well, but she didn't understand. He thought she was happier that he was home alive than for what he'd accomplished in the name of patriotism. He'd gone through hell for a purpose, and now that his dues were paid, it was time to collect. Maybe mothers, like the Army, didn't always appreciate their heroes.

"Why don't you just do nothing for a while," Alycia suggested. "You don't have to go to work right away, do you? Rest. Get your bearings. I'm happy to cook for you, wash your clothes . . ."

Jean reconsidered his appraisal of his mother. Maybe she did understand him, after all. "That would be great," he said.

Every morning he slept late, and no matter what time he wandered downstairs, his mother was there to fix breakfast. They began to talk about the war and what he'd been through. Sometimes they'd take in a movie or a concert at the Hollywood Bowl or the Greek Theater. It was surprisingly easy to communicate. After years of fighting, he and his mother were finally getting along.

When he wasn't home, Jean spent his time driving through the city. So many changes in two years, he thought, awed almost everywhere he looked. Los Angeles was in another growth spurt, downtown especially. He drove by every one of his father's old properties. What were they worth today? He tried not to feel too sick about it. Why hadn't his mother had the foresight and courage to hold on to them?

Sometimes he'd stop at his old after-school hangouts to meet girls, a process greatly facilitated by his Corvette and his easy smile. Often he'd spend the night in a strange apartment, but his mother never showed displeasure when he came home with a hangover or the girl on his arm. After a month he met a redhead at the beach and began living with her in a funky house in Malibu Canyon. He no longer called home, but he would drop by once in a while to visit, just as he did with his grandmother.

"Jean, there's something I have to tell you," Alycia said one evening after she'd fixed him dinner. They sat on the patio overlooking the lake.

Jean tilted back lazily in his chair, not really listening. Upstairs he could hear his sister opening and closing drawers. Miss Organization was already packing for school and she didn't leave for another week.

"I didn't want to bring this up right away, not after you just got home," she began. "I wanted you to rest, and get your feet on the ground."

"Bring up what?" he said, suddenly curious.

"While you were away, certain things happened to me. I had some unpleasant encounters with people, people I used to count as friends."

"Like who?" He dropped his chair to the ground and listened more carefully.

"Almost everybody," she said, sounding upset.

"Electra?"

"Yes."

"I thought she was your best friend."

"Not anymore. Do you want to know what she wrote about me in the newspaper? Do you know what it feels like to be totally ostracized? To have everyone think you're a kook?"

"Hey, Mom, take it easy. Do you ever think you might be exaggerating? I bet this is just like the lawsuits. You've brought a lot of this on yourself."

Jean thought his mother had been feeling sorry for herself ever since his dad had died. Somehow he'd thought she'd snap out of it, but she seemed more disgruntled than ever. Jean didn't have a lot sympathy. He had survived Vietnam; why couldn't she overcome this?

"What did you want to tell me, anyway?"

"I'm starting a new life," she said, "just like you are."

He nodded, yet something made him suspicious. "This doesn't have anything to do with that monk, does it? What's his name?"

"Brother Andrew."

"Well?"

"No," she said, almost sadly. "This is all my decision. Jean, I want to move away from here."

"Move?" Jean thought that was the craziest thing he'd

ever heard. Why was his mother acting so hurt? If she was feeling ostracized, what was moving going to prove? Was she really going to find new friends? "Where?" he asked.

"Palm Springs."

He started to laugh. "Why—because nobody knows you there? What are you going to do?"

"I don't know. I'll decide after I sell the house and get my affairs organized."

Jean straightened in his chair. "Wait a second—sell the house?"

"I know you have a lot of warm memories here, but I only seem to have bad ones. I can't live here anymore—"

"What are you talking about? This is my home too! I won't let you sell it." He heard the defiance in his voice.

"You don't understand, Jean. It's almost as if this house is haunted."

"Haunted?" He rolled his eyes.

"There are ghosts here. Your father, your grandfather—"

Jean groaned. "Christ, this is ridiculous. Just give the house to me. Because I won't let you sell it. No way. Dad would never approve."

"Your father isn't here to approve or not approve. It's my decision. If I thought I were depriving you or Felice of something, I'd feel differently. Felice understands what I'm doing. Why can't you? I'll pay for your education, and I'll give you money to start a career and a family. But I don't think staying in this house is good for either of us."

"Who says?" he almost shouted. "I'll decide what's good for me, okay? I want this house because it means something to me. It means a lot. This was my father's house. Whatever he had, a part belongs to me."

"I want to sell it, Jean. It's time for both of us to move on."

Cold fury swept over Jean. Why was she doing this to him? Who had she been talking to? In some way, that monk still had to be influencing her. Jean felt his anger spilling over.

"If you sell this house," he threatened, "I don't ever want to see you again, Mother."

Alycia sagged in her chair. "You don't mean that."

"You've done this to me before, when you sold Dad's buildings. This time I won't accept it. I want to come back to this house whenever I want to—that's my birthright."

"Your birthright was to be loved by your mother and father, which you were," Alycia answered.

"I'm warning you, Mother. You're betraying me. What else is rightfully mine? I wonder. Look at you, so pale and still. Why don't you tell me what you're thinking?"

"I'm thinking only that I love you. I want you to know that. I'll do whatever I can for you, always. But I don't think you have the right to get angry with me about the house."

Jean felt his face redden as he waited for his mother to yield, but she was firm. Well, then, so was he. "Then it's good-bye," he announced, burning underneath. His mother looked miserable as he rose from the table. He gathered a few possessions from his room, tossed everything into his new car, and brushed past his sister in the hallway without a word. Why should he waste one breath on that little twerp? She'd never taken her brother's side. His mother tried to kiss him at the door, but Jean ducked away.

Driving off, his rage deepened. How could his mother do this? His happiest memories had just been ripped away from him. He wanted them back—he needed them back, he thought, because without them he wasn't whole. This wasn't the end of the matter. His mother might not want anything to do with her past, but Jean swore he'd find a way to get his back.

Within a week he'd broken up with the redhead, rented a tiny studio apartment in Westwood, not far from UCLA, and turned his thoughts to the future. He bought a couple of suits and a nice stereo system—what else did he need? Every morning he devoured the *Times*'s real-estate section and help-wanteds. Nothing looked terribly promising. When Jean typed his résumé it looked so skimpy he was embarrassed.

To test the waters, one day he phoned a dozen real-estate firms. The few times he charmed his way past the secretaries, the response from brokers was unequivocal—he was too young, too inexperienced. He explained what he'd done in Vietnam, but there was only a polite silence. Jesus, he couldn't believe it. He'd almost died on that stinking mountain, and no one gave a shit? This was how heroes were treated? He saw how the middle class was finally turning against the war—the whole thing was wrong, Jean knew that more than anyone—but why should people take it out on *him*? He'd served his country like he was supposed to. Then he told the brokers about his father, how much he'd taught Jean about real estate in Los Angeles. Reactions were even cooler. Jean slammed down the phone. This was his mother's fault. She was keeping his father's name alive in infamy. She was making it hard on everyone.

It was almost Christmastime before his luck and persistence paid off. Jean landed a job with a Beverly Hills firm called Bomer and Walton. Just in time, he thought. His bank account showed $27.34 and he was behind on his rent. He celebrated by cadging some grass from the kid in the next apartment and getting so stoned he thought he was back in Nam. No more peanut-butter sandwiches for dinner, no more cold nights without heat. But in his heart of hearts he had liked the feeling of a close call. He could have been totally broke and he still would have found a way to survive. It wasn't unlike the firefight on Hill 642, the thrill of putting everything on the line. Risk and salvation. Either you accepted the idea of fate and were happy, Jean thought, or you denied it and lived in misery.

Bomer and Walton's main office was off Rodeo Drive, in the pampered, expensive heart of Beverly Hills. The firm had spent a mint on furnishings—subtle grays and blacks mixed with expensive antiques with rich patinas, and everything was spotlighted by overhead cans. The clientele arrived in Mercedeses or Cadillacs or chauffeured limousines. Jean could smell the money. His role was strictly Mickey Mouse gofer stuff, with some research and secretarial thrown in, just like at the Irvine Company. At night he studied for his broker's exam; when he passed that, the partners had promised, he'd become an associate and earn regular commissions.

It was his charm and good looks that had won him the opening, and to stay and prosper here, he knew he had to play a role. He lavished his entire first paycheck on a Pierre Cardin suit and Gucci shoes because that's what most brokers wore. He had his hair styled, began lifting weights in a gym, and saw that his nails were manicured weekly. He turned in his Corvette for a Cadillac. The "in" bar or restaurant changed every month, but Jean kept himself current. He wasn't much of a drinker—had never been—but it was important to be seen by the right people. What was more difficult was finding ways for someone else to pick up the check. When he did get stuck, or he took out a date, he usually could charm his way into the restaurateur's heart and get a tab started. When it climbed too high by the end of the month, he'd starve himself a few days, use his next check to pay the tab, and begin the cycle of credit anew.

Jean did not navigate the curves on the road to sophistication by himself. An associate broker named Kirby Willis had taken Jean under his wing almost from the first day. In many ways Kirby was not a typical Beverly Hills broker. He was from the Midwest, only twenty-seven, and had the stocky, muscular build of a linebacker. Like Jean, he had come to Bomer and Walton virtually broke and with no connections. But he was handsome, with large dark eyes and a pensive smile, he had a silver tongue, and he knew how to hustle. The wives of Beverly Hills loved him. Jean suspected Kirby took half his clients to bed, but he never named names. In this town, discretion was as vital and powerful as its cousin, gossip. Kirby was also a master politician within the firm. He knew what to say to whom, how to give and receive favors, to step over people he didn't like and to stay close to those in power. All his ploys he shared with Jean, and more. He showed his young friend where to shop for designer clothes, to pick up wealthy girls, to buy the best French wines cheaply. Over lunch he'd educate his protégé about real estate. What Jean already understood about listings and financing he could stick in a thimble compared to what Kirby knew. The education of Jean Poindexter was not without its interruptions— Kirby put his own deals first—but Jean was a quick and grateful student.

On his own time he read everything he could on real-estate law and practice. He passed his exams in a wink and found himself a fledgling salesperson. Working with his first clients— referrals from Kirby—he had no time for anything but real estate. His mother called almost every week but Jean would just hang up. It was too late for reconciliation. In a letter she even offered to take the house off the market for now. Jean felt some satisfaction but he didn't take the bait. His mother would change her mind again. He wasn't going to be anybody's fool.

One March weekend, Kirby invited Jean to see the beach house he was building near Ventura. On the drive up, Kirby, as always, dominated the conversation. He liked passive, receptive audiences, Jean knew. Kirby saw his duty as educating the world to his strong, sometimes unorthodox views. He disliked black people because he thought they were even lazier than Mexicans. He considered religion the opium not just of the masses but of otherwise intelligent people. He found the Russians so much smarter politically than Americans that he predicted they'd control the world by the twenty-first century. Kirby was a little full of himself, but Jean was impressed with anyone who, before he was thirty, had saved over a million dollars, owned several apartment complexes, and did almost anything he wanted.

"What a house," Jean remarked as they walked through the half-finished structure that sat not fifty yards from the ocean. Kirby had brought a picnic lunch with exotic cheeses, fruit, and the inevitable French wine. By now Jean knew every good cabernet sauvignon of the last twenty years. They lounged back in their bathing suits in the sand. With an overcast sky the waves looked gray and uniform, as if they'd been cut out of cardboard.

"To the good life," Kirby toasted in his mellow voice, raising his glass. "Unfortunately, in the next ten years this will all become commonplace," he added with a sigh.

"This? That's crazy," Jean said, looking back at the beach house.

"No, it's not. In the seventies everyone our age is going to be so sick and tired of protest and rebellion they'll become like the older generation they despise. You know what I mean—they'll want Porsches and beach houses and whatever trendy things come along. But you and I, we're ahead of them, aren't we?" He was suddenly gloating. Kirby could change moods on a dime.

"I don't think I'm ahead of anything," Jean spoke up. "I'm behind. I feel left out. Like I've got a lot of catching up to do." It felt good to be honest.

"You're not even twenty-one," Kirby scoffed.

Jean shrugged. "Maybe it was Vietnam. It was like I aged ten, fifteen years there. Part of it was that I thought no one cared about me."

"No one did care. And they still don't. You were a chump."

Jean stirred uncomfortably. "I did what I thought was right," he said, glancing away.

"So much for your judgment. Maybe now you'll get a little smarter." Kirby was suddenly staring at Jean's leg. "Hey, what the hell is on your thigh?"

Jean felt embarrassed and dropped his arms over his leg. "Nothing," he said.

"Nothing? It's a picture of a goddamn anchor."

"I had it done in Okinawa. I was just bored, waiting to be shipped to Germany."

Kirby was suddenly howling. "Jesus Christ, a *tattoo*! You

want to sell million-dollar homes in Beverly Hills and you have a *tattoo*? God, if this ever gets out—''

"Lay off," Jean warned. "No one can see it."

"Don't be so uptight, kid—"

"I'm not a kid. And I don't like people who knock the Army or what we did in Vietnam."

"Oh, my, I almost forgot. You're a hero."

"I'm warning you, man—"

"'*Man?*' Jean, we must do something about your vocabulary. When you sell an estate on Doheny Drive, you do not close the deal by saying, 'Hey, man, here's a nice pad, dig it?' " Kirby's shoulders trembled with laughter.

"Why are you doing this, Kirby? Just shut up, okay?"

Kirby shook his head in wonder. "That's something else we can't have—a temper. I see I've got a lot of work ahead of me."

"Lay off, I said."

"Let me see that tattoo again," Kirby needled.

"Fuck you—"

Kirby raised a deflecting arm but he was too late. Jean's fist landed just above his eye. Kirby squealed in pain and rolled in the sand. Jean thought he looked pathetic, a big guy like that groveling. He was ready to punch him again but there was suddenly so much blood over his eye that Kirby was too stunned to do anything. Jean refused to apologize. Without a word he hitched back to Westwood.

Monday morning he found a note on his desk directing him to the president's office. Jean gave Mr. Bomer his best smile as he dropped into one of the elegant chairs for visitors. The large, energetic man with thick-framed glasses was gracious, but his message was succinct: the young sales associate wasn't carrying his load and should look for employment somewhere else. Wounded, Jean looked for Kirby. The coward, dirty work done, wasn't around. Jean cleaned out his desk and marched out the door.

Big fucking deal, he thought when he got back to his apartment, trying to hold in his temper. He would survive this, and find a better firm. He didn't regret what he'd done to Kirby, and at least the guy had taught him a lot. The want ads for the next week produced nothing. Jean began calling his original list of firms, with predictable results. The few that were interested asked for a recommendation from Bomer and Walton. By May Jean saw the handwriting—he was

broke. He called his grandmother, apologizing for neglecting
her, and hinted at his predicament. But when Harriet offered
money, Jean changed his mind. He was too proud for a
handout. He would get out of this mess by himself.

He took a selling job in the men's Casual Corner at Bul-
locks, intending it to last only until he found the right real-
estate firm. He was dismissed after a week when store
management realigned its departments. He lasted longer waiting tables at Hamburger Hamlet, then quit for a better job
selling encyclopedias door to door. He could palm off ice on
Eskimos, he knew, but after splitting his commissions with
his boss, Jean's first month's take-home was less than four
hundred dollars. Lighting a joint in his apartment, he would
sit between his two prized speakers and turn up the volume.
The grass eased his frustration and fortified his confidence.
He was living on the edge, right where he liked it, he
thought, and at any moment things would break for him.

A letter came the next week from the Pentagon, informing
him he would not, after a formal review of the facts, be a
candidate for the Congressional Medal of Honor. Jean was
assured, however, that his actions as a soldier would never be
forgotten by the American people. "Right," whispered Jean,
lighting a fresh joint. Even the Army was deserting him. He
remembered what his mother had said about being ostracized.
Maybe she'd given up, but he wouldn't. One day he was
going to be a goddamn real-estate mogul and own more of
this city than his father and grandfather combined.

Still, he found leaving the apartment every morning harder
and harder. By summer he abandoned his encyclopedia job
and sold the Cadillac. Vietnam revisited, he thought when he
began taking hits on a water pipe in the morning, at noon, at
three, and after his usual dinner of soup or macaroni and
cheese. Sometimes he would take a bus downtown and walk
by the buildings his father and grandfather once owned. The
air jangled with change. New buildings were going up in all
directions. Downtown was a crucible of opportunity. On
Flower Street north of Sixth he paused in front of a clean-
lined three-story brick structure with an American flag billow-
ing from its crown. He was stoned and he thought the flag
was the most beautiful thing he'd ever seen. There was no
name on the building, but a passerby informed him this was
the California Club. Kirby had told Jean all about it. The
California Club was the top of the prestige ladder of the city's

all-male social clubs, a rung or two above the University Club
and the Jonathan Club and the Petroleum Club. Even Kirby,
who was dying to belong, didn't have the credentials for
admission. He was too young. The California Club was a
bastion of old wealth and conservatism. Members thought the
greatest President of the twentieth century was Calvin Coo-
lidge, said Kirby. Jean faced the flag and swung his arm up in
a sharp salute. Pedestrians gave him glances of pity or derision. God damn, let's hear it for patriotism, he thought,
unashamed as a tear rolled down his cheek.

"Young man . . ." a voice called.

Jean turned and faced a stranger in a three-piece banker's
pinstripe. The gentleman looked in his seventies, his slender
face deeply weathered, but his alert eyes searched Jean with
interest. In his dirty chinos and pulled-out shirt he felt like a
slob.

"It's a pleasure to see a young man pay homage to our
flag. I'm Ransom McAlister," he said, approaching with his
hand out.

"Jean Poindexter, sir." He tried to focus. His stomach was
churning from too much weed. The whole city was wobbling.

"I'd like to take you inside and buy you a drink, son."

"Sir?" Jean's eyes swam up the imposing edifice. The
building looked so stolid and quiet, it was hard to believe
anyone was actually inside. "You're a member here?"

"Different location then, but my father joined the California Club in 1917, after he came home from the war. Rode side
by side with General Jack Pershing. I became a member in
1946, same damn thing. How about you, son? Were you in
the Republic of Vietnam?"

"The Republic . . ." For a moment Jean didn't know what
the man was talking about. "Yes, sir. Infantry."

"Wounded?"

"Yes, sir."

"Killed any enemy?"

Mr. McAlister was enjoying this. Jean nodded. "I was
awarded the Silver Star and the Distinguished Service Cross,
for a firefight near Cambodia." He was half-bragging, half-
embarrassed, but he couldn't stop himself. "Lost ninety-five
percent of our company, but we stopped the enemy."

"Tell me, son, what are you doing here?"

"Looking for work, sir."

An arm wrapped around his shoulder and he was escorted

into the inner sanctum. The corridors of wealth were dignified and imposing. Walls were adorned with expensive oils lit by small brass lamps that hung from the tops of the frames. Dozens of staff in starched uniforms scurried around to empty ashtrays or run the elevators or carry someone's luggage. Private rooms for members and their guests shared the top floor with a gymnasium and a sauna. On the main floor were reading and card rooms, lounges, a sumptuous dining room, and a mahogany-paneled bar where Jean suddenly found himself facing several more members whose deep, craggy faces were lined with history.

Jean struggled to come alert. Waves of nausea flooded over him. He waited out the silence until he understood it was *his* stories they wanted to hear. He told them about life in the war zone, how sneaky Charlie could be, but how brave the American fighting man was—every last one he'd known would give his life to preserve democracy and freedom.

As Jean piled on the shit, a smile of approval and gratitude rode up McAlister's face. "That's right, that's right," he kept saying. The liberal media, inspired by the New York *Times*, the old man swore, were disparaging and distorting the war effort, glorifying American boys who refused to fight and hamstringing the brave troops like Jean who weren't. The chorus of pasty-faced octogenarians agreed with every word. Jean was incredulous. Someone actually thought the war was right?

"I think we can help you out." McAlister finally turned to Jean.

"Sir?"

"If you need work, this club would be happy to employ you. I'll see to it. It won't be anything fancy, but I won't let a young man of your character drift on the streets."

"Thank you, Mr. McAlister."

"When can you start?"

"Tomorrow."

Jean was too startled and grateful to ask what the job would be, but when he showed up the next day he found himself in the underground garage parking members' cars. Maybe it wasn't glamorous, he thought after the first week, but he had a paycheck again and tips were generous. He bought some clothes and cleaned himself up. The members liked him.

The novelty lasted a full month before Jean began pondering his future. How was he going to make his millions, put

his real-estate empire on the map, by parking cars? He waited for
Mr. McAlister or one of his cronies to offer him a job in the
business world, but they only waved and smiled each day and
occasionally passed on a stock tip. Whenever Jean thought
about quitting, he had to consider the job market. Except for
these freaks at the California Club, no one seemed to want to
help him, starting with his mother. If she'd only let him stay
in the house, he thought, feeling anger again, this scenario
would never have happened.

One morning he came to work stoned. No one seemed to
notice. When it became a habit, the days passed in a harmless
blur, soft edges that buffered an internal agitation. He was convinced he was the victim of a conspiracy—not a personal one,
but an implicit plot against all Vietnam vets. They had come home
to an indifferent, even hateful public. People like Kirby wanted
Jean to languish and suffer. He could be a car jockey the rest of
his life and that would be hunky-dory with humanity. The fury
built inside him like a fire growing on itself, a private conflag-
ration that raged in his soul and was soon out of control. And
somebody was to blame for this, he knew, somebody had to pay.

On a rainy, cold afternoon an avocado-green Mercedes 450
SL presented itself in the California Club garage. Its driver
stepped out smartly in a gray suit, blue shirt, and yellow tie.
The attire was flashy by club standards, and so was the
middle-aged man: tall, with self-important good looks, deeply
tanned. His companion was a girl half his age, blond and
beautiful and in a miniskirt. The club allowed women for
lunch on certain days, and this babe was going to cause a few
cardiac arrests, thought Jean. Her companion thrust the Mercedes
keys into Jean's hand with a friendly wink.

"Take good care of the car, son."

"Yes, sir."

"Here, I mean it."

Jean pocketed the ten dollars, but not without looking into
the man's eyes. Whatever had clicked, and something had,
bothered Jean the rest of the day. Maybe he was just stoned,
he thought, but a voice told him this was not some hallucina-
tion. His memory was hiding something from him, betraying
him. When the gentleman returned for his Mercedes, Jean
had the same feeling of *déjà vu*. The man began to show
regularly for lunch, rarely bringing the same girl twice. He
was always impeccably dressed, the teeth wonderfully white
and straight, a splash of cologne lavished on his face.

Frustrated, one day Jean flipped open the Mercedes' glove compartment. Jesus, he thought in shock. What the hell was happening? His hand trembled as he slipped the registration back. How could he not have recognized the man? Was he that stoned? He felt nauseated the rest of the afternoon, but when his anger crystallized he had never been more sure of himself.

In a compelling moment of illumination he understood not only why and at what moment his life had gone wrong but also how he could correct it. Redemption was still possible; for the rest of the world too. Jean knew he had been appointed by forces unnamed to wipe this scumbucket off the face of the earth. His father would finally be avenged, and his own life would begin anew.

The next morning he purchased a .38 at a downtown gun store and secreted the weapon in a crevice at the rear of the garage. Walter Mandrake did not appear for the next six days. Jean made cautious inquiries. Was he off making some movie? Had he dropped out of the club? Jean told himself to be patient. The moment of reckoning would come. To calm his nerves he began to smoke on his breaks. He was possessed by his anger. It swept and churned through his blood like a flooding river. He didn't care about the consequences of murder. Walter Mandrake had destroyed his father. Justice had to be served.

The immaculate avocado-green Mercedes squealed into the garage on the afternoon of the seventh day. Jean's heart leapt as he turned and ran for his weapon. When he returned, out of breath, he found Mandrake alone, leaning over the car's windshield, using his fingernail to scrape off the carcass of an insect. Jean held the gun in both hands, crouching as he aimed. He shouted his enemy's name.

"What the fuck?" Mandrake said angrily when he turned. He stared at Jean as if he were an apparition.

"You know who I am?" Jean demanded.

"You're a wacko, kid."

"I am the avenging angel. I'm sending you on your way to another life. But before you go, you can kiss my ass."

"Put down that stupid toy—"

"I'm Jean Poindexter, asshole! You remember my father? Do you?"

His shouts echoed through the empty garage. For a moment

he thought Mandrake actually looked sorry and full of despair. Jean knew it could never match his own.

The first bullet slammed into the slender shoulder, spinning Mandrake around and dropping him like a puppet. Jean pumped in four more rounds until the body was still and the pressed, immaculate suit an abstract canvas of blood. The last bullet he saved for the Mercedes, though he had no idea why. The windshield shattered like a block of ice, its thousand fragments frozen together.

Jean slipped out the entrance of the garage and kept running. The gun was ditched in a drain gutter. Within minutes he heard the sirens. He had all of $163 in his pocket, his entire savings, and he knew only that he couldn't return to his apartment.

Free, he thought, free at last.

Alycia arrived at Harriet's Bel Air home to say good-bye on the last weekend in July 1969, a sun-baked, smoggy morning without a wisp of a cloud in the sky. The whole city was talking in paranoid terms about the grisly slaying of actress Sharon Tate, wife of Roman Polanski, and her friends, by what appeared to be hippie drifters. The mood of ugliness and uncertainty only added to Alycia's conviction it was time to leave the city. In her back seat sat a single cardboard box filled to the top, covered and tightly bound, which Harriet had agreed to keep. It contained Alycia's personal possessions she didn't want to take with her. She was keeping them only because she had no right to throw them away, she thought, as much as she was tempted. She had sold the house to a family from Connecticut, finally cutting all ties to her past, but these tenuous fragments remained, and as unpleasant as they were, they represented unfinished business. Someday, somehow, Alycia hoped, the family would make peace with all of it.

Alycia climbed the stairs and deposited the box in Harriet's attic. She was out of breath when she came down. Harriet held up two glasses of iced tea.

"You're a mind reader, Mother," she said, collapsing in a chair and gulping the tea. She was finally ready to leave, but glancing at Harriet, she couldn't help but feel guilty. Jean had made her feel like she'd deserted him, and now so did her last good friend.

"Would you like a refill?" Harriet asked.

"No, sit, I'm fine. Mother, you look tired. Is there anything I can do for you?"

"I've seen better days, dear. A little arthritis, some gout, and this house gets bigger every day. But I've survived this long, why not forever?" She gave a triumphant smile. "You don't have to worry about me. I'll be fine. Is everything taken care of? You're driving to Palm Springs today?"

"As soon as I leave here."

"I've made a room up for Felice when she comes home from school."

"Thank you, that's wonderful. I don't know if she'll need it. She's become very independent, by the sound of her letters. I want her to come to Palm Springs, but all she talks about are summer art classes back east."

The pause was delicate and awkward. Neither wanted to talk about Jean. Harriet had sympathized with and consoled Alycia throughout her battle with her friends, and over the lawsuits, which had finally been settled, and about Brother Andrew. But over Jean their ranges of tolerance, their levels of expectation, were very different. No matter how serious the storm, Harriet saw a light shining in the darkness. Alycia had begun to feel that maybe Jean was the darkness. Her fears did not diminish her love for him, but she wondered if anything or anyone could save him. She understood his frustration and torment, but she did not understand why they dominated and controlled him. Had Red's death done it? The war? Had she?

When Jean tried hard, when he was motivated, he could accomplish anything, Alycia knew. He had the identical drive and persistence of his father, but he also had his own demons. Fortunately for everyone, Walter Mandrake had recovered—miraculously, his doctors said. Jean was still a fugitive from the charge of attempted murder. No one had heard from or seen him. The media, obsessed with the Tate murders, had not given Jean much attention. Only one piece had mentioned Red and Alycia. Members of the California Club had expressed surprise and regret, but no one had taken a personal interest in the young man. Maybe that was the demon that nagged him the most, Alycia thought.

"Mother, I think I should get started," Alycia said in the silence. She gave a sigh of mixed emotions that both understood. Alycia walked over and embraced Harriet. "I'll call you tonight, I promise."

"I'll miss you, dear."

"We don't have to be strangers. I can visit. And you can come to Palm Springs. I'll send a driver—"

"I don't know, all that desert heat," Harriet said. "Los Angeles is bad enough."

"If Jean contacts anyone," Alycia found the courage to say as they walked outside, "I know it'll be you."

"Rest assured I'll call you right away."

At the car they hugged again, tears in their eyes. "Mother, if you do hear from Jean," Alycia said at the last moment, "no matter how sorry you feel for him—and I know this might be hard—please don't tell him about the trusts from Owen. When I get to Palm Springs I'm going to decide what to do about the money. I have a lot of thinking ahead of me."

"I promise," Harriet said, and waved good-bye.

The drive to Palm Springs took Alycia near the San Bernardino Mountains, where city smog finally began to dissipate, and into the oven air and desert terrain of the Coachella Valley. Palm Springs was the winter capital for wealthy golf-loving Angelenos, but every summer the town emptied out, which Alycia liked as much as the cathartic heat and pink-champagne sunsets. Trailer parks lined the outskirts, giving no hint of the spectacular homes that filled the town's interior. Palm Springs, in season, had almost as much wealth and social climbing as Beverly Hills—Bob Hope and Frank Sinatra had residences here, and Walter Annenberg's famous Sunnylands estate, with its own golf course, welcomed the Washington crowd—but Alycia felt far away from all of it. The house she'd purchased, in a quiet subdivision miles from the trendy shops on Palm Canyon Drive, was as isolated and unpretentious as the Toluca Lake home had been grand and lavish. No one would know she existed.

Palm Springs was largely a mid-century creation of Los Angeles developers, but its earlier history was what appealed to Alycia. In the late 1800's a judge named John Guthrie McCallum arrived from the East in the sleepy Indian settlement of Agua Caliente. Hot mineral springs bubbled through the desert crust, for which the Indians had no great use, but McCallum found the mineral baths, along with the warm, clean air, perfect for his tubercular son. Falling in love with the desert, the judge purchased six thousand acres, leased additional land from the Indians, and engineered an aqueduct to bring water from the mountains. McCallum began to grow figs, oranges, and grapefruit, prospering as much as any citrus farmer eighty miles east on the outskirts of Los Angeles. One year an uncharacteristic drought dried up his aqueduct and killed his dream, but he refused to sell the land. On his death, it passed intact to his only daughter, Mrs. Austin McManus. Shrewd and perceptive, the woman hired a hydrologist. When it was discovered her six thousand acres rested on a series of huge underground freshwater lakes, the future assumed a different complexion.

Sharing her father's love for the desert, Mrs. McManus guided the growth of the town for the next thirty years, selling to developers only if they agreed to her restrictions to preserve the character of the desert. The great woman had recently passed away, Alycia had heard, but maybe her legacy of care and concern endured.

Her first weeks in town, Alycia thought not infrequently of Mrs. McManus. She would take sunrise walks through the dry lavender hills, spotting snakes, jackrabbits, and spectacularly shaped cacti whose names she found at the library. The environment had not changed dramatically in the fifty years since Mrs. McManus walked it, but Alycia guessed that fifty years hence it would be unrecognizable. In town she heard people talk about nearby developments named Indian Wells and Palm Desert and Rancho Mirage. Golf courses and swimming pools would flesh out the landscape. Blocked by the Pacific, Los Angeles would journey inexorably east until it ran into Arizona.

In the heat of the day Alycia stayed inside and read. She was the local library's most faithful patron under the age of sixty. There wasn't much else to do. Her phone was as quiet as it had been in Los Angeles. Harriet would call, and so did Felice, and there were occasional solicitations from gardeners and golf clubs and department stores, all of which Alycia politely declined.

There was no word from Jean. Sometimes a caller would hang on the line, as if waiting for the courage to speak, then click off. "Jean, is that you?" she asked more than once. Waking in the night, she would hear something and think Jean was in the next bedroom and call his name. In town she would spot him at the supermarket, or strolling down a

sidewalk, or working at a gas station. After a while she
stopped looking so hard. She tried to get a perspective on
Jean in the same way she kept her distance from the town,
becoming the judicious and objective observer of her own
flesh and blood. She was torn between feeling anger for
Jean's incredible insolence and guilt for abandoning him,
between strict censure and all-accepting love. If she did find
him, she wondered, would he reject her again? His disappearance had been the ultimate blow. He was punishing her by
not giving her the chance to reconcile or help him. She had
been left powerless. Acceptance of pain came no more naturally to mothers than it did to their children.

A story in the local paper at the end of September broke the
monotony of summer. A twenty-one-year-old drifter named
Jason Carter Brannon, without the blessing of the city fathers,
had set up a tent in a well-manicured park not a block from
Palm Canyon Drive. The unsightly hand-painted hippie abode
and lingering smell were taken by tourists and wealthy residents as a sign of the Apocalypse. Charles Manson and his
friends had been arrested in Los Angeles for the murder of
Sharon Tate, but people in Palm Springs smelled conspiracy.
Twice police escorted the soft-spoken Jason Brannon from
town, and twice he had returned and bivouacked in the park
again. "The park belongs to the people," he had told the
police officers when they finally arrested him.

Alycia drove to the city jail one morning and asked to see
the young man. A perplexed deputy begrudgingly allowed her
entrance. She did not really expect to find Jean, but she had
to be sure. The boy's face was hard and distrustful, the blond
hair dirty and matted, but the blue eyes were full of hope.
When she offered to pay bail and give him a place to stay,
Jason Brannon declined but thanked her softly. On her second
visit he relented. He was a college dropout, an Army dropout,
a family dropout, he confided to Alycia, but he was trying to
get his act together if people would just stop hassling him. In
the chambers of the municipal judge Alycia was politely
advised to put her checkbook away. The young man's bail
had been raised to one hundred thousand dollars. Charles
Manson paranoia was as strong as ever.

"Fine, I'll pay it," Alycia said without hesitation.

"Madam," the judge whispered as they sat facing each
other, "who are you?"

"Alycia Poindexter."

"Are you a resident of Palm Springs?"

"I just moved here."

"Are you related to the defendant?"

"No," she answered.

His large florid face showed incomprehension, then exasperation. "I don't know your motives, but if this young man is released, he's either going to jump bail and burn you or going to stay in this town and cause trouble. We don't want trouble in Palm Springs. Am I clear?"

"I'll take my chances," Alycia said, getting out her pen.

"Why?" the judge asked.

"I think he's right. Why shouldn't the park belong to everyone? It shouldn't matter that Jason Brannon doesn't have Gucci shoes or drive a Mercedes or belong to a local tennis club."

Alycia digested the judge's look. She was being taken for a dotty eccentric, or a Communist out to undermine the American way.

"I'm raising the bail to a quarter-million dollars," the judge said.

Unflinching, Alycia started a new check. The judge's hand jumped on top of hers. "Madam, I will raise the bail as high as I have to."

Alycia sat up. "I'm not a lawyer," she said, "but I've been around enough of them to know that bail can't be set in excess of the nature of someone's crime, which in this case is loitering."

"Then I'll deny bail altogether. I'll find a way."

"So will I," Alycia promised, and she turned and left the chambers.

The next day she found herself on the front page of the local paper. She had come to Palm Springs wanting only to be a stranger and had ended up in the vortex of controversy. References to her and Jean's contretemps in Los Angeles followed in the next edition. When she cooked a meal for Jason Brannon and brought it to jail, an enterprising freelance photographer captured the moment for posterity and sold it to the Los Angeles *Times*.

At least this was a different kind of fight—it didn't involve her personally. Alycia hired an attorney to defend Jason and started a petition to free the young man. Signatures were hard to come by. Alycia heard herself referred to as a carpetbagger and a hippie-lover, but that only spurred her to work harder.

She visited Jason every day. They discussed Vietnam and the campus protests from Berkeley to Columbia, and why it would be a dandy idea if the politicians of the world were drafted to fight in wars, because that way any conflict was sure to end quickly. Jason talked about his parents and how they had thought he was a lazy dreamer. He'd tried to find a decent job in Seattle and San Francisco; counter work at McDonald's was all he was offered. He didn't like school. His wife had jilted him. Alycia listened to every word. At first she was reluctant to give advice—she expected fierce pride and defiance—but after a few days the young man was receptive and trusting. He looked at her queerly when she slipped once and called him Jean. She would do anything to help him, she knew, which was when she realized this fight was personal after all.

Pressured by the mayor and city attorney, and running out of maneuvers, the judge levied a fine of fifty dollars on his hippie prisoner and released him. At the jail Jason gave Alycia a warm hug. He refused her offer to stay and work around her house, but he did accept a hundred dollars, which he promised to repay along with the fine. "Wow, you don't know how good it is to be free," he said, walking outside. Yes, Alycia told herself, she did. It was easier than she had expected to watch him walk away.

A phone call came late that evening as Alycia was readying for bed. The voice was familiar, yet her memory faltered. "Who is this?" she asked.

The caller paused. "Maybe I shouldn't be bothering you," he teased.

"Please—"

"Okay, I surrender."

"Who is this?" Alycia repeated.

"It's me . . . Scotty."

Alycia gulped a breath. "Scotty Madigan?"

"I've been following your little war in the local rag. Character is fate, right? Well, bully for you, I say. This town has more hypocrites per capita than Hollywood and Beverly Hills combined." He laughed good-naturedly.

"Scotty, you live in Palm Springs?"

"I've been practicing here for seven years. Do you want to have lunch?"

"Do I? You don't know how nice it is to hear a friendly voice!"

There were crow's-feet around the sensitive eyes, and his chin had begun to sag, but Scotty had a wonderful tan and his off-center smile was the same. He was dressed casually, as if just off the golf course. They laughed as they hugged. The patio of the restaurant was empty. A light breeze rippled the umbrella and made the fall heat bearable.

"You look wonderful," Scotty said. "I mean it. Are you enjoying Palm Springs?"

"If I'm not run out on a rail."

"I thought you were great. This town needs a little shaking up. Why did you move here?"

"Probably for the same reason as you. I got tired of L.A."

"Amen."

"So here I am," she said, "picking fights again. What about you?"

"I'm fine, I think. Haven't touched a drop of liquor in five years. Got my surgery license reinstated. My practice is flourishing. My golf's improved. What else in life is there?"

She threw up her hands. "I don't know. I really don't. I moved to the desert to find out."

Scotty ordered them both the poached salmon with dill sauce and a bottle of mineral water. "I was sorry to hear about Jean and all his troubles," he said when the waiter had left.

Alycia nodded. "One day he'll be all right. I sound like my mother-in-law, but that's how I honestly feel now. I suddenly have that faith."

"You've always been strong. Stronger than me. You sure needed something to get through your fight with Electra. I don't know what happened to her. She was never that mean with me, or maybe I didn't really know her. We hardly speak anymore. Anyway, we don't have to discuss any of *that*," he said, looking relieved.

"Tell me about you, Scotty. Did you remarry? Do you have a girlfriend? Are you the town's most eligible bachelor?" Alycia blushed. "I'm sorry. I'm getting carried away."

"Absolutely not. The answers are no, no, and no. I date occasionally, but there's no one special. I don't look for much in a relationship. That way I'm not ever disappointed. If I can keep straight with myself, that's enough."

"It sounds like you're on top of everything," she said, but

she looked away. The talk drifted to Scotty's children and
Felice. Alycia dug down for courage. "There's something I
have to tell you," she said when there was a pause.

Pain suddenly glinted in Scotty's eyes, as if he knew the
subject. He didn't want to hear it, Alycia thought, but she
would tell him anyway. "I just want to say this once," she
told him. "We don't have to discuss it."

"If this has to do with Red, maybe we should skip it." He
was suddenly a wall. All the warmth and trust emptied out of
him.

"No, we do have to talk about it."

"Why? I almost didn't call you because I was afraid this
would come up."

"Scotty, listen to me. What I have to say will help you.
It'll set the record straight."

He drew up his shoulders.

"You didn't kill Red," she said.

His lips moved soundlessly, mimicking her words.

"You didn't, Scotty. Red knew there were bullets in the
gun. He killed himself."

His eyes glazed over. "I don't believe you."

"You knew Red as well as any friend did. He had no
tolerance for failure, particularly his own. He wrote me everything in a letter."

Scotty waited for the thought to penetrate. "But why?" he
demanded. "Why were you silent so long?" His agitation
was close to anger. "Do you know how long it took me to get
over the incident? Do you think it's easy making peace with
yourself when you're sure you killed your best friend?"

"Scotty, I'm sorry."

"That's not a reason."

"I had Red's memory to think of. And my children. The
death was hard enough on them without their knowing it
was suicide. I still haven't told them."

Scotty pushed away his food. "Jesus, this is crazy."

"And then you disappeared, I couldn't find you," Alycia
explained.

"I wish it were that simple."

"Scotty, from the bottom of my heart, I'm sorry," she
whispered. "Please accept that. I can't offer anything more."

He touched his fingers to his temples, deliberating. "Christ,
Red used me," he said, growing even angrier.

"We have to forget."

"How could he have done that to me?"

"Scotty, it's over."

He looked like he didn't believe her as they sat awkwardly. No one finished his meal. Alycia felt bad, but there was nothing she could add. When they said good-bye they promised to stay in touch. Somehow, Alycia knew, small town or not, they'd never see each other again.

Los Angeles was never a city that extolled tradition over improvisation. It liked miracles, came to expect them, and the more improbable and outrageous, the more rabid and accepting were their followers. The consciousness of Hollywood, the art of illusion, permeated the whole city. A Disneyland could not have first been built in Kansas City or Peoria. Famous Amos could not have started selling his chocolate-chip cookies anywhere but Los Angeles. The Watts Towers belonged only in one town. New ways to make money or achieve power or gain attention were acted out every day. Businessmen, artists, interior decorators, street mimes, and restaurateurs competed against each other because they vied for the same audience. Who could be the boldest and wildest and most original? The city was a harsh and fickle judge, but the winners reaped rewards that could exceed the imagination.

The first Mad Man Marvin stereo wholesale discount store opened on Sherman Way in the San Fernando Valley in September 1970. The modest storefront was in a small strip mall, squeezed between a meat market and a vacuum-cleaner dealership, and consisted of no more than twelve hundred square feet. The merchandise was strictly imported—names like Sony and Toshiba that Americans were not overly familiar with, and certainly did not trust as they did General Electric or RCA. Mad Man's demo models were cluttered on improvised shelving and connected by untidy wiring. The day he opened his doors to the public he had no ad spots on radio or TV, no banners or bunting above the store; the telephone wasn't even connected. Rain pelted the streets all day.

Mad Man himself was the store's sole employee, and he knew very little about stereos. He did know how to be personable and engage a customer. He also knew that the San Fernando Valley, which in 1950 had been the nation's twenty-fifth-most-populous urban center, and ninth in 1960, was now, with three million sun-loving fools, the third. One-fourth were under twenty-one, a wild, antiestablishment, Wood-

stock generation of music-lovers who could appreciate a great
sound system but rarely had the money to afford one.

Three months earlier, Mad Man had picked up a stereo
trade magazine in a barber shop and read an ad from a Japanese wholesaler looking for a foothold in the U.S.-manufacturer-
dominated market. The wholesaler was so hungry he extended
Mad Man not only credit on his initial shipment but actual
cash to tie up a lease for six months. The reputation of
Japanese electronics was still to be proven to the world.
Japan's manufacturing sector was more imitative than innovative, and stereos were already a competitive market everywhere. But the merchandise Mad Man was shipped, thanks to
a weak yen and a cheap labor market, was ridiculously inex-
pensive. Even with a generous markup for himself, Mad Man
could undercut retail competitors by thirty percent. He also
was willing to extend credit to any kid who could make a
down payment or get his parents to cosign a note.

His first day in business Mad Man didn't make a sale until
after lunch, but it was to the first customer who walked in the
store. A heavyset boy with braces had shuffled in seeking
shelter from the rain. His eyes bugged out at the prices. His
friends returned an hour later and bought three more systems—
amp, tuner, and speakers—thanks to Mad Man's easy-credit
policy. By the end of the week he had sold his demos and
was ragging his distributor for more goods.

The shipments kept coming, barely keeping up with Mad
Man's whirlwind pace and unspeakable luck. Concentrating
on the lucrative Valley, he opened a second store within three
months, two more by his first anniversary. His cash flow was
incredible. He began advertising, calling himself "the stereo
king," whose prices positively, absolutely could not be beaten.
His picture appeared in the *Times*'s display ads every day,
young and handsome with a full reddish-blond beard and
piercing blue eyes—balancing a Sony speaker high in each
hand as if about to hurl them out of the picture . . . he was so
crazy he was giving these speakers away! He did radio spots
for rock stations that began "This is *Maaaaaad Man Marvin*" against a soundtrack of bedlam as if from an asylum.
There were TV spots where customers would stand alongside
Mad Man and sing his praises. Sometimes he got celebrities
to give the testimonials. Nobody major—a local golf pro or
radio deejay—but famous enough. People in L.A. paid atten-

tion to celebrities. They trusted their taste and bought what they bought.

Mad Man Marvin was becoming a minor celebrity himself. He could walk down a busy street and someone would ask for his autograph. The recognition left him glowing. A fan club sprang up at a Valley high school. Letters came to his store asking him to run for mayor. In a city that loved the offbeat and the eccentric, Mad Man Marvin was the epitome of success. He was making enough money to live comfortably in the flats of Beverly Hills, and he didn't mind if the world knew it. In an interview with a pop magazine he dwelled at length on his poor, rural childhood in Florida. His father had died when he was young and he had to work as a stevedore in New Orleans, sending home money to support Mama. Then one day he'd visited L.A. and just *knew* this was the land of opportunity.

By Easter 1972 Mad Man Marvin had opened nine stores, each grossing over $100,000 a month. When he couldn't get his hands on merchandise fast enough, he flew to Tokyo to see his manufacturers. The plants were so efficient and the management so dedicated that Mad Man realized Japanese electronics were not a fluke. In the United States, research and plant modernization were almost dirty words; management skimmed off every free nickel for salary and bonuses. Instinct fired Mad Man's dreams. It was time to expand his market and take anything the Japanese would make—televisions, cameras, copiers, watches, typewriters. These guys were doing state-of-the-art. He had found a star to hitch his wagon to.

One sunny June morning Mad Man stepped into the Wells Fargo branch in North Hollywood where he'd opened his first account. In two years his assets had multiplied so dramatically that whenever teller lines were too long, one of the bank officers gladly handled its star customer's business. But this morning Mad Man had a special appointment. He breezed past the tellers and several secretaries and dropped into a deep leather chair in the office of the president.

"Good morning," he began, crossing his legs. He flashed his charming smile. "I need a million dollars."

The president, a friendly and appreciative man, knew his prize customer well. But now he curled his hands in his lap and his lips stretched reflexively over a band of smoke-stained teeth. Words failed him. The bank did make commercial loans in modest amounts, but a million dollars?

"What did you have in mind, Marvin?" he asked delicately, picking up a pencil to take copious notes.

"I can't explain it, really. I just want to expand. I want to make a huge warehouse—a consumer emporium. I'm going to call it Little Japan."

"I never heard of any such thing," the president said.

"That's what makes this idea great!"

"The loan committee would need details. Site plan, blueprints, cost estimates . . ."

Mad Man betrayed impatience as he struggled half out of the deep chair. "I told you, I don't have details. I have my dream. That's how I got started in the first place."

"I see."

"If you like, I can take my business elsewhere."

"Nonononononono," the president said, showing those yellowed teeth again and holding up his hands as if to physically prevent the outflow of bank assets. He pulled out a loan application. "If you'd be kind enough to fill this out . . ."

The stereo king of Los Angeles scanned the questions with private amusement. *Name . . . age . . . date of birth . . . place of birth . . . mother's and father's names . . .* He produced a gold Cartier fountain pen from the breast pocket of his hand-tailored suit and wrote MARVIN HARP at the top, then without a second thought filled in the other blanks. He was amazed by the string of small, insignificant lies that he'd woven into a fabric of such credibility that at times Mad Man Marvin seemed more real to him than Jean Poindexter. Nobody much remembered—or cared to—the troubled young vet who'd tried to murder Walter Mandrake. The media no longer wasted a drop of ink on Jean. The police probably thought he'd bolted to another state. Jean was determined the fiction would endure as long as Mad Man Marvin. The memory of fleeing from the California Club and living for a year like a hunted animal, scrounging from restaurant garbage cans and sleeping in alleys, still made him shudder.

Looking back, he understood that he'd not been of sound mind. Too much weed had fueled his paranoia and frustration, boiling them into a volatile and lethal mixture. When he'd read that Mandrake had survived, Jean decided he'd been lucky, had been given a second chance, and it was time to mend his ways. Still, he didn't regret shooting the man who destroyed his father. The creep had deserved death. Recovery had not come without some revelations for the Hollywood executive, too. The gossip columns still carried stories of how Mandrake, finding peace with himself, no longer was seen at splashy parties or making mighty back-room deals. He had repudiated his whole sinful life of excess, starting with his Mexican vacations and bevy of twenty-year-old women and become a rather shy, spooked soul. Remorse did not seem sufficient punishment to Jean, but he knew he'd never really understood that emotion.

A year after the shooting, Jean began taking chances. At a Salvation Army mission he found a bed and a hot meal a day, and eventually took a job washing dishes in a pizza joint. He was still a fugitive but he no longer felt like the object of a manhunt. Los Angeles' Finest had thousands of criminals at bay—why should they focus on him? To be safe, he grew a beard and put on weight. When a waitress had once asked his name, "Marvin Harp" slipped off his tongue. Poor Lieutenant Dumbfuck would live on after all. Without great difficulty Jean obtained a social-security card, driver's license, and passport—thoughts of fleeing the country occurred in moments of paranoia—and he slowly inched his way into the world of the living. When he leafed through the stereo magazine at the barber shop, when the brainstorm had struck, he knew he'd found a way to save himself. What had been impossible to foresee was the magnitude of his success.

Jean left the completed loan application with the bank president and strolled out into the brassy morning to his Mercedes. He remembered his father's story of how he'd once forged Owen's signature. The precedent only made Jean feel more secure. He wondered what his father or grandfather would think of him now. They would have to be proud, wouldn't they? He'd gone through hell and come out on top, was, in fact, still climbing to a summit they would have thought unimaginable for him—or themselves at his age. The bolder he grew, the more risks he took, the more things happened for him. The light was green all the way to the end of the world.

By a quarter to ten he was on Laurel Canyon, navigating the windy, heavily trafficked tongue of road with impatience, heading to an apartment complex on Santa Monica Boulevard in West Hollywood. His Friday-morning assignation always lasted through lunch. It was an inconvenience to Jean—time off from business was precious—but he allowed it in the name of an unmitigating obsession.

Almost a year ago a teenager in tight faded jeans and a T-shirt had ventured into his store asking directions to a girlfriend's house. Jean had escorted her the three blocks to her destination, scarcely letting his eyes swim from the wondrous face. It was the face of a naïf, a little girl with peaches-and-cream complexion and inquisitive brown eyes and a pouty mouth. Her thick brown hair was swept back from her high forehead. She was no more than five-foot-three, slim and taut, with pert breasts and a voluptuous bottom. Jean, with his gift of charm, elicited the vital information. Leslie Mae Cummings was nineteen years old, a high-school dropout from a small Nebraska town, and had been in L.A. less than a year. With a perky, innocent smile she informed him she was an aspiring model. There was nothing arrogant in her manner, as if she'd told Jean she was a waitress or a student. He discreetly inquired where she lived, if she had any boyfriends, what she did in her spare time. Jean hung on her every word.

In the weeks that followed, the better Jean got to know Leslie Mae, the more certain he was of his initial feelings. The girl's uncontrived innocence, her uncomplicated sincerity, were a healing balm to him. There was not one bone of deceit in her. Being with her made him feel better about himself, helped cleanse from memory his anxious past and self-doubts. In a city that swarmed with ambitious, scheming souls, Leslie Mae was unaffected, an island unto herself, and a refuge for Jean.

After six months he considered telling her he was not Mad Man Marvin. He wanted Leslie Mae to accept him totally. On two occasions he almost succeeded, but something held him back. What if she didn't like his duplicity, didn't understand his need to lie, or was afraid of this Jean Poindexter? Honesty would have to wait, he thought as he showered her with presents and dinners at quaint restaurants. When she began to reciprocate his affection, hers was so pure it was like a bottomless crystal-clear spring that Jean could never drink enough of. She wanted nothing from him. She was exactly the opposite of his troublemaking and nagging mother and his meddlesome sister. There were no strings attached to Leslie Mae's love, no need to make a public display of her emotions, no discontentment with the world.

Nothing seemed to faze the uncomplicated girl. There were thousands of fledgling models in L.A., all at the mercy of exploitative agents and directors and ad agencies, and like most, Leslie Mae was buffeted from one hostile shore to another. She landed a job now and then, but nothing seemed to last or build to a career. Most girls gave up after a few years, but Leslie Mae told Jean she had no plans to quit. Things would work out, or so she hoped. Anyway, she wasn't going to worry. Whatever was, was meant to be.

After a single knock, the apartment door swung open and Jean found Leslie Mae in her negligee. The soft smile seduced him instantly. "I missed you," she said as she pulled him inside. Jean's heart melted as her lips brushed his. He wondered how he had lasted a whole week without her.

She took his hand and led him to the bedroom. The simple apartment was decorated with wicker furniture and throw rugs from discount furniture stores. Picasso posters brightened the walls. She'd taken a class in stained-glass-making and one of her pieces hung from the ceiling. In the bedroom she helped him out of his clothes and saw that he was already hard. Pulling back the sheets, she took him in her arms.

Jean never knew how long the lovemaking would last, just that he had a way with women and that his own patience and mood dictated the longevity of the morning. Even before he had had Kirby Willis as a mentor and hung around the Beverly Hills lounges, Jean was a competent lover. By instinct he not only knew where and how to move his hands, to position his body, but also had the gift of timing that elevated sex above mere mechanics; he was always in control, always the leader who never doubted himself. He listened now, enthralled, to the crescendo of Leslie Mae's tiny, sweet gasps. She was so beautiful, so fragile. He would never let anything happen to her. Times like this, he knew he couldn't live without her, and wasn't that the same as being in love?

"Do you want a baby?" Leslie Mae suddenly asked when they rested for a moment.

He struggled to make sense of the words. She had caught him off-guard. He thought Leslie Mae had somehow found a baby and wanted a home for it.

"Don't worry, I'm not pregnant," she assured him. "I was just wondering, Marvin, if you ever thought about things like that."

"Should I?" Why was she bringing this up? How could he think about babies or even marriage when he had business on his mind? But moments like this, he was more vulnerable. He was capable of giving up everything, he thought, to please Leslie Mae.

"Maybe it was your childhood," she said thoughtfully. "Sometimes people who were treated badly as kids don't want to have children of their own."

"That must be it," he murmured. For an impressionable Leslie Mae, Jean had embellished on his background beyond what the media wrote. The rural Florida of his childhood had been a war zone. After his father died, a hard-drinking uncle had lived with the family and beaten the kids frequently. That was really why Jean fled home. And his mother was no saint. She had been a cold, emotionless woman who never paid attention to her children. The words came so effortlessly that Jean felt they were the truth.

"You know, I really like babies," she went on.

But you're too young, you're like a baby yourself, Jean thought. Instead, to humor her, he asked, "What would you name it?"

"I'd like a boy. He would look just like you, very handsome," she said happily. She kissed Jean on the lips. "His name would be Daniel, or Robert, or Michael. Those are my favorites."

"Daniel," Jean voted, for no particular reason.

"He would have your sweetness," she went on. "That's what I like best about you."

"Mad Man Marvin is sweet?" Jean said, astonished. "He's a crazy man!"

"No, he's sweet and gentle. He's the sanest person I know. He only pretends to be ambitious—"

Jean laughed nervously. Was Leslie Mae just a romantic, or could she really see things in him that Jean could not? How could she say he wasn't truly ambitious? If he wasn't ambitious, what was he? He was too afraid to ask her.

"Come on, let's get lunch," he said.

"Do you love me as much I love you?" she asked, stopping him.

"What?"

"Please tell me."

She looked vulnerable suddenly. Jean had seen the face before. Leslie Mae wasn't totally uncomplicated. She was insecure about being loved and accepted, maybe no more needy than him, but needy enough for Jean to know that all his little presents and romantic dinners wouldn't be enough to satisfy her forever. Now he understood her talk about babies. His mind spun quickly but he couldn't think of the right answer. What would Mad Man Marvin say? Or Jean Poindexter? "Of course, I love you," he said, the easiest thing, and got into his clothes.

Leslie Mae lingered on the bed. The pouty mouth turned down another degree. Her eyes glazed over in self-pity. Whenever she thought she was neglected, or Jean was insincere, she was like a flower in the snow, withdrawing her beauty like retracting petals. Jean put his arm around her, and with a slow, appreciative kiss, revived her.

They dined as usual at a quiet, chic French restaurant off Little Santa Monica called Auberge. It was Leslie Mae's choice but Jean had grown fond of the rich sauces and he certainly knew wines. A generous tip to the maître d' ensured they were always seated in the best room. Jean peeked from his menu, nudging Leslie Mae with an elbow.

"Look," he whispered. "To your left. No . . . over there."

"What?"

"Don't stare. It's Paul Newman."

Leslie Mae finally got her bearings, and nodded, but Jean saw she wasn't impressed. The actor looked so young. For a moment, Jean was sure, Newman glanced at their table. Had he recognized Mad Man? Jean couldn't be positive, but there was a glint in the actor's eyes. Jean took out a business card and had the waiter deliver it with a bottle of Mouton Rothschild 1948.

"Tell him it's from Mad Man Marvin," Jean instructed.

"Why did you do that?" Leslie Mae asked.

"Why? Because he's an important actor. He's a celebrity. Wouldn't you like to meet him? I'd love to have him in one of my commercials."

"I don't care about celebrities," she offered, thinking about it. "What's so special about them?"

Jean couldn't believe the question. "What's so special? They made it to the top! They made it where I'd like to be. "

Leslie Mae looked disapproving and hurt. "I don't know if I could love you as much if that happened. Because I don't think you'd still love me."

"Hey, what are we talking about? You think I wouldn't care any more about you?" he said smoothly, taking Leslie Mae's hand, but his thoughts were still on Paul Newman. What would it be like to have a celebrity sitting at his table?

He didn't understand Leslie Mae. Or maybe he did. Jean understood why she'd never be successful as a model. She just didn't care. She didn't own an ounce of ambition. When she got calls from her agent, half the time she was having her period or had invited a girlfriend for lunch or was on her way to cooking class. So what if a rival got the shooting assignment, she'd tell Jean. Her personal life and feelings came first.

After a minute the waiter sallied back to Jean with a handwritten note from Paul Newman. Jean was astonished. The actor thanked him for the fine wine, and would have his secretary send Jean a pair of tickets for the preview of his new movie.

"How about that?" Jean said, gloating as he read the note to Leslie Mae. He carefully folded and preserved it in his pocket, and didn't worry about Leslie Mae's indifferent gaze.

Jean's million-dollar loan was approved within three weeks. The site for his emporium was in the ever-expanding San Fernando Valley, but this time so far out on the Ventura Freeway, in a rural area known as Woodland Hills, it seemed halfway to Bakersfield. In the middle of orange groves, he could purchase five acres for fifty thousand dollars—a tenth of what it would cost him in a more populous location—and it was right next to an off-ramp, visible from the freeway. He wasn't entirely alone in his act of faith. Another developer had purchased fifty acres nearby for a shopping mall, but he had yet to break ground for lack of anchor tenants. Jean had no intention of waiting for anybody. If his idea was good, people would come to him. Hadn't his father told him the story of Disneyland?

When his rezoning was approved, he erected a single-floor steel-girder building with aluminum sides, a cavernous space that measured just over fifty thousand square feet and could have accommodated a couple of football fields. There was nothing frilly inside. A couple of miles of shelving, a loading dock and storage space in back, a dozen cash registers at the exits. He was saving as much money as he could for inventory. Leslie Mae helped him decide on the name: Little Japan in America. Jean liked the ring of it. They also decided it was best to keep his stereo chain intact; the new emporium would carry everything else.

Plans for opening day were dramatically different from

when he'd sold his first hi-fi. For a full week Jean orches-
trated a media blitz that outspent Safeway, Ralph's, and
Piggly-Wiggly combined. No shopper in Los Angeles languished in ignorance. There were TV spots of Mad Man
Marvin surrounded by tottering stacks of copying machines
and typewriters and televisions. "I'm *giving* this stuff away,"
he shouted, raising his arms beseechingly. "All you have to
do is drive to Woodland Hills and take it!" Free gifts were
promised for the first one hundred customers, and hot dogs
and sodas for everyone. Nobody would be refused credit.
What you couldn't cram in your station wagon, Little Japan
would deliver for free.

When the doors opened at eight, employees stood ready.
Gaily colored pennants hung from the eaves. A nervous Mad
Man Marvin hunkered in front of his million-dollar dream. A
small voice warned him he really was crazy. Was this going
to be the biggest flop since the Edsel? But the very uncertainty made his adrenal glands pump overtime. He loved it.
Hadn't his whole masquerade since shooting Mandrake been
so ridiculously reckless that he should have already been
caught? It only proved that no one was going to catch him
now. The bigger the risks, he reminded himself, the greater
the destiny.

Cars began trickling off the freeway, built to a steady
caravan by nine, and an hour later spread over the two-acre
parking lot. The store became a frenzy of thrusting hands and
careening shopping carts. Lines at the cash registers snaked
back into the store. To defuse tempers, girls dressed like
carhops circulated with the soda and hot dogs. It was one big
glorious orgy of consumption. When the store closed fourteen
hours later, Jean had sold almost a third of his inventory. He
estimated his one-day profit at $100,000. Jesus Christ Al-
mighty, he thought with palpitations.

The second day was hardly anticlimactic. Cash continued
to come in by the wheelbarrow. Jean's biggest headache was
keeping his shelves stocked. One afternoon as he roved the
store he spotted a familiar face. He couldn't pull out the
name, but the older man with stark wide eyes and bushy gray
eyebrows had played dozens of television roles. He could
hardly be poor, but here he was with the masses, looking for
a bargain. Jean stopped him at the cash register.

"Hi, there, I'm Mad Man," Jean said, extending a friendly
hand.

"Oh, yes, of course. Gordon Glouver." The character actor was more pleased to meet the celebrity store owner than he was to be recognized himself, thought Jean.

"Did you enjoy shopping here?" Jean asked candidly.

The actor's bushy eyebrows raised like a curtain. "The rich don't want cheap steak, but they want steak cheap."

Jean laughed with the old actor, and then he savored the concept. He refused to let Mr. Glouver buy anything. Everything was compliments of the house. "Say hello to your friends for me," Jean offered as they said good-bye.

Within days he received a warm thank-you letter from Gordon Glouver. Jean placed it in a folder with his note from Paul Newman. Going through customer checks every evening, he began to notice other celebrities were shopping at Little Japan. He sent a gift to every one. Along with gracious thank-you notes came complimentary passes to television game shows, movies, fine restaurants, hotels, private golf clubs for a day. Whenever he met a celebrity in person, Jean always bought him a drink or extended another gift. One Friday morning he burst into Leslie Mae's apartment with a wide grin.

"What is it?" she asked, startled.

"Get out your best dress. You and I are going to a party next weekend."

"What are you talking about?"

Jean understood. Except for their Friday lunches, he was always too busy to take her out. Now she wasn't sure what to think. "At the Beverly Hills Hotel, darlin'. I got right here an invitation from good ole boy Kenny Rogers . . ." Jean held up the thick folio invitation like a kid with a straight-A report card. He took in Leslie Mae's look of skepticism. Why couldn't she ever act a little thankful or impressed?

"I don't like it when you talk like a hillbilly," she said.

"I was just having fun," Jean explained, "and Jesus Christ, we're talking about Kenny Rogers. Don't you want to go?"

Leslie Mae slumped in a chair. "No."

He was shocked. "Why not?"

"Never mind."

"This is not some impersonal charity benefit. This is a private birthday party for intimate friends. The man likes me, he shops at my store, I've played golf with him, and you think I'm not going to his party?"

"Why do you want this so badly?"

Jean threw up his hands. "Because I like being seen with famous people. It makes me feel good." He wheeled on Leslie Mae. "I don't understand you—"

She looked pained to disappoint him. "I just don't like that kind of thing," she said.

Making love didn't change her mind. Jean had to buy her a new dress, flowers, and promise they'd be home early before he could get her in his Mercedes the next Saturday. When he ascended the hilly entrance to the famous hotel, his excitement pushed his head in all directions. It was like a movie set. Hadn't his father been here many times? His eyes drank in the exquisite cars and the people that stepped from them like porcelain dolls. He'd never seen so many celebrities in one place, and when the parking valet addressed him by his name, Jean knew he belonged here.

Escorting Leslie Mae into the Maisonette Room, he felt her arm trembling. Jesus, this was pathetic, he thought, but he wouldn't let it sour him. He brought Leslie Mae a glass of champagne and left her with a free-lance photographer who'd just shot a spread for *Vogue*. What else could he do for her career? As Jean circulated by himself, he felt no self-consciousness, no inhibitions. These customers were now his friends. Hands reached out to shake his, to grasp his elbow, arms were slung over his shoulder in tipsy camaraderie. It was as if he'd been one of them all his life.

"Hey, Marvin, come here," a sandpaper voice coaxed as Jean lifted a glass from a caterer's tray. He stared into the wan, chubby face of a record producer and sometime golf partner named Harvey Crisp.

"What's up, Harvey?" Jean inquired pleasantly.

The executive's smile resembled a lopsided sliver of a moon. "You, Marvin," he said. "Your name keeps coming up everywhere. You're a wanted man."

"Better than being a nobody," he joked.

"Have you ever heard of the California Club?"

Jean pushed back his shoulders, a distraction to cover the surprise that he was sure covered his face. "Who hasn't?"

"Then you know it's the most prestigious club in the city. I've been a member since my third divorce. It's a great place but a bit too stodgy. I got myself on the membership committee last year. We all got to talking. There was a consensus—we need younger blood in those antiquarian halls."

"Really?" said Jean with perfect detachment.

"We want you, Marvin." The moon smile waxed brilliant. "I mean, if you want us, your friends . . ."

"I'm touched, really," he said, still in control, "but isn't the California Club pretty conservative? I mean, would I fit in? The public thinks of me as a wild man."

"The bottom line, Marvin, is you're very successful at what you do. That's all that counts."

"I see."

"I sense some reluctance on your part. If it's about that regrettable shooting some years ago, please forget it. It's our only black eye."

Jean waited for panic to flood his brain, a paralysis to set in, but he was fine, really, in total command. Was that a sign he should join? Mandrake was ancient history. Ransom McAlister and his cronies, if they were still alive, would never recognize him. And, of course, he wanted to belong; this was an honor, an invitation to more contacts with the famous and the rich and the powerful. A bridge to his own destiny. His eyes jumped back to Harvey. "I'd love to become a member," he allowed with all his charm.

"Good!" Harvey pumped his hand. "I'll formally nominate you next week."

"I'm sure there's paperwork, questions about my background," Jean added cautiously.

"Don't worry about details. I'll take care of it all."

"You don't know how grateful I am, Harvey. Are you free for golf next Sunday?"

He told Leslie Mae the good news in the car. Her delayed response annoyed him, even if it came with the perky smile he was in love with. "That's nice," she said.

"That's nice," he repeated. "What's wrong now? I got you out of the party early, didn't I? I set you up with a fashion photographer—"

"Do you know who Orville Faubus is?" she asked. Leslie Mae looked hurt now.

Jean sighed as he tried to think. Faubus, Faubus. He'd had too much champagne. What the hell was this about, anyway? "I don't know. I think he had something to do with the blacks and segregation. Yeah, that's right. I did a paper on him in prep school. He was the governor of Arkansas in the fifties."

Leslie Mae looked at him. "You were in prep school?"

"No, no, not a prep school," he corrected himself hastily.

"A private school, and just for a semester. After I ran away I got placed with a family briefly, and they put me in school. What about Orville Faubus?"

"Who's George Foster Dulles?" Leslie Mae continued, looking more crestfallen by the second. "Or Arthur Miller, or Robert Oppenheimer, or Whittaker Chambers?"

"They all had to do with the Cold War and spying, and who had Communist sympathies and who didn't. Leslie Mae, what in the hell are you getting at?"

"I stood around all these people tonight and I didn't know what they were talking about! I pretended I did, but they could tell I didn't. It was humiliating."

"Maybe they were just a bunch of name-droppers. Some people are going to be pretentious—"

"These were your friends," she reminded him, cutting him again. "All these successful, smart people, and I'm a stupid high-school dropout. I knew it would be like this, I knew it! Now do you understand why I didn't want to come?"

Jean studied the sincere, proud face that was now a river of blue and red tears. Her makeup was down to her chin. She dropped her trembling jaw in the hollow of his shoulder, snuggling closer. Her body was so warm, the flesh so fragrant. Jean fastened his free arm around her like an anchor.

He suddenly felt remorse for the last few years, the lies he was perpetuating that Leslie Mae would undoubtedly find as wrong and upsetting as the pretensions tonight. No, she would find them worse, despicable, he thought. If she knew the truth right now, she'd never want to see him again. A dam of anxiety broke inside him. He could not lose Leslie Mae. He didn't totally understand the reasons for his fear, but he thought it would be like losing his own soul.

Holding her tightly, as the Mercedes weaved among the cruisers and sightseers on Sunset, Jean swallowed any urge to confess and buried his secrets even deeper. When they reached her apartment, he walked Leslie Mae inside and laid her gently on the bed. Her dress was unfastened button by button, and when they were both naked and lying on top of the soft sheets, nothing else seemed to matter.

The formal letter of invitation to meet the membership committee of the California Club arrived within two weeks. Jean wore his most conservative suit and met Harvey Crisp at the club doors promptly at seven. As he was ushered down the quiet, somber corridors of privilege, his eyes skated to the familiar paintings and carpet. His ears picked up the clicking of dominoes from the game rooms. Nothing had changed. He entered a small room with elegant wainscoting and sat comfortably before a half-dozen men who inquired into his life. Jean assured them he loved the city of Los Angeles, abhorred communism, was a religious man in his heart, and swore to keep secret what went on inside this hallowed club.

"Congratulations, you've been accepted," Harvey told Jean in the club lounge where he waited afterward.

"That was so quick," Jean allowed. "I feel great. Thank you. Thanks for everything."

He walked Harvey to his car in the club garage. Lit by a single sodium vapor light, the cavernous space was filled with flickering shadows, as quiet as a tomb. A skinny kid no more than eighteen ran for Harvey's car and returned it with a tired smile. Haunted, Jean stared at the young man, then, before Harvey could react, lifted a ten from his wallet and pressed it into the boy's hand.

The sight of a tall, well-tanned woman in shorts and hiking boots, a colorful bandanna around her neck, sometimes carrying a walking stick as she traversed the dry sand beds and mountain ridges, was a daily occurrence to anyone who was out early enough in the desert to observe it. But nature pilgrimages at dawn were not on the agenda of most Palm Springs residents. They preferred their sun at poolside and at hours respectable enough to include a cold beer. No one in the town, however, expected normalcy from Alycia Poindexter. She had won her spurs by choosing to side with a hippie wanderer, and almost three quiet years later the label of eccentric had not left her. Besides trekking through the mountains, she was observed in town at the library or supermarket, and occasionally she attended a city-council meeting, where everyone held his breath. Some women in town, strong and individualistic to a degree, had invited her to lunch at their clubs, but they were always turned down.

Alycia roamed where and how she pleased, much as Mrs. McManus had, and like the town's founder, she was determined to keep her life free of cluttering schedules. She had never felt better. The rigorous walks had increased her stamina, and the sun, limited only to early-morning exposures, had turned her skin a deep, soft gold. She had lost some weight too, and whenever she caught herself in the mirror as she emerged from her bath, she thought her figure belonged to a woman in her thirties.

The physical pleasures were a distraction from an anxiety that never quite faded. Jean came into her thoughts when she least expected it. Where was he, and why hadn't he been in touch with her or Harriet? Like Harriet, Alycia believed he was alive and well, hiding somewhere. It was only intuition, because the facts belied it. Alycia had hired a succession of private detectives who each concluded that her son was either dead or out of the country. No phone-company, social-security, insurance, or tax records showed the existence of Jean Poindexter. Falling between the cracks of society wasn't impossible, and Alycia was consoled that if Jean did trip up and surface, he would be found.

Whenever she was down, Alycia turned her thoughts to Felice. The senior at Oakley Academy was studying art history and creative writing, earning almost a four-point average. In her several visits east, Alycia found that not only did her daughter not date much, she didn't like any extracurricular activities. Her few close friends were just like her—they sequestered themselves in the library or took in a movie or went out for pizza. That was their social life. Their communication didn't focus on boys or career plans or going on shopping sprees. They were young intellectuals who wore jeans and T-shirts every day and talked about existentialism and abstract art and Marxist communism. They threw ideas back and forth like seals bouncing a ball to each other. But they could be intimate and supportive too, in the way almost all women were. When one of Felice's friends had gotten pregnant last spring, the others kept her secret and raised money for the abortion. When Felice told her the story, Alycia kept her judgments to herself. Making choices and taking risks was the only way for Felice to become independent and form her own values.

On her Christmas break, Felice flew to Palm Springs and Alycia took her to lunch at a quiet restaurant far from Palm Canyon Drive. She had decided it was time to reveal the truth. As they sat over glasses of wine, describing Red's suicide wasn't easy, but afterward Alycia was glad she'd done it.

"Why didn't you tell me before?" Felice demanded, searching her mother's face.

"I didn't think you were old enough to understand. Now you are."

Felice digested the story without outward emotion, but Alycia could tell she was agitated. "Was Daddy that unhappy?"

"In a way, yes. It had nothing to do with you or Jean. He loved you both very much. But he was too hard on himself. His standards were too high."

"And there were pressures from Grandfather," she said perceptively. "No one told me directly, but I could feel them."

"Yes," Alycia said.

"You never told Jean this?"

"I was too afraid. If he ever comes back, we'll have a lot to talk about."

Felice slipped her hand consolingly over her mother's. "Don't worry. He'll come back."

"There's something else you should know," Alycia went on. "Your grandfather left you a great deal of money. It's in my care, and I'm not sure what to do with it . . . what's best for you . . ."

"Money?" Felice looked puzzled.

"A very substantial amount."

"Like how much?"

"Nine million dollars."

Felice's face broke into a smirk. "What? Nine million dollars?" She began laughing. "Wait till my friends find out. They'll think I'm a capitalist and never talk to me again!"

"Seriously, I don't know if I'd tell anybody," Alycia said. "When you have money, that's all people ever judge you by."

Felice pondered her mother's words. "But what are you going to do with all that money? All I know is, I don't want to be unhappy like Daddy or turn out like my brother. Money and success were all Jean ever thought about."

"Then I hope I have the wisdom to decide for you," Alycia said, but she knew there were a thousand other things she'd rather think about.

When Alycia returned from her desert walk one morning, she found a bouquet of flowers resting against her front door. The wildflowers of brilliant colors had been handpicked from the nearby mountains. There was no note.

"Alycia . . ."

Even before she turned, she knew the voice. She had almost anticipated it, even its nervous timbre, but what she hadn't guessed was her reaction. She turned and let her eyes parade over the handsome figure and the kind face with the trim beard that was now all gray. Andrew stood as tall and proud as ever, but he looked pale under the intense sun. She couldn't speak. As often as she thought of Jean and Felice, she also had fantasized about Andrew. She had forgiven him for what had happened at the monastery, pretended, in fact, it had never occurred. They were still in love. They had been separated by circumstances. And one day they would be together again.

But as she stared now at Andrew she felt no understanding or forgiveness. She was not in love. An anger swept over her that chased away her nervousness. How could he dare approach her? Did he come to apologize or explain? What could he possibly say to make her feel differently? She had been abandoned by the one person she'd been sure would never abandon her, her one anchor in an unending sea of infidelity.

"I have no business intruding in your life," he said, keeping his distance. "I know you feel betrayed by me. But I wanted to see you again." His weight shifted, and the gentle, wise eyes settled on her as if he'd never been away.

"How did you find me?" Alycia asked.

"I knew you had moved. I even knew when. The family who bought your house was kind enough to tell me. Are you well, Alycia?"

"Fine, thank you," she said, still disturbed.

"I spoke to Harriet yesterday. She told me about Jean," he continued. Sympathy shone in his eyes. "I'm very sorry, but I hope you've not given up on him."

"No. I've always taken your advice to heart." She pushed the hair from her eyes. "And what about you? What have you been doing?"

"Time flows like a river. I'm afraid sometimes I lose track of where I am. For the last two weeks I've been in Los Angeles, raising funds again."

"Then I'm an afterthought to you," she observed.

"That's not true," he said quickly. He was ready to say more, but he saw the distrust and disappointment in her eyes. It was what he'd expected, and he couldn't blame her. He was an unwanted trespasser, and perhaps no words would ever make him welcome. "Perhaps I should say good-bye now," he offered, turning contritely.

"If you really want to explain things to me," she stopped him, "I'll listen."

She wanted to be fair, she thought. As they moved inside, Andrew asked for a glass of water, then settled on the living-room couch opposite Alycia.

"I know I let you down," he began in his measured voice, "but what has happened in the last three years has not been easy for me either. Sometimes I think I'm only full of self-pity and that God must take me for a fool. The day you came to the monastery to visit me, I was there, I overheard your voice—"

"Then your abbot lied," she said, shocked.

"He did not want you there. Forgive his expediency. He believed, with all the wisdom he could summon, that my soul was in danger. You must remember the context of how you and I met. Brother Manning took a great risk in sending me to raise money. He came under harsh criticism from other Trappists—our vows, after all, require strict separation from the material world. It was one thing for him to take liberty with that stricture, quite another to find that I was receiving so many letters from you. Benefactor or not, you were suddenly a danger. When Brother Manning learned you were to visit, he grew concerned."

"You let him do that to you," Alycia protested. "You told him."

"I had to, when he asked. He is my abbot."

"But you'd just written me you were in love with me, and suddenly—"

"Alycia, what could I do? When I joined the Cistercians I took a vow of strict obedience. To God, to my superiors in the Church, to any voice of authority I willfully serve."

"So because of your abbot, or your conscience, you forgot me?"

"No! That is not true," he said emphatically. "Every day I thought about you. I realized how strong my heart was, perhaps even stronger than my conscience."

"What are you saying?" she asked.

"My abbot does not know I'm here. I was told never to see you again, no matter how much money you might donate."

"Then why are you here?" Her heart pounded. She had to repeat herself. She wanted Andrew to be perfectly clear.

"Because I'm still in love with you."

Alycia's eyes cut away from the monk. He had told her what she wanted to hear, but now she was sorry she'd asked.

"Why do you look so unhappy?" Andrew demanded.

"Because what happened between us once can happen again. Because I don't want to be disappointed anymore. Because we have no future."

"I see," he said. He was hurt. He could think of nothing to say. "Alycia," he finally spoke, "at least know that I never forgot you—and never will. After you left the monastery, Brother Manning, seeing my distress, did not allow me to travel in the States again until now. I was sent back and forth to the Amazon. I was forbidden to contact you, even to think about you, Alycia. But my heart would not let go. I would phone you at this house, and then, feeling the burden of Brother Manning's words, lose my nerve and hang up."

"That was you?" she said, remembering the calls. "You took the trouble to find out I had moved?"

He squared his shoulders in frustration. "It did me no good, did it?"

She could feel Andrew's torment, and her own shame for being angry with him. There was no one to blame.

Andrew rose awkwardly. "I pray that God forgives me, Alycia. I've come to realize I'm not as perfect as I would like to be. Perhaps I do not fall short if measured by most yardsticks, but by God's, and my own, I am a disappointment."

The torment flickered across Andrew's face as he turned and walked to the door. Alycia watched him duck into the sunlight.

"Andrew," she called. He pivoted as she approached. She entwined her arms around his waist and buried her head in his shoulder. For a moment Andrew hesitated. Then he returned her embrace.

"Can't you stay?" she asked.

"Alycia—"

"Just for a while. I have an extra bedroom. If you've taken the risk of disobeying your abbot, what would it hurt to stay a few more days? I haven't been fair to you."

"You told me you didn't want to take a chance—"

"I don't want to think about the future now. I just want you to stay. Please?" she said.

Just having Andrew's arms around her was comforting, Alycia thought, and to see and talk to him for a few days was something she needed. That afternoon they worked in her garden, laughing and exchanging stories, and later Andrew helped with house repairs. By default, he was his monastery's handyman, he said good-naturedly, and he told her he liked to sing Italian arias as he worked. Alycia made him sing now, clapping after each rendition.

The next morning she took him on her constitutional walk in the desert. Alycia pointed out geological formations and exotic wildflowers, but Andrew knew them better than she. He told her about plants and animals of the jungle and life along the Amazon, the constant presence of malaria, the tyranny of the Brazilian government, which sold land to foresters and mining companies without regard to the rights of the Indians. Not only did he have to fight the government over the land issue, he had to teach the Indians to become farmers. It wasn't an easy transition for a people who since immemorial time had been hunter-gatherers.

"Do you ever get lonely?" she asked over dinner that night. "It seems everything you do is a solitary endeavor. You don't get much help."

"God is my help. But it's true," he admitted, "my work is mostly done alone."

"It doesn't bother you?"

"Why should it? I'm used to it."

"But there's a void sometimes, isn't there? Just you and God—is that enough?" she prodded. She often thought of how difficult Andrew's life had to be. How could a world of so much silence be bearable? To Andrew it was more than that, she thought; it made him happy.

"Of course, being close to God is not always a comfortable feeling," Andrew volunteered. "I always feel accountable to him. Nothing I do or think or feel goes unnoticed. I am aware of every slip and error I make."

"Do you ever think of quitting?" she suddenly asked.

"Quitting?"

"The Cistercians."

He thought for a moment. "I would not be human if I said I hadn't. I think most brothers at one time or another have been tempted. Being a monk is not easy. It means years of complete and unrelenting self-denial. There is a great peace in surrendering your soul, but the rigid routine often means losing touch with your feelings. Any emotion you have must be directed to God. And in the monastery God manifests himself in rigid theology, Latin Masses, ponderous scholastic treatises. An air of intellectual martial law rules, I'm afraid. There is no room for argument or doubt in the abbey, at least not out loud. To this day I carry that sense of bloodless duty with me.''

Alycia was puzzled. "Then where is the joy in what you do? I know you're a man filled with joy. I've seen it.''

His soft smile warmed the room. "In spite of my training, in the last ten years I've come to see that God is also a spirit of understanding and forgiveness. He knows we are not perfect, no matter how hard we might try. It has been said there are two Gods of Christianity. The one of the Old Testament, who is full of wrath and retribution. And the New Testament, a God who understands and forgives our transgressions. I prefer the latter. Because it is by knowing my own weaknesses that I can best understand and help others, and thus do the most good in the world. That is what fills me with joy. Does that make sense?''

"Why do you say in the last ten years?''

"Perhaps it was part coincidence, but it was after I met you that I began to examine my own feelings more closely. And on our second visit, it was definitely you who wakened in me a different sense of love and commitment.''

Alycia tried to keep the anxiousness out of her voice. "What do you mean?''

"I told you in my letters. You are a very special person to me. I fell in love with you.''

"And how do you feel now?''

"Nothing has changed. Time has not dulled my heart. Nor,'' he said, looking more troubled, "has it quieted my anxiety. There is still a war in my soul. Perhaps there always will be.''

"And you can live with that? It's my fault. I torment you—''

"Alycia,'' he said in the gentle but firm voice she knew so well, "we will not discuss this further. I am here to visit you and be your company. Nothing more. Let's take pleasure from that. And now,'' he added, rising, "if we are to be up early for that walk I enjoy so much . . .''

He approached and kissed her on the forehead. Alycia could feel the conflict in Andrew, and in herself. The anger she had once felt toward the monk she now directed to his vows of denial that shut her out of his life as if she were nothing but a temptation. She was more than that, she thought. She was someone who loved and cared for him.

Andrew spent the entire week. The dawn treks through nearby canyons were supplemented by evening picnics, and in between they read and talked. On one level Andrew was a man of simple honesty and direction, but on another Alycia wondered if she truly understood him. She peppered him with personal questions. He dwelled on his mother, whom he had loved deeply but had been too busy to show it. He told of certain monks in the abbey whom he counted as his truest and strongest friends. Of his plans for making the Amazon project a showcase for other Indian settlements.

After dinner one evening, Andrew stirred his coffee self-consciously. His eyes moved everywhere but to her at the table. "Alycia," he finally said, "I'm afraid I have something to tell you."

She looked up.

"I must be leaving soon. Tomorrow."

She scrambled for what to say. "But why? Do you have an appointment?"

"Not exactly. I'm returning to the Amazon in a month, and there's so much preparation—"

"I understand," she said, cutting off her feelings She was too upset to try to forestall the inevitable. She made an effort to pick up her spirits as she said good night and disappeared into her bedroom. Drifting in a gray, fitful sleep, she woke with a start. No, she could not let him go, she thought, not like this. Everyone else whom she'd loved had fallen out of her life. She would not lose Andrew too.

She rose and drifted into his bedroom. A priest—a man of God—what right did she have to tamper with that? She did not want to be a temptress. But what about her own needs?

She sat on the edge of the bed and studied Andrew as he slept. The rugged face was for the moment without torment or conflict. When she stroked his beard, his eyes flicked open. No one spoke as his hand traveled to her cheek and rested there. Gently he pulled her on top of him. Her lips brushed against his. Andrew hesitated, then kissed her back. It felt like more than a reprieve from her loneliness, Alycia thought. She felt passion, too. She shed her nightgown and slipped between the sheets.

Tentatively Andrew guided his hand to her breasts and

down her belly. When he moved on top of her, she dropped her arms around his sloping shoulders and kissed him hungrily. Her fingers glided down the muscular ridges of his arms. Alycia expected one of them to be unsure, but Andrew became as lost in the flood of passion as she. His kisses covered her face and neck. Alycia let herself go completely. For these exquisite moments she wished away all her independence and defiance. All the years of waiting were worth this intimacy.

"That was magical," she breathed when they were still. She couldn't help smiling. Had this really happened? She propped herself on an elbow and looked at Andrew. He seemed lost in his thoughts. "Are you all right?" she asked.

"What have I done?" he said, gazing back at her. A stunned, embarrassed smile broke on his lips.

"Please don't regret this," she said, suddenly worried. "Are you still in love with me?"

He folded her hands in his and kissed her tenderly. "I was thinking that not only am I in love with you, but that I want time to stop. Right now, this instant."

"That would be wonderful," she whispered.

"I imagined this moment for so long," he said, facing her. "I never had the courage to seduce you, nor the courage to resist, it seems."

"None of that matters," she assured him.

"And I always wondered how I would feel afterward. If there would be such crushing guilt that I couldn't face myself—"

"Is there?" she asked. She wondered if she felt guilty herself.

"I am in love with you. How can I regret what feels natural and fulfilling? If I have sinned in God's eyes, I pray he forgives me and shows this has happened for a purpose."

"A purpose?" she said, intrigued. Andrew's gaze was suddenly vacant. "What is it?" she asked.

"Nothing."

"No. Please tell me."

He paused. "I've always wondered what it would be to father a child."

Alycia bit her lip. "Really?"

"Why, are you surprised?"

"I don't know. I never thought a monk would think like that. But now, knowing you, I understand."

"To have my own child, to teach him or her what I think is wonderful and valuable about life—how can there be any higher pleasure? I know the heartaches you've endured as a parent, Alycia, but often I think I'd like the chance."

Moved, Alycia lay beside him. "Would it be absurd for me to want to have your baby?"

He stroked her shoulder. "No, it would be wonderful. But it is not possible. Our circumstances . . ." He had to smile.

"I've never met anyone like you," Alycia said. "You look at life in the most basic, simple way, yet you're a complex man. Is that what it takes to be content with having so little?"

"I have everything I need," he said with a calm she envied.

"Society looks on you as some kind of aberration. You're tolerated, but no one takes your views seriously. Everyone thinks you're naive. The world is really a hostile, aggressive place."

"I don't disagree. The world has always been that way, Alycia."

"But you try to change it."

"Of course."

"If everybody didn't care about their houses and cars and how much money they had . . . can you imagine? If everyone suddenly thought like you?"

"For me," Andrew said, "I realized long ago that possessions are only burdens. I grew up with so much, and it turned out to be an empty life. What does it profit a man if he enjoys a worldly kingdom but loses his soul? Wasn't it Thoreau who wrote that one is as rich as the things he can live without?"

"Why must you leave?" Alycia suddenly asked in the quiet. She blinked back a tear.

"I don't want to, you know that." He traced his finger over her lips. "But no matter what has happened tonight, no matter how strongly I feel about you, I am still a servant of my church and God. I am supposed to return to the Amazon. I want to return, Alycia. My work is my happiness."

"Then I want to go with you," she said.

Andrew's eyes narrowed in surprise. He took in Alycia's earnest face. "Why?"

"Because I'm in love with you. Because I have nothing to do here, and because I want to learn to live like you. I don't know if I've ever been truly happy in my life. Some times were happier than others, but there were always tensions and troubles. I want to try something different. I want to be free."

"Alycia, are you running from something? From memories, from Jean—"

"No. I've thought about this for so long. I can't change the past, and I have to do what's right for me. I think this is exactly that."

"There are problems, Alycia—"

"No, there aren't," she said stubbornly.

"Life in the Amazon is not like Palm Springs. You may be used to solitude, but on the river our days are very long, the heat and humidity intense. There's sickness, frustration. We never have enough money. The government harasses us."

"I don't care. You can't discourage me."

"I won't always be there. I must go where my abbot sends me. I never know, and to leave you alone would be irresponsible."

"At least let me try. Maybe I'll learn to be as independent as you. You'll be my teacher."

"What about Brother Manning?" Andrew asked with a sudden chuckle. "I don't think he would approve."

"He doesn't have to know. If I fly to Brazil on my own, would you turn a volunteer away?"

"You've already made up your mind, haven't you?" he said, amazed.

It was Alycia's turn to smile.

"That's one thing I've always admired about you," Andrew confessed. "You do what you want."

"There's something else," she put in delicately. "I know this will come as a surprise, but you're the only one I'd ever trust. You just talked about being burdened by possessions . . ."

Andrew struggled up in bed, scrutinizing her now.

"Please don't think I'm being rash," Alycia went on. "I'm not losing my senses. If anything, I'm finding them."

"Go on," he said, not certain he wanted to hear.

"I want to give you my money. Virtually all of it. Even the trusts that Owen established. I want you to give it away for me."

His face flushed. "Alycia—"

"You know how I feel about organized charity. I won't give another dime."

"And you expect the Church to fill that void?"

"The money is not to go to your abbot or the Church. I don't even want them to know. I don't trust them. They'd be swayed too much by politics, face too many temptations. The money is to go to you. You alone will have the power to dispense it."

"This is impossible," he said, staggered.

"Nothing's impossible. I'll leave Felice and Jean and Harriet something, but I want my money to do some good in the world. It's only caused my family pain. And I trust your judgment."

"You know I cannot accept this."

"Tell me why."

"I just cannot. It is too much to ask of any person."

"Won't you at least consider it?"

"I'm truly sorry. I love you, but this has nothing to do with love."

Alycia turned away. Andrew released a breath. He knew Alycia was too stubborn to back down. She would bring up the idea again, and again. It was not a question of whether he would surrender, he supposed, but of when.

"Perhaps," Andrew allowed cautiously, "if the sum is not too great, I could find ways to spend it without Brother Manning knowing. If he never asks me, I suppose I don't have to tell him. And your money *would* do some good in the world."

"My own net worth is twelve million dollars," Alycia informed him after a beat. "The trusts for Jean and Felice have appreciated to almost twenty million."

She had never seen a face pale so quickly. Andrew's hands froze in midair.

"I'm flattered by your faith in me," Andrew said when he'd recovered, "but I am a man of only modest talents. I am not a banker. I would have no idea what to do with that sum of money. But I am a decent judge of character, and I can tell you, should our secret be exposed, that I would be in peril. Your former friends would say I exerted undue influence over you, which would undermine my efforts to put your funds to good use. Jean would demand his trust money back. And my abbot would probably have me censored for deliberately deceiving the Church."

"I wouldn't let those things happen to you. I love you too much."

"Alycia, there are some things we can't control, despite our intentions."

"I'm not afraid," she said, "and you shouldn't be either. I don't care about public opinion. It's never been my friend. The point is, the money is mine to do with as I choose. I want it to do some good. How can you refuse that? Isn't that what you want too? The secret will never get out. The only ones who know are Harriet, Felice, and my attorneys."

"It is so much money, Alycia. So much responsibility!"

"You don't have to spend it all at once. My lawyers will draw up papers giving you complete discretion over the money."

"Alycia, you once told me that there were too many secrets in your life."

She nodded, remembering all too clearly.

"Secrets mean risks," he reminded her.

"Maybe there're times neither can be avoided. Didn't you tell me that our lives are full of imperfections?"

Alycia's lips pressed gently against his. Her warmth and aroma aroused Andrew again. He felt the stirring of guilt, but as he took Alycia in his arms, any residue of doubt was washed away in the tide of commitment. The pleasures of the flesh were only an echo of the needs of the soul. He did not have to stop time, he realized. Love between a man and a woman was a bond that triumphed over the ravages of time. It was something no one but God could take away.

Over breakfast he told Alycia everything he could about the Amazon, the projects they would be working on, the tasks still to be started. A new generator for the settlement was needed; so were tools, a boat, books, clothing. His voice trembled with hope.

"Then my money can definitely help," Alycia said.

"If we are careful and discreet," he said. "This shall be a rather bold experiment, don't you think?"

"We won't fail," Alycia promised. "You'll see."

Andrew remained at the house another week. He could not pull himself away. Every time he made love to Alycia his joy suffused his heart and soul. He told her that their love was so complete and powerful it would triumph over all obstacles. But when waking in the middle of the night, Andrew felt hesitation and doubt. He asked God for forgiveness. He could not help himself. If physical love was but an extension of a natural emotional bond, how could it be a sin? Maybe even his emotional attachment to Alycia was wrong in God's eyes.

Maybe God wanted him to live in a vacuum of purity, an ideal for others to look up to. Wasn't that the original doctrine of the Cistercians? Yet it was his abbot who had dispatched Andrew into the world, to live among those who took no such vows. How could he be expected to remain so aloof and pure? Brother Manning would never see the contradiction. Andrew wondered if God would understand. The monk was a man with needs—did that make him any less able to work among the poor and spread the Gospel?

Andrew's torment came and went, but he always kept it from Alycia. She had suffered enough. His shoulders were wide enough to carry her secrets as well as his. He had not been in contact with his abbey in over two weeks. Would Brother Manning be suspicious? What if he confronted Andrew with specific questions? Andrew dreaded the prospect of having to lie. The path of the future was suddenly full of perils and challenges. The monk prayed that God would provide him the wisdom to negotiate it.

When the time came to say good-bye, Andrew wrapped Alycia in his arms and consoled himself that she would be joining him in the Amazon within a month. He pushed away his anxiety and apprehension. Their love for each other would shine like a beacon in the darkest crevasse of the darkest night. And if its light could never be extinguished, he thought, what was there to fear?

Alycia wasted no time packing. Loose ends were tied up, and she placed her Palm Springs house on the market. She instructed her attorneys to put all proceeds from the sale into a new trust, together with the rest of her assets and her children's twenty million dollars, naming Brother Andrew sole fiduciary and trustee. Alycia was immediately advised against such folly. She reminded her attorneys that everything was confidential and that her decision was final unless she notified them otherwise. When the new papers were drawn, she drove to Los Angeles for dinner with Harriet.

"Oh, my," Harriet replied when she heard Alycia's plan to join Brother Andrew in the Amazon. "Are you sure you know what you're doing?"

"I'm more than sure, Mother." Alycia leaned across the table. "For the first time in years I'm excited about something. I feel free. It's a new life for me. I can't wait."

"South America is so far away. When are you coming back?"

"I don't know, honestly," Alycia admitted. "I don't think it matters." She caught herself when she saw the hurt on Harriet's face. "I'm sorry. I know I have responsibilities to you and the children. But things will work out."

"Did Brother Andrew talk you into this?" she inquired, still unconvinced.

Alycia controlled her smile. "It was the other way around."

Harriet was disturbed anew, but she saw a glow in Alycia that had been absent for years. And she could understand the excitement of a new adventure—for so many years she had wished one for herself. Now she could live this through Alycia. She decided not to worry. If anyone had proved she could survive adversity, it was Alycia.

"Could Brother Andrew use another volunteer?" Harriet teased.

"You're welcome anytime, Mother."

"I have a friend who just joined the Peace Corps at seventy-nine. One never knows."

After dinner they settled in the cavernous living room where Alycia had been first introduced to Red's family. Her gaze locked on the sunset. A fireball was exploding on the blurred edge of the horizon. Alycia could suddenly see Red standing by the bar, waiting to talk to his father while she hovered in a catatonic state on the couch, worried about her makeup and the liquor on her breath. Owen appeared, handsome and impeccably dressed, the judgmental eyes sweeping over her.

"Alycia, are you all right?"

She pulled herself out of the reverie. "I'm just tired, Mother." She retrieved a notepad from her purse and wrote the address and phone of a church office in Belém. In case of an emergency, someone there could reach the Trappist settlement by radio. Then Alycia pulled a check from her wallet and handed it to Harriet.

"What's this?" Harriet asked, putting on her glasses.

"A gift."

She scrutinized the check and handed it back. "Alycia, thank you, but it's not necessary," she said. "I live adequately."

"Please. It would make me feel better."

"I don't want you to feel guilty at going. I can see now that you would feel much worse if you didn't go."

"I want you to have something from me. What about my jewelry?"

"Are you afraid you'll never see me again?" Harriet asked perceptively. "I don't plan on leaving this earth just yet."

Alycia felt her face color. "Mother—"

"We'll see each other again. Give your jewelry to Felice. Just be sure to think about us. Especially Jean. You know, something strange happened the other day . . ."

Alycia hunched her shoulders. "Tell me."

"I was going outside to turn on the sprinklers. Across the street was this car—an old Lincoln convertible, but restored, deep burgundy, just like the one Red bought when you were first married. I thought it might have been the same one. Is that possible? Do you remember what happened to that car?"

"Red sold it to some dealer. It could still be around. A car like that was an instant classic. No one in his right mind would scrap it."

"Did Jean know Red had the car?"

"I'm sure Red told him."

"When I moved closer," Harriet continued, "the driver turned on the engine, hesitated, and drove off. He looked young, and he had a beard. I was sure for a moment he was going to talk to me."

"You think it was Jean?" asked Alycia, rushing her words.

"It could have been. There was something familiar about the face. I know I've seen it. I tried to get a look at the license plate, but I'm too slow these days. I keep thinking he'll come back."

Alycia felt a surge of hope. It was always her feeling that Jean might contact his grandmother. Both she and Harriet kept in touch regularly with the detective agencies. Every so often a clue would turn up, but nothing ever came of it, and in general Jean's trail was icy cold. Alycia finally believed he had fled the country. Had he come back now?

Harriet toasted the tantalizing possibility with a nightcap of Courvoisier. Harriet was to contact Alycia at once if Jean reappeared. Then they toasted their futures. Alycia wiped away a tear as she rose to leave.

"I'll miss you, Mother," she whispered as they hugged. "You've done so much for me."

"And you for me, dear. Will you promise to take care of yourself?"

"I'll be fine. What about you?"

"I think after all these years I'm entitled to call myself a survivor."

*   *   *

Alycia stayed at an airport hotel to catch the first flight in the morning to Philadelphia. She'd considered calling Felice at Oakley Academy ahead of time, but the idea of surprising her was too tempting. She was almost free now, she thought in the plane. She wondered how Andrew was, and if he missed her as much as she longed for him. She hoped Felice would understand.

"Mom, what are you doing here?" Felice exclaimed when she found her mother outside her classroom. Alycia couldn't take her eyes off her daughter. She was suddenly a young woman, ready for college, ready for the world. But suspicion burned in Felice's eyes, as if sure her mother's unannounced presence indicated something wrong. Mother and daughter strolled along a manicured lawn surrounded by tall, lush hedges that moaned in the spring breeze.

"Is this about Jean?" Felice finally asked.

"No. I haven't heard anything," Alycia admitted, "not of substance." She relayed Harriet's story, but Felice could make no more sense of it than Alycia had.

"I wouldn't hold out too much hope," Felice volunteered. "Jean was always good at hiding when he wanted to."

"Please don't say that. Maybe he was never easy to get along with, but I hope that when he appears, you'll find a way to accept him."

"You know I'll try," she said, "but we have nothing in common."

"You're brother and sister, Felice."

"That's not enough. Really, I hope Jean is all right, but I don't want him in my life."

"Felice, I need to discuss some things with you," Alycia changed the subject. Her daughter gave her another searching look. "Remember on my last visit we discussed money?"

"I remember. The trusts."

"I've finally made up my mind. I want to know if you'll be resentful. I've set up an account for you for five hundred thousand dollars. That's for college and graduate school and to get started afterward. I've done the same for Jean."

"Mom, that's more than I'll ever need. Why should I be resentful? I told you, I'm not like Jean."

"Then you wouldn't object if I told you I'm giving most of what I have away?"

"I don't think so. To whom?"

"Since my last visit, I've been in touch with Brother Andrew." She watched the smile widen on her daughter's face, as if Felice had known this was going to happen. "I'm going to join him in the Amazon. There's a project I'll be working on, and I want my money to go toward it. You mustn't tell anyone, Felice. That's for Andrew's sake. You should also know I might be gone for a long time."

"You're going to live in a jungle?" Felice asked, incredulous.

"I'm going to start a new life. I'm a different person, Felice. At least I feel like one."

Felice looked away.

"You don't approve," Alycia said, anxious

"No, it's not that, really. I'm just surprised. Anyway, you don't need my approval. You don't need anybody's. You've always done what you wanted with your life. That's why I admire you so much. I like to think I'm the same as you, but I'm not sure."

Alycia looped an arm around her daughter. "I have all the faith and confidence in the world in you. You're strong and capable, Felice. And please don't think I'm disappearing. We'll keep in close touch."

Felice threw her head back, smiling. "This is like a novel that Electra should have written."

"Maybe one day you'll write it," Alycia said.

"Maybe." She started to laugh.

"What's so funny?"

"I've got something to tell you too, Mother."

It was Alycia's turn to look concerned.

"I want to take a trip myself. I was going to ask your permission. Now I don't see how you can deny me."

"What kind of trip?"

"*Qu'est-ce que tu pense? Je veux voyager à Paris. Comme tu—*"

"Paris?" Alycia was stunned.

"Just for the summer, before I start college. Princeton's already accepted me, so why not? I can take a class or two at the Sorbonne. I feel so confined here—I want to get out and explore. You always promised to take me to Europe someday."

"Felice, you're only seventeen."

"Eighteen in July," she corrected.

Alycia was besieged by memories. Her father teaching at the Sorbonne, living on Place San Michel, the long war, meeting Red. Part of her wished she was a teenager again, or taking this trip with Felice. "And here I was worried that you still needed a mother to take care of you."

"I can take care of myself, I swear, Mom. Just like you. We'll both be fine. Now, tell me, are you in love?"

"What?"

"With Brother Andrew. And did you sleep with him?" she asked.

"Felice . . ." But Alycia knew she had no business being shocked. She was glad for her daughter's candor. She wondered if Felice had any boyfriends she was intimate with. She gave her daughter a look. "You're sure I don't have to worry about you?"

"About men? No, Mom," Felice said with a small laugh. She pushed her arm through her mother's. "Come on, let's have lunch and you can tell me everything about you and Andrew. I won't let you say good-bye until you do."

In June 1981 the claim of tallest building in Los Angeles could be made by the new First Interstate Bank Building. The crown jewel on Wilshire Boulevard was sixty-two floors and commanded majestic views of the fastest-growing city in the country. Its first tenant had leased the entire top floor, twenty-two thousand square feet, before a single shovel had broken ground and without quibbling over the thirty dollars a square foot annual lease. The interior-decorating tab ran over a million. The one hundred and twenty-nine employees of Harp Enterprises, Ltd. enjoyed not just finely appointed offices but a sophisticated network of computers with access to the city's tax rolls, building-department permits, and real-estate sales histories. Harp Enterprises spared no expense in impressing clients that it was the center of a very important and dynamic universe. Real-estate development was a crowded, competitive field, but according to the Los Angeles *Times* and other media, Marvin Harp, president and CEO, genius founder of Little Japan in America, friend of the stars and important people, was king of the mountain.

Marvin Harp was no longer Mad Man Marvin. The crazy-man image had been shed years ago, replaced by a more mature and astute businessman whose market was not pimply-faced stereo junkies but the educated and wealthy. On a silvery June afternoon, Harp Enterprises' boyish president stood confidently in his leather-and-chrome conference room before a group of investors. They included one of America's favorite late-night television entertainers, several sports personalities, the owner of a Beverly Hills restaurant, a successful woman novelist, and two brothers who had started a health-and-fitness spa that was so successful clients waited a year to get in. The common denominator of the group was money and a deep respect for a man who had made them still richer. Marvin Harp was their friend, mentor, financial guru.

"What I'm proposing is the biggest cineplex in the country." The president spoke in his golden-throated voice, pointing to a chart of bright graphics and numbers that no one paid attention to or understood. "Los Angeles is the entertainment capital of the world. Billions of dollars are generated by the film industry. People don't read books anymore, they go to movies. The cineplex concept has already proved successful in shopping malls. Now is the time to go a step further—an eighteen-screen complex combined with video arcades, gourmet-food outlets, boutiques, specialty stores. The more exotic, the better. Sources of instant gratification. Because entertainment today means spending money. It doesn't matter what you spend it on. What counts, psychologically, is spending. Shopping is a fix. The act of spending money is the second-most-powerful drug our society has invented. The most powerful is making it. For our cineplex I've targeted an entire block in Westwood, not far from UCLA. Twenty thousand college students are a gold mine. My people have purchase agreements on all but one of the properties. Four and a half million will take the block. Another four to build the facility. We can be open by the fall of eighty-two."

Jean knew he could talk forever. He loved the sound of his voice, but now he paused to take in the rhapsodic and eager faces. No one could wait to pull out his checkbook. Had his father found it this easy? Jean fielded the usual questions: What kind of return could everyone expect, what about tax write-offs, was there any competition . . . ?

"Those who know me know I don't worry about competition," Jean said. "When you're the best, you don't mind taking chances."

"But I understand," the woman novelist interrupted, "there's a Japanese group buying a lot of property in the city, and they're trying to start some super shopping facility in the Valley."

"You mean the Kitmitsui Group? Samurai in business suits," he quipped. As Jean's eyes cut across the silent room, he saw looks of genuine worry. What was it with the Japs? They were scaring everyone. He didn't get it. Who had won Pearl Harbor, anyway? "Kitmitsui won't build. I know the Japanese. I worked with them for years. And have I ever been wrong?" he asked the group. "Have I ever let you down?"

His golden voice exorcised all doubts. Jean felt the trusting, revering eyes again. He was their leader, their savior, and he would not disappoint them. When the meeting adjourned, he shook hands warmly and returned to his private office that was more high-tech than the cockpit of the sleekest bomber. He had come a long way in a relatively short time. Little Japan in America, an obscenely generous cash cow, had provided the springboard into real estate. At first he had kept his acquisitions simple. A strip mall in Santa Monica. A movie complex in Reseda. A couple of office buildings in Ventura. Within a few years he was building his own malls and movie complexes and commercial centers. He had ventured out of L.A., into Texas, where forty-dollars-a-barrel oil was sending local economies into the stratosphere. A Houston savings and loan he'd paid dearly for would be his private gusher. He was also buying "air rights" anywhere in the country where downtown property was at a premium. The empty space *above* a building could be purchased and resold to another developer, who, otherwise impeded by zoning restrictions, could utilize that additional height for his own building.

Money, Jean saw clearly, was the river of life that ran through this whole country.

Jean stared from his office window, keeping any anxiety at arm's length. Despite what he'd just told his investors, he knew the goddamn Japs and Arabs and Chinks were drinking from that river too. Not just drinking, they were bathing in it. The Kitmitsui Group *was* ready to steal Jean's cineplex concept—and they weren't the only foreign syndicate buying property. Los Angeles was becoming a League of Nations. In the fifties, the city had been mostly white, growing at a controlled, responsible pace, steered by a social conscience. A decade later, induced by the sixties' favorable tax climate for real estate, the institutional investors rushed in—the insurance and pension companies, the banks and big corporations. Almost overnight Los Angeles became known as the city where money meets the sea. That's what had brought the foreigners in. In the seventies, the wealthy and elite from troubled countries saw the United States as not only a safe political harbor but the best place to preserve and increase capital. The humbled masses felt the same. Rich or poor, if one had to pick a city, why not one with a great climate? The white flight from downtown Los Angeles after World War Two that had inspired his father to move to the Valley was, after a considerable reversal, happening again. White business in the civic center was alive and well, but after five and on weekends the canyons of commerce emptied, and downtown belonged to a mosaic of peoples.

Four years ago Jean had finally sold his Little Japan in America out of disgust for his suppliers. Once his friends, the Japs had become ruthless and piggy, raising his prices without warning and selling at a discount to his competitors. He had been furious at the betrayal. Who had helped make names like Sony and Mitsubishi more liked and trusted than RCA and General Electric? This was their way of thanking Jean? At times he felt like he was back in Nam, standing guard on a lonely hilltop to prevent a tide of slant-eyed gooks from overrunning his land.

He sat at his desk and scrawled on a legal pad.

Dear Tom:

I thought I would drop this note to express my growing apprehension about the pattern of growth and change in our beloved city. You and I have known one another for over five years, and while I have supported your mayoral campaigns with my pocketbook and have an obvious economic self-interest in your success, I also consider us good and trusting friends. What is happening now, Tom—with the influx of foreign money, the purchasing of American property by the Arabs, Japanese, Koreans, French, and Latin Americans—is scaring the hell out of me, and should scare you too.

My feelings have little to do with racism or even patriotism—they are about economic survival. These foreign buyers are changing the complexion of our great city. I know a lot of this impinges on federal laws, but as a metropolis, Tom, we must set an example for the rest of the country—foreigners cannot be allowed to buy up our real estate as if this was some international Monopoly game. As bad as the situation is now, I feel by 1990

it will become a crisis so severe that it will be con-
ceived as a war greater than World War Two. We're losing control of our destiny. Local developers like myself
do not have the financial resources to compete with Arab
princes so flush with petrodollars they can purchase half
of L.A. on the strength of revenues from a couple dozen
rigs. We need laws to preserve American real estate for
American citizens. I know this sounds like typical California Club polemic, of which as a member I plead
guilty, but others in the city have raised the same cry,
though admittedly not enough.

Please let me have your thoughts.

Sincerely,
Marvin Harp

Jean called in his secretary and asked her to type and
hand-deliver the letter to Mayor Bradley's office before the
end of the day. He had thought he would feel better, but his
anxiety lingered. The Kitmitsui Group was like an octopus—if
something wasn't done, it would strangle the city, strangle
him. What made Jean especially furious was its duplicity.
Everyone thought the Japs only bought established properties
and businesses, but in East L.A., the third-world manufacturing heart of the city, there were entire blocks of sweatshops
with blackened windows. Jean knew the Kitmitsui Group was
landlord or equity partner in several. One particular site,
where transmission parts were manufactured and sent to Detroit, at the end of the assembly process the country of origin
was stamped on the parts. To conceal their very profitable
operation, the Japs were putting on "Brazil" or "Hong Kong"
or "Korea" and faking the bills of lading.

In the next three days Jean contacted the Immigration and
Naturalization Service, the Occupational Safety and Health
Agency, the Internal Revenue Service, and the mayor's Task
Force for Equal and Fair Employment. He made sure of his
facts, and asked for strict anonymity. On the eve of the raids
of four separate sweatshops, he discreetly alerted both local
and national media.

The raids went without a hitch. Overnight the name Kitmitsui
became synonymous with slumlord and violator of human
rights, abuser of American labor practices and standards.
Jean approached the Valley property owners where Kitmitsui
wanted to build its entertainment complex. Few words were

necessary to persuade them not to sell to a bunch of sleazeballs. City councillors were already speaking out on the need for Los Angeles citizens to control their own economic destiny. Jean reported back to his investors that everything was fine with his Westwood project.

To build his real-estate empire, Jean had always put in twelve- and fourteen-hour days, six- and seven-day weeks. In the early days, that had meant hard work and ingenuity, and often working alone. He never minded. At least he was always in control. As his organization had grown, however, there'd been problems. Security was especially worrisome. He didn't like being a spy, but if he were alone at the office at night, he peered into executives' files and wastebaskets. One surveillance had turned up a note crumpled at the bottom of his vice-president's chair with the private number of a competitor bidding on the same property as Jean. The vice-president was fired the next day. Paranoia seized Jean and wouldn't let go. Who else was trying to screw him? A memo was circulated to all staff. Handbags and briefcases were subject to inspection by security personnel at any time. Jean didn't care about popularity. His people were well-paid and they had better be loyal.

One July afternoon he tidied up his desk and left the office early. The company limousine was waiting at the building entrance on Wilshire. The driver quickly opened the rear door and Jean scooted in. Leslie Mae looked radiant as she leaned toward him for a kiss. Like a little girl, the petite figure was perfection itself, and the innocent, sensitive eyes trusted him implicitly.

"Where are we going? What's the surprise?" she asked, excited. The limousine swung into traffic. "You said today was special."

"It is," Jean said succinctly.

"Aren't you going to give me a clue?"

He smiled playfully. "Okay. It's expensive, but I would pay ten times the price if the seller asked."

She pressed her lips together. "A new car? We don't need anything like that."

"Then it must be something else."

"That's all you're going to tell me?"

"That's all for now."

Leslie Mae was easy to string along and to please, Jean

thought. His infatuation for her had not dimmed in the seven
years of the relationship. He had thought many times of
marrying her, but Leslie Mae didn't seem to care one way or
the other, and when things worked, what was the point of
fixing them? It was her simple core of happiness that still
attracted him. Leslie Mae was his sanctuary, his sanity. Sweet,
uncomplicated, and undemanding, she was his opposite, and
as long as he had her and her approval, Jean knew he was
safe from his darker side. Leslie Mae only knew a handsome,
hardworking, and generous man who had asked her to live
with him in his Beverly Hills home, who could and did make
love to her anytime she wanted, praise her for her fitful
modeling career, and knew every thought and impulse that
passed through her.

"You know I'm terrible at guessing," Leslie Mae finally
said as the car headed north. She looked anxiously at Jean.

"We're going to buy a house," he gave in.

The childlike face was vexed. "We already have one."

Jean snuggled an arm around her. "This one is better.
We're moving."

"I don't understand."

"I've been keeping an eye on this property for years, in
case it ever came on the market. Today it did. We're the first
buyers to see it."

Leslie Mae began to feel Jean's excitement as she peered
out on the blur of houses, wondering which one if any was
the surprise. The car glided over Laurel Canyon and into the
Valley, down Riverside Drive, across Lankershim, and soon
Jean was pointing out the homes of Bob Hope and Henry
Winkler. She recognized the area now. They had been to a
cocktail party or two here. The neighborhood was called Toluca
Lake. The limousine rolled along the wide, pretty streets and
finally stopped in front of a handsome, imposing two-story
Tudor.

"Is this it?" she asked with a catch in her voice. "It's
lovely." She stepped out and took in the full panorama of
lawn and flowerbeds. "It feels like we're in the country."

"Wait till you see the pool. And the view of the lake. We
can watch the sunset every night."

"How did you know about the view? I thought you hadn't
seen the house."

She knew Jean had heard her, but he was in a trance as his
eyes swam over the front yard. Finally he took her hand and

led her inside. The rooms were huge. She thought everything about the house was gorgeous and tasteful. Jean took her upstairs to one of the bedrooms. Relatively small, it was lined with bookshelves on one side. The carpet marks showed where a desk and bureau had been.

"What are you staring at?" she asked. "It's just an empty room."

He was too absorbed to answer. He turned and walked downstairs. She followed him as he stopped at the threshold of a study.

"What is it?" she asked again.

"Who painted these walls?" he said, almost angry.

"The blue's not a bad color."

"But the original wood was beautiful."

She looked at him. "Original wood?"

He wet his lips, flustered for a second. "Original wood is always preferable."

Leslie Mae deserted Marvin and took her own tour. The kitchen was especially light and spacious, and Marvin was right about the view from the patio. She watched, delighted, as a caravan of ducks ventured onto the lawn. In the garage she saw there'd be plenty of space for their old Lincoln convertible. It was Marvin's favorite car, but he didn't drive it much. He preferred keeping it in storage, immaculately clean and polished, as if saving it for something.

"I love the house, Marvin," Leslie Mae said when he joined her on the patio.

"This is perfect, isn't it?" he asked, gazing on the lake. "You know how happy I am this moment?"

"Are you?" she said, pleased but wondering why. She asked him.

He gave a peculiar laugh. "I just am."

After a minute Jean drifted alone down to the silvery lake where he had once skipped rocks and navigated a rowboat and swam in the heat of summer. He had always done those things alone, not with friends. He never had friends then. He remembered his mother's parties and the elegant couples dancing under the stars and a band playing until three in the morning. He could still hear his father's carefree, intoxicated laughter that signaled everything was right with the world. Sometimes Jean had sneaked downstairs and hidden in the bushes, spying on guests, wondering what it was like to be an adult, what he would be like as one, if he would ever escape the prison of being a child.

But he had escaped, he reminded himself now. He already entertained lavishly in Beverly Hills, and his Toluca Lake parties would be even splashier, affairs as glamorous as anything his parents had hosted. With his money he had carefully cultivated favors and friendships among the famous, a process Leslie Mae still viewed with disapproval. In his heart of hearts Jean wanted her to understand. There were times he'd almost confessed everything, but whenever the impulses of love and faith moved him to honesty, they were countermanded by doubt and fear. Leslie Mae would be outraged by his years of deceit. She would not understand that her love for him was not enough to make him happy. She would reject him, and tell the whole world of his duplicity.

The thought of being exposed chilled Jean. He had perpetuated a charade that had taken on, in his own mind, heroic proportions. He had won against incredible odds. He had made himself into a legend, only half of which his friends were aware of—and all of it could crumble in an agonizing instant.

The first week of August he closed on escrow and moved with Leslie Mae into his old house. His father had bought the property in the late fifties for about sixty thousand dollars. Jean had just forked over, happily, more than half a million dollars. The first thing he did was to have the study stripped to its original wood. He shopped until he found furniture identical to what he remembered of his father's. On one wall he placed his various mementos from celebrities—the first note from Paul Newman, framed, was at the top—but otherwise the room, along with the rest of the house, was slowly and painstakingly returned by workers to its original condition. A puzzled but happy Leslie Mae joked about Jean's fussiness, and when she asked when he'd be done, he didn't know what to promise her. His memory kept turning up old details. Everything had to be included, everything had to be right.

Jean had no difficulty finding someone to sponsor him for membership at Lakeside. His first time on the course he surprised his foursome with his knowledge of the greens and how to play the traps. He saw that the clubhouse and men's locker room had been redecorated, but the feel was much the same. After a month he dropped his membership at the Los Angeles Country Club. Lakeside became his second home.

The fresh-faced kid with tousled hair who had been his father's caddy was still around carrying bags and shining shoes. He had a head of gray now and his shoulders were stooped. Jean used him faithfully. He coaxed from him stories of Red Poindexter's generosity and sense of humor, the many friends he had had, drinking rounds, outrageous golf bets.

"I heard he was a great man," Jean said as the two walked the back nine one afternoon.

"He was one of my favorites," the caddy averred.

"Do you remember his children?"

"Sure, Mr. Harp."

"What were they like?"

"The girl—I forget her name—was a very together kid. I remember being impressed by her. She was friendly, and very sure of herself—"

"And the son?" Jean interrupted.

The caddy frowned. "With me he was always very polite, charming. But I saw him in unguarded moments. With his mom, for example. Then he was moody, withdrawn, kind of unhappy—"

"Maybe that's because no one really understood him, except for his father," Jean suggested.

"You know him, Mr. Harp? I thought he'd just disappeared. There was that shooting at the California Club—"

"This time it's going to be different," Jean went on, ignoring the comment.

The caddy angled his head. "What's going to be different?"

"This time his father isn't going to die."

"Mr. Harp?"

"And no one's going to take his house away from him."

The confused caddy turned quiet as they played out the last hole. Jean said nothing further. His thoughts swam away from his father to Harriet and Felice and his mother. Grandmother Harriet was still in the same Bel Air house, forced by her arthritis to use a cane but otherwise in good health. His mother, according to her Palm Springs broker had gone to South America; her mail, what little there was, was being forwarded to a missionary outpost in the Amazon. Jean saw the influence of Brother Andrew, but if his mother wanted to spend the rest of her life being the monk's fool, that was her business. Felice was in graduate school at Princeton, living with a young man who was a faculty lecturer. Jean had made a number of attempts to contact each of them, but there was always a failure of nerve. Why was he so afraid? He had courage and hope inside him, he knew it. He just needed something to bring them out.

At the clubhouse Jean bestowed a generous tip on the caddy and went straight home to Leslie Mae. He wrapped his arms around her with tenderness. "I love you," he whispered.

She kissed him back.

"I want to make love to you," he said.

"That's very romantic of you, but I'm cooking dinner."

"And don't wear your diaphragm."

Leslie Mae's mouth dropped. "You want me to get pregnant?"

"Yes."

"This is a joke—"

"I said yes. We have this huge house. Why not start to fill it?"

"We're not even married."

"I want a son. We said we were going to name him Daniel, didn't we?" Jean remembered. "A baby first, then we'll get married." He wondered if the proposal was crazy, but having a son was suddenly the most important thing in the world to him.

"You never wanted a baby before. You had an unhappy childhood, remember?"

His smile had a glow. "That's why I want to make everything different. I want to pretend the past never happened. I want everything to be perfect."

"You really want a child?"

He saw how pleased she was. Having a son would change everything, Jean knew. A baby, a new life—it was the fresh start he was looking for. He would become a new man capable of telling the truth. A feeling of hope began to shine in him. After dinner they went upstairs and turned off the lights.

Every night he came home ready to make love. He knew the length of Leslie Mae's cycle and the most opportune time for conception. Sex took on a new meaning. Whenever it came time for her period, he held his breath.

Two months passed, then three. The spring weather buoyed Jean's hopes, but another side of him felt desperation. What was taking so long? A friend recommended he consult a psychic. Jean started to laugh but he made the appointment. The young, graying Dr. Banyon called himself a New Age doctor of healing—whatever that was—and after an hour with Jean he predicted the birth of a son before the end of 1982. "That's going to take a miracle, it's already March," Jean quipped.

That evening he told the prediction to Leslie Mae, who was not nearly as skeptical. She was late for her period, she said. She had an appointment tomorrow with her obstetrician. Jean called her every hour the next afternoon. Leslie Mae didn't answer, and Jean couldn't reach the doctor. Worried, he rushed home. Leslie Mae was in the kitchen. She turned and kissed him passionately on the lips. No words were necessary. Jean fell to the floor and raised his arms in thanks to the gods of procreation. When he'd opened a bottle of champagne, he told Leslie Mae to be prepared to pamper herself the next seven months.

"Why?" she asked happily. "I feel fine."

"Because our baby is too important to take risks over."

"You expect me to stay in the house for seven months?"

"Leslie Mae, yes."

"Can I cook and clean?"

"Maybe a little."

"What if I get bored? What about modeling assignments?"

"You're pregnant, remember?" He smiled with delight. "A fat lady."

"My manager says agencies are always looking for pregnant models who look wholesome."

"I want you to look like a cow," Jean declared.

"Marvin, I don't want to feel tied down. You know how I like to come and go—"

"Hey, why are we arguing?" Jean interrupted. "This is the happiest moment of our lives!" Like a bridegroom, he picked her up and carried her upstairs to their bed. He cooked dinner for them and then lay next to her on top of the sheets, stroking her belly. He could imagine it swelling like a small mountain, the sweet struggle of life inside, a gift to the world, to him.

The first trimester and half of the second passed uneventfully, except for Jean's excessive attention to Leslie Mae. Fresh flowers were delivered to the house every morning. Over Leslie Mae's objection, a Mexican girl was hired to live in, to cook as well as clean. Eating the right foods was essential for mother and baby, Jean said emphatically. He refused to let Leslie Mae sit more than an hour in the direct

sun, and puttering in the garden was equally limited. Books
and magazines came weekly, even though Leslie Mae protested she wasn't much of a reader. Jean let her watch television and call her friends, and go for an occasional drive if she
promised to avoid heavy-traffic hours. How could he forget
what had happened when his mother was pregnant with Isabel? With each day Leslie Mae's face grew a little rounder,
brighter, incandescent with joy. Jean was always inquiring
how she felt. The obstetrician, the best and most expensive in
Beverly Hills, was consulted over the smallest worry.

One evening Jean came home to find a note on the fridge.
Leslie Mae apologized, but she'd gone out for a drink with
her agent.

"What were you doing?" he demanded when she appeared
after midnight. He heard the temper in his voice. He'd been too
upset even to watch television. Leslie Mae's skin was flushed
and she was wobbly. "How much did you drink?" he asked.

The smile vanished from the radiant face. "I didn't mean
to do anything," she whispered. She half-stumbled into a
chair. She was genuinely sorry. She couldn't believe this was
the man who loved her. He looked furious.

"Didn't mean to?" he said. "You're not supposed to
drink, dammit. You're not supposed to be out late—"

"I'm sorry." He was scaring her. She'd never seen him
this way.

"Never again," he said, "do you understand?"

She folded her arms tightly. A tear brimmed in her eye.
"You're making me upset."

"Go to bed. This is over."

"I wanted to talk to you," she said bravely.

"In the morning."

"I've been offered a magazine shoot for Friday. Just one
day—"

"Absolutely not."

"I feel like a recluse here. Why can't I get out once in a
while—"

"No," he insisted, and he waited for her eyes to drop in
surrender before he calmed down.

Jean would never have found out that she'd disobeyed him
if the housekeeper hadn't let the secret slip. If he was enraged
the first time, now he was beside himself.

"Why?" he said tersely, when he ran upstairs that evening.
"You promised—"

In her pajamas, Leslie Mae scooted up on the bed. "Because I wanted to," she found the words. Marvin looked like he wanted to hit her, she thought. "I told you, I feel smothered . . ." She brightened suddenly, thinking this would please him. "Do you know the art director said I was fabulous? Really. He told me pregnancy brought out my color and made my eyes sparkle."

"I don't give a shit what any art director thinks. You're carrying around *my* child, not his."

"Please don't talk that way."

"I'll talk any way I want."

"You sound mean. You sound like you don't love me anymore."

"Will you shut-up?" Jean picked up a vase and pitched it against the wall. The shards exploded like a grenade. He immediately wished he hadn't done it, and would have apologized, but Leslie Mae was already running down the stairs. When he heard the garage door open he shouted her name. A car horn sounded, a shrill stab that mimicked him. He rushed down and watched her car careen backward down the street, swerving like a drunk. The headlights lurched up and down, stabbing him in the eyes as he gave chase. He could see the frightened face behind the wheel. Jean made a final lunge, but the car was accelerating now, and he stumbled and fell.

Furious, he stalked back into the house and washed the blood from his face. When Leslie Mae didn't return by morning, he notified the police. They took the information about a pretty pregnant woman in silk pajamas driving a Cadillac, but Jean was informed he had to wait forty-eight hours to file a missing-persons report. An associate recommended a private detective he knew in Beverly Hills. Jean supplied the man names of Leslie Mae's friends, and expected her home by dinner. A week passed and no one knew anything. He fired the detective and found another. The police, involved finally, were accused of indifference and inefficiency. He was an important man, he let them know; why weren't they helping more? Mayor Bradley and half the city council were called. Couldn't anyone do anything? Jean placed ads in the personal columns. The housekeeper was always by the phone. Why didn't Leslie Mae at least let him know she was all right?

He could sleep only an hour or two at a time, if he was lucky. Focusing on business was impossible. He was sorry, didn't Leslie Mae know that? He'd lost control, gotten carried away, that's all. He loved her.

And she had his baby.

To distract himself, he would stop by the California Club after work and hang around the bar. One evening he tried a massage and sauna on the third floor. A gentle man with beefy hands would bring relief to his knotty muscles, and then Jean would sit naked on a redwood bench and let the steam seep into his pores. He began repeating the routine every night. It was the only way to keep his mind off Leslie Mae. One evening in the sauna a gentleman parked himself on the opposite bench—large, stocky, soft in the belly, hair turning gray. His dark eyes riveted uncomfortably on Jean. He'd been in the sauna once before, Jean thought in his haze, but the familiarity of the face went even deeper. Jean peeked up again, struggling to identify the face. The man, however, was focusing on Jean's leg.

"Aren't you Marvin Harp?" he finally asked.

"That's right."

A savage smile floated to his lips.

"Are you a new member?" Jean asked, perplexed.

"Sure enough. I've been waiting forever to get in the club."

"Well, welcome."

"Pleased to meet you, Mr. Harp," the man replied, and started to laugh.

Jean jumped up almost too quickly and moved to the door. But Kirby Willis was quicker. "You can never remove a tattoo, can you?" the Beverly Hills broker called out. "Oh, my, Jean Poindexter, wait until the world hears about this."

August 3, 1982

Dear Felice,

I image your Princeton weather is a lot more idyllic than mine. Spring in the Amazon is virtually indistinguishable from the other seasons—it's our fall, slightly cooler than summer, but the humidity is so intense it doesn't matter. After almost six years here I've learned to accept and like the exquisite heat, even would miss it if I had to move away. The feel and smell of human sweat seem so natural that when I first came with a deodorant and showed it to the Indians they were intrigued, and filled with laughter! I still practice hygiene, but I understand their reluctance. Here, even mirrors seem pretentious.

The new Indians in our settlement (we seem to be growing every day) are a happy, self-contained people, but
hard to discipline in a Western sense because their rhythm
of life is far different—and perhaps more logical. They
work when they wish, then watch us finish up what they
start, with both amusement and appreciation. Odd, how
I am looked upon as being energetic and ambitious when,
relative to life in Los Angeles, I feel so lazy now! Andrew and I have been joined recently by another monk—a
Jesuit—named Sebastian, and together we are putting
finishing touches on a meeting hall. My money has already provided for a generator, a library filled with books
(I teach English to the children), medicine, several good-
size boats, and a handsome secondhand plane which both
Andrew and I have learned to fly, courtesy of lessons from
Brother Sebastian. Improving the Indians' lot is not easy,
no matter how much money we have, because getting materials delivered here takes a century or two. The government doesn't make our task easier. Fearful we're giving
the Indians false ideas about independence and power,
suddenly they are requiring permits for our most mundane
acquisitions. Whenever I feel discouraged I look at our
food gardens around the settlement. Despite unending bouts
with insects and the inbred tradition of hunting, the Indians are learning to become farmers, and there's nothing
the government can do about that!

Sebastian thinks we can reclaim acres and acres of jungle if we put our minds to it. He is as good-natured and
even more of a bullheaded optimist than Andrew. I think,
though it's never been spoken, he understands why I'm
here. Officially, of course, I am just a hanger-on at this
settlement, a nondenominational volunteer. Andrew's abbot still does not know about me. Sebastian reveres Andrew so much that nothing Andrew and I could do would
upset him truly or undermine his faith. I do understand
his feelings of respect. Andrew is like no man you've
ever known, Felice. I'm sorry you two have never met.
When I visited you last year at Princeton, I tried to bring
him along, but problems here prevented him from traveling. One day, I'm sure, your paths will cross. Then I
hope you'll be impressed. I don't mean just by Andrew's
honesty and sincerity. Beyond that, he cares about so
many people—he knows every child in this settlement by

his Christian *and* Indian name, every grandmother, every relative who's ever come to visit! I wonder how anyone can have a heart so caring, so filled with light.

Whenever he's called to travel somewhere by his abbot, I miss Andrew terribly, but I've learned to distract myself with work or reading, and the pleasure of my own company. My days are very simple. I rise early, eat with Andrew or Sebastian, meditate, work, rest, and meditate some more. There is something about solitude that very much agrees with me. I can think and understand things so much more clearly now, especially my own life. There really are patterns that possess us, but we must not be afraid. There is strength in peace. Anyway, here I live virtually without stress. Problems arise but we solve them. There is no feeling of fighting time or meeting deadlines or adhering to schedules. There is no sense of missing out or being deprived, or having to please anyone but ourselves. We have our own world here. If I were to die tomorrow, I would only miss seeing you and Jean and Harriet, nothing else. Perhaps I am guilty of becoming something of an eccentric—with my wide-brimmed hats and colorful neckerchiefs the Indians consider me a character—but I don't want to leave here. Whenever I think back to Los Angeles I wonder how I could have lived there so long.

Felice, I have read your last letter about Jean with great care and concern, of course, along with the newspaper clippings from the *Times*. When I received your envelope I was in shock for days. Suddenly not only had the outside world intruded, but in as hurtful a way as I could imagine. Jean is being crucified, and Red's and my names have surfaced once more, as if to paint a portrait of more than one generation of misfits. I hate so much being treated like an insect on a specimen board, pinned and labeled for the whole world to judge. What do they know about me? Or Jean—or any of us? I can understand an outsider's curiosity—even I don't know how Jean could have successfully masqueraded as someone else for so long—but not disrespect for our privacy.

I am hurt even more, of course, by Jean. How could he have not contacted at least one of us during those long years? On the one hand I'm very sympathetic to what he's going through now—I know all about the breath of scandal— and I'm deeply worried about the district attorney bringing him to trial for shooting Walter Mandrake. But on the other hand, Jean has never assumed responsibility for his actions. The day after I received your letter I flew to Belém and spent several days trying to reach him. He wouldn't take my calls. I've written several letters since, which have all gone unanswered. What good would it do me to fly up? Since Jean has now been in contact with you and Harriet, maybe you could find out what he expects from me. I think he blames me for everything bad that's ever happened to him. And he doesn't trust me, as if certain at any given moment I'll turn against him again, if I ever did in the first place.

All my love,
Mother

Felice tucked her mother's letter into her handbag and stole one last peek in the mirror, rubbing her lips together to smudge her lipstick. She could hear David's car idling in the drive as he waited to take her to the airport. Normally as mild and forgiving as a lamb, David La Porte was cross at her sudden leaving. After a decade of silence, Jean had called Felice a half-dozen times in two weeks. It wasn't easy to get off the phone. His last call was to say he was sending Felice a first-class round-trip ticket to L.A. He needed her to testify on his behalf at some court hearing. Jean wouldn't be more specific. She didn't understand, except that Jean had pleaded with and cajoled her, and on top of all his troubles with the law she'd felt sorry for him. She was dropping everything for her brother—a Christmas trip to Maine with David, work on her thesis—and so far Jean hadn't even said thank you. Ten years, and nothing had changed.

"Am I going to make my plane?" Felice asked as she squeezed in next to David and her suitcase in the MGB convertible. She looked at him and sighed. "David, I'm sorry. I'll be back as soon as I can."

"You know, you look like you're going to a party. What's so captivating about your brother? Overhearing your phone conversations, I thought he sounded like a jerk."

"I wish I knew what's so captivating. Maybe just that he needs help. That's a novelty for him."

"What's Jean like—besides pushy and overbearing, I mean," David said dryly.

"For starters? Brash, cocky, dominating, insecure—"

"Just the opposite of you. How in the world do you explain the gene pool?"

She had already told him about her family in depth. David applauded her mother's Amazon adventure but could find nothing redeemable about a brother as sneaky and self-centered as Jean. Felice was trying to find something. She was always doing battle with her old feelings of suspicion and dislike for her brother. Maybe she had to give him a chance. Mistakes of the past were not a guarantee of the future. Jean could change. Blood ties meant she had at least to root for him.

David jiggled the radio to a classical-music station, as if to find something soothing for both of them. Felice snuggled an arm around him and knew he wouldn't stay mad. She loved David, she thought. There were so many wonderful things about him. He was a real political-science scholar but totally unpretentious. He was more content staying home than partying. He could cook *and* make love. He understood her. What more could she want? David was too tall for the MGB with its top up, but he looked great in it just the same, like some spy with his narrow, chiseled face and trim black beard. He'd been her instructor for a senior poly-sci elective, and she'd fallen for him even before he'd asked her out. She liked men who looked like James Bond, she had teased him—it was the playful, imaginative side of her, the one that never got acted out much but was a larger part of her than most of her friends knew.

In Paris, where she had stayed, not for one summer, as she had promised her mother, but for three years, Felice had discovered that she might be perfectly content hanging around Left Bank cafés the rest of her life. Even if Shakespeare and Company was no longer the haunt of writers and artists of Hemingway's and Gertrude Stein's Paris, Felice found the scene impossibly magical. A bearded poet she might not give a second glance to in Los Angeles was, in a dim café on Rue Gisbert, the incarnation of Baudelaire. Her studies at the Sorbonne were abandoned after a month. Paris was her classroom. She had needed to leave the United States almost as badly as her mother, to escape and let her imagination run. She had not been promiscuous in France, but she had been open to adventure. Getting involved with a man was always self-discovery. Relationships, the way they could begin on notes of such hope and promise and end in utter despair and sadness, fascinated her in the abstract. Truth was always relative when Felice wanted it to be absolute, and unfailingly absolute when she needed it to be relative. Unlike for her father or brother, the world was not for her to conquer, Felice had decided, but just to be made sense of.

Four years ago she had finally enrolled in Princeton after more than one prodding in her mother's letters. Reentering the world of structure and expectations wasn't easy, but Felice knew she had some advantages. Three years older than most freshmen, and far more worldly, she had a certain presence and sophistication. She had no trouble making friends—or dating grad students and instructors. She wrote poetry and some of it was published in an undergraduate magazine. David thought she had promise. Felice wasn't sure. The outside world, her future, were unknowns. She had confidence from Paris, but something inside her was still intimidated by what she couldn't understand.

"Good-bye. I love you, I'll miss you," Felice said when they reached the airport. She threw her arms around David. He kissed her back with even more passion. "Me too," he whispered.

At Los Angeles International Airport Felice trailed off the plane to find a slim mustachioed chauffeur holding up a placard with her name.

"This must be a mistake," she said, but the driver insisted he was sent by Jean Poindexter, and inside the limousine were fresh flowers and a card from her brother. The familiar cityscape of clogged freeways and smoggy air added to her anxiety. She was glad she didn't live here anymore. She was even more baffled about Jean when the car pulled up at an elegant restaurant in Beverly Hills called the Bistro Gardens, its front curb crowded with shiny Mercedeses and Porsches. On the phone Jean had practically cried about his fate. He had been kicked out of Lakeside and the California Club and ostracized by most of the celebrities he had steadfastly courted. Honor besmirched, cashiered from the corps, Felice would have thought he might be holed up somewhere licking his wounds. Instead, here he was at a chic restaurant playing the old games of self-importance as if nothing disgraceful had ever happened. Where were his pride and his honor? Something similar had happened to their father, who had felt the sting of shame and infamy. Jean had written himself a different scenario. Was it just the difference between a father and a son? Felice wondered. Or was everyone today simply more self-forgiving?

The maître d' escorted Felice to a corner table. Jean rose and like a gentleman kissed her hand. She studied the tan baby face that had aged gracefully and was at once angelic and unrepentant. She would not have recognized him in a crowd necessarily, despite her gifts of observation and memory. She thought of him as a chameleon as she sat and ordered a drink.

"How are you, Felice?" he began warmly. "You don't know how good it is to see you. You look terrific. How long has it been?"

"A long time. I think I should ask how you are."

He put his hand on top of hers. "Never been better."

"On the phone you sounded—"

"I'm celebrating, Felice. I just learned the district attorney isn't going to prosecute. The statute of limitations on my crime is too ambiguous. There're evidentiary problems too. All the cops had was a lot of circumstantial smoke. I never admitted to shooting Walter Mandrake." He offered a smile of triumph.

"Congratulations, that's wonderful," she said, though she didn't feel as much joy as she would have thought. "Please write Mother right away. She'll be relieved."

"Really, do you think?"

"You know she will. You should see what she writes me about you." Felice started to pull out her mother's last letter, but Jean waved her off. "She's hurt you haven't written back or taken her calls," Felice said more strongly.

"Mother betrayed me, Felice. Don't you know that? She's never understood me, never been on my side. Or on Dad's."

"That's not true!"

He laughed at her. "I could tell you so many stories your head would spin. Did you know our sainted mother was having an affair with some doctor while Dad was still alive?"

"Stop it," Felice said angrily.

"Oh, excuse me. I forgot. You two are very close."

Felice started to rise, but a look of such remorse swept over Jean that she halted in wonder. "Please don't go," he said. "I need your help."

She dropped back in the chair and braced herself.

"I have a child now." He spoke quietly. "A son."

"Come on—"

"It's true," he swore.

"When did this happen?"

"The baby was just born, last month. His name is Daniel. His mother refuses to give me custody. She's claiming I wouldn't make a decent father. Her case wouldn't have stood a chance until my past came out. Now she calls me violent, untrustworthy, a liar. She has all these witnesses—like a banker I took a loan from when I was Marvin Harp—a lot of folks who will call me deceitful. But you know better."

"I don't understand," Felice said, still startled. "Who is this woman? Are you married? How did it all happen?" She listened as Jean told about a fashion model named Leslie Mae, the old Toluca Lake house he'd bought back, and restored, his sudden inspiration to have a child and change his old ways—and begin a new life. Felice couldn't believe it. Jean had bought back the old house? What was going through his mind? But he spoke with a sincerity that bordered on reverence for this magical baby he'd yet to lay eyes on. Leslie Mae had baby Daniel hidden with friends. Jean was undaunted. He had retained the best child-custody attorney in Los Angeles, and he would get his son back.

"I don't know what to say," Felice admitted as she tried to digest everything. It all seemed as incredible as the deception Jean had perpetrated. She wondered if she really knew her brother anymore.

"I need you to testify for me," Jean said. "Tomorrow morning, in family court."

"Testify?"

"To a judge. He decides who gets custody of my son. Harriet has already spoken for me."

"What did she say?"

Jean's brow shot up in dismay. "What did she say? What do you think she said? That I was an upstanding citizen, a kind, wonderful grandchild of great promise, a man of integrity and love and responsibility . . ."

Felice knew Grandmother Harriet had always believed in Jean. She had seen only light where Felice had glimpsed shadows. "And what am I supposed to say?" she asked carefully.

"The truth, of course."

"The truth," she repeated in a whisper.

"You're my younger sister. We were always great and

trusting friends. We grew up together sharing everything. You knew me as well as my parents did—no, you knew me even better. I was never violent, crazy, or depressed like Leslie Mae's attorneys are claiming. I was normal, fun-loving, outgoing. I had a lot of friends . . ."

Felice pulled her eyes away. Was Jean just putting her on? When she studied him again she suddenly saw something—a crack in the facade of confidence, a festering wound probably invisible to anyone but her. For a moment he looked so humiliated, so defeated. The scandals he'd been through and tried to brush off as if just so much inconvenience had hurt too much to conceal. They were a link to the part of his past he wanted to shut out forever.

"Jean . . ." she said.

The look of defeat suddenly vanished. He met her gaze, daring her to contradict him. "I was a warm, loving human being and still am, Felice," he insisted, as if knowing what she was thinking. "Vietnam messed me up, that's all. It messed up a lot of people. This country is just waking up to that fact. It's time we got more sympathy. Particularly me. I was a war hero, remember? I made sure the judge knew that right away. Anyway, we're all entitled to go through rough periods. Look what I've accomplished since. You know how much real estate I own in this city? How much I'm worth?"

"Jean, I can't help you," she said, summoning all her courage. "Your memory is very different from mine."

"A few details here and there—"

"No. You and I never got along."

His chest pushed out. His tongue peeked nervously between his teeth. "Felice, you have to help me."

"I can't. I don't want to lie. And what about Leslie Mae? I don't know anything about her. Maybe she'd make a good mother. Maybe she's as entitled to Daniel as you are."

"Whose side are you on?" he demanded. "Felice, I *need* you." His voice grew more agitated. "Without your testimony I'm never going to get my son. Is that what you want?"

"No," she had to say.

"Do you want me to be happy?"

"That's not fair."

"Do you?" he insisted.

"You know I do."

"Then what choice do you have?"

She wished now she'd never flown here. Jean had concealed things from her. He was taking advantage again, manipulating and intimidating her as he'd always done. Her brother had not changed at all. He would not let her out of his grasp, he would not give her peace again, until she surrendered.

"I just don't want to lie for you," she said.

"Felice, help me this one time—*just this once*—and I'll never bother you again. You won't even have to see me again if you don't want to, I promise. We'll go our separate ways."

"You've said things like that before."

"This time I mean it."

Her temples were pounding. Why couldn't Jean just disappear?

"All you have to do is say a few kind words about me. That'll be enough, according to my attorney. Is that asking too much? Is that so painful for you? Don't I deserve a second chance? We're brother and sister. We have to help each other—"

Felice looked away. Why was it so difficult for her to get a perspective on herself? She could distinguish truth or falseness in strangers as readily as the color of their eyes, but she had a blind spot about herself and her family.

"All right," she heard herself say, just to be left alone. Her stomach and head were spinning. She hated being a coward but she couldn't find the courage to retract her words. As she left the table, all she could think of was what she'd once told her mother, what she would always believe because it was one of those absolute truths: Jean was a tempest striking down everything in his path.

BOOK FIVE

The late-afternoon shadows had already crossed the swollen river and were cutting toward the portico of the school building. From nearby trees a bevy of dark birds took flight, cackling like witches as they skimmed overhead. Most of the children in the village played by the river, rarely gazing back anymore to Brother Andrew and his visitor under the portico. In exquisite handwriting a little girl had written on the school blackboard—November 9, 1986—as if to impress the stocky, heavyset archbishop with his magnificent white hair and bushy eyebrows. Otherwise, no one paid him attention now.

Neither Archbishop Rationi nor Brother Andrew had, except for a brief interruption for lunch, stirred from his chair since morning. The bright silver plane sat tranquilly in the river, in no hurry to leave. Andrew wished otherwise. Hours of explaining had left him tired and spent. He remembered how he had once told Alycia that confession was good for the soul. Now he was less than sure of that truth.

"Is there anything else you wish to tell me?" Rationi asked in the silence, shifting his weight in the uncomfortable chair.

"I can think of nothing else, your Eminence." Andrew's head was swimming. What else was there? He had told everything, and all of it the truth. Falling in love with Alycia, sleeping with her, becoming sole trustee of her substantial fortune. . . . He had expected Rationi to react strongly to some of his statements, but behind the hooded reptilian eyes the archbishop had carefully concealed his feelings. The stoicism was a sign of a seasoned listener—a priest accustomed to hearing confessions—and a discerning intelligence, but it hardly eased Andrew's anxiety. He could taste his vulnerability like a bitter herb.

"Brother Andrew, before we finish, I want to be very clear on certain issues. Please remember I am not here to judge

351

you, but to render a strict and accurate accounting to Rome.
Your story differs dramatically from Jean Poindexter's.''

"I am not surprised," Andrew allowed.

"You and he never got along?"

"As I told you," Andrew said, "Felice was very accepting
of me, according to her mother, but Jean saw me as some
kind of interference. He did not want me near his mother, or
to have anything to do with their lives. He was very
distrusting.''

"And knowing this, how did you feel?"

"I still tried to like Jean. We haven't seen each other in
many years, of course, but he was always in my prayers. And
I would like to see him now. I wish he had sought me out
here before taking Alycia.''

"According to Jean, he did try to locate you. He wanted an
explanation.''

"For what?" Andrew inquired.

"He came down planning only to visit his mother, inform
her of Harriet's death, but when he found her in such a
miserable state he felt he had no choice but to take her home.
He wanted to know what you had done to her—''

"Done?" Andrew said, shocked. "I . . . did nothing.''

"Did you not realize how sick she was?"

"Yes, of course I did. I warned Alycia repeatedly to take
better care of herself. But I was not always in the settlement—I
traveled at least half the time. The last month I was concerned
enough to bring in a Swiss doctor, but by then Jean had
already left with Alycia. You have to understand what kind of
woman Alycia is—very stubborn, very independent. She does
as she pleases. She simply didn't pay enough attention to her
body—there were always more important things for her—''

"Jean has suggested," the archbishop interjected delicately,
"that perhaps she was influenced into not caring.''

Andrew straightened in his chair. So this was Jean's gambit. The monk tried to stay calm. "That is simply not true.
Why would I ever do that? I love Alycia.''

"Jean showed me letters his mother had written him—I
read them myself. To my unprejudiced eye, I thought they
revealed a woman who was more than independent or even
eccentric. I did not think she was in full command of her
faculties. She spoke of visions of blinding light, of a sense of
being out of her body and into another world. She said she
fasted willfully and often to put herself into this state. And

she always mentioned you, Brother Andrew, as her inspiration, the object of her devotion.'' The archbishop raised his chin gravely. "Were you not fully aware of all this, Brother Andrew?''

"I was aware that she loved me, just as I loved her. But I did not influence her behavior, your Eminence. Alycia is intelligent and strong-willed. She is her own person. In the settlement she did as she pleased. Her life, as I told you, has been extremely difficult. Here, at last, she was very happy. It is true that she fasted, to purify her mind and soul, and maybe she did have some kind of visions—I find no fault with that, your Eminence.''

"Nevertheless, Brother Andrew, Jean Poindexter believes you exerted undue influence over his mother.''

"For what purpose?'' Andrew demanded.

"To get total control of her money.''

For the first time since the archbishop's arrival—for the first time in his recent memory—Andrew felt an uncharacteristic flame of temper in his patient soul. "I do not believe I am culpable of anything, your Eminence, except for my relationship with Alycia. Even in that instance I cannot see that love, falling in love, is really a sin. I have been tormented about this, and I have prayed for God's guidance, but my honest judgment is that following one's heart leads one to more compassion for others. Can that be wrong? As for the money, personally it means nothing to me. It is only a tool to do some good in the world.''

"Please be calm, Father. You act as if you think that I consider you somehow weak or unworthy as a servant of God. I do not. Sins of the flesh, like the other cardinal sins, result not from any fundamental evil in us but from our fundamental goodness running to excess.''

Andrew listened impatiently. He already knew traditional Catholic dogma, and he also knew, more crucially, that his carnal relationship with Alycia would be only a peripheral issue in the eyes of Rome. Something to weaken his credibility, of course, but not enough to damn him. Only one thing could do that.

"I do not have any regrets about my role as trustee of Alycia's money," Andrew reiterated clearly, suddenly eager for a confrontation. He would never be a politician, he realized. He had no real gift for strategy or maneuvering. He only wanted Rationi to be as honest and straightforward as Andrew had been with him.

"I'm afraid you're speaking too impetuously now," Rationi warned. The reptilian eyes bored straight into Andrew. "I, for one, think that in regards to the money you have erred rather seriously."

Andrew allowed himself a faint smile. Finally he'd gotten an honest response. "Faced with the same circumstances all over, your Eminence, I believe I would do exactly the same. As I've already related, over the years I've spent only a tiny fraction of the interest earned on Alycia's principal. Every penny went either to the Trappists' work in Brazil or other spots I have visited—not one cent was wasted, I promise you. I have never invaded the principal. Alycia doesn't even know that. First, it is so much money, and second, I thought Alycia should always have the option to take it back, should circumstances warrant it."

"But the fact is, Brother Andrew, at this moment you are still the sole trustee," he replied, edging forward in his chair to make his point, "for what is more than seventy million dollars."

Andrew heard the discomfort in Rationi's voice. "The investment firm I chose has done well with the money," Andrew said modestly. "I am proud that none of it's been squandered."

"I would not be too proud, Father. You have willfully concealed from your abbot and the Church what is a sizable fortune."

"I was entrusted by Alycia Poindexter to tell no one, not even the Church. I was only obeying her will."

"And what of the will of your order?" Rationi replied, not attempting to disguise the sharpness in his voice. "Must I remind you again of your vows of obedience? Do you not yet realize that you have grossly deceived those to whom you pledged total honesty and devotion? By not being forthright about your confidences, let alone spending money that you had no right to assume personal responsibility for, you have erred badly. Whatever belongs to you, belongs to the Church."

"The money belongs to no one but Alycia. I have kept a copy of the original letter she gave her attorneys, appointing me as trustee of all her funds. I have done exactly with her money—no more, no less—as she instructed. If Alycia wishes me to give the money back to her, or to her children, or to the

Church, I will be happy to comply. Until then I can do nothing.''

Andrew rose with an effort. He was shaking from a combination of anger and fatigue and worry. ''Forgive my impertinence, your Eminence, but in your blind loyalty to the Church, there is a principle you are not seeing.''

The archbishop's eyes firmed on the recalcitrant monk. ''And you are not seeing what is so painfully obvious to everyone else, Father. You have no choice here. This is not a matter of debate. Until the matter is straightened out with Jean Poindexter and his sister, you must immediately turn over the money—every penny—to the Church.''

Andrew sighed deeply. He suddenly wished he had not forced this confrontation. He was tired, not in control. Yet he knew that even fresh and in full command of his thoughts, his answer would be the same. ''In all sincerity, I cannot do that.''

''You just told me that the money personally meant nothing to you—''

''Archbishop Rationi, I am not a troublemaker. I do not wish to earn your or the Church's rebuke. But I promised Alycia I would carry out her wishes—that her money would go directly to the poor, and to no one else. That is what I have done and will continue to do.''

''All because of a woman you fell in love with. That you slept with,'' the archbishop said with barely disguised cynicism. ''You have been compromised, Father. You have already embarrassed yourself and the Church, and now you're about to do more harm—''

''I believe this is a matter of conscience,'' Andrew interrupted firmly.

Rationi was now up, arms folded impatiently over his round middle. ''Father, which is more important to you—your conscience, or allegiance to the very body you swore to serve faithfully and forever?''

Andrew thought for a moment, but he already knew his answer. ''My conscience is the whisper of God.''

The unhappy archbishop cast a final and stern glance at the monk, giving him a chance to recant. When there was only an incomplete silence, Rationi turned his gaze on the river. ''Until you hear further from me, Brother Andrew, you are not to leave this settlement. Is that clear?''

''But why?'' he said. Andrew was dumbfounded. Had he

not been hurt and insulted enough by Jean's accusations?
Now they wanted him to stay put, as if afraid he would make
more trouble. "How long will that be?"

"Are my instructions clear, Father?" Rationi repeated. "If
you become restless, I suggest prayer and meditation. Recit-
ing the Nicene Creed would not do you any harm either."

"Could you at least tell me where Alycia is?" Andrew
asked. "You said she was in a hospital. Is she doing better?
Has she said anything about me?"

The archbishop ignored his inquiries, signaled to his pilot
in a nearby clearing, and walked toward the dugout that
would ferry him to his plane. The children who had been
playing by the river joined in procession, but there was not
the same gaiety as this morning. Andrew followed reluctantly, trying to find something to pick up his spirits. Rationi
had said he was not here to judge anyone, but clearly the
archbishop had made up his mind. Andrew's stubbornness
had only sealed the judgment against him. He thought now of
all the things he should have told Rationi—such as, if Jean
were truly the faithful and concerned son, why had he never
once written to his mother? Andrew thought, too, of asking
Rationi for a special Communion, a private Mass, but such
futility hung in the air that he could not summon the words.
He felt terribly used. Trust me, just as I trust you, Rationi had
told him.

Andrew watched as the dugout carried its august visitor
through the water, the paddles of its two boatmen dipping in
and out without a sound. A strong, clear voice suddenly rose
from a bend in the river, not far from the plane. Andrew
followed the archbishop's gaze to a second dugout and the
strapping figure of Brother Sebastian. The Jesuit priest, part
Indian, part Spanish, part Portuguese, had been away for a
week, and Andrew was happy now to have him return. He felt
a small wave of relief and comfort. They could discuss
Rationi's visit with total candor. Andrew always valued the
young Jesuit's opinions and perspective. He was thirty years
younger and filled with a corresponding level of energy. A
favorite of Alycia's, too, Sebastian was known for hundreds
of miles along the river for his infectious smile and buoyant
spirit. The Jesuit hierarchy had all but forgotten him here,
which was how Sebastian liked it.

The exchange between the Jesuit and the archbishop was
predictably one-sided, Andrew observed. As the two boats

pulled alongside one another, Sebastian dwarfed the prelate not only physically but also in conversation. Rationi only seemed anxious to leave, distrustful of the effervescent and charming Jesuit who, along with Andrew, had kept Alycia Poindexter hostage here.

Now *he* was the prisoner, Andrew suddenly thought with great sadness, and he could only wonder what waited for him next.

Room 413 on the top floor of Cedars-Sinai Medical Center, despite the large picture window and the autumn light of Los Angeles, despite the constant attention and expensive care of the city's finest nurses and doctors, was a mirthless place. Jean Poindexter knew that more than anyone else. It was not his wish that his mother be so unhappy—it was her own doing. He visited often—sometimes three times a day—but nothing he said could alter his mother's spirits or make her cough up a single word, as if she thought she were somehow invisible, or the rest of the world was. She simply would not speak to anyone. Yet Jean knew her mind was hardly silent. She was planning something. Reminding doctors of what some already believed, that his dear mother was not a hundred percent in the head and was perhaps even capable of hurting herself, he insisted hospital security keep close watch on the room twenty-four hours a day.

On a chilly November afternoon Jean strolled into Room 413 looking, to the shift of nurses and orderlies who saw him every day, cool and dapper in his Saville Row suit and Gucci loafers. He stopped to joke with a candy striper in the hall, charming her with his usual smile, and asked for a vase to hold the fresh-cut daisies he had brought, as customary, for his mother. Everyone in the hospital thought he was Mr. Wonderful, the dutiful son. Gossip had informed the staff of his past troubles—the years of masquerading as Mad Man Marvin, the alleged episode with Walter Mandrake, a custody battle for this son—but in light of his current behavior they readily forgave him.

What they could not see, under Jean's veneer of charm and concern for his mother, was a financial desperation that all but prevented him from sleeping and eating. There was only so much suffering a Southern California suntan could hide, Jean knew, and if he lost another few pounds or his face grew any puffier there would have to be more gossip, more specu-

lation. The hounds of doom were snapping at his heels. Four
years ago, when his identity was exposed, he had barely
survived a scandal that had left him badly scarred. For weeks
the *Times* carried stories about him until he couldn't stand
it. He'd sworn he would never be humiliated again. Yet
now came another crisis. The Houston savings and loan he
had purchased when the Texas economy soared as high as its
oil rigs, was suddenly, along with much of the state, near
financial collapse. Until oil prices started to plummet, Jean
had been too busy and too successful to pay attention to the
books; suddenly he saw millions of dollars of energy and
real-estate loans in jeopardy. As the savings and loan's major
shareholder, he had originally mortgaged several of his properties to invest in the institution. Biting the bullet of humility,
he'd just sold his downtown parking lot—to a Korean
syndicate—to keep the S&L afloat. Jean's accountant had
called this morning. Another ten million dollars had to be
raised before year's end.

It wasn't fair, of course. He'd been bushwhacked. Right
from the start, the way Jean saw it. If his mother had given
him the trust money when it was due him, none of this would
have ever happened. In his mind he had rewritten his life a
thousand times.

"Hello, Mother. How are you?" he began, as he always
did, standing with the flowers by the side of her bed. Sometimes, as now, she would give him a glance, then stoically
turn her head away. She looked, Jean thought, better than
ever. Her skin had color, she had put on some needed weight;
physically she was totally recovered. "I would appreciate,
Mother, if you wouldn't try to sneak out any more letters to
Brother Andrew," he said, holding up as evidence, though
she wasn't looking, the latest missive, which a nurse had
intercepted from the hospital mail.

Jean had read the letter twice, but like his mother's first
letter to the monk, this one shed little light on anything
meaningful. He'd hoped to learn more about his father's
suicide; instead, his mother wrote of her love for a monk Jean
had never liked, and her distaste for Los Angeles, which she
compared to Babylon. She longed to return to the Amazon.
There was a family she worked with—she asked that Andrew
look after them in her absence—a mother and father and nine
children so destitute that Jean couldn't believe it. The father

had been hurt in an accident and couldn't work. One of the kids had cancer, another was chronically sick.

Jean thought of those magazine ads with black-and-white photos of impoverished children and captions that said "This little boy can be fed for $18 a month." That was another world. Maybe it existed, maybe it didn't, he didn't know. Was it Jean's responsibility? Everyone got dealt a hand, and one played it the best he could. That was the challenge— either you overcame your fate or you were defeated by it. That other people were starving wasn't Jean's fault. Why should he help them? Who had helped him? Not his mother, not when she had so much herself to give.

His mother's letter to Andrew had ended with a long-winded prayer that was not unlike what she'd written Jean from the jungle. References to the spirit and the body, life and death—he was sure she'd gone over the edge.

"Brother Andrew will never find you, Mother," Jean spoke up, "not unless I help him. And I can't do that until you help me."

Jean knew that he was essentially talking to himself, which only added to his feelings of foolishness and anger. Still, there were moments when he sensed he was making a breakthrough.

"You can't keep silent forever, Mother," he continued. "You may despise me all you want, but at some point you have to talk to me. All I want is what's mine, you know. My share of the trust money. Is that asking too much? Remember, I saved your life. You were dying in that jungle. Is that the thanks I get?"

He had said the same things over and over, but he leaned still closer, unwilling to surrender. "I want to make up with you, Mother. I know I haven't been the best son. But my life hasn't been so easy. In some ways it was just like yours—full of rejection and humiliation—can't you see that? And I always felt you in particular didn't love me. There was always a chasm between us. You couldn't reach me, I couldn't reach you. We can change that now."

He watched as his mother's head shifted on the pillow. She was listening. "You know from Felice's letters to you that I have a son. Your grandson. His name is Daniel. He just turned four. He looks a little bit like you. He has your wonderful blue eyes. He's so beautiful, and he makes me very happy. I had to win custody of him in a fight with his mother. It was the greatest victory of my life. I don't know what I'd do without Daniel. Don't you want to see him, Mother? Don't you want to feel like a family again?''

Jean honestly expected his mother at least to turn now and face him. He knew her—she would very much want to see her only grandson. Instead her eyes stayed focused on the wall. A wave of incomprehension swelled up from nowhere and overwhelmed Jean. Why was she rejecting him like this? How dared she?

"Mother, you're making me very angry," he whispered. "I don't deserve this treatment. I'm your flesh and blood. And I'm desperate. Do you know what it means to be broke? A business deal went sour for me. It happened to Dad, too, remember? Don't you have any sympathy?"

The silence only pushed his temper up another degree. "I'm going to tell you the truth now, Mother. You want to know how I found out about the trusts? You thought it would be a secret forever, but Harriet told me, just before she died. I know, you had sworn her to silence, but she had a change of heart. She deserted you, Mother. She loved me more than she loved you. She believed in me over you."

It was only a glimpse, but Jean saw it clearly, the pain crossing his mother's face, the hurt and disbelief. "After Harriet died," he went on, pushing in the sword, "I went through her attic. In a box you'd left not only your scrapbooks but Dad's gun and his letter to me. Why did you hide them, Mother? So many secrets. Dad wanted me to have the money, it's clear. And his suicide—what right did you have to keep that from me? He was *my* father. You told Felice, I know that. Why were you afraid to tell me? Did you think I couldn't handle it? Maybe you didn't think it was important enough. It just shows how much you didn't love me, doesn't it?"

Jean turned and left the room, enjoying the triumph of finally showing his ace. He'd given his mother something to think about. Maybe now she would capitulate, whether from guilt or attrition or a desire to reconcile, Jean didn't care. The point was, his mother would finally see that he was deserving of more than the half-million dollars her attorneys had finally handed over. She owed him a lot more than that.

In the hallway Jean found himself staring at a young man of medium height with fair hair and tortoiseshell glasses. He quickly bent over a drinking fountain, but Jean knew he'd

seen him before. The man hurried on. Furious with hospital
security, Jean made a mental note to chastise whoever was in
charge, then said a brief prayer to whatever god ruled over
reporters. Don't let this guy be one, don't let a city of five
million strangers into my life again, he whispered.

Jean met Felice in an unpretentious hotel in Santa Monica
that same afternoon. With her half-million, his sister could have
afforded much better, but it wasn't Felice's nature to be even
slightly extravagant. Jean pitied her.

"How was she?" Felice asked anxiously as they sat over
coffee.

Jean smirked. "The same. She won't talk to me."

"Something's bothering her. She won't talk to me either.
I'm worried."

"For whom?" he shot back. He couldn't believe it. Jean
had confided his financial woes to Felice, but all she cared
about was their mother. Since flying in from New Jersey, she
was at the hospital even more than Jean. "I really don't
understand you. This is your money too—"

"We don't have to get into this discussion again," she cut
him off. "All I'm concerned about is Mom. I don't want her
rushed out of the hospital to some attorney's office to sign
papers, no matter how desperate you are. This is her decision,
Jean. You can't pressure her."

Jean threw up his hands. How could he even talk to his
sister? Married to David and entrenched in her own academic
career, she was more isolated from the real world than ever.
She only liked to talk about artists and writers. She had
published some poetry in several serious magazines, always
about her childhood, abstract verses which Jean could make
no sense of, to the point that he wondered if Felice was really
his sister. Hadn't they grown up together? Then why didn't
he understand what was she writing about? *A lake that breathed
fire in my dreams,* she had written once, and *my father, the
artist of love gone wrong, the architect of an empire with no
heirs. . . .* What the hell was he, Jean wondered, if not
an heir?

Jean summoned all his patience. "Felice, I want you to
come with me to the hospital tomorrow. I want us to confront
Mother together."

"I can't do that."

Jean squinted at her, holding in his anger. "Why not?
What, is it me? You don't want anything to do with me? I

invited you to stay at my house, and you turn me down for a dump like this . . . that's it, right?''

"No," she said again, looking unhappy. "This has nothing to do with you. When I visit Mother, I want to be alone with her. It's personal, that's all."

"I don't understand you, Felice. We're brother and sister. We have to stick together in this."

"The last time I helped you—winning custody of Daniel—you said it would be the last. We'd go our separate ways. Those were your words."

"How could I have anticipated this? This is different. *We* have a problem—why don't you accept that?"

"I've never thought of my mother as a problem," she said firmly.

"Oh, beautiful. How come you always take her side, Felice?"

"Jean, you and I are different people. When will you accept *that*?"

"I always have," he said, suddenly bitter. He thought of his father's suicide again. Felice acted like she already understood it, could live with it, was resolving all the distortions and meanings in her poetic soul. Well, it wasn't that easy for him. He'd resolved nothing. Jean resented that their mother had confided the truth to Felice years ago, when she was still in prep school. Jesus, she'd always favored his sister.

"Look," Jean announced impatiently, "if Mother doesn't come around within a few days, I'm going to have to do something about it."

"What do you mean?" she challenged. "Why are you pushing so hard?"

"Dear sister, I am practically broke. I am squirming like a fish on the line. A Houston savings and loan that I own is about to drown me."

"How much money do you need?" Felice asked. "I can lend you something—"

He scoffed and gave her his accountant's estimate. Felice didn't seem impressed. Jean laughed inside—what did a poet know about money, anyway?

"I have every right to have Mother committed," he informed Felice.

"Committed?"

"We're talking about a woman who refuses to speak to

anyone. A woman who lived in a rotting jungle for over ten years and slowly went crazy. Look how I found her. Look at the letters she wrote home . . . do you honestly think she's sane?''

"I don't know if her letters are that strange. They're filled with biblical prophecy. Does that mean she's crazy? Toward the end of his life, Sir Isaac Newton was consumed with the same thing. And whatever they are, Mother has her reasons for staying quiet. I'm sure of it. I think you don't care enough about her to want to know—"

"If *you* care so much, Felice, why aren't you doing anything?"

"Because maybe Mother needs time—"

"Not in a hospital that's costing me two thousand dollars a day."

"Then I'll take care of her."

"Is that right?" he said, almost delighted. "Besides paying the bill? What else? Are you going to take her back to your one-bedroom Princeton apartment? What will David say? Who's going to look after Mother every day?"

"I will."

"I've already spoken to the top probate attorney in Los Angeles," Jean went on, not even listening anymore. He rose to leave. "He thinks we've got a real shot at filing a petition with the court to appoint you and me as conservators to run Mother's affairs."

"Which wouldn't just happen to include her money, would it?"

"If you're so concerned, come to the appointment Monday. Two o'clock."

He handed Felice the attorney's business card and left. He had no more patience with his sister. She was as blind and stubborn as their mother.

Jean was back in Toluca Lake before six. Daniel was on the front lawn with his full-time nanny, and jumped up excitedly at the sight of Daddy's car. He waved and giggled and waved some more. Jean picked up his son and swung him by his feet in a wide arc until the four-year-old, half-laughing, half-yelling, begged to be released.

Jean let Daniel sit in his lap as he collapsed back on the grass, suddenly exhausted from a day in which he'd done little except to worry about money and try to deal with his mother. His days were all the same now. His business, without his full time and attention, was floundering. He didn't date much. He didn't read or watch television. Only Daniel brought him real peace.

In another month, for a week at Christmas, the boy would be visiting his mother in San Francisco. Leslie Mae had become something of a celebrity model. She was always in magazines, shown at parties with famous people. Jean still couldn't believe it. After all the crap she'd given him about Paul Newman . . . Her first break had come when she was pregnant with Daniel. Suddenly she was on the cover of *Glamour, Mademoiselle, Cosmopolitan*, and a dozen European magazines. She had married a wealthy older attorney who managed her career, and they had a little boy of their own. Daniel saw his mother every summer for a month, as well as Christmas and Easter. Whenever he left, Jean missed him terribly.

"What do you say, young man? Shall we go to Disneyland tomorrow? It's Saturday, and you don't have nursery school."

A delighted grin came to the handsome face. "I wanna go all day, Daddy."

"All day? You'll get tired."

"No-no-no-no . . ." He shook his head so earnestly and with such conviction that Jean drew a breath of surrender.

"Okay. We'll see how you do."

Jean took his son's hand and led him inside. The housekeeper had already prepared dinner, and while the nanny tidied Daniel's room before leaving, Jean pulled out a book and read to his son. He was extremely bright—Jean had seen that right away—and athletic too. Jean remembered how his father had usually been too busy to spend much time with him, but the occasions they did share were always special. He was determined to do the same with Daniel.

After dinner, putting his son to bed, Jean sat on the patio and gazed on the lake. He saw himself again as a boy, his arms churning through the dark waters, the sun blazing on his shoulders, and it was easy to imagine Daniel in a few years crossing the same stretch of lake.

The call from Archbishop Rationi shook Jean from his reverie. Just back from the Amazon, he apologized for not being the bearer of happier news. Brother Andrew would not cooperate. He refused to surrender control of the money. Before Jean's anger could build, the archbishop quickly allowed that he was not overly worried. More pressure was about to be brought on the stubborn monk, and sooner than later he would have to yield. Rationi sounded confident as he gave Jean the details of what was to come. A pause followed, and Jean knew to fill it with the same assurance that had first prompted the archbishop to take an interest in his problems.

"I look forward to making a substantial donation to the Church, Father," he said quietly, and hung up. How much of the seventy million dollars, Jean had never indicated, but he thought Rationi had high expectations.

The gleaming glass-and-steel tower in downtown Los Angeles, with its foyer of Italian marble and a two-story atrium of exotic trees, struck Felice as something out of a future she wanted no part of. She had been uneasy all morning waiting for the appointment with the probate attorney, and now she was in his lair. She took the elevator to his suite of sumptuous offices—more marble, leather furniture as soft as butter—where she had another troubling thought: this was Jean's world too. These power-loving men in their exotic fortresses—this was the new Los Angeles. Was L.A. much different now from Manhattan, which she visited with David sometimes for theater or museum exhibits? When it came to power and money, the country was like a barbell, weighted disproportionately on both ends.

Before she had a chance to reconsider and flee, Felice was told her brother had already arrived. She was ushered into the attorney's inner office. Her pulse raced, her stomach was in knots. She still wasn't totally clear why she'd come—except to protect her mother's interests. Jean couldn't do anything without her approval, she knew, but she wanted to be armed with more than knowledge. Her eyes paraded to the expensive kilim rugs and walls hung with Hockneys and Stellas. Jean rose graciously to greet her. His charming smile was reproduced almost exactly by the attorney, a wiry man with eyes as blue as his rugs and sandy hair parted so squarely in the middle that Felice was reminded of a road in the desert.

In enemy territory, Felice deemed it wisest to sit and listen. The rhetoric from the attorney did not break new ground. A maverick monk had virtually enslaved Alycia Poindexter, almost let her die—and who knew what he would have done with Alycia's money if she *had* died. Eyes jumped to Felice.

"Brother Andrew did not manipulate her," she heard herself say. "I know that from my mother's letters. She may have been devoted to him, but she was her own person too."

"All right, Felice," Jean said, amused. "For argument's sake, let's say the monk didn't exist. Mother still went crazy. She might as well have been living in outer space."

"I should point out, Mrs. La Porte," the attorney interjected, "that we're only asking the court to appoint a probate investigator to determine if your mother is competent to handle her affairs. This is not the same as saying she *is* incompetent. That determination will be made by an independent observer—"

"Impartial or not, I wouldn't trust him," Felice spoke out. "He doesn't know anything about my mother."

"Mrs. La Porte, I would be more than comfortable if you chatted with the investigator first. He'll want to hear everything you can tell him."

"What about what he learns on his own? And I know what my brother is going to tell him. This city's newspapers have their own story to tell too. I think it's all a setup."

"Then you mean you won't give your permission?"

"No."

"Mrs. La Porte, I know you feel close to your mother . . ."

Her heart was pounding.

"Felice . . ." Jean rose impatiently and gave her a glance of undisguised pain. "Could we talk a minute in private?"

"What?" she said as they navigated to a corner. All she wanted was to leave this stifling office and never return.

"Felice, I'm begging you," he whispered. "What's it hurt to say yes? It's only a preliminary investigation."

"I won't go along."

"You must really have something against me."

"That's not the point."

"You want me to keep on suffering, as if I haven't suffered enough."

"Jean, will you stop it?" she asked. Incredibly, she thought, he believed what he was saying.

"I don't understand. Why won't you help me? I want us to remain friends. No more fighting. Brother Andrew will end up turning over the money anyway."

"I don't think so."

He smiled, delighting in his secret. "You'll see."

"What do you mean?"

Jean decided there was nothing his dear sister could do to interfere. She was a coward anyway. "The archbishop is summoning Andrew back to Boston tomorrow. One way or another, I'm going to win, Felice. So why keep fighting?''

"Because I want to do what's right for Mother," she said, feeling even more helpless. What was going to happen to Brother Andrew?

"We're a family, Felice. Mother's a part of it. Something has to be right for both of us. You don't think I'm capable of change, do you? When I get what's mine, I'll be a different person. I'll reform, you'll see. All I need is some hope in my life.''

Felice smiled tightly. She could never get a perspective. She didn't want to be used by Jean, but she didn't want to be so coldhearted as to completely desert him either. Hadn't her mother always asked her to get along, putting personal differences with her brother aside? He sounded lost and desperate now. Was it an act if he really believed what he was saying? Felice supposed, too, that her mother might really need help. As much as Felice didn't want to accept it, her mother had been as distant and mysterious to her as she had been to Jean. If she agreed to become co-conservator of her mother's affairs, she could be more effective in keeping an eye on Jean than if she stonewalled everybody.

Her gaze swam back to the attorney. The papers were in plain sight, ready to be signed. She moved toward the desk. Jean padded behind as the expensive fountain pen scratched across the pages in her hand.

"Thank you, Mrs. La Porte," the attorney offered when everything had been signed.

"You won't regret this, Felice." Jean leaned toward her to give her a brotherly kiss, but she pulled herself away and left without a good-bye.

Jean was home early that afternoon to pick up Daniel. He excused the boy's nanny for the rest of the day and buckled his son in the passenger seat of his Mercedes. Four bouquets of red roses rested in the back. The weekend Disneyland excursion had been a major success—Daniel had tired only the last hour—but today's trip Jean knew might not be as comfortable. Still, it was important for Daniel to understand certain things at an early age.

"Daddy, were you at the hospital?" Daniel asked as they drove.

"No, son. Not this afternoon."

"Where were you?"

"At an attorney's office."

"What's that?"

"An attorney is someone who helps you when you have a problem."

"When do I get to see Grandma?"

Jean knew to be patient. Daniel was at a stage when his curiosity knew no boundaries. Question followed question without rhyme or reason. Jean thought he remembered when he was that age.

"You'll see Grandma soon. When she's all better."

"Goody," he said, smiling foolishly. "Is she like Mommy?"

"What?"

"Is Grandma like Mommy?"

Jean started to tell Daniel he was confused, that Grandma was Daddy's mother and not Leslie Mae's, but the truth went deeper than that. When he had first met Leslie Mae it was her simplicity and sweetness that had attracted him. She had been the very opposite of his complicated and complicating mother. Now he wasn't so sure the two women weren't mirror images of each other. By deserting him that night, Leslie Mae had complicated his life as much as his mother ever had. And when the scandal of his identity broke, Leslie Mae was nowhere around to help or sympathize. She had that judgmental, superior side to her too, it turned out, just like his mother. She could never be trusted.

"Grandma has nothing to do with your mother," Jean finally said. "They don't know each other."

"Will they?" he asked.

"Know each other? I don't think so."

"Oh," Daniel said, disappointed.

The drive to Forest Lawn cemetery took only a few minutes. A morning wind had pushed away the smog, and as Jean took Daniel's hand and went up a grassy knoll overlooking half the Valley, he felt as peaceful as the view.

It was the same peace he had felt when he used to bring Daniel to visit Harriet. The two were an instant match. Harriet had always baked cookies for her great-grandson and let him have the run of the Bel-Air house. Throughout the week before she died, Daniel had hovered with Jean by her bedside, his small face stricken with worry. A stroke had virtually paralyzed Harriet, but she could utter a few words, and her shining eyes betrayed a still-keen awareness of the world. They would follow Daniel wherever he roamed in the room, and she would not allow the nurse to chase him away. Jean did not leave either. If alive, his father would have been here, and it was Jean's role to take his place. He loved his family. He would not betray his duty or trust.

One afternoon Harriet had beckoned Jean closer to her bed. The frail white hand gripped his arm with surprising strength and the lips moved to whisper something urgent. Her eyes had stayed on Daniel, absorbing strength and energy from the little boy, as if seeing in him the light of redemption for the entire family. Then she had told Jean. His grandfather had established a trust for him. Alycia was the trustee. It was supposed to be a secret, but Alycia was very close to Brother Andrew . . . If anything ever happened to Jean or Daniel, if money was ever needed . . .

Her words had come out slowly and with great difficulty. Afterward, exhausted, she managed to put her hand on the boy's head. As she closed her eyes, Jean had heard Harriet ask Alycia to forgive her. He had said nothing, his thoughts still spinning with his mother's duplicity.

"Put the flowers in the ground, in the metal containers," Jean instructed Daniel gently as they knelt by the four graves marked with simple stones. "Don't be afraid . . ." The little boy was sweating from the walk up the knoll. He looked unsure, but Jean guided his hand first to Owen's, then Harriet's, then Isabel's, and finally Red's.

"They're all dead," Daniel announced, suddenly realizing the situation.

"These are people who loved you even before you were born," Jean answered.

The boy's smile dimmed and he looked perplexed.

"And they love you now. They will always love you."

"They're dead," he said again, confused, looking at his father.

"No. Not their spirits."

Daniel cocked his head. "What's a spirit?"

"Someone you can't see but you can feel. Someone who is a part of you."

"The spirits love you too?" Daniel asked with a child's wisdom.

"Yes. Me too." And Jean had cried.

*   *   *

Holy Cross Cathedral in Boston, the archdiocese of New England and the long-standing throne of Archbishop Rationi, was a massive, gloomy neo-Gothic edifice. It was hardly the architectural equal of the great cathedrals of France or England, but it had the same stolid, medieval appearance and feel. With its spires arching up like arms to heaven, and its cold, cavernous interior, the visitor was quickly humbled. There was a sense of importance and righteousness in even its darkest corner; man was mortal, the cathedral was not.

This was not Brother Andrew's first trip to Holy Cross, but none had been less enjoyable. Tired from his journey from Rio, he skirted the basilica and edged down a long and lightless corridor. At the end loomed a faded, cracked oil of St. Peter holding up the keys to heaven—the stormy eyes burned through Andrew. Where was the light and warmth of Christ in this imposing church? Chancery staff breezed by without giving the monk in his simple habit the courtesy of a smile. His sense of being in a sacramental community was not as strong as that of witnessing a business going about its day. As instructed by the archbishop, Andrew again repeated to himself the Nicene Creed—the Catholic doctrine of sin and salvation—and stopped in front of a carved wooden door.

He was a good hour late for his appointment, but somehow he had thought that was not important. He was too nervous to worry about anything but what he would say to the archbishop, who had summoned him from Brazil with only the briefest of messages. Andrew was to attend a special conclave and explain his position regarding Alycia Poindexter's money. What more was there to add? he had wondered on the plane. What hadn't he already explained? Did they think he would change his mind? And no one had yet had the decency to tell him anything about Alycia.

He took a breath and opened the door. His eyes jumped to the high vaulted ceiling and then to the table whose large proportions dwarfed the room. The walls were covered with more oils of pale saints and martyrs. Brother Manning greeted his rebel monk with a reserved embrace, then backed away to allow Andrew access to his more illustrious company. Around the table sat no fewer than six bishops, as if this were a private synod, and another half-dozen heads and members of curial departments within the archdiocese. Andrew's heart began to pound. He had never counted on this. Rationi, seated to the right, cast a wary eye as the monk gravitated to the empty chair at the end of the table. Someone bade him sit. Andrew studied the handsome, radiant face—the first light he'd seen in this gloomy cathedral. The tall, imposing man had wide shoulders and an infectious smile. He also wore a biretta, the three-cornered red hat of a cardinal.

"Your Eminence," Andrew said, starting to rise again.

"Please sit, Father," the cardinal exhorted in his mellow voice.

"Thank you."

"Father, do you know who I am?"

Everyone in his abbey knew of the bishop from the St. Louis diocese, Andrew thought. Robert Easton was one of only three cardinals from the United States, and its youngest, appointed by the pope before the prelate's forty-fifth birthday. He was a crack canon lawyer. His reputation had been earned by settling disputes between the pope and several recalcitrant bishops who'd taken exception to papal doctrines or Vatican Council decrees. A tough and clever negotiator, self-deprecating, always loyal to Rome.

"I do," Andrew replied.

"And I know who you are," the cardinal joked. His smile lit the room. The other bishops seemed to relax. Andrew felt some relief as well, as the prelate filled the air with humorous anecdotes about Rome. He made one like him right away, Andrew saw. Still, the monk knew to be careful.

"Brother Andrew," he finally said, "I understand that you've accomplished some remarkable things in your service to the Church. Your work among the poor is legendary within your order, and beyond. I congratulate you."

"Thank you," Andrew said, "but I've only done what my abbot has asked of me."

"And done it far better, far more selflessly, than most of your brethren. Your fund-raising efforts have enabled your order to expand its work."

"I am glad for that," he replied simply. Andrew knew he was being set up with praise. He was not fooled. The cardinal was a much more skillful sparring partner than Archbishop Rationi.

"Your background is unusual for someone who has chosen such a stringent order. You came from a very wealthy family, I believe."

"I did."

"Do you miss that life, Father?"

"No, I don't think so."

"You're certain?"

"I have no interest in money, your Eminence."

"Really?"

"Yes."

The silence told Andrew he had dug himself into a little hole. "I have no interest in money for myself," he clarified. "But I appreciate the good that, if wisely used, it can accomplish in the world. Perhaps that's why I was somewhat successful at fund-raising."

"You were particularly successful with one individual, were you not?"

"Do you mean Alycia Poindexter?" Andrew spoke up.

"You have been friendly with the woman for two decades. You know her very well."

"She believed in our cause, your Eminence."

"Some would say that she believed in you."

"I think that is irrelevant. She saw the work I was doing and admired it. She wanted to help. I cannot see anything wrong with that, your Eminence."

"Brother Andrew, do you value the esteem of your colleagues?"

"Of course."

"And mine?"

"I am honored just to be in the same room with you."

"You respect me, then?"

"You are a leader in the Church. You are a man of great power and wisdom," Andrew answered carefully. "How could I not respect you? I certainly would not wish to offend you."

"Does that mean you would comply with my requests?"

"You are my superior."

"If I asked you specifically to relinquish control over Alycia Poindexter's money—"

Andrew pushed back in his chair. He was almost relieved the subject had finally come out. He liked and respected Cardinal Easton, but he had not liked all his evasive maneuvering, as if this was some Harvard debate. "I believe that you, and everyone in this room, know that Archbishop Rationi asked me the very same thing," Andrew said. "You also know my position on the subject."

"I have the archbishop's report. Now it is I making the request. You realize, Father, that my presence here indicates the gravity, and perhaps historical uniqueness, of this situation."

"I do, and I am no more happy about it than you appear to be," Andrew said frankly. "And I don't believe there is any more that I can add that has not already been said."

There was another silence that made Andrew's heart begin to pound again. Looking at the stony, friezelike faces of the bishops, Andrew began to understand just how major an embarrassment he had become to the Church.

"Brother Andrew," the cardinal said, shifting his tone delicately, "you do not have to be confrontational. Let us assume a different perspective. You've proven that your abilities obviously suit you for a higher position within the Church than being a monk. Most of us in this room believe that you are deserving of far more than you have. And I believe you know that."

Andrew pondered the thought. "Honestly, there's nothing I want," he said.

"You mean that if I were to offer you a position within my curia . . ."

"I would be most flattered, but I am more than content with the obligations I have now."

"You have no ambition?"

"Not of that nature. My only ambition is to help as many people as I can."

"And if you were offered something in Rome . . ."

Andrew hesitated. The cardinal repeated himself. Andrew knew he'd be a fool not to say he wasn't tempted. Maybe he did have ambition. He had just never thought of himself basking in the light of fame and power—but he had never been approached by a cardinal, either. Andrew had no doubt the prelate was sincere. He meant well. Yet what the cardinal basically wanted—what everybody wanted—was much clearer to Andrew than was his ambition. "Thank you, your Eminence, but I am happy with what I'm doing."

"Then, conversely, Brother Andrew," Cardinal Easton went on, hardly skipping a beat, "if your lack of cooperation would hurt you in the eyes of the Church . . ."

"I would feel badly," Andrew offered.

"And what would you do, Father?"

"I would still not change my mind about Alycia Poindexter's money." He wished he did not have to say it. He wished he did not like Cardinal Easton, or that the warm smile was not so strong and unyielding. He wished he were anywhere but here. "I will never change my mind about that, your Eminence."

"Brother Andrew, I am not here to find fault with you, or castigate you for your sins. I am here to reason with you as a fellow servant of God. What happens here today, I must report to Rome. My high personal regard for you notwithstanding, I cannot influence Rome's decisions or actions. I can only beg you to understand that your recalcitrance has angered people more powerful than I, and there has been talk that the Holy See will order your dismissal from the Trappists. Further, your chances of being excommunicated from the mother Church grow every day." The cardinal paused to let his words sink in. "I do not believe you wish that. I certainly do not wish it for you."

The threat seemed to have come from nowhere. Andrew was totally surprised. It felt like he'd been clubbed on the back of the head. Was money this important? Was the Church so embarrassed by one man, and a simple monk at that, that it was doing everything in its considerable power to bring him to his knees? Andrew stumbled for words. "I do not wish it either," he spoke up. "I don't understand. Didn't you just tell me that I have served the Church beyond what most men would ever do? I do not understand how I can be punished for obeying my conscience. I have confessed my sins, but this is not one of them. I tell you this with great reluctance: I cannot yield to you because it contradicts my deepest feelings of right and wrong."

Andrew looked to his abbot for support. Their eyes met, agreed on nothing, and drifted apart.

"Do you have anything else to say, Father?" asked the cardinal, visibly upset now.

Andrew wanted to feel good about his courage—some surge of peace or hope that came with his defiance—but the coldness and animosity in the room were overwhelming. "I would like to know where Alycia Poindexter is," he said.

"Brother Andrew, you will return to your abbey immediately and pray to God that he enlightens your judgment. You profess to love and serve the Church. We shall see. In two days—Wednesday evening—you'll return here and tell us what you've decided."

"Where is Alycia?" he repeated stubbornly, but his words

were drowned in the shuffle of chairs and rustling of robes. The room abruptly emptied and the monk was left alone in his chair, as if to taste the isolation he was in danger of being punished with. For a long moment he could not move. He'd been asked to pray to God for enlightenment. What was Cardinal Easton thinking—that he wasn't praying already?

Andrew suddenly wondered if prayer would help him stand up to this pressure. He saw, with great clarity and pain, that courage took him only so far, that he had never been tested like this, and he sensed that he could not hold out forever. Who could? His weaknesses had always scared him, but never more than now. He hated being helpless. Of course, he knew something of church law himself, and he would demand an eccelesiastical hearing if he were threatened with excommunication. He did know how to fight, and would, but he also had the wisdom to see that he was only one man, and that the Church, when it wanted to be an adversary, could crush the mightiest armies of the world.

The door swung open to the empty room. Andrew turned with only half-attention, then could not alter his gaze. The sight of a woman—young and beautiful—in the doorway of a room reserved for male clergy did not startle him as much as the woman herself, or rather her distinctive features, which were unmistakable. Andrew rose awkwardly, still galvanized. He had never met Felice, only seen her photographs. Andrew was unable to speak as he held her eyes now. She approached slowly, too, then they wrapped their arms around one another.

"You are so beautiful, just like your mother," Andrew finally said when they broke apart and sat down. His spirits picked up. He couldn't stop thanking God for this moment. "How are you, Felice?"

"I'm fine."

"How did you know I was here?"

Felice pushed a strand of hair from her eyes and tried to quiet her pounding heart. This really was Andrew. She had found him after all. Jean had only revealed that the monk was being called back to Boston—it had required some sleuthing to learn where and when. She had done a lot of investigating the last few days. To see now the man her mother was in love with was worth all the effort, and more.

"The important thing," she began, "is that I did find you. And that you go to my mother right away. She's at Cedars-

Sinai Medical Center in Beverly Hills. You'll have to sneak in somehow. Security is very tight."

"How is she?" Andrew implored eagerly.

"I don't know. She won't talk to anyone. That's why you must see her. I'm very worried . . ."

Andrew's mind raced. A cardinal had ordered him back to his monastery. The woman he loved was languishing in a hospital in Los Angeles. "Jean is keeping her there?" he asked.

"He wants to have Mother committed. He's ruthless. And somehow I can't make myself stop him. You've seen what he's done to you."

"Everything has happened so fast, Felice. I'm still trying to make sense of things. First, please tell me why Jean needs the money so badly," Andrew asked.

Felice nodded knowingly. Ever since her father had died she had willingly made herself a prisoner of a small, hermetic world that she could control. The poetry she wrote, the art she studied, they were safe and unassailable. An internal world that enabled her to ignore conflict and stress. Fight or flee, said the conventional wisdom. Jean rampaged like a bull through life, and she expended all her energy avoiding him. It had brought her happiness and peace, but after seeing her mother in the hospital, troubled and vulnerable, Felice had grown uneasy with her cowardice.

Maybe there was meaning and peace in meeting her brother head-on for once, she decided. For so many years she had admired her mother for her strength and courage. Felice knew she had her mother's looks and intelligence, but she didn't think she had been given that courage. Now she knew differently. She had made this trip to Boston. Jean would be outraged when he found out, and accuse her of betraying him. She could handle it. She would not be intimidated any longer.

"For the last few days," she told Andrew, "I've been looking into Jean's business affairs. It wasn't easy for me. I know so little about loans and hard assets and cash flow. That was always my father's world. I've never cared that much about money, nor has my husband, David. But the other thing you should know is, I don't think money is that important to Jean either."

Andrew was astonished. "How can that be? He's always wanted to be rich."

"No," Felice corrected, "he's wanted success and esteem.

Money was just the tool, just like it was for my father. What I learned from talking to Jean's bankers was that my brother's net worth far exceeds his liability for his Houston bank. He could sell a few more properties and everything would be fine. He'd still be a wealthy man. He just doesn't want to sell anything. He wants the power and prestige and reputation of being a success. He's still trying to prove himself to a father who's no longer alive. You have to understand our whole family to understand what drives Jean. And he is driven. He's haunted by the thought of failure and humiliation. He wants all the adulation and acceptance he can find."

"Your mother feels that money is something else, something damning," Andrew said, trying to put this in perspective for himself. "She says it's done nothing but hurt your family."

"I agree with that," Felice said. She told the monk everything that had happened to Jean the last ten years.

"Then what I don't understand," Andrew finally confessed, "is why Jean never could accept your mother's love at face value. She gave him plenty, I know that. Why did he construe love as having to be his old house or his father's properties or a reputation or money?"

Felice sighed. "I don't know for sure. I've thought about this a lot, believe me. In some ways Jean is like our father and our grandfather. There's a mixture of nobility and baseness in him. I can't explain it better than that. Some things are never easily explained, but that doesn't mean they aren't real or believable. I'm not afraid of Jean anymore," Felice added, "but in the abstract he still scares me."

Andrew laid a concerned hand on her shoulder. "Your brother is very difficult, I understand that. But I still feel for him."

"So do I," said Felice. "I always have. That's why he's been able to manipulate me, and my mother, and probably everyone else in his life. Jean's had some hard times, a lot harder than I have. I'm convinced now it's not just Mother who needs help, but also my brother. He takes everything so personally, so dramatically. Every victory or defeat is magnified. As guilty as I've been for being locked into my small world, Jean's is even smaller—and I really don't think he's in control. Events control him."

Andrew absorbed the words. "I'll leave for Los Angeles first thing in the morning," he said, giving Felice an embrace. "I will speak to Jean. I'll do everything that I can. And nothing will keep me from Alycia. Thank you again for coming here, Felice."

Despite his anxiety, for the first time in weeks Andrew felt a surge of hope. That he would earn the displeasure or even the censure of Cardinal Easton bothered him greatly, but he had made his choice. As they walked out together, Felice told Andrew she had to be with David tonight at Princeton, but she would fly to Los Angeles late tomorrow. Andrew clasped his arms around her again and promised she would be in his prayers.

At the end of the day, Jean powered his fire-engine red Mercedes out of the underground garage with the relief and exuberance of a man buried so long in darkness that seeing daylight again almost made him weep. He could barely contain his happiness. He had had his first good day at work in months—concentrating, making deals, putting money into the bank instead of taking it out—and at the end of the afternoon he'd received a call from a movie star who for years had acted like Jean had disappeared from the face of the earth; now Jean was being invited to the man's dinner party. What goes around comes around, he thought. He had stared down the spectre of his defeat and not blinked. He had more than survived; he had triumphed over obstacles that would have crushed other men. With his share of the trust money he'd bail out his Houston bank and have enough left to purchase an office building he coveted in Santa Barbara. The upcoming dinner party would be the first of many. There was a woman he was thinking of asking out. Developers were coming back to him. Goddammit, he was a hero again!

The Mercedes weaved in and out of rush-hour traffic. Jean was impatient to see Daniel—they would have to celebrate tonight. Taking the curb lane to the freeway entrance, he nearly ran over an emaciated man with a scraggly beard, arms stacked with copies of the evening edition of the *Herald Examiner*. The liberal newspaper publisher was playing the Good Samaritan, hiring the homeless right off the street for vendors, but Jean didn't see social redemption in the ploy, he saw politics. The man spun out of the way of the rushing Mercedes, but the final image in Jean's mind was of the newspaper he held up as if to protect himself. The subliminal flash of a photo and a headline—no, it was impossible.

Ten yards before the freeway entrance Jean made a wobbly U-turn and drifted back. He bellied his car up to the curb and snatched a newspaper from the surprised man. Jean did not hear his high-pitched cursing or the blaring horns as cars swerved around him. He could only focus on the photo of his mother in the hospital room. Grainy and blurred, it had been taken quickly, a hit-and-run job. The paper burned in Jean's hands. . . . dying in the Amazon, saved by her son but mysteriously kept a prisoner at Cedars-Sinai Medical Center . . . mother and son have never gotten along . . . the questionable finances of Jean Poindexter . . .

Back on the freeway he couldn't hold his lane. Something pushed down on his chest . . . he could barely breathe. Who else had that reporter talked to besides some interns and nurses? Electra maybe, or that countess his mother used to hang around? Did it matter? Jean knew he would be held up to ridicule again. He could smell the new scandal in the air like a coming storm. His name would be whispered in derision by millions of strangers. Chances of success in probate court had just been reduced to minus zero. What had he done to deserve this?

It was his mother's fault, of course. Maybe he should never have brought her back to Los Angeles. Wherever she walked, scandal followed. It was like a goddamn law of nature. The Mercedes swung off the freeway at the Universal City exit and promptly went out of control. It careened off a telephone pole, bounded slightly into another car, and righted itself. A pain burned in Jean's right shoulder but he kept driving.

At home his housekeeper and Daniel's nanny looked at him with concern. Politely and in control, Jean asked them not to return for at least a week. He wanted some time alone with Daniel, he explained. In his study, he sat motionless behind the desk, his eye roving slowly around the room, wondering where he was. This was his father's study, he thought, confused. What the hell was he doing here?

The phone rang. The caller took ten seconds to identify himself as a reporter; it took Jean only three to hang up. Daniel appeared at the doorway. His tiny fists rubbed his eyes. Waking from a nap, he seemed to sense that something was wrong.

"Go away, Daniel," Jean said coldly. "I want to be alone."

Pretending not to hear, the boy sidled up to the couch and took a seat.

"Go, Daniel. Now."

"Why can't I stay?"

"Do as I say."

He shook his head bravely.

Jean's eyes blazed into the little boy. "I won't warn you again, Daniel."

"I don't want to leave," he answered defiantly. "I want to be with you."

"Go—or you'll be punished!"

Daniel didn't budge. Jean rose from his desk. He seized his son roughly by the arm and marched him upstairs to his room. "You will stand here in this corner for one hour. You will not move. Not one muscle. Not until I come and get you. Is that clear?"

A tear rolled down the boy's soft cheek. Fear and incomprehension mingled in his stare.

"Don't you dare cry," Jean ordered. "You're not a baby, you understand? You're my son."

Somehow the boy stopped his trembling jaw. Jean turned and left the room.

As soon as Andrew drifted into the visitors' lobby of Cedars-Sinai he realized he could not have picked a worse evening to try to see Alycia. He had just read the front page of the *Herald Examiner*. Badly embarrassed hospital security officers were as ubiquitous now as the nurses. It was obvious that no visitor was going anywhere without a pass.

Deception had never come naturally to Andrew, but he forced himself to confront an attractive older woman at the central nurse's station and quietly declared that he was visiting one Selma Bernstein—a name his eye had caught on a patient folder. It was a foolish gambit, Andrew considered the instant he spoke—what would a Jewish woman want with a Trappist monk? But his face and voice must have registered more sincerity than not. The nurse surrendered a pass, Andrew logged his name into a visitors' book, and he was off down the hall. Felice had given him the number of Alycia's room. At her door he found two more guards. They denied him entrance. Andrew protested that he had been sent to visit Mrs. Poindexter by a higher authority. The joke eluded them, but they looked at one another and, figuring there was no possible harm a monk could do, let him pass.

Andrew pushed open the heavy door. It was not yet nine, but Alycia was already asleep. Her gentle face was lit by the amber cast of the emergency light above her bed. He wondered if he should wake her. He was relieved how rested and well she looked. Around the room were a dozen floral arrangements. One basket was from Electra, he saw, another from Evan Chambers. Inspired by sympathy, or amnesia, or perhaps the politics of the rich, old enemies had suddenly become old friends. Andrew was sure there'd be a provocative piece in the morning *Times*. What would Alycia think of that? He knew she wouldn't be fooled. He hovered over the woman he loved more than anyone in the world and took her hand. When her eyes opened they fixed on Andrew with the certainty that he was an illusion.

"Alycia, it really is me," he whispered. He leaned over and kissed her. Her hand reached up and stroked his cheek.

"Andrew—"

"I'm here."

"I've missed you so much." Alycia levered herself up in bed and folded her arms around him. "I can't believe this," she said.

"Felice told me where you were. She said you won't talk to anyone. She's very worried."

"I know, I'm sorry," Alycia answered. "It was painful for me not to say anything to her. I can explain everything." She pulled back to get a full look at Andrew. His face was lined from fatigue and worry. What had he been through? She could only guess Jean had made as much trouble for Andrew as he had for her.

Sorting her thoughts, starting from the beginning, Alycia told Andrew everything. She had been so angry at being kidnapped, stuck in a hospital among strangers and in a city she despised, that she decided not to speak to anyone, to pretend none of them existed. She hoped that if she kept silent, everyone would leave her alone. The effect was the opposite. Jean came to her room three or four times a day, determined to break her silence as if it were some code. Each day of failure brought him closer to rage. She had overheard him whisper to a doctor that he wanted her committed to a psychiatric hospital. As painful as it was not to confide in Felice, Alycia knew that if she'd spoken one word to her daughter, Jean would have found out and hounded his sister. She had hoped to stay in the hospital until she reached Andrew, but Jean had intercepted her letters. She had not known what to do. This evening, out of nowhere, had come the flowers, as if someone had waved a white flag of surrender, of peace. She was now a celebrity again.

"And you should see the story in the evening paper," Andrew said with a chuckle. "I think your enemies have forgiven you."

"I don't want to be forgiven," Alycia answered. "I did nothing wrong to be forgiven for. The flowers are just society's way of grabbing attention for itself in the media. I don't want attention."

A smile warmed Andrew's tired face. "Everyone was afraid you'd gone off the deep end. I didn't believe it, but it's nice to see for sure you're the same Alycia."

She squeezed his hand in gratitude. "Maybe people had a right to think that. I did let myself go physically. I'm in my sixties—what does physical beauty matter anymore? It's the spirit and soul that endure. And now I want to go back to the Amazon."

"Alycia, I forbid you to be in such a rush. You must make sure you're well this time."

"I miss so many people. The Indians depend on me. How is my family?" she asked.

"For all their struggles and tragedies, very well, I think. Brother Sebastian is looking after them."

"I wish Jean could see them. Then he'd understand what it means truly to have nothing."

"I don't believe the suffering of others makes an impression on Jean," Andrew said. "He is too full of a sense of his own suffering." He related everything Felice had told him about her brother.

Alycia sifted through Andrew's words. He was concerned about Jean in a way that she couldn't put a finger on, but it gave her a new sense of uneasiness. She had always known of Jean's vulnerability, but lately all she'd seen was his wild, angry side.

"How is Felice?" she asked, diverting herself.

"She's fine, really. You should thank her for bringing me here," Andrew allowed. "She's as courageous as you."

"I want to see her."

"She'll be here soon."

"How did she find you?"

"Jean let slip that I was in Boston."

"Boston? What's happening there?" she said with fresh concern.

"It's my archdiocese. I'm being put on trial, I'm afraid. At least it feels like it. Maybe Jean already told you—the Church wants your money too. It pains me to say it, but I think more and more that Jean must have promised someone something."

"What will happen to you?"

Andrew described Archbishop Rationi's visit to the Amazon, then the interrogation from Cardinal Easton, and his ultimatum. Andrew had to be back in Boston tomorrow evening.

Alycia closed her eyes. She felt terrible. She had done this to Andrew. She had been irresponsible. The trust money had come back to haunt her again. Andrew's pressure from the Church was Jean's doing, but it had all started with her. She had put Andrew in jeopardy by asking him to administer the funds. He had warned her things could go wrong. She should have listened.

"What happens to me is not important," Andrew insisted. "I promised you I would take care of the money, and I will."

"No, I won't do that to you," Alycia said. "You've been put in enough jeopardy, none of which you deserve."

"You're forgetting that I love you."

"Love should have nothing to do with money," she answered knowingly.

Andrew realized their voices were carrying. His glance swung to the door. "I don't know how much longer we have together," he whispered. "Every second is crucial. There are decisions that must be made."

Alycia rose and strolled to the window. The nightscape of twinkling lights belied her roiled emotions. "I know," she said. "And the most important is about Jean. I don't want him to hate me. I don't want him to suffer. I feel so much guilt as a mother already. If he were honestly in trouble, I'd gladly give him the money. But you said he's not destitute. Not by any definition except maybe his own. Even if he promised he'd never touch the money but save it for Daniel, I wouldn't hand it over. From the beginning, the trusts have meant nothing but disaster. Money has been confused for love in this family. I haven't even seen Daniel, but I won't risk ruining his life. The chain has to be broken. It's up to me to break it.''

"I agree," said Andrew, "but just how do you propose to accomplish that? What will you do with seventy million dollars? If you gave me a clue, I'd know what to say to Cardinal Easton.''

`She turned to Andrew. "I want to leave this hospital I can't think here.''

"Jean would be called immediately if you even suggested checking out. You'd have to prove to some psychiatrist that you're of sound mind. That could take days, even weeks. We don't have that time, Alycia.''

"You have to be in Boston tomorrow night?''

"Yes, but that doesn't concern me now. It's Jean I'm most worried about.''

Alycia's uneasiness swept over her again. She turned back to the view of the city, trying to gather her thoughts.

"I'm sure Jean's seen the evening paper," Andrew explained, "and he'll probably take this as a terrible defeat, since his chances of forcing your hand now are greatly reduced. His gamble has failed. He'll be in a very anxious and frenzied state." He put his hand on Alycia's shoulder. "I think I should see him as soon as possible. I have as good a chance as anyone to be accepted, and to reason with him. I want him to understand how much you love him.''

"Then I'll come with you. Felice wrote me how he'd bought back and restored our old house . . . maybe that's where I should be meeting with him, not in this hospital.''

"Let me go alone, Alycia, at least this time. Jean's feelings for you are too explosive right now.''

"You don't have to fight any more of my battles. You've done enough for me.''

"Let me fight this one. I want to get through to Jean. I believe I have a chance. I'll be back for you tonight—then we'll find a way to sneak you out of here.''

Andrew drove straight to Toluca Lake. Was he doing the right thing? What words could he find for Jean? Reaching through the young man's layers of despair and frustration, earning his trust, would rightfully take someone years. But Andrew's strong sense was that he had to act tonight. He had not wanted to alarm Alycia, but he sensed some urgency. Preparing himself psychologically, Andrew fought his natural dislike for Jean. He was good at that, he considered—resisting

his own tendencies, repressing, sublimating, reaching beyond
the reality for the ideal. His training as a monk had served
that end well. It was a side of himself he did not always
like—falling in love with Alycia had been a direct rebellion
against it—yet this disciplined self was a part of him too, a
good and necessary part. Now it would be put to use.

It was almost eleven when Andrew reached the Toluca
Lake house he would never forget. He wondered if Jean
would still be up. He walked across the dewy grass and
knocked firmly on the front door. He could swear he heard a
voice inside, but no one came forward. Andrew knocked
again.

"Hello!" he shouted. "Jean, it's Brother Andrew! May I
come in, please?"

Andrew stepped back for a better view. There was a light
upstairs, and one in the study. Making his way through the
flowerbed, the monk perched on his toes, giving him a clear
view into the study.

The glass fogged under his breath. He watched as Jean,
behind his desk, peered into an atlas. His finger turned one
page at a time, eyes sweeping over the different countries.
Across the room, stiff and quiet as his father, was a handsome blond boy in only pajama bottoms. His face was dirty
and streaked with tears. Andrew was alarmed by how exhausted he looked, how unnaturally still he held himself; his
eyes pointed at his father.

Andrew rapped his knuckles against the window. Daniel
glanced up first. The monk had a warm smile for the boy.
Then Jean rose. The stare he aimed at Andrew was so con-
temptuous, so accusing, that Andrew froze for a moment. He
had never seen such meanness, such desperation.

"Jean, I have to speak to you," he said, raising his voice
to be heard through the window. "Will you listen to me? I
have seen your mother tonight. We spoke. She wants to see
you. Will you come with me now, back to the hospital?"

Andrew felt foolish. Jean's gaze was blank, as if he hadn't
heard a word. Still, the monk persevered. "I know you think
she has failed you as a mother, Jean. Sometimes she thinks
the same thing, but I disagree. She and your father gave you
all the love they had. But despite best intentions, despite all
the love in the world, no one can control another human
being or his destiny. You must accept that. You must accept
that you are loved by your mother and sister, and that in spite

of your bitter disappointments, you must also learn to love yourself.''

The force of Jean's eyes pushed him back. Had not one of his sentences made an impression? Could Jean be that hardened? Andrew knew he could not leave. Whatever Jean was planning, whatever the needs of his soul, it was also Daniel, he sensed, who was in peril.

The monk knocked again on the glass. The fury on Jean's face did not shift or bend. ''Daniel,'' Andrew shouted, trying to get the boy's attention. Afraid, the boy glanced away.

What am I to do? Andrew thought, immobilized. He was badly shaken. Maybe there was nothing he could do, no matter how anxious he felt. Perhaps he was wrong to have come at all, or to think he could help. Maybe the crisis here was exaggerated in his imagination. Should he call the police? He had witnessed no violence, no provocation. As he edged away from the window, still struggling with his thoughts, he saw Jean rise, take Daniel by the hand, and turn off the lights.

Andrew retreated to his car. He was dismayed by his lack of resolve and courage. He had never felt so helpless, and he prayed to God to have his strength and wisdom back. What did all this mean—was he just tired and confused? Was God punishing him by taking away his ability to help others? He tried to fight off his paralysis as he thought of all his problems, the decisions still to be made, but he couldn't find even the tiniest crack of light.

The dark-complexioned young man in the wire-transfer department of the Wall Street investment banking firm of Ernst and Gulbranson arrived at work, as usual, promptly at eight. He wore an English-tailored suit that far exceeded his budget, imported Italian shoes, a silk tie from Saks, and a custom pinstripe shirt. He was ambitious and tolerated his menial job only because one day he hoped it would lead to an account position. His desk in the corner of a small windowless office was stacked with a sheaf of client orders that had come in during the night. With a cup of black coffee, the young man stifled a yawn and perched at his computer terminal.

Carefully he made the proper keystrokes that would ensure the unimpeded flow of millions of dollars from well-known banks in Geneva, Paris, London, and Rome to a depository in New York, and the reciprocal exodus of money from New

York to points abroad. The routine usually lasted several hours and ended with the dispatching of last-minute orders that fell on his desk during the morning. He paused at only one, toward the bottom of the pile, puzzled by its destination. He double-checked the code for accuracy. Who knows, he thought, it was a crazy world. Without hesitating, he punched the keys that in minutes sent more than seventy million dollars to an obscure bank in Brazil. The only identifying name on the new account was that of a Brother Leon Edward Sebastian.

The chill of the November evening remained in Andrew's bones long after he'd entered Holy Cross Cathedral. He paced outside the conference room, fighting his fatigue from a sleepless night and today's flight from Los Angeles. The thick door precluded any chance of overhearing the discussion of the bishops inside, which surely centered on Andrew's latest acts of disobedience. He could only wonder again how this had all happened. Andrew had lived most of his adult life in willful obscurity, before a chain of events had pushed him into a spotlight no one could envy. He longed to escape into the shadows again.

He was still badly shaken by what had happened at Jean's house. Returning to the hospital had been even more devastating. Alycia's room was empty. Hospital security was as puzzled and agitated as the monk, as he searched the hallways and other rooms in vain. What had happened, and why hadn't Alycia at least left him a note? He'd been so full of despair he had considered not showing up in Boston.

The door opened and Brother Manning beckoned Andrew. The abbot had developed a talent for showing disappointment with only the slightest shift of his eyes. Andrew expected to confront the same pantheon of lofty and austere judges, anchored by Cardinal Easton. He was not disappointed. Yet entering the room he also found twenty brethren from his own abbey lining the walls. One ventured forward to pull out a chair for Andrew.

"We applaud your courage—other abbeys know of you too!" the young monk whispered to Andrew.

The words heartened him, but they were no match for the stoic faces that surrounded him like a wall. Cardinal Easton's look of disappointment bore right through him. The prelate's large hands were folded in front of him, his bishop's hat of authority so splendid on the broad head that Andrew's eyes couldn't leave it.

"Brother Andrew," he began, "we are convened here again, amid our prayers and hopes, to learn of your decision. All of us were dismayed that you did not return to your abbey as instructed. Do you not realize the consequences of insubordination? You need God's firm guidance now more than ever—"

"I realize everything," Andrew said quietly, "including my own thoughts and feelings."

"Would you begin by telling us where you were the last two days?"

"I went to Los Angeles," he admitted, though he was sure everyone in the room already knew from hospital security.

"To accomplish what?"

"I visited Alycia Poindexter. I presented the situation, and your point of view, as fairly as I could. I told her I would do what she wanted."

The cardinal stirred uncomfortably. "Are you aware, Brother Andrew, that Alycia Poindexter disappeared from her hospital room sometime last night?"

"I am," he said.

"Were you responsible for helping her?"

Andrew knew the question had been inevitable. So were the bishops' judgments. They all thought he was guilty. He surveyed the hushed room and spoke clearly. He had visited the hospital the previous night, around nine, talking his way past the security personnel. He had returned, shortly before midnight, to find her room empty.

"She was not found?" the cardinal iterated.

"Not to my knowledge," Andrew said.

"Do you know where she is now?"

"No, your Eminence. I wish I did."

"Did she return to Brazil?" the cardinal pressed.

"I do not know."

"Did she promise to meet you somewhere?"

Andrew shook his head. He resented this badgering. He knew nothing. They could see he wasn't lying. His agitation was too great.

"What happened when you last saw Mrs. Poindexter?" the cardinal continued, hardly finished.

"She said she wanted very much to relieve me of the

burdens she had imposed, and that she needed to leave the hospital in order to think."

An enlightened smile came to Cardinal Easton. "You are telling us, then, that she spoke to you. To everyone else, including her own children, she didn't utter a word, and suddenly with you she is lucid, alert, fully capable—"

"Exactly," said Andrew, pleased with the conclusion.

The cardinal's eyes cast around to the bishops before returning to Andrew. "But she is not around now. No one knows where she is. Isn't that correct? No one can be sure what she's thinking or what she's up to. I would submit to you that someone in full control of her faculties, someone who truly wishes to help you, Brother Andrew, who has nothing to hide, would not be so rash or evasive."

"My observation, to the contrary," Andrew spoke up, upset, "was that I had never spoken to anyone more lucid or in control than Alycia Poindexter. There are reasons for everything she's done."

"I would not exactly call you an impartial witness," the cardinal replied.

"Nor would I you," Andrew answered.

One of the monks from the abbey smiled his satisfaction too openly at the retort. It did not go unnoticed by Brother Manning. But it was Andrew's irreverence that stirred the room. He could feel the cardinal's anger. The prelate's wit and understanding had been replaced by impatience and disbelief. The room grew warmer. Andrew straightened in his chair. After his failures last night, he wondered if God was still there to hear his prayers.

"Your Eminence," Andrew spoke up, "I came here today not to fight with you or to pass judgment on Alycia Poindexter, but to tell you simply that I have not changed my mind. The funds will remain under my control until I am instructed otherwise by the same woman who entrusted me with the money. I regret the pain this decision brings me and everyone in this room, but I have searched my conscience, and I stand by my decision."

Andrew tried to ignore his thudding heart. The unreality and embarrassment of his defiance prompted the cardinal to rise and stand behind his chair, his elegant hands wrapping around its scrolled top. His eyes locked on Andrew's. It was impossible for the monk not to feel the full weight of the cardinal's authority, and his own insignificance and helplessness.

"And what about passing judgment on you, Father?" the cardinal said in the hushed room. "Do you honestly expect me to accept your stand and do nothing?"

"I still believe, your Eminence, that I have done nothing wrong."

"Are you not aware that despite your claims of conscience, your position in the eyes of the Church is fully untenable, and your fate, with the full authority of Rome, is now in my hands?"

"I am," Andrew answered. He knew this was his last warning. The cardinal's voice had turned cold and aloof. Gone was the compassion Andrew had felt from their first meeting. Matters had been reduced to expediency, to politics, the layers of which did not allow for sympathy. Still, Andrew thought, he could not recant.

"Brother Andrew, do you have anything more to say?"

"I do not."

"Then, as of this moment, I am relieving you of your work in the Amazon, and all fund-raising duties for your order. I have already discussed this with Brother Manning. You will spend the next five years in East Africa under the direction of the Trappist abbot in Nairobi. You will not be allowed to travel. If at any time you disobey me, I have no choice but to recommend that you be removed from your order."

Andrew was staggered by the words. He looked up defiantly. "But you are making me a prisoner, your Eminence. And to sever me from my abbey, or my work in the Amazon, is like severing my arm or leg—I would be lost." His shoulders sagged at the possibility.

"I also order you to relinquish every penny of the money Alycia Poindexter gave you. It belongs to the Church, not to you, Father. If you do not comply, I have no other choice but to request your excommunication from the Church."

There were murmurs of disbelief from many of the monks. Andrew could not manage a word. They cannot do this to me, he thought. He would demand an ecclesiastical trial. How could anyone dare think of excommunication for him? Was he a heretic? If Rome had told him he would not be allowed to administer the sacraments, Andrew could understand, but to have the doors of the Church closed in his face because he believed that his conscience was a clearer and purer voice of God than any order from the Holy See . . .

And what of all his years of service that the cardinal had

commended him for? Did they not count for anything? Crushed, Andrew dropped his head in disbelief. Everything felt like it was disintegrating. He began to feel the full burden and misery of failure. He had failed Alycia, failed Jean, failed his church—what was left for him?

It was Andrew's turn to rise, though he was not sure what he would say. His legs trembled. Did they expect him to beg for mercy? He would not. He would tell them that even if they punished him, God would not desert him. As ineffectual as he'd been in service to the Church, he did not doubt that God still loved and forgave him.

"Your Eminence . . ." He looked first to his fellow monks for support, only to find that not a single eye was trained on him. Andrew turned and followed their stares. The door had opened without a sound. The two visitors entered and stood behind Andrew, undisturbed by the startled silence of the male enclave.

"Alycia," Andrew breathed.

She wore a plain cotton dress, as did Felice, and their heads were covered by scarves. Alycia glanced at Andrew, smiled softly, then faced the incredulous cardinal, who had returned to his chair.

"I'm Alycia Poindexter," she said in a firm, clear voice, "and this is my daughter, Felice."

Cardinal Easton raised a temporizing hand. "I don't believe you belong in this room, Mrs. Poindexter."

"For the moment I don't belong anywhere but this room."

"I'm sorry, I must ask you to leave."

"I don't want to be here any more than you want me," she answered. "The hypocrisy and the greed of the Church offend me. But I have something to say."

Andrew saw that the cardinal and his entourage did not wish to hear it. The bishops flashed glances to one another.

"I want to prove to you that I am physically and mentally well, and that you have no reason to impose any punishment on Brother Andrew—"

"*That* is the business of the Church," the cardinal stopped her.

"Very well," she said, "do as you wish. But Brother Andrew is no longer in control of my money."

The cardinal hunched forward. The startled face struggled to recover. His glance swept to Andrew, as if suspecting a conspiracy. Andrew could only look back blankly. He honestly knew nothing.

"Mrs. Poindexter," Cardinal Easton said carefully, "perhaps you are not as recovered as you think. The money has not disappeared, has it?" ·

"No. It's just been transferred out of Brother Andrew's account. Further—"

"To where?" Cardinal Easton demanded, not believing her. His handsome face froze.

"Further," she continued, "I have formally relieved Brother Andrew of all legal responsibility for the money. I have a copy here of my letter to my attorney . . ." Alycia pulled an envelope from her pocketbook. "Brother Andrew cannot turn over to the Church what he doesn't possess or control."

Alycia left the letter on the mammoth table, then turned and followed Felice out the door. The prelates were in an uproar. Amid the startled looks and voices, as dumbfounded as anyone, Andrew slipped away.

"Alycia . . . Felice . . ." he called, half-running down the hallway.

In the busy corridor he caught up and wrapped one arm around each of them. The mutual embrace was so full of relief and happiness that Andrew didn't care who was watching or what anyone thought.

"How," he asked when he finally pulled back, his smile widening, "did you get out of the hospital?"

"Felice came just after you left. She brought a nurse's uniform for me to slip on. The guards at the door weren't paying very close attention . . ." Alycia smiled now at the memory. "I should have left you a note, but we were worried about leaving clues. Besides, I knew I would see you soon."

"Thank you for coming. I was shocked," he admitted. "I still am!"

"I told you—I wasn't going to let you down anymore."

"Just think," Andrew said, lifting his eyes in thanks, "after all these years, I don't have to wake up tomorrow worrying about whether someone has found out about the money."

Andrew wanted to celebrate, but his joy was eclipsed by Alycia's sober countenance.

"I haven't totally saved you, have I?" she said.

Andrew realized he'd almost forgotten. His own mood turned more somber. "You overheard?"

"I opened the door a crack."

"I've been ordered to spend the next five years in Africa. I shall not be able to leave."

"They can't do that to you," Felice objected. "It's pointless punishment now."

"I don't think Cardinal Easton will change his mind—he can't. After all I've been through, I know a little something of the logic and politics of Rome. I was insubordinate, and there's a question of precedent."

"Will you go?" Alycia asked in a pained voice. "You can come back to the Amazon with me."

"Alycia . . ." His eyes cut away. He could leave his order and be free to do anything, go anywhere with Alycia. He was so tempted. But hadn't he just defied a cardinal on the principle that serving God and his church was his life's work? How could he leave voluntarily? It would be as hypocritical as if the Church had turned its back on him. He was, despite his contradictions and weaknesses and doubts, a man of God. As imperfect and impure as he was, his desire to serve God was not. He was sure Alycia would understand. His love for her had not been diminished by these weeks of torment, nor would it be by separation of ocean and continent. If love was true, it endured.

"I must do as Cardinal Easton has ordered me," he said, holding Alycia gently by the shoulders. "But I know we will be together soon. In our hearts we are always together. And can you not visit me?"

Alycia felt a tear glide down her cheek. She blinked back another and forced a smile. She had to distract herself. "Don't you want to know what I did with the money?"

Andrew pursed his lips. "I'm afraid to ask, but I'm too curious not to."

"Brother Sebastian has it," she whispered, looking around the hallway. "I wired him everything this morning. I think he'll accept the challenge. That's the way he is. Bullheaded like you. And while the Jesuits are under the leadership of Rome, they're very independent politically. I don't think Sebastian will have any problem, even if word does get out."

"You are a clever, determined woman, as I know so well," Andrew observed, hugging her again.

"I think it's my turn to surprise everyone now," Felice broke in.

Andrew and Alycia watched one another's expressions as

Felice milked the suspense. "Guess who's going to have a baby," she finally said.

"You're pregnant?" Andrew echoed, throwing up his arms. "Oh, my, this is joyous . . ."

Alycia's eyes lit up, and she threw her arms around her daughter. "That's wonderful! I'm going to be a grandmother again!"

"You'll have to come home more often now, Mother."

"Oh, I will!"

Andrew watched the joy steal over Felice's face, but there was only a current of sadness in him. Not just because he would be in Africa and not lay eyes on Felice's child for five years. Something deeper, he realized. He had felt this pang of deprivation before, had discussed it once with Alycia. Now the desire returned stronger than ever. To father his own child, to know the joy of creation, to teach a son or daughter all that he had learned, signified, to Andrew, everything that was holy. The irony that he pursued a life of purity and idealism, yet denied himself this ultimate miracle, filled him with an overwhelming futility.

"Will you send me photos of the baby?" he asked.

"I'll do better than that," she said. "If it's a boy, I'm going to name him Andrew. What do you think of that? David's already agreed."

The monk felt his face warm. "You can't."

"Why not?"

"I don't deserve it. And surely a poet's imagination can come up with something better."

"You deserve it, and more," Felice replied. "Andrew is a beautiful name. And you've helped all of us so much. I wish I could do more."

Felice gave Andrew and her mother a long embrace, and a final wave as she hurried on her way. Andrew walked with Alycia out of the cathedral into the evening shadows. He was suddenly quiet, stilled by Felice's kindness and love, by the ability of life to constantly surprise. Yet when he thought of Felice's unborn child and all the hope and promise that a new life could bring, his thoughts jumped to another child.

"Alycia," he said, turning to her on the cathedral steps, "I saw Jean last night."

"What happened?" she said anxiously.

"And Daniel too. He's a beautiful little boy."

"Did Jean speak to you?"

"Not exactly. Jean wouldn't let me in the house. We looked at one another through a window. I tried to talk to him. He was very agitated."

"What do you mean?"

"Something wasn't right. The way Daniel looked at Jean . . . I could tell that he loved and adored his father, but he was terrified of him too. I'm afraid I failed, Alycia. I thought I could help Jean. These last weeks have shown me how frail I am, how many limitations I have, but by standing up to Cardinal Easton I've also learned that I have my strengths. I want to try to go back. I can't give you one reason, but Daniel seems very special to me. I want to make sure he's all right. And if Jean can be helped, I must help him."

Alycia took in Andrew's words. Old feelings of guilt and inadequacy kept her from focusing her thoughts right away. What was Andrew saying? Was Daniel in serious jeopardy? And Jean? Free now, she had to explain to him why she'd hidden his father's letter, why she'd handled the trusts as she had. There had been so much misunderstanding. She wanted to make a peace with Jean that would last. She would try to undo the damages of the past. Maybe her judgments and actions hadn't always been correct. She had responded to the pressures in her life with as much wisdom as she could. It wasn't a life she had necessarily wanted, but she had done her best.

"I'll go see them right away," Alycia said.

"May I come with you?"

"I'd like that very much, but it's now my turn, Andrew. I have to see Jean alone."

"At least let me wait outside in the car—"

"No, I'll be fine," she promised, giving him a final hug. "Call me tomorrow night. I love you." Alycia gave him the name of a hotel in Los Angeles and was gone.

Alycia had prepared herself not to be shocked when she saw the old Toluca Lake house, but when her cab pulled up to the curb she felt a tremor of disbelief. The annuals in the flowerbeds, the painted birdhouse atop the willow tree, the weather vane on the east roof—everything was the same.

A lanky blond boy with a beautiful face darted out from behind the bushes, playing some game that looked like it had no rules. He would cast menacing looks at an imaginary enemy, then flap his arms like a bird taking off. Alycia couldn't stop staring. Daniel looked so much like Jean that for a moment she really thought she had slipped back in time.

She stepped from the cab and went toward him with an open smile. Closer, she saw his face and arms were filthy, as if he hadn't had a bath in ages. His jeans and T-shirt looked like they'd been slept in.

"Hello, Daniel," she called.

He spun around, startled, cocking his head at her with a suspicion reserved for strangers. "Who are you?" he said.

"I'm your grandmother."

"My grandmother?" he asked, still dubious.

Alycia wondered what Jean had told him about her. "I'm your father's mother. I've been away for many years. I wanted to say hello. You know, you're a very handsome young man. It's a real pleasure meeting you."

Alycia held out her hand.

"You're really my grandmother?" He debated her veracity only for a moment. With total trust he walked up and took her hand, stretched to his toes, and kissed her on the lips as Alycia bent down.

"I knew you'd come," he said, beaming.

"You did?"

"Daddy said you'd never come, but I knew you would. I knew it."

"And did you know that your grandfather and I used to live in this house—a long, long time ago?"

He nodded earnestly. "Uh-huh. Daddy talks about him a lot."

"Your grandfather? What does he say about him?"

Daniel shrugged. Suddenly he looked anxious. "I don't know. I don't understand sometimes."

Alycia put her arms around the boy. "Is everything all right?" she asked. Daniel didn't answer. She stroked his head, then stood back and looked at him with a reassuring smile. "You remind me so much of your father at your age. Andrew was certainly right. You are a very special boy."

Pleased, Daniel shook off his mood. "Who's Andrew?"

"A good friend of mine. He came to visit you and your father late the other night. He peeked in the window and saw you. Do you remember?"

Daniel nodded faintly, troubled again.

"And right now I want to visit your father. Is he inside?"

The boy didn't have to answer. His stare suddenly pointed

behind her, his eyes brimming with caution. Alycia could feel Jean, but she didn't turn yet. "Daniel," she said as she bent down, "go find some bread in the house, then feed the ducks by the lake. That's what I used to do with one of my daughters. I'll come see you in a few minutes."

The boy scampered away. When Alycia turned and faced Jean, she was alarmed by his puffy eyes, the red, patchy skin. He looked like he hadn't slept in days.

"Hello, Jean."

"Mother." The voice was flat and cold. His hands were stuffed in his jeans pockets, elbows angled out. "Why are you here?"

"I don't want to intrude. And I know what you must be thinking about me. But I'm going back to South America soon, and I wanted to settle some things between us."

His face twisted cynically. "So now you're talking? I'm impressed. All better, huh?"

"Jean, you had no right to take me from my home in the Amazon. You wanted something from me that I wasn't prepared to give. The love that I was always ready to give, you didn't want. That's why I didn't speak to you. Maybe I was wrong. But I want to talk now."

"It doesn't matter anymore. It's all over, Mother. Everyone's laughing at us again."

"I've never cared about public opinion."

"You might have," he interrupted. "Then maybe none of this disgrace would have ever happened."

Alycia sighed. She had to get through to him. "Jean, may I come inside?"

He led her into the house. There were several open suitcases in the entry, clothes piled inside carelessly. The kitchen was a disaster area. She didn't have to see the bedrooms to guess their condition. Alycia sat on the couch in Red's study and studied the movie-star memorabilia on the wall. Otherwise, uncannily, the interior of the house was identical to when Red and she had owned it.

"You're planning a trip?" she asked.

"*Was.* Then I realized there's no place to go. You can't run from yourself, can you?"

"You don't have anything to run from," she said. "You're fine. You just have to believe that."

"I'm a failure, Mother. The whole world knows it."

"Why are you so hard on yourself?" Alycia said, distressed. "You create these impossible standards for yourself. They're too high and unrealistic. What are you trying to prove, Jean, and to whom? Is it still your father?"

"My father?" he whispered. "Now, that's an interesting subject. My dear father, who I always thought loved me. Maybe you and Felice didn't, but he did. I could always count on that one certainty in this fickle world. And you're right—I worked so hard to please him. I thought he would love me even more if I did. Then one day I found out that my father didn't love me at all."

"That's not true! You meant so much to him, Jean."

"If Dad really loved me," he said carefully, "then why did he kill himself? How could he do that to me? I adored him, I needed him—he knew that."

"Jean, for a long while I thought the same thing. It was hard for me to forgive him too. Even though I loved him, I was angry. Then I began to understand. Like you, Red set impossibly high goals for himself. He didn't allow himself to fail because he wanted to show *his* father how strong and successful he could be. That terrible pride—it consumed him, and he refused to recognize it. Maybe that's why it took control of him. He wanted too much, Jean."

"Just like me, Mother? Is that what you're saying?"

"Yes," she answered.

"Well, I don't want anything anymore. Absolutely nothing. Every success I've ever earned has been pulled out from under me. I've been held up to ridicule . . . I live in a world of strangers . . . and you've never cared, Mother—"

"I do care! You act like you're the only one who's suffered in this family. After your father's death you thought I rejected you—and I'm sorry for every bit of agony you've gone through—but I also felt that you were rejecting me. I know parents are supposed to be stronger and wiser than their children, but when you came back from Vietnam and suddenly turned your back on me—"

"I turned my back on you? You sold this house!"

"That wasn't the real issue, Jean. And in your heart you know that."

Jean's dark laughter filled the room. "You're still trying to reach me, is that what I'm supposed to believe? That's why you're here? A mother never gives up hope?"

"I want you to take Daniel and leave this house," Alycia said, standing now. "Move out of Los Angeles if you have

to. I know you have the money. If you don't, I'll give it to
you. Go anywhere, make new friends, start a new life. It's
best for you, and best for Daniel. Felice did it, I did it—you
don't have to live at the mercy of strangers and ghosts.''

Jean seemed to look right through her. His jaw worked
back and forth in deliberation. Like she had seen Daniel do in
the front yard, he was fighting an invisible enemy.

"The same thing would only happen all over again,'' Jean
whispered in a tired voice. "There's nothing I can do about
it.''

"You're wrong. You have to have hope. History doesn't
have to repeat itself. Think of Daniel.''

"He doesn't belong to me anymore.''

"Don't ever say that! He's your son—''

"The dream's been ruined. Go away, Mother. I want to be
alone.''

"We can leave right now if you want,'' Alycia suggested,
trying to stay calm. "I have a taxi outside. Lock up the house
and we'll worry about everything later. We'll get Daniel and
leave this moment . . .''

She approached the desk and tried to take Jean's hand. He
pulled back and froze her with a look of such pride and
contempt that she understood what Andrew had witnessed.
She was not his mother to him anymore, Alycia thought. She
was just one more stranger.

"Get out of my house,'' he ordered again.

Something stirred behind Alycia. She turned cautiously.
Daniel was standing just inside the study door. How long had
he been hiding? His cheeks were stained with tears, his tiny
fists balled at his sides. Jean seemed barely to notice him. His
vacant eyes roamed over his son as if Daniel meant no more
to him than did Alycia. She hurried over and wrapped her
arms around the boy.

"Daniel, you have to come with me now,'' she said softly.

"No. I want to stay with Daddy.'' He began to struggle.
Alycia tightened her grip.

"We won't be gone long, Daniel. Your father's not well.
He can't really take care of you. We'll come back when he's
better.''

"No,'' he yelled as Alycia picked him up and moved to the
front door. With a broken heart she gazed back on Jean, then
she hurried with Daniel into the sunlight.

*   *   *

Jean watched his mother vanish. Gone forever, he thought. Peace now. He opened the top drawer of his father's desk. He had taken pains to arrange it exactly as he remembered from that terrible day. Stamps, paper clips, scissors, notepads, old letters. His father's silver-plated revolver was in the corner, handle toward him. It came out easily into his grip.

Now, he thought, he would never have to remember it again.

The story of Jean Poindexter's suicide was carried by the Los Angeles media, but with none of the prominence or infamy that had characterized his father's death. Jean's impact was more that of a footnote, somewhat sad and inevitable but unworthy of sparking gossip that lasted more than a few days, as if to prove what Jean had always thought of his place in the world. Alycia stayed in her hotel room for days and wept bitterly. She was consoled by Andrew and Felice, who looked after Daniel, but nothing anyone said could soothe her pain. It bored into her like a parasite and lodged in her heart. Tears did not loosen it, nor memories, nor prayers.

The funeral service and burial took place at Forest Lawn on a raw, overcast morning, the day before Thanksgiving. On Alycia's instructions, the public was not invited, though elaborate floral arrangements came from many of her old friends. Leslie Mae and her husband flew down from San Francisco and stood behind Alycia and Felice and Andrew at the graveside. Alycia watched as Daniel knelt with daisies he had picked and laid them across his father's casket. Then he placed a single rose by Harriet's stone, another by Red's, a third by Isabel's, and a final one by Owen's. He marched back bravely and took his grandmother's hand.

"Daddy told me everyone here is alive," he whispered anxiously.

"No, Daniel," she said. "It's not true. They're not alive at all." Alycia trembled a smile for him. "That's all in the past. You and I must think about the future now."

"Why did Daddy kill himself?" he asked.

"I think he was very unhappy about some things. But I know they had nothing to do with you. He loved you very much. You must always remember that. Promise me?"

Daniel looked unsure. Alycia put her arms around him and gave him a hug. "I love you too, very, very much," she said. "That's something else you must never forget."

He was disconsolate for a moment but managed to raise his chin. "I won't forget," he said, and gave her a teary kiss.

Andrew stepped forward with an open Bible. In a voice that had the strength and clarity of a sonorous bell, he sang the Twenty-third Psalm.

He waited till the wind stopped gusting before he signaled everyone to bow his head. "In the name of the Father, the Son, and the Holy Ghost," Andrew said, "we deliver the suffered soul of Jean Poindexter and ask your mercy upon it. We do not understand the wisdom of your providence, only the frustration of our hearts and the pain of our grief. Help us be patient, help us heal. Absolve us of guilt, and fill us with hope. Jesus said, 'Come unto me, all ye that labor and are heavy-laden, and I will give you rest.' Thou are a God ready to pardon, gracious and merciful, slow to anger, and of great kindness.

" 'In my father's house are many mansions,' it is written in the Gospel According to Saint John, 'I go now to prepare a place for you.' "

Andrew closed the Bible and encircled Alycia and Felice with his arms. As they left together, the wind blustered and sang with bitterness, but Andrew knew to listen only to his heart.

EPILOGUE

Dear Grandma,

Thanks so much for the birthday check—I went out and
bought myself a new bike *and* a skateboard! Mom took
a photo of me on the bike. She's mailing it to you when
it's developed. San Francisco is a great city for going
downhill, but unless you're Superman it's a bummer ped-
aling back home. Grandma, did you get my last letter?
I actually won my school spelling bee—I got "chihua-
hua" right and Suzie Hendrickson (I think she has a
crush on me) missed "embarrassed." Everyone asks how
I got to be such a great speller, and I just tell them I
read a lot of *Mad Magazines*. Now that I'm almost twelve,
Mom wants me to think about going away to prep school
next year. She says I'm bright and I should get the best
possible education. My dad can afford it, I know, but
the truth is, I don't think I want to go. Maybe when I'm
older, but not now. I like my friends here, also my room,
dog, canary, new bike, computer, basketball, video games,
drum set, and my set of Chinese checkers. I also think
Mom would miss me if I was gone very long.

Are you going to come back and visit? My friends think
it's pretty radical to have a grandmother who lives in a
jungle. Maybe one day I can visit you there. Oh, I almost forgot—Brother Andrew came for dinner last week.
He was great—he told me all these stories about Africa. I think I really want to travel when I grow up. He
also wanted to know all about my school and what I
was doing. I like him a lot. He talked to my dad for hours
about *pro bono* (whatever that is) legal work Dad does,
and he said he's eager to visit you, Grandma.

Well, so long for now. I'm supposed to be going to a

movie— *Godzilla Meets Arnold Schwarzenegger*. I love
you!

Daniel

   With a smile Alycia folded the letter and placed it in a
small crammed basket with her other letters from Daniel. He
wrote almost every month, and Alycia had saved them all.
She kept few possessions in her small house that sat back
from the river, but they all meant something: the letters;
photos of Daniel and of Felice's three boys—the oldest,
Andrew, was now seven and, according to his father, the next
Mickey Mantle; small, exquisite pieces of art that Andrew
had sent from Kenya; handmade gifts from the many Indian
children she had taught over the years; and an old typewriter
for her letters to the world. There was nothing else she valued
enough to keep.
   She rose from her chair and stepped out into the humid
afternoon. She was tired today, she thought, but happy. A
few children splashed in the river; a family was working in
the vegetable garden. Tomorrow Andrew would be coming,
and the day after that was her seventieth birthday. Brother
Sebastian insisted, over Alycia's objections, on giving her a
party. The monk had wangled a portable phonograph from a
local trader, and he swore he knew how to get his hands on
two Tommy Dorsey albums, the kind she had in Paris after
the war. She gazed at the timeless river and imagined something far away. All the gala balls, dancing with Red, the
lunches with Electra, Harriet, Owen. She thought of Jean
more often than she did of anyone else, she supposed, but
now there were a peace and an understanding that came with
the mercy of time.
   She sat at her typewriter and wrote back to Daniel.

About the Author

Michael French is the prize-winning author of over a dozen works of published fiction, including the national best-sellers *Abingdon's, Pursuit,* and *Indiana Jones and the Temple of Doom.* A native of Los Angeles, he has also lived in New York and Europe, and currently resides with his wife and two children in Santa Fe, New Mexico. The author is a graduate of Stanford and Northwestern universities. When not writing, he is active in real estate development, which was the basis for FAMILY MONEY.